CURTAIN CALL

CURTAIN CALL
Graham Hurley

Severn House Large Print
London & New York

This first large print edition published 2019
in Great Britain and the USA by
SEVERN HOUSE PUBLISHERS LTD of
Eardley House, 4 Uxbridge Street, London W8 7SY.
First world regular print edition published 2019 by
Severn House Publishers Ltd.

British Library Cataloguing in Publication Data
A CIP catalogue record for this title is available from the British Library.

ISBN-13: 9780727892331

Severn House Publishers support the Forest Stewardship Council™
[FSC™], the leading international forest certification organisation. All
our titles that are printed on FSC certified paper carry the FSC logo.

MIX
Paper from
responsible sources
FSC
www.fsc.org   FSC® C013056

Typeset by Palimpsest Book Production Ltd.,
Falkirk, Stirlingshire, Scotland.
Printed and bound in Great Britain by
T J International, Padstow, Cornwall.

To
Lara, Harri, Enya, and Cormac

Tirez le rideau, la farce est jouée
Ring down the curtain, the farce is over

—the last words of François Rabelais

One

The neurosurgeon has a fondness for metaphor. 'The Reaper comes knocking at every door,' he says. 'I'm afraid yours might be one of them.'

I'm staring at him. Pale face. Pale eyes behind the rimless glasses. Pale everything. Half-dead already, he could be an apprentice ghost. Another metaphor.

'Should I lock the door? Hide? Pretend I'm not in?'

'Any of the above.' The eyes drift to the PC screen. 'Next of kin? A husband maybe?'

'He's in Stockholm.'

'On business?'

'He's about to re-marry. It might be the same thing.'

'I'm sorry.'

'So am I. The last thing the poor woman needs is Berndt.'

He reaches for his keyboard and taps a line I can't read. Is he making notes about some drug or other, some brave attempt to stay the Reaper at the corner of the street? Or is he having trouble spelling Berndt? I did once, so I wouldn't blame him.

With a tiny sigh he glances up, as if to check I'm still there. Then he half-turns to consult a calendar on the wall behind him. The calendar features a child's painting, stick figures in crayon,

1

mainly red and yellow. There's a football, and birds, and a big whiskery sun. I rather like it.

'Do you have enough Percocet?'

'Yes.'

'Good. No more than one tablet every six hours and lay off the booze. Before we make any decisions, I'm afraid I'll need to see you again.' His finger has settled on the end of next week. 'Would Friday be convenient?'

'Friday would be perfect.' I manage a smile. 'My place or yours?'

Crying in public is something I try to avoid, in this case without success. This is a bar I've never been to before. It helps that everyone is a stranger. Moist-eyed, I order a large vodka and stare at my own image in the mirror behind the optics. In truth I feel undone, a parcel ripped apart by unseen hands inside me, but that's a complicated thought to share with anyone and thankfully no one seems very interested.

Less than two weeks ago I went to the doctor with a persistent headache and a problem with the vision in my left eye. Now, it seems, I ought to be thinking hard about a hospice. Private medical insurance definitely has its blessings but no one tells you how to cope with news this sudden and this final.

The neurosurgeon I've just left showed me the MRI scan they did on Thursday, tracing the outline of the tumour the way you might explain a new route home. I followed his thick forefinger as best I could, trying to imagine the cluttered spaces of my own throbbing head, but none of it made much sense. At the end, when I asked what next, he came up with the line about the Reaper. Now I leave my glass untouched and head for the street. Coping is something I've done all my life. Until now.

Home is a sixteen-pound cab ride to Holland Park. I live on the fourth floor of a 1930s block of flats with a sunny view south and the constant assurance from local estate agents that serious cash buyers are only a phone call away. The place is safe and beautifully maintained. I've spent the best years of my life here, even with Berndt, and until this morning it's never occurred to me that one day I might have to leave.

My immediate neighbour has lived here even longer than me. Her name is Evelyn. She's West Country, from a small village outside Okehampton. She's wise and kindly and Berndt always said she belonged in a homestead in frontier America with a rugged husband and an army of kids. Berndt was wrong about that because she's never married, probably never had a man, and maybe as a consequence she puts a great deal of thought into nurturing relationships she values. I flatter myself that I count as one of her friends.

Evelyn has sharp ears for the arrival of the lift but always waits until I've settled myself in before knocking lightly on the door. These calls are always for a purpose, another reason we get on so well. Since I've known her, she's worked as an editor for one of the smaller London publishing houses. People I know in the business tell me she's become a legend and I tend to believe them. She certainly knows that less is more, an editorial rule she applies unfailingly to her own life. She stands at the open door, a thick Jiffy bag in her arms. The pencil behind her ear is a signal that she's busy.

'I took this in,' she says. 'I think it's from your agent.'

She gives me the Jiffy bag and then pauses before stepping back into the hall.

'Is everything OK, my lovely?'

'No, if you want the truth.'

'Anything I can do?'

'No.' I force a smile. 'But thanks.'

She nods, says nothing. She'll be there if I need her, I know she will. But not now.

I put the kettle on and toy with making a cup of tea but give up, overwhelmed yet again by what's happened. I'm thirty-nine, shading forty. I'm in my prime. I jog round Kensington Gardens three times a week. My serious drinking days are long gone and I can't remember when I last had a cigarette. Only a week ago, a casting director swore he'd never seen me looking better. Now this.

Shit. *Shit.* Normally, I'm good at self-analysis. I can distinguish at once between a sulk and something more worthwhile, but this ability to read myself appears to have gone. Is this anger I'm feeling? Or bewilderment? Or, God help me, simple fear? The fact that I don't know only makes things worse. Helpless is a word I've never had much time for. It smacks of giving up, of surrender, of weakness. And yet that's as close as I can get. Helpless? Me?

4

I open the Jiffy bag. Evelyn's right, it's from my agent. It's a French-Canadian script and she rates it highly. The producers are still looking for finance, and despite everything it's good to know that my name attached might help them find the right kind of backer. So what do I do here? Do I lift the phone and tell my agent to hold all calls? Do I fess up and say I've joined the walking dead? Or do I just breeze on and hope that I can somehow make it through? In certain kinds of script we call that denial. Denial, under the current circumstances, sounds perfect. And so I pop another Percocet and curl up on the sofa.

My agent's right. Even with my mind still wandering up cul-de-sac after cul-de-sac, I give the script enough attention to know that it's very, very good. I play a French academic on a one-year sabbatical in Montréal. I fall in love with a handsome campus drunk who turns out to be already married. Life gets very difficult, and then impossible, but a clever plot gives me the chance to exact a little revenge in the final act.

The writing is serious and comic by turns, and the dialogue alone has won me over. By the time I've given the script a second read, I've already made that strange alchemical step into someone else's head. I *am* the woman on the page. I cut my bastard suitor far too much slack and I'm punished in subtle and inventive ways that bring a smile, albeit rueful, to my face. But Fate, thanks to the gods of the cinema, comes to my rescue. My jilted beau ends the movie on the very edge of Niagara Falls, contemplating a messy suicide, while I accept the applause of my peers for simply surviving. *If only*, I think.

Another knock on the door. It's Evelyn again, this time with a bottle in her hand. Very unusual.

'Good?' She's nodding at the script.

'Very good.'

'Tempted?'

'Oh, yes.'

She's brought whisky. I pour two measures, adding ice, aware of Evelyn monitoring my every move. On occasions, she can be very direct.

'So what's happened?' she asks.

I tell her everything. It doesn't take long. I'm sharing my brain space with a tumour. Soon it will kill me.

To my relief, she doesn't move. No arms around me, no whispered consolations, no invitation to share the pain. Just a simple question.

'And do you believe this man?'

'*Believe* him?'

'Yes.'

'You think he's kidding me? Some kind of joke? You think the guy's a sadist?'

'I'm just asking exactly what he said.'

I do my best to remember, word for word. Mention of the Reaper brings a scowl to her face.

'He said that?'

'He did.'

She nods. She clearly thinks it's unforgivably crass, even cruel, but she's also wondering whether he'd recognized me. I tell her my medical records are in my married name, Enora Andressen, but she doesn't think that's a factor.

My last movie, a screen adaptation of a decent novel, has been doing good business in London art-house cinemas.

'Men can be funny around fame,' she says. 'Especially alpha males. I see it in the office sometimes. When we stoop to celebrity biogs, and the lady concerned pays us a visit, the Head of Sales always makes a fool of himself. It's primal behaviour. It belongs in the jungle. If I were you I'd ignore it.'

'That's a hard thing to do when he tells me I'm going to die.'

'He said *might*.'

'He did. You're right.'

'So hang on to that.'

A silence settles between us. It feels companionable. Warm. I think I love this woman. When things got really tough with Berndt and he started throwing the furniture around, she offered nothing but good sense. *Change the locks. Get yourself another man. Preferably someone bigger*. As it happens, I did neither but just now Evelyn is offering just a glimpse of something that might resemble hope.

'Did he talk about treatment at all?'

'No. I've got to see him again on Friday.'

'No mention of an operation?'

'No.'

'Radiotherapy? Chemo?'

'No.'

Another silence. I gulp the whisky, draining the glass. I haven't touched Scotch for years but I'm glad she's brought the bottle. The fierceness of the burn in my throat creeps slowly south.

I'm alive. Everything's still working. Fuck the tumour.

'More?' She refills my glass, not waiting for an answer.

I nod. I'm gazing at her. My eyes are moist. I very badly don't want to cry. Not in front of Evelyn.

'And Malo?' she says softly. 'You think you ought to tell him?'

Malo.

I hold her gaze as long as I can and then I duck my head, holding myself tight, rocking on the sofa, letting the hot tears course down my face, howling with the pain of my grief.

Malo is my son. He's seventeen years old, impossibly handsome, impossibly difficult, and impossibly remote. I can forgive Berndt most of the stuff that went on between us, but not for stealing Malo. By the time he eventually left, far too late, I finally realized what he'd been doing with our son's affections. My ex-husband was always clever. He had a way with words. As a successful scriptwriter, he understood the magic of language. His move into direction taught him how to ramp up the pressure. His obsession with *noir* gave him the meanest of streaks. My poor Malo was putty in his hands. Given any kind of choice, what seventeen-year-old wouldn't opt for a penthouse apartment in Stockholm and the company of a blonde starlet with a huge Scandi fan base? Drunk, towards the end, Berndt had talked of trading me in, one washed-up actress for a younger model, but in my darker moments I wondered whether Malo hadn't shared the same thought. From what I can gather, Annaliese makes perfect cheesecake. Job done.

Enough. Evelyn is sitting beside me on the sofa. Practical as ever, she's found some tissues. I tell her that I've no intention of sharing my news with anyone, least of all Malo or my ex-bloody-husband.

'A secret, then? Just you and me? Until you're better?' Evelyn is smiling. I can tell she's pleased. She puts the cap on the bottle and suggests I go to bed. Anytime, day or night, all I have to do is lift the phone. I do my best to thank her, to apologize for the tears, but already she's on her feet.

At the door, struck by a sudden thought, she turns back.

'I forgot,' she says. 'You had another caller this afternoon. He knocked on my door as well. Mitch, he said. Mitch Culligan. Ring any bells?'

I shake my head. The name means nothing.

'He said he'll give you a ring. He must have your number.' She nods towards the bedroom door. 'Sweet dreams, my lovely.'

Sweet dreams? It's eighteen years ago. For the second time running, a picture of mine is up for a major award. My mum and stepdad have trained it down from Brittany in case my movie makes the Palme d'Or. Expecting me to meet them at the station in Cannes, they take a taxi to the Carlton in time to catch me deep in conversation with Berndt Andressen. Berndt is hot just

9

now. He's just penned a script which will – in time – open the floodgates to a torrent of Scandi crime *noir* and he's in town to court some of the international finance people who might make his script happen.

Like everyone else in Cannes, I've read about Berndt in the weightier trade magazines, but in person he comes as a bit of a surprise. He's a decade older than me but it hardly shows. He's slim, quiet, and decidedly opaque. He has a thatch of blond hair and the good taste to wear a carefully rumpled suit instead of the designer jeans and collarless linen shirts that have become standard combat issue in certain corners of the media world. We've been talking non-stop for hours by the time my parents show up, which is a weak excuse for not meeting their train. I've never been able to fool my mum, no matter how hard I try. Berndt is courteous and attentive to them both, and insists on buying a bottle of champagne to toast their arrival. 'You'll marry that man,' my mum tells me later when Berndt has left for yet another interview. And she's right.

We slept together that night. My movie didn't win the Palme d'Or but I was way past caring. If Berndt's *noir* script measured up to his talents in the sack then he was heading for stardom. The second time we made love, in the way that only a woman can sense, I knew that Berndt and I had made a baby. As it happens, I was wrong but that – as they say in La La Land – doesn't play well on the page.

The rest of the festival we talked, drank, swam a little, and compared endless notes. That summer

10

I'd been along the Côte d'Azur for a month already, holed up in Antibes waiting for a French production team to finish a rewrite before shooting extra scenes for a gangster movie in which I'd won a smallish but important role. The script work went far too slowly and at the very end of the shoot some of us had fallen into bad company aboard one of the grosser cruisers docked in the marina. This was nothing I especially regretted – in those days I could put anything down to research – but at Cannes a day later it was wonderful to be in the company of someone thoughtful, someone who knew how to listen, someone whose interest in yours truly extended beyond the taking of yet another scalp. Berndt had the kind of attentive curiosity I've yet to meet in any other man. It took me years to realize how predatory that can be, but by the time the festival came to an end I knew I was in love.

Berndt and I said our goodbyes at the airport. His flight to Stockholm was the first to leave. I remember standing in the hot sunshine on the balcony at the airport, watching his plane climb away into the blue and wondering whether I'd ever see him again. Eight days later, on the phone from Copenhagen, he proposed. We were married in London a week before Christmas. By then, I was well and truly pregnant.

My alarm is always set for 06.30, a habit I picked up on countless locations. For most of the night I've been dreaming about my father. He's been dead for a long time now, a victim of throat

11

cancer, but when I was a child he used to entrance me with puppet shadows on the wall. He'd make shapes with his hands, sometimes one, occasionally two. The shapes would be a barking dog, or an owl with flappy wings, or some nameless beast with three heads, and my world was all the richer for these sleights of hand. At the time he called them *trompe l'oeils* but it was a while before I realized they were simply optical illusions.

Now, a thin grey daylight washes across the big double bed. For the first time in weeks, I realize that I haven't got a headache. I silence the alarm clock and think hard about the stillness inside my skull. Has the tumour taken fright and left me for someone else? Do I owe my life to Johnnie Walker Black Label? I get up, moving very carefully, the way you might carry an overloaded tray. Last night's glasses are still where I left them in the sink. Gratitude smells of stale Scotch.

The phone rings at one minute past nine. I'm on my third cup of tea, still pain-free, still marvelling at this small moment of release. The voice on my mobile phone belongs to a stranger: northern accent, bit of a cold.

'Enora Andressen?'

'Who is this?'

'My name's Mitch. Mitch Culligan. You're OK to talk?'

Culligan. The name rings a bell but I can't think why. 'How did you get my number?'

'Friend of a friend.'

'Like who?'

'Can't say. Sorry.'

'So why should I talk to you?'

'No reason at all. I'm in a car outside your block. Red Fiat. Seen better days. If this sounds creepy, it isn't. Fancy breakfast?'

I have to take the phone into the spare bedroom to check the street. A tallish guy, visibly over-weight, gives me a wave. Grey anorak. Battered day sack. Baggy jeans. Terrible hair. I'm staring hard at his face. I saw him once on *Newsnight*. He's a journalist. And he once did a couple of decent articles on the land mines issue.

'Are you the guy who called on my neighbour yesterday?'

'Yes.'

'So what do you want?'

He won't say, not unless we have a proper conversation. In my job, exchanges like these come with the territory. Normally I'd bring the exchange to an end rapido but the land mines issue was important to me, still is, and in any case yesterday has done something to my normal sense of caution. Time, for one thing, has become a commodity I can no longer take for granted. What the hell.

'Breakfast,' I tell him. 'On you.'

We go to a wholefood cafe off the Bayswater Road where they know me. At my insistence, we walk. He's much taller than I am. He has a strange gait, lumbering, flat-footed, body thrust forward, hands dug deep in the pockets of his anorak, as if he's heading into a stiff wind. When I mention land mines he nods. Angola. The

Balkans. Afghanistan. Any country touched by conflict has been left with a legacy of buried mines and a generation of kids who've stepped on them.

'You know about this stuff?' He seems surprised.

'I do. Not first-hand but through someone close to me. There are charities who work in the field. I've always done my best to help.'

He nods in approval. We're definitely on the same page here. Nice to know.

The cafe is comfortably full but there are generous spaces between the tables. Wealth has its own smell, in this case freshly brewed Java Pure.

My new friend studies the chalkboard in disbelief.

'They do bacon?'

'No.'

'Sausages?'

'Only soya.'

'Anything edible?'

We order scrambled eggs on five-grain wholemeal toast. En route to a table at the back, I accept an air kiss from an Iranian art dealer who owns the gallery on the corner. Word on the street suggests that nothing costing less than $10,000 gets out of his door.

We settle at the table. Mitch, his day sack tucked under the table, is taking a lively interest in the cafe's clientele. I'm beginning to be intrigued by this man. In my business you spend half your life pretending to be someone else and unconsciously or otherwise you're forever on patrol, watching other people, making mental notes, tucking away their tiny idiosyncrasies – little giveaway tics – in case they might prove useful later.

Mitch, unusually, offers few clues. His lumber-jack shirt, which is missing a button, could do with an iron. He badly needs a proper shave. His lace-up boots are caked with mud. But this air of neglect doesn't appear to trouble him in the least. On the contrary, he seems to be a man thoroughly at ease with himself – not as common as you might think.

He wants to know what I thought about the recent election sprung on us by Theresa May. The question takes me by surprise.

'Nothing,' I tell him. 'I was on location in the States.'

'Trump?'

'A buffoon. And allegedly a serial groper.'

'You ever get to see him in the flesh? Meet him, maybe?'

'Christ, no. That man puts his smell on people. He's a dog. I'd be washing him off for a week.'

He grins at me, his big face suddenly younger. He says he spent the three weeks before the election touring parts of the UK, taking the pulse of the place, looking for clues.

'And?'

'This country's a crime scene. Make that a plural – crime *scenes*. We've been screwed by neglect, by clever lies, and by a long list of politicians who should have been paying more attention. Behind them is an even longer list of

15

names you've never heard of and they're the ones you really need to watch.'

'You write about all this stuff?'

'Of course.'

'So should I have recognized your name?'

'Depends what you read.'

'Very little, I'm afraid. I gave up on the press years ago. If a girl wants fiction she should stick to novels.'

He shoots me a look. I think I've offended him. Then he tells me he's recently gone freelance after years with a major broadsheet. Facebook and the rest are killing the print business but there's still money to be made.

'Is that what this is about?' I nod at the space between us. 'You're after some kind of exclusive?'

This time I know I've hurt him. Worse than that, he's got me down as a spoiled celeb, tucked away in Holland Park, protected by a thicket of agents, publicity machines, and very big ideas about myself. He's talking about the recent election again, how three weeks on the road talking to people about the kind of lives they lead should be compulsory for every politician.

'But it is. That's what elections are about. No?'

'No.' He shakes his head. 'It's a comedy show. These people are looking for votes but they have no time. Here's a sticker. Nice dog you've got there. Lovely baby. Remember my name.' He scowls, leaning forward over the table. 'This country is dead on its feet. The ones with money might vote. The rest have nothing to protect. On some levels, believe me, it's scary. And you know why? Because the system doesn't work any more. Because the system is fucked. I could spend half a day in some run-down shopping centre and not meet anyone who had a clue what to do with his vote. Either that or they couldn't be arsed. This country has become world class at giving up. Not here so much. Not in London. But up there. You ever been to Burnley?'

'Once. I was playing in a Rattigan at Blackburn. You?'

'Born and bred. My dad was a vicar. Can you believe that? Burnley was a proper place. Once.'

He makes space on the table and sighs while the waitress delivers the food. He watches her return with a carafe of mango juice, on the house. My new friend is impressed.

'Are they always this nice to you?'

'Always.'

'Why?'

'They like my films.'

'Good. I've been meaning to tell you. That scene at the beginning of *Arpeggio* – you seriously underplayed it. The rest of the movie? Excellent. But you were nuts to kick it off that way.'

I take this as a compliment, partly because I'm warming to his bluntness but mainly because he's right.

'That was the director,' I tell him. 'I wanted to play it full-on. He thought we'd lose the audience.'

'You nearly did. And I'm a fan.'

We talk movies while he demolishes

17

the scrambled eggs. To my slight surprise, his knowledge of films is huge, his taste impeccable. Early Chris Nolan. Anything by Almodóvar. Sean Penn in *21 Grams.* Perfect.

'Not hungry?' He's looking at my brimming plate. I've barely touched it. His interest is obvious.

'Help yourself.' I reach for the mango juice. 'And while you're at it you might tell me why we're here.'

He forks scrambled eggs on to his plate and then bends to the day sack. Moments later I'm looking at a thickish file. Handwritten on the front is a single word: Cassini.

Already I'm intrigued. I've come across the word recently but I can't remember where. *Cassini*?

Mitch wolfs several mouthfuls of egg and then opens the file. Sheets of text hide a pile of photos. He's about to show me one of them but then his hand pauses. Long fingers. Cared-for nails. No rings.

'This is a long story,' he says. 'Which is rather the point.'

'I like stories. But what's this got to do with me?'

'That's my question, I'm afraid.' He pauses, looking up, catching something in my voice. 'You OK?'

I'm not. I have a sudden, blinding pain behind my left eye. I can see two versions of Mitch, both of them shading into grey, and the tables around us are blurred beyond recognition. Mitch is already on his feet. I'm clinging on to the

18

edge of the table now and I'm dimly aware of throwing up on to my plate. Somebody – Mitch? – is holding me from behind. I try to lift my head. The pain is unbearable. Then everything goes black.

Two

The next few days are lost to me. Time expands, condenses, wriggles around, expands again, and then snaps like some worn-out elastic band. My first moment of consciousness comes in the back of an ambulance. After that, I'm adrift again until a face swims into focus at my bedside. Only slowly do I associate the rimless glasses and the paleness of the face with my neurosurgeon. He's wearing blue surgical scrubs and a white face mask dangles beneath his chin. Costume drama, I think dimly. Death-bed bye-bye scene. Not good.

The face fades, only to return later. It might have been a couple of minutes later, it might have been the following day, I've no idea, but this time we have a conversation.

'It went well.' He's sitting on the bed. 'Much better than we expected.'

I try to speak. Frame an answer. Make some kind of comment. Nothing. I start to panic. An exposed nerve in my poor failing brain? A parting *billet-doux* from the tumour? A slip of the scalpel cutting whatever goes to my vocal chords? I try to swallow. Find it nearly impossible. What kind of future awaits an actress who can't speak? Can't even breathe properly? Then comes a soft pressure on my lower arm and it takes me a moment to realize what it is. Reassurance. Comfort. Kindliness.

'You've still got tubes down your throat,' the face says. 'Don't try and talk. Just nod or shake your head.' The face smiles. 'Any pain?'

I shake my head.

'Nothing? No discomfort?'

A tiny shake this time.

'Just a bit?'

I nod.

'Good girl.' The hand on my arm, again. 'Take it easy. No dancing. I'll be back tomorrow.'

Bless him. Bless them all. My first visitor is Mitch. He lumbers into the High Dependency Unit, his big face invisible behind an explosion of blooms.

'Lilies,' he says. 'My dad used to swear by them. Dark properties. Keeps the devil in his place.'

He disappears to find a nurse and a vase, and returns within moments. No anorak today. Apparently an Indian summer has descended on West London.

'OK?' His eyes are mapping the tangle of leads that keep my vital signs on track.

'Fine.' I can talk now. The tube has gone.

'And?' He wants an update, a prognosis. No messing.

'They say I might get better.'

'Might? That sounds a bit provisional.'

'Might,' I confirm. 'All these conversations depend on where you start. They wrote me off the other day so I can definitely handle "might". In fact "might" could become my very best friend.' I lie back and close my eyes. My little speech has exhausted me.

21

When I come to again, Mitch is very close. He's found a chair. He's been eating garlic.

'This has been going on a while? Only I feel a bit guilty.'

'You mean the cafe?'

'Yes. Dragging you out. Bothering you.'

'It was good you were there. It would have happened anyway.'

'How do you know?'

'I don't. I'm just being nice.'

'Appreciate it.' His hand lingers briefly on my shoulder. Then he's on his feet again. 'Anything I can bring? Next time?'

My hand goes to the bareness of my scalp where they shaved me before the operation.

'A beret?' I suggest. 'Maybe red?'

After Mitch, a succession of friends and relatives arrive. Evelyn is first, bearing a box of Belgian chocolates she knows I'll kill for. Then my agent and the actor who played opposite me in *Arpeggio*. The news that our movie has been short-listed for a BAFTA sparks a big smile from the nurse who's sorting my tablets. Next day, my parents arrive from Brittany. Evelyn has given them the key to my flat and my mum will be here for as long as I need her. She stays all afternoon and she can't wait to tell me the news from Stockholm. Malo has been on the phone. He's had a big row with his father. His love affair with Sweden is over. This is very good news indeed.

'He's coming back to London?'

'He didn't say that.'

'What, then?'

'He wants to travel a little.' She's frowning. 'I told him he should still be at school.'

School has been a festering sore between the three of us – Berndt, myself and Malo – for some time. Malo bailed out of the local comprehensive last year. My marriage was in ruins and I admit to taking my eye off the ball, but it was months before either Berndt or I realized that on many days he simply wasn't turning up. When I confronted him, he said that the teaching was crap and he was wasting his time, but I think the real reason was that he just couldn't cope. Under the circumstances, our circumstances, I couldn't really blame him. Then he went to Sweden and what was left of his education became Berndt's problem.

'So what did he say on the phone?'

'He wants to borrow five thousand euro. I told him to ask his father.'

My smile is unforced. I've learned recently from my stepdad that my Christian name was my mum's choice. Enora is Breton in origin, homage to a saint of the same name. St Enora is celebrated for entering a convent on the day she got married. Maybe I should have listened harder and picked up the hint.

'So where does Malo want to go?'

'Polynesia. He says it will improve his French.'

'His French is fine already.'

'*Bien sur.* But he says that would make New Caledonia a kind of university. *Pas stupide, notre Malo.*'

She's right. Despite his academic record, Malo

has always been bright, as well as manipulative and feckless, but given the chance I'd write a cheque here and now for both of us. Two tickets for New Caledonia? Two glorious months in the sunshine with my lovely boy? Ten thousand euro for the pair of us? A steal.

Mum has had a word with the neurosurgeon.

'He says you're doing OK. Maybe you should come back to France with us.'

I do my best to smile up at her. There are worse prospects just now than an autumn in their manor house overlooking the beach at Perros-Guirec. My mum cooks like a French mother should and I've never had a problem with my stepdad. He used to be a consultant engineer in the oil business, which is where all the money came from. His career made him a perfect role model for my son but his occasional attempts to talk Malo into doing something useful with his life have so far come to nothing.

I say I'm grateful for the offer.

'You mean no?'

I nod. For now, I tell her, I need to be in London.

'For the doctors?' Her eyes flick towards the nursing station. 'Just in case?'

'Of course. And maybe one or two other things.'

Mitch is back a couple of days later. He's knocked at Evelyn's door again and on her instructions he's arrived with my iPad, plus a beret she's found in my wardrobe. I seize the iPad greedily. I want to know where to find some of the stuff he's been writing.

'You're serious?'

'Always.'

He directs me to a handful of websites. One of them is the *Guardian,* another the *New Statesman.* A third, the most interesting, is a web-based digest of investigative journalism that calls itself Finisterra.

'It's Latin,' he explains. 'Posh. It means the end of the world.'

'Light reading? Something to keep the kids amused?'

He smiles. We've met just three times, the first a near-death experience, but we seem to have already developed that unvoiced kinship that can happen between two strangers who share the same sense of humour. In my drowsier moments I wonder whether it bears any comparison to my early days with Berndt, but I know already that this is something utterly – and thankfully – different. We're older. We've knocked around a bit. We've left footprints in the sand. Not that I know the first thing about this man, except that he makes me laugh.

'Tell me where you live.' It's early evening, rain streaming down the window, the hiss of rush-hour traffic from five floors below.

'Hither Green,' he says.

'Where's that?'

'South of the river. A Tesco Express and a couple of decent pubs. Old working-class London plus young couples on the make. You're getting the picture?'

'Alone? Married? Kids? The whole shtick?'

'Once.'

'And now?'

'Just me and a Syrian guy from Aleppo. He's a refugee but he's got leave to remain.'

I nod. I badly want to dip into the websites this man's tallied for me but I like his company, too. Tough call.

'You want me to take a walk? Find a coffee?' He's nodding at the iPad. 'Then come back?'

I gaze up at him and nod. This man reads my mind. Remarkable.

I start with the *Guardian*. Mitch Culligan turns out to be an occasional contributor to the Opinion page. A couple of his pieces deal with the aftermath of the election. They're punchy, beautifully written, closely argued, full of attitude. His pre-election tour of the kingdom, as I already know, filled him with a bewilderment verging on despair. Now, to everyone's astonishment, Corbyn has pricked the Tory bubble and the electoral future, just for a month or two, looks a great deal sunnier. Brexit, in Mitch's book, remains a huge own goal but the kids are at last on the march and Jezza has given them some sense of destination.

I find myself nodding. I met Corbyn once at a college in North London where I was doing an acting workshop. He struck me as sincere and companionable in ways I've never associated with politicians. He was also, like Mitch, a bit of a film buff.

I scroll through the rest of the *Guardian* pieces, then sample an offering or two from the *New Statesman*. By now, Mitch's preoccupations are very clear. He detests, in no particular order,

Donald Trump, Steve Bannon, Margaret Thatcher, Liam Fox, fiscal favours to public schools, the rotting corpse of UKIP, and the whole swamp of corporate greed. He suspects Theresa May is no great brain and he'd very much like to ride to work on a re-nationalized railway. He also thinks, joy of joys, that the Tory party is about to implode, and that a judicious poke or two might reveal the blackness of its soul. 'Expose these people for who they really are,' he writes, 'and they'll be out of power for a generation.'

I've found the investigative website by the time he returns. He must have been gone at least an hour. Some coffee.

'I had to make a couple of calls,' he grunts. 'Most days it would have been twice as long.'

I take this as a compliment. Then I mention Finisterra. This website, as I understand it, is Mitch's little allotment, the place where he can plant whatever thoughts he wants and share them with a wider world. Fair?

'Completely. Allotment is right. I take all this produce to market and wait for takers. That's the magic of the internet. You can kid yourself you've put the mainstream media out of business until you take a proper look at the traffic figures.'

'So why the Black Death?'

'You mean the piece on Boccaccio? The Decameron? The week the plague came to Florence?'

'Yes.'

'Because no one else would take it.'

'I understand that. I'm asking you why you wrote it in the first place.'

'Easy. It's the stats. One in two of the population died. Not just Florence, everywhere.'

'Here?'

'Everywhere. Do the sums. The Black Death gave you a fifty per cent chance of making it through to the weekend.'

These are odds I can relate to, thanks to my neurosurgeon. His playful introduction to the Grim Reaper still rankles, though more recently he appears to have saved my life.

'You've studied this stuff?'

'I have. I know it makes me a sad old git but maybe you should put it down to perspective. Grief's an easy sell these days. Why? Because there's serious money in other people's pain. Some lunatic goes bonkers on Westminster Bridge and the whole country – the whole fucking planet – wrings its hands. This is heavy stuff. Wrong time, wrong place. But we need to get a grip because these are buttons the bad guys know exactly how to press.'

'You think we should just ignore it?'

'I think you should log on again,' he nods at the iPad, 'and read about the Black fucking Death.'

This conversation is getting nowhere but I have the sneakiest feeling that Mitch is right. Living with Berndt's fevered imagination bothered me for years. He wrote like an angel and knew exactly how to tighten a plot until the audience was gasping for air. These are genuine talents but like everyone else in the marketplace he was aware that movies and books and everything else we call entertainment had to get blacker and blacker. Cannibalism. Animal rape. Multiple sex with Siamese twins. Anything to keep the cheques rolling in. I shudder to think about the impact on kids, and on Malo in particular. Serious money in other people's pain? Too right.

Mitch is delving in his day sack. Out comes the sweetest umbrella, powder blue, plus the cable to charge my iPad. Apparently the rain's in for the evening and Mitch has to make an event in deepest Camden. The four-way debate will be exploring the proposition of something called the Deep State. When I ask who's on the panel, he gives me names. One's a Labour MP. One's a rebel cleric. Another guy is a Venezuelan academic I've never heard of.

'That's three,' I say. 'Who else?'

'Me.'

Ouch.

Instinctively I reach out for him but he backs away. Then, just in time to delay his departure a little longer, I remember the name on the file in the cafe.

'What's Cassini?'

He looks at me a moment, then checks his watch before nodding down at the iPad.

'Google *Death Dive*,' he says. 'And wish me luck.'

Cassini turns out to be an inter-planetary space probe launched to investigate the rings of Saturn. It's done most of its business and just now it's barely weeks away from a final plunge towards the planet's surface. With the batteries all but dead this last act may reveal just a little more about Saturn's secrets before its atmosphere burns it alive. Hence the term 'Death Dive'.

Death dive? I'm trying to connect the dots here. Mitch is a campaigning journalist with a national reputation. He has talent, motivation, a squillion media contacts and thus a sizeable audience. People read his stuff, probably lots of people, and so they should. But what has any of this got to do with little me? I circle the question all evening, a bit like the poor space probe, getting no closer to an answer. Mitch has made no promises to come back to the hospital and in any case I may be discharged within days. Is this the last I'll see of him? Or might there one day be a chance to get a proper look at his mysterious Cassini file?

Next morning they get me into a wheelchair and take me several floors down to see my neurosurgeon again. This turns out to be the office where we first met, but by this time we've become old friends. He takes me through the operation and shows me scans and surgical images the way you might share holiday snaps. The tumour, it seems, was a glioblastoma, malignant, aggressive, difficult to get at. Pressing on my optic nerve, it was responsible for my headaches and my wonky eye. Untreated, it would undoubtedly – in time – have killed me.

'You got it all out?'

'We think so. We can't be absolutely certain but the chances are good.'

'So it won't come back?'

'It may. We never say "never". We'll be scanning you every three months to check.'

'And if it does? Come back?'

'Then we may have to pay it another visit.' A thin smile. 'The Reaper shouldn't have it all his own way.'

Under the circumstances, I later reflect, the comment is as close as I'm going to get to an apology. When I told the Reaper story to my mum she was horrified. It was my stepfather who had a private word with the hospital management and I imagine they did the rest. Either way, I'm genuinely grateful for everything this man and his team have been able to do for me.

'You saved my life,' I tell him. 'At least for now.'

Back home, I find three more Jiffy bags awaiting me. My stepfather has gone back to Brittany but my mum has truly made herself at home. My appetite for her very distinctive take on onion soup has returned with a vengeance and I'm even able to help her out with a decent bottle of Sauvignon.

Two of the Jiffy bags have come from my agent. Both contain scripts and both are duds. Of the French-Canadian project there's so far no news though these things take forever to develop so I'm far from disappointed. In any case, the last couple of weeks seem to have loosened my career's grip on me. Things I once viewed as important – an evil review, for instance – have joined the rest of the background static in my life. No longer will my precious future be threatened by a critic's crap judgement or a casting director's inexplicable failure to see me as the obvious choice for the female lead. No, from now on – just like everyone else on the planet – I'm simply a billion cells in loose formation, any one of which could turn rogue at any moment.

This realization, to my surprise, comes as a bit of a relief. All told, I've done OK. I've been in some quality films. I've won some devoted fans. I've made more money than I ever dreamed possible. I might even get to live with my precious boy again. Not bad. Not bad at all.

One evening, late-ish, I try to explain some of this to my mum but, like most French women of her generation, she's fiercely proud of what I've achieved and refuses to accept it might be over. In time, she tells me, I'll get back to my old self, maybe put on a bit of weight, start looking for new roles to conquer. I nod, and agree, mainly to keep her sweet but later, after she's finally retired to the spare bedroom, I stand by the window in the lounge, staring up at the night sky.

Thanks to the street lights and all the other pollution there's very little to see but I know that out there, way beyond the creamy blob of the moon, a tiny little morsel of high-tech is readying itself for its final curtain call. I've read the websites. I'm word perfect on the script. One last fizz of data transmission. One last fuel burn. And then the plunge into oblivion.

I hang on to the thought for a moment and

then remember the third Jiffy bag. I've a feeling it might have come from Mitch and the moment I open it I know I'm right. He's sent me a framed shot of Saturn from the Hubble telescope. The image is truly beautiful, the huge blue planet girdled in mystery. I hold it at arm's length, and then return to the window.

Poor Cassini.

Three

Two days later, it's Mum who takes the call.

'Malo,' she mouths, bending to the phone.

My angel child is at Stockholm airport. His flight is due to take off in half an hour. By mid-afternoon, he should be in Heathrow. Any chance of a lift?

'Ask him which terminal.'

My mother gives me the phone. I put the question myself. Malo says he hasn't a clue. He sounds sleepy.

'Give me the flight number,' I tell him. 'It'll be on the ticket.'

There's a long silence. My pulse quickens. For a moment or two I think I've lost him. Finally he gives me the flight number. Then he's gone.

The last time I saw Malo was more than a year ago. Berndt had moved out after a particularly vicious row. He'd come at me with an empty bottle of vodka he'd smashed on the edge of a kitchen work surface and after I'd locked myself in the loo, I called the police. Malo stayed in contact with his father after the exclusion order and disappeared within the month. No farewell hug. No note of explanation. No forwarding address. Not even a hint that Berndt's credit card had bought him a ticket to Sweden. At the time, it had been hard to forgive either of them. Now, though, I'm telling myself that Malo is my best chance to rescue something from the ashes of the past couple of years.

At the airport, my mum is the first to spot him among the tide of incoming passengers.

'Malo!' she shouts in her throaty Breton twang. I follow her pointing finger, her madly waving hand. The same mop of black curly hair. The same adolescent slouch. The same ripped jeans. But something has happened to his face. The hollows are deeper, more sculpted. He's started shaving in earnest. To my slight surprise, I'm looking at a man.

My mum, like me, has always been a sucker for the sudden warmth of Malo's smile.

'*Tout va bien, mon petit?*'

Malo accepts her hug and assures her he's fine. His voice is deeper, his French perfect. So far, he hasn't even looked at me.

The stream of incoming passengers is thinning. Malo stoops to retrieve his bag. Soft red leather. Not cheap. Like his father, my son has always travelled light.

'Why Einstein?' I'm gazing at the image on his T-shirt.

Malo ignores the question. He can't take his eyes off the neat line of stitches across my shaved head.

'Some kind of accident?'

'In a way, yes.'

'You OK?'

'I'm fine.'

I resist the urge to kiss him, to tell him how wonderful and unexpected it is to see him again, how the best news always takes you by surprise. Instead, I tell myself that this is a scene best played long. Life has moved on, his and mine. We need to take our time.

On the way back into London I insist that Malo sits up front with my mum. She's always been a natural with Malo, ignoring his reticence, filling his silences with a blizzard of news from home. This is a knack I've never been able to master, not least because to me gabbling is always a sign of nerves, but by the time we're back home I realize that nothing has changed. My son is as gorgeous, and opaque, and impenetrable as ever. Except when there's something he needs in a hurry.

It's late evening. Before retiring, my mum has broken the news that she's off back to Brittany the day after next. I've told Malo about the operation, and the various tests to come, and it's clearly Mum's expectation that her grandson will take over as my guardian and nurse. This responsibility Malo appears to be ready to shoulder. With one proviso.

'I've got a friend, Mum. From Stockholm.'

'He? She?'

'She. We could share the spare bedroom after Gran's gone, yeah?'

Her name, he tells me, is Eva. She's just graduated from university with a degree in psychiatry. She speaks perfect English. Better still, she has a driving licence. Perfect for running me around.

He presents the proposition with a yawn, and wanders into the kitchen to make himself a coffee. My agreement is evidently a given, a technique

I suspect he's picked up from his father. Irked, I call him back.

'How old is Eva?'

'Twenty-six.'

'And how long might she be here?'

'Dunno.'

'Weeks? Longer?'

'Depends.'

'On what?'

'Loads of stuff. You'll like her. She's cute.'

'Cute' is a word I don't recall Malo using before. New, as well, is his invitation to join him in a spliff or two. The coffee abandoned, he produces a bag of loose tobacco, a box of papers, and a cube of resin untidily wrapped in silver foil.

'You brought that through customs?'

'Yeah.'

'You're crazy. These days they lock people up for less.'

He shrugs, doesn't react. I watch him rolling the joint. He does it quickly, deftly. For the first time in days my head is beginning to throb.

'If you really want to smoke you'll have to do it outside, preferably on the pavement.' I nod towards the door.

'It's raining.'

'I don't care. The choice is yours. I hate smoking. You know that.'

He studies me for a long moment and I sense something in his eyes that I've never seen before. My precious son is full of rage.

'Tell me about this thing with your father.' I reach for the spliff and put it carefully to one side.

'What do you want to know?'

'Everything. What happened between you. Why you decided to leave. What drove you out.'

He gives me that same look but this time the inference is clear. This is none of my business. I try again, same questions, different phrasing, and this time – briefly – I spark a response.

'The man's a dickhead,' he says. 'But I guess you'd know that already.'

I want to know more about the dickhead, about Eva, about his year and a bit in Stockholm, but Malo is already on his feet. He picks up the spliff and heads for the door. Moments later, he's gone.

It must be twenty minutes before the phone rings. Thinking it might be Malo locked out in the rain, I'm already heading for the panel in the hall that houses the entry phone.

'Enora? That you?'

It's Mitch Culligan. Before I get a chance to say anything he's apologizing for the lateness of the hour. He's been tied up with a bunch of Marxists who don't know how to end a sentence. He'd have phoned earlier but he couldn't find a way of putting the conversation out of its misery.

'That bad?' Despite myself, I'm laughing.

'Worse. Two of them belonged in a museum. The other was borderline deceased. Marx never knew what he started. How are you?'

'Terrible, if you want the truth.'

'It's come back? The headache? All the rest of it?'

'No. Yes. Oh, shit . . .' I'm staring at the video camera. There's no one at the main entry door but where the gardens lap against the exterior wall I can make out a slim figure, bent over a cigarette, sheltering under a tree. It's an image that makes my blood run cold. To me it speaks of something beyond pathos. It has to be Malo.

'Enora? What's the matter?'

'Nothing.'

'You're crying.'

'How do you know?'

'I can tell. It's a man thing. A night with a bunch of Marxists tells you everything you want to know about grief. That's a joke, by the way. You want me to come round?'

I know the answer is yes. Just now, I'd like nothing better. But an evening with my only child, the only human being I'm ever likely to bring into the world, has taught me what a crap mother I must be.

'No,' I say as firmly as I can. 'Give me a ring tomorrow.'

Malo, when he finally returns, is soaking wet. I let him in at the main door downstairs and fetch a towel while he walks up to the fourth floor. His curls are plastered against the whiteness of his scalp, and his T-shirt and jeans are wet through, but he's calmer, even talkative. He seems to have realized that I hold the keys to the flat, that I own the place, that I might conceivably have ideas of my own, and this – at last – prompts the beginnings of a conversation.

'It must have been scary,' he says. 'Nearly dying like that.'

He's standing in the middle of the living room,

naked except for his boxer shorts. I want to towel every inch of him dry. I want to make him hot chocolate and French toast just the way he used to like it. I want to have the two of us back together again and maybe have another go at getting it right. Instead I ask him to tell me more about Eva.

'I met her through Dad. He says he went to her for advice on some character or other but that's bullshit. When I turned up he was giving her this big line about a part he had in mind. You know the way he can be? Close but not too close? Hanging back? Pretending he isn't interested?'

I nod. I know exactly how Berndt plays scenes like these, artful, canny, seemingly disengaged. He once boasted to me that he could talk any woman into bed without laying a finger on her.

'This was in the apartment? The penthouse?'

'Yeah.'

'So where was Annaliese?'

'She's been on location in Russia. Before that, she was doing some movie or other in Hamburg.'

'So she's away a lot?'

'Most of the time.'

'And is that a problem?'

'Not for her. She's got a brain in her head. A couple of weeks living with Dad and she couldn't wait to get on the road again.'

'But they're going to get married. Have I got that right?'

'No. That was the plan. They'd made the big announcement. Then Annaliese told Dad she'd prefer to wait a bit.'

40

'Why?'

'She never said. Not to me.'

'So will they ever get married?'

'No chance.'

'And your dad?'

'He never mentions it. Eva calls it denial. You mind if I have a shower?'

He disappears towards the bathroom without waiting for an answer, leaving me alone in the living room, gazing at the wet footprints on the carpet. I'm grinning. The news from Stockholm is excellent. Not just me, I think. Her, too.

In the kitchen, I put the kettle on. The last face-to-face conversation I had with Berndt took place at a pub we occasionally used in Soho. He was days away from moving back to Stockholm and he wanted to settle what he quaintly called 'our private affairs'. In terms of money and possessions this boiled down to a simple split. He'd keep his place in Stockholm, everything he owned personally, and the contents of his several bank accounts, while I would end up with Holland Park, my accumulated savings and investments, my three-year-old Peugeot, and anything else with my name on it.

At the time, I didn't believe him. I'm worth a great deal more than Berndt and I thought that this was a big, splashy gesture calculated to belittle me. In the world of Berndt Andressen, he seemed to be saying, money counted for nothing because only his work, that sequence of movies stretching from here to eternity, really mattered. That was why he was so glad to be shot of me. That was why he couldn't wait for us to get formally divorced.

Thinking about it that night, back in Holland Park, I tried to imagine what would happen next. Berndt would talk to his lawyers. They'd point out I was worth a bit and that a bit of pressure might entitle him to half the joint estate, maybe with some kind of adjustment for Malo. At that point he'd nod and agree, and we'd then settle into our respective trenches, hunker down, and await the opening bombardment.

My lawyer said much the same thing. He seemed to have been dealing with divorces for most of his professional life and in his view my soon-to-be ex-husband was suffering from something my lawyer called 'shaggers' remorse'. This boils down to guilt at the break-up and there are some men who believe that a generous settlement will wash all that nastiness away. To be frank, I never thought Berndt was one of them. Deep down, as his darker plots might suggest, he's a selfish, narcissistic, ruthless bastard, and as the weeks passed without any word from his lawyers, I began to wonder if I was fated to spend the rest of my life in this matrimonial twilight. When I discussed this with my own lawyer, he counselled patience. Early days, he said. Better to wait and see.

Nothing happened. Neither then nor now. There's still been chatter in the trade press about Berndt's forthcoming nuptials but unless he's planning on becoming a bigamist I can only believe that the journalists have got it wrong. Now, thanks to Malo, I know that yet another relationship in his busy, busy life has crashed and burned. Annaliese, bless her, has seen through the man. Soon enough, in her own interests, she'll probably be gone. Either way, I'm very glad he's out of my life. The only thing he had that mattered to me is my precious son and just now he's within touching distance. Berndt, to be blunt, is history.

Malo joins me in the kitchen. He's wearing my dressing gown he must have found in the bathroom. The tea's nearly brewed.

'So what happened with Eva?' I ask. 'When your dad wanted this advice?'

'She turned him down. She told him she didn't believe in the character and neither did he. Dad's not used to women answering back. Not these days. Not with his reputation.'

I pour the tea. I can imagine this conversation in every detail. Malo's right. Berndt always had the upper hand.

'You think I was like that?'

'Like what?'

'Compliant?'

'Never. You fought back. If you want the truth it was horrible being around you both.'

'But why did you go with him?'

'Because he did the same number on me. And I was stupid enough to believe him. Talk to Eva. She's the one who's seen through all the bullshit.'

I nod. Grin. I want to give my wayward boy a hug. By some miracle I don't properly understand we seem to have become comrades in arms, refugees from the same dark presence I should never have let into my life. Looking for the sugar bowl I wonder whether I owe my son some kind of apology for the madness of the last couple of years, but when I begin to explain just how things got so bad so quickly he shakes his head and turns away.

'Mum . . .' he mutters.

I feel a sudden blush of embarrassment. Playing mother is a tough gig. I've gone too far, too fast. I ask again about Eva. Does he have a photo? He fetches his phone from his sodden jeans next door. I find myself looking at an urchin face caught in bright sunshine as if someone's just called her name. Wide smile. Perfect teeth. Punk hair. There's a tram in the background, and a priest on a bicycle.

'Twenty-six, you say?'

'I know. I couldn't believe it either. Sometimes I think she could be my kid sister.'

'And your father?'

'He couldn't handle her. Or us, either. Once he knew we were screwing it got really ugly.'

'Is that why you're here?'

'Yes.'

'Because you've got nowhere else to go?'

'I didn't say that.'

'But is it true?'

'No.' He blinks and looks away, embarrassed by this small admission. I want more. I want him to tell me he's glad to be away from his father. I want to know he's going to be around for a while. I want him to call this cave of mine home.

At last, I pour the tea. Malo always had a special mug, a souvenir from a muddy weekend the two of us shared at Glastonbury, but he barely touches it. Instead, he begins to yawn. I do my best to reignite the conversation but it's obvious he's no longer in the mood.

He's looking round the kitchen as if he's never lived here, never even seen it before, and then he notices one of the photos I've pinned to the corkboard. It comes from way back and it shows the pair of us, Malo and me, on the South Bank. He'd accompanied me to a rehearsal at the Old Vic and afterwards I'd taken him for coffee at the Festival Hall. These little get-togethers were much rarer than you might imagine, one of the reasons I've found space on the corkboard, and Malo seems fascinated by it.

He was still a boy then, pre-adolescent, vocal, curious, prone to mischief and wonderment in equal parts, and I still treasure the memory of that afternoon. He'd sat in the stalls in the theatre while we went through a sequence of key scenes in the last act and he'd been fascinated by the play of light on the set when the director was experimenting with a couple of effects. I suspect this was the first time he'd properly grasped the idea of theatre and there was pride as well as curiosity in the questions he fired at me over the strudel. Who was Ibsen? How come I'd got the part of someone who kills herself? Was I really crying when I was crying?

We were with another actress friend of mine at the time and she thought Malo was really sweet. She was older than me, with two grown-up sons, and when she produced her camera to take a shot of the pair of us she told Malo to

45

cuddle close to me. Good as gold, he did exactly as he was told and next day, back at the theatre, she told me how envious she'd been. Seven's a magic age, she said. You'll spend the rest of your life trying to get back to that moment.

At the time, I'd thought nothing of it. Malo had always been trusting, as well as tactile, and I'd somehow thought that would last forever. Now, in the kitchen, I ask him whether he remembers that afternoon in the empty stalls at the Old Vic.

He's still gazing at the photo. I think I catch the faintest nod though he won't answer my question. Finally he steps back from the corkboard. For whatever reason, he won't meet my eyes.

'I'll crash on the sofa.' He turns towards the door. 'Have you got a couple of blankets?'

Four

I phone Mitch Culligan two days later. After a second night of broken sleep, Malo has swapped the sofa for the privacy of my bedroom during the day and Mum is out scouring the local shops for goodies for my stepdad. Life without certain foodstuffs is a hanging offence in their house and she's dangerously low on Marmite and decent marmalade.

Mitch is on a bus, stuck in traffic somewhere near the Elephant and Castle.

He tells me we need to meet.

'Why?'

He won't say. When I mention Cassini, he just grunts. Whether the doomed little explorer has become code for something else I've no idea but the realization that Malo may be around for a while has given me a whole new take on my immediate future. I have responsibilities here. One of them is to get better. Another is to my wayward son. And the third is to find out exactly what Mitch Culligan might be after.

We agree to meet. He has an appointment with his agent to discuss a first-draft submission. This is the first time I become aware that he writes books, as well as tub-thumping, bravura pieces for the left-wing press, and I'm back on the internet within seconds of ending the call. Two crime novels and a biography of an ex-Navy diver I've never heard of, a man called Joe Cassidy. A visit to the Amazon site reveals a four-star average reader score for the latter with sixty-three posted reviews. Impressive.

We meet, as planned, at the office of his agent in Putney. I'm curious about the biography.

'Why Joe Cassidy?'

'I did an interview with him back in the day. He was involved in all kinds of mischief over the years and he fascinated me. I never believed in greatness until I met that man. He was still middle-aged but he'd been through a lot of stuff in the Falklands War and he was so *wise*. Fame had passed him by, not that he seemed to care a toss, and I thought that was a shame. When I suggested a book he wasn't keen, but if you ask the same question often enough you'll end up with the answer you want. I think he said yes just to get me off the phone. After that everything went like a dream.'

'He didn't disappoint?'

'Not at all. And he even seemed to like what I made of him.'

At this, he gets up and leaves the borrowed office. Seconds later he's back with a copy of the book I recognize from Amazon. It's slimmer than I expected and the photos include a shot of a cadaverous man in baggy shorts sitting on the edge of a harbour wall.

'He's only got one leg,' I point out.

'Exactly. Yet he still swam year round, every morning, without fail. He ran a dive business, too. Still does, as far as I know. Amazing bloke.'

'A kind of homage, then?' I'm still looking at the book.

'Definitely. A privilege to meet the guy. He became a kind of friend.'

I nod. Hand the book back.

'You'd rather not?'

'I'd like you to sign it. Do you mind?'

'Not at all.' He's looking pleased. He finds a pen and pauses a moment before scribbling a line and then adding his signature. When I get the book back, his handwriting is indecipherable.

'What does it say?'

'It's a quote from Joe. *Never let the bastards have it all their own way*. I think that's what kept him going. That and Scotch.'

'Bastards?'

'Bastards.'

'Anyone in particular?'

'Plenty. He was a good hater, Joe. He liked to recruit an army of enemies and see them all off. It was a while before I realized he was a blunter version of what kept this country going. Stubborn as you like. Brave. Stoic. Difficult. Unforgiving. Brilliant man.'

I nod, not altogether convinced.

'Last of a breed?'

Mitch nods, smiles, says nothing. I thank him for the Saturn photo.

'You like it?'

'I love it. September fifteenth? The final plunge? The death dive? Am I right?' I want him to get the file out, the one with *Cassini* on the front. Once again, he seems to read my mind, stooping to his day bag.

Then he pauses. I know exactly what's coming next.

'Last time we did this wasn't good,' he says carefully. 'Are you sure you can handle it?'

As a question, this has its drawbacks. Handle what? Mitch acknowledges the question with a frown. His fingers have already slipped inside the file. Moments later he produces a sheaf of photos.

I'm looking at a shot of a middle-aged man in an expensive suit. He's posed against a group of younger women who look like models. The setting, maybe a hotel, could be some kind of fashion event. He's on the short side and he needs to cut down on the lunches but he has the look of someone unbothered by the opinions of others. He holds himself like a boxer, squat, nicely balanced, ready for anything. The grin is wide. There isn't a thread of grey in his curly black hair and the three-day stubble is camera-perfect. He has his arm around the nearest of the women and the fact that she must be at least a couple of inches taller doesn't bother him in the least. Confidence, I think. And maybe serious wealth.

'Do you recognize him?' Mitch asks.

'No. Should I?'

Mitch lets the question ride. The guy's name, he says, is Hayden Prentice. He pauses, looking at me.

'No?'

'No.'

'His mates in the early days used to call him "Saucy". Some still do.' Another pause. 'HP? Saucy?'

50

'I'm sorry.' I shake my head, still staring at the photo. 'He's in the rag trade? Some kind of businessman?'

'Only as an investor. The guy's a moving target. Think fingers. Think pies. He made his first fortune in the Alps. Affordable ski holidays for the nearly rich. Some say he got lucky with the exchange rate and perfect snow but if that's true then he's been lucky ever since. Just now he has a big fat portfolio of businesses. They range from a stake in a major entertainment complex to a couple of niche insurance companies, and every one of them makes him money. Luck, I'm afraid, doesn't cover it.'

I'm looking harder at the face in the photograph. Something is stirring deep in my poor brain. Maybe a long-ago conversation. Maybe more than that.

'Alps, you say?'

'Yeah.'

'The French Alps?'

'Courchevel. Chamonix. Les Houches. Combloux. Draw a circle round a decent airport. Talk to the locals about weather patterns. Get the chalet offer right. Suss the nightlife. Nothing's fucking rocket science, not if you know what you're about.' He pauses, looking for another photo. 'That's him talking by the way, not me.'

This time Prentice has been snapped on the deck of what looks like a sizeable yacht. It might be the south of France, Sardinia, Marbella, anywhere with that overwhelming blue of sky and sea. Prentice is squatting on the deck with a handful of sun cream. Lying full length on a

51

turquoise mattress is a naked blonde with huge Guccis, and an all-over tan. Whoever took the photograph seems to have taken Prentice by surprise. He's looking up at the camera, visibly annoyed. His own tan matches his companion's and I'm right about the boxer bit. He's carrying a couple of pounds he doesn't need around his belly but his shoulders are broad, his chest lightly matted with black hair. This is someone who plainly works out, someone you'd be wiser not to upset.

'Well?' A tiny edge of impatience has crept into Mitch's question.

I'm still looking at the photo. Especially the chest.

'He speaks French? Prentice?'

'Not a word. Wouldn't hear of it. Mark of weakness in his book.'

I nod. Sit back. Close my eyes. It's all coming back, every single detail. *Saucy*, I think. Fuck.

Five

It's the summer of my first appearance at Cannes, my first glimpse of Berndt Andressen, the summer when I prefaced my film festival moments with a lazy, paid-for month shooting a movie at Antibes. With the budget on its knees, the French production company put us up in a fleapit *pension* in a back street near the station. According to the director, an ageing *faux philosophe* still looking for his first major breakthrough, the experience was meant to sharpen our appreciation for the class of criminal around whom his sagging scenario was constructed. We all knew this was an excuse to save a few more precious francs and when the invitation arrived for drinks aboard a newly docked vessel in the marina, we gladly decamped from the cafe-bar which we'd made home.

The boat was clinching proof that no one with any money has any taste. It was big, sleek, and very white. It had the kind of lines a child might have drawn if he wanted to turn a series of waves into a boat. You boarded via a gangplank that looked as box-new as everything else. A uniformed lackey who probably doubled as a bodyguard met you at the other end and when you stepped down into the salon, along with a blast of air-con came gusts of an overpowering perfume I can only describe as emetic. The name of the boat was everywhere: on the bow, on the stern, on the lackey, on the lifebelts, embossed in brass on the bridge controls, even appliquéd on to the thick courtesy towels in the closet. *Agincourt.* Subtle.

Smirking in French is easy. You put on your brightest smile, shoot a look at your buddies, and murmur that you think the whole thing is *impressionnant.* In this context *impressionnant* means *merde.*

Our host was a man called Dennis who apparently owned a football club along with some huge construction company. He was tall, thin, and rarely smiled. Unlike everyone else, he'd forsworn shorts for a suit. The pastiness of his face was untroubled by the sun and within minutes of our arrival, having muttered instructions to the lackey about the champagne in one of the huge fridges, he made his excuses and left for the airport at Nice.

At this point we were beginning to wonder quite why we'd ever been invited but minutes later the rest of the party arrived. They'd spent most of the afternoon in a harbourside bar and it showed. They were all English, mainly men. They tramped aboard and there was a blizzard of oaths when one of them lost his footing on the deck. This turned out to be Saucy. My first impression was slightly marred by the blood pouring out of a gash on his cheek. In another life I happened to have done a first-aid course.

A woman we hadn't seen before was already on hand with a towel and a handful of plasters but Saucy ignored her. He liked what I'd had to

say about ice cubes. The woman fetched a bucket-
ful from down below while Saucy sprawled on
one of the hand-stitched leather banquettes. I
had the towel pressed hard against the side of
his face. He couldn't take his eyes off me.

'I've seen you before, ain't I? Give us a
name.'

'Enora.'

'I meant the film. The movie. Starts in London.
Two dykes in bed. Not you, love.'

'*Kalendar*.'

'That's it. You were good. You were great.
Easy with that ice, eh?'

The bleeding stopped within minutes. I closed
the wound, which wasn't deep, and applied the
biggest of the plasters. All the while, Saucy was
telling me about the movie, about what happened,
as if I'd never heard of it before. Finally he
swung himself up into a sitting position, fingering
the plaster. By now everyone was up on deck.
Drinks had been served and there was a great
deal of laughter. When I suggested we join them,
Saucy shook his head.

'You got a bloke with you? One of that lot?'

'No.'

'Good. A gal needs looking after. The least I
can do.'

Cold on the page this sounds less than enticing,
but there was something about him, a cheekiness
or maybe a hint of vulnerability that I liked. He
was bouncy, like a dog you'd be happy to have
around, and when he said he'd fix us a proper
drink, not poncey Krug, I said *oui*.

'You speak the lingo?'

55

'*Oui.*'

'Wash your mouth out. Now tell me you like a decent margarita.'

'*Oui.*'

'Yeah? We like that. Stay there. I'll be back.'

I did what I was told, trying to decide which of the framed sunset shots I loathed most. The margarita, when Saucy finally returned from below, was excellent.

'So tell me about you,' I said. 'You're a friend of the guy in the suit?'

'Yeah. Like brothers on a good day, me and Den. Other times it ain't so sweet, but who's keeping score?'

'And this is his boat?'

'Every nut. Every bolt. Every gold fucking door knob. Hideous, innit?' Laughter suited his face, even when blood began to seep beneath the plaster. He told me about Den, about the money he'd made, about the way he couldn't keep his hands off all the gold clobber. He made this obsession with self-advertisement sound like an addiction, which in a way I suppose it was. Finally we got round to the question I really wanted to ask.

'And what about *your* football club?'

'Pompey. Till I die.'

'Pompey?'

'Portsmouth.'

'And you own it? Like Den?'

'*Own* it?' More laughter. 'Fuck me, I'm just a punter. Tell you the truth, it ain't going too well just now but disappointment never hurt anyone.

56

We miss Ballie big time though he lost it towards the end.'

Ballie? I hadn't a clue what he was talking about but it didn't seem to matter. I'd finished the margarita and my new barman was down below fixing another. By the time he came back, to my slight regret, we had company. The new arrival, a refugee from the drinks party on deck, had yet to introduce himself. Saucy spared me asking.

'This is Terry,' he said, 'And he's about to fuck off back upstairs. Right, Tel?'

Terry spared me a nod, told me to watch my arse, and did what he'd been told. Saucy and I were back on the banquette. Already the first margarita had gone to my head. When I asked Saucy about his last port of call he described a city that could only have been Nice. A single night tied up alongside a boat full of partying Russians. Total oblivion.

'You never went ashore?'

'No point. Vodka's fucking vodka. Especially when it's free.'

I couldn't think of an answer to that but Saucy didn't want one. Instead, he asked me what it was like to be an actress. This is a question we thesps get less often than you might imagine. Strangers often want to know about a particular performance, or a favourite fellow actor, but what they're really after is gossip. Saucy wanted something far more interesting.

I remember doing my best. I told him I'd always liked make-believe: reading it, watching it, doing it. Sit in the darkness in the cinema, put yourself into the hands of a good director, and you can find yourself mapping a whole new world. Not just outside but inside.

'What the fuck does that mean?'

'It means you can become someone else. Which is what an actress does.'

'That's good.' Saucy appeared to be thinking hard. 'I never thought of it that way.'

He seemed genuinely impressed. He said he liked movies, make-believe, all that shit, but that nothing could beat real life.

'Where I come from,' he said, 'you get one chance. Either you take it or you spend the rest of your fucking life sat on your arse.'

'And you?'

'I took it. Big time.'

'So what did you do?'

'Back then I was an accountant. Don't laugh. It's not what you're thinking. In life you follow the money and the guys who know the best route up the mountain are people like me. All you need is a bit of nerve, a head for heights, a bit of bottle.'

This wasn't what I'd been expecting. Saucy came at you with the force of an express train. It wasn't just his physique, the way he held himself, but there was something in his eyes, a hint of apartness, that I've only ever associated with people who've made the big time, either through wealth or fame or – more usually – both. Marquee names in showbiz have it. A top French politician who used to fancy my mum had it. These are people who trust their own judgement, who always know which

58

gambles pay off, and who never entertain a moment's self-doubt.

I don't know why but I didn't want this conversation to end. Saucy had swallowed the last of his second margarita.

'Are you rich?' I asked him.

'Yes.'

'But accountants don't get rich. Not properly rich. Not drifting-round-the-Côte-d'Azur-getting-pissed rich.'

'This one does.' He put the glass to one side and kissed me softly on the lips. Then he stood up and tugged at his shorts. 'Later,' he said. 'Then we'll have a proper chat.'

We joined the revellers on deck. More bottles of champagne. More stories traded back and forth. More extravagant toasts to passing strangers on the marina pontoon. Then, as the sun set, the arrival of a mountain of take-out from a *resto* on the quayside. By now, we were all royally pissed. Thick wedges of anchovy, olive, and tomato pizza made little difference. By this time, Saucy had abandoned an Italian actress who was part of our little *equipe* and was back at my side. Some of my buddies were trying to negotiate the gangplank. In the warm darkness, totally blitzed, they looked like battlefield casualties and when Saucy suggested I stay the night and spare myself the embarrassment of following them it seemed like a totally reasonable proposition.

He was occupying a stateroom next to his mate Dennis. I remember giggling when Saucy confirmed that the sheets were silk and I think there may have been mirrors on the ceiling overhead. Either way, Saucy was a considerate lover and didn't seem to mind when I went to sleep on him. By the time I awoke, nursing the grandmother of all hangovers, it was daylight again and he'd gone.

Six

Mitch is impressed by my recall.

'Word perfect,' he says. 'So why didn't you recognize him?'

There are more photos on my lap. Saucy snapped on a busy street of what looks like London. Saucy at the wheel of a rally car. Saucy blowing out the candles on a huge cake. I count them, still thinking about Mitch's question.

'He's really fifty?'

'Yes. Last month. He was abroad at the time so the big party's still to come.'

'He lives in London?'

'Dorset. He bought a pile a couple of years back and spent a fortune doing it up.'

'You've been there? Seen it?'

'Not personally but someone I trust got an invite down. She says he's done it beautifully. Bought the right interior design talent. Got the décor spot-on.'

Mitch produces another photo, this time scissored from a copy of *Country Life.* The house – Flixcombe Manor – looks comfortably Georgian. Seven bedrooms. Two reception rooms. Sauna. Inner courtyard. Heated indoor swimming pool in adjacent stable block. Self-contained guest cottage. Timber-framed barn. Sherborne six miles.

I look at the house again, trying to imagine it at the hands of the man I met so briefly all those years ago in Antibes. Mitch, I suspect, is wrong. Saucy would have masterminded the job himself.

'It was eighteen years ago,' I tell Mitch. 'We were different people, both of us. That's why I needed the name.'

'I get the impression you liked him.'

'I did. You're right. He was real. In those kinds of circles that's rare.'

'You saw him again?'

'No.'

'Never tried to make contact? Never went back to the boat?'

'There was no time. They'd finished the re-write on the script and I was back to work. The next day I went along the coast to Cannes. By that time, if you want the truth, I'd forgotten about Saucy. It was an interlude. An amusement. I met someone else at Cannes and that was completely different.'

Mitch nods. So far I've never mentioned my ex-husband and I sense this isn't the place to start. Instead, I ask how Mitch had made the link between me and Saucy.

'I'm writing a book about him,' he says, 'and I've been talking to loads of people. Some of them were on that boat and a couple remembered you.'

'There's a book in Saucy?' I'm staring at him.

'Yes. Saucy and one or two friends of his. Like-minded folk.'

'How come?'

He won't answer the question, not yet. My phone is ringing. I fetch it out and check the caller.

'You want to take that?'

It's my agent, Rosa. She checks I'm OK – a question that has suddenly become more than a courtesy – and then says I'm up for a BBC radio play. She names a writer she knows I admire. It's a one-off, an hour long. Rehearsals are scheduled for a couple of weeks' time. Might I be interested? I say yes without really thinking. She sounds pleased. She'll put the script in the post.

'Head OK, sweetness?'

'Head's perfect.'

Rosa hangs up and I'm back with Mitch. He's found yet another image. This time it's on his iPad. He passes it across. I blink, look harder. This has nothing to do with Saucy or two-million-pound properties in rural Dorset. The segment of a black orb, delicately edged in silver, pushes in from the top left-hand corner. It looks both sinister and beautiful. Beyond it, the curve flatter, is a biscuit-coloured girdle that seems to act as a shield or a fence against the infinite blue-black background. Look harder, and this yawning void is faintly pricked with tiny points of light.

'Saturn.' I look up. 'Has to be.'

'You're right.'

'Taken from Cassini?'

'Right again. But that's not the point.' He gets up and crouches beside me. His finger finds one of the bigger points of light. 'That's us,' he says. 'That's Earth.'

For a second or two I don't believe him. Then I remember the stats I've picked up from the various websites: twenty years in ever-deeper space, a journey of three and a half billion kilometres. No wonder we've reduced ourselves to just another twinkle, one among trillions.

I shake my head. Little Cassini has given us a truth we've all found so hard to grasp, or even imagine. Our own planet, our own teeming world, is – in truth – nothing more than a speck of bluish light: small, frail, lonely, steeped in darkness. For a split second, madly, I'm tempted to relate all this to the cellular vastness of my own brain, equally frail, equally vulnerable. In both dimensions, inner and outer space, we never get the real picture. We kid ourselves we're unique. We tell ourselves we're important. We even pretend we're somehow in charge. When all the time we're the merest smidge from oblivion.

Just now, just here in this small moment of wonderment and revelation, I owe little Cassini everything.

'When are they putting her to death?' I ask.

'Next week.'

'We should hold a wake. Raise a glass or two. Thank her from the bottom of our feeble hearts.'

There's alarm in Mitch's face, as well as puzzlement. He asks my agent's question.

'You OK?'

'I'm good.' I nod at the iPad. 'And I'm serious about the wake.'

It's at this point that I realize how seriously Mitch is taking my welfare. He's collecting the shots of Saucy and returning them to the file. When I ask why, he says my getting better is way more important than anything he might have in mind. When I realize he means it, that he's acting as a kind of guardian, this becomes a real piss-off. I'm hooked on Saucy. I want to know more. I want to know what he's done to merit an entire book and I want to know what role Mitch might have in mind for yours truly in whatever happens next.

Mitch has ignored every one of my questions. He's busy with his iPad. He lifts his head and checks my email address. Then he squints at the screen and hits Send.

'Take a proper look when you get home,' he says. 'And have the rest of the day off.'

I don't move. If this is my cue to leave it has to be on my own terms.

'Just tell me one thing,' I say. 'Tell me why you've put the word "Cassini" on the file.'

Mitch nods, like he's been half expecting the question. Those long fingers return the image to the screen. He seems to brood for a while. Then he smiles.

'Some said the mission was impossible,' he murmurs. 'Saturn up close and personal? A robot parked on one of her moons? Clues to what made the universe in the first place? Turns out they were wrong.'

Seven

I show Malo the Cassini image when I get home. My mum is packed and ready for the airport. Evelyn, who'd volunteered to drive us, has been called to some kind of emergency meeting and so it's going to be me behind the wheel. This is exactly what I shouldn't be doing, not if I'm paying attention to my neurosurgeon, but I haven't shared his sensible advice about not driving with either my mother or my son, and in any case Cassini's take on little us has revised my view of more or less everything.

'Neat.' Malo has spared the image a glance on my iPad. 'Cool.'

My mum, in her practical French way, finds the stats difficult to grasp. She's also a devout Catholic. God created the universe and she believes we unpick its mysteries at our peril. She's also worried about missing the flight.

'You don't think that's incredible?' I'm still looking at my iPad.

'I don't think anything, *cherie*. It's Friday night. The traffic will be *penible*.'

She's right. Her flight leaves at 18.35. It's already nearly four. At the airport, thanks to the latest terrorist attack, we should add an extra hour for the queues at security but a check on my iPad tells me that traffic on the M4 is moving sweetly west.

We join the motorway at Chiswick. My iPad lies. All I can see are three lines of traffic inching forward. It's too late to look for a diversion. We crawl up the feeder lane and barge our way into stalling traffic. My mum, who has an acute instinct for impending disaster, is already convinced that we've missed the plane.

'The Tube,' she says. 'Drop me at a station.'

Easier said than done. My knowledge of exits on the M4 is less than perfect but I've a feeling I can get off at the next junction and try and find the Piccadilly line at South Ealing. Mum is only too game to take on Heathrow alone but I use the airport a lot and I know the kind of shortcuts that might still get her on to the plane.

The traffic has come to a complete halt. Tension has a way of killing conversation and this is the perfect example. I try and find something on the radio. Sarah Dunant interviewing Rosamunde Pilcher. Steve Wright in the Afternoon. Simon Rattle conducting Poulenc. Anything. My mother isn't fooled.

'We should have gone straight to the nearest Tube. This is crazy.'

I can only agree. Mile after mile of traffic seized solid? Mad. All that filth pumping into God's good air? *Fou.* The most expensive city on earth moving at less than the speed of a horse and cart? *Incroyable.* I tell myself to relax, to ignore the growing pressure in my head, to concentrate on that lonely speck of brilliance in the deepness of space. Cassini, I say softly. Cassini.

Like a one-word prayer, it seems to work. Very

slowly, stop-start, the traffic is on the move again. By now, my mother has become fixated by the digital clock. She's winding backwards from the moment when they close the departure gate. She wants to know how often the trains run on the Piccadilly line.

'All the time,' I say. 'One every minute.'

She knows I'm lying but she also knows I'm doing my best. And more than that, she's begun to blame herself for putting me in this situation. Her hand settles briefly on my arm.

'I'm sorry,' she says simply.

Minutes later, we're off the motorway and heading north. South Ealing station is less than a mile but there's no parking.

'How's the time?' I ask her.

'*Pas de problème.*'

'I don't believe you.' I steal a glance at the clock. Nearly quarter to five already. This is going to be very tight.

I wait for a break in the oncoming traffic and haul my little car into a U-turn. I can't see a kerb without double yellow lines but this isn't the moment to lose one's nerve. I park outside a florist, grab my mother's heavier bag, and hurry her across the road. The driver of a Polish truck brakes in time to avoid killing us both. Glancing back, I catch him crossing himself.

'That was God's doing,' I tell my mum. 'Three more Hail Marys and we might make it.'

We do. Just. At Terminal Two, I have a second and a half to plant a kiss on my mum's cheek and tell her I love her before she's swallowed by the queue for Departures.

Exhausted, I find a bar. I haven't popped a Percocet for a couple of days now and I tell myself I've earned a drink. My head is thumping but I put that down to stress. When the barman slides into view I wonder what to order. Memories of Saucy tempt me to ask for a margarita but there's something slightly shameful about a lone woman drinking cocktails at half past five so I settle for a glass of San Miguel and find myself a table with a view out across the concourse. Moments later, I feel a pressure on my shoulder and look up to find an actress friend of mine called Fern. Her flight to Rome has been delayed by an hour and a half. Would I mind if she joined me?

We drink for the best part of an hour. Fern knows nothing about my tumour, about my operation, or even about Cassini. I'm wearing a beret that hides the stitches and I realize at once that I can pretend nothing's happened. This, believe it or not, is enormously liberating. We talk about a movie part she's just landed. She tells me a very rude story about a gay director we both adore. And when she enquires what's next in my busy, busy life I'm more than happy to talk about the radio script.

'Brilliant,' she says. 'No lines to learn. No hanging around. Bosh-bosh. Done.' She glances at her watch. 'Shit.'

She takes a quick peek at her make-up mirror and seconds later she's gone.

'*Addio*,' I whisper, turning to watch her running for the departure gate.

By now, I'm pissed. Under normal circumstances

a pint and a half of Spanish lager would impart nothing but a cosy glow but something troublesome seems to have happened to my balance. Finding my way back to the Piccadilly line is a lot more difficult than it should be. On the train I pick up a discarded *Metro* and feign interest in a story about some Brexit deadline. By South Ealing, I'm trying very hard not to throw up. I emerge from the station and look in vain for my precious Peugeot.

Hopeless. It's gone.

The flower shop, as it happens, is still open. I join the queue of customers selecting blooms for their Friday date. Every transaction takes an age – scissors to trim the stalks, showboat ribbons for the paper, those little sachets of plant food to keep the dream alive after the weekend – and by the time I get to the head of the queue, I'm nearly as exhausted as the owner.

He's late middle-aged, thickset, heavy foreign accent. When I ask whether he noticed a red Peugeot parked outside his shop, he nods.

'I phoned the council,' he says. 'The guys with the truck took it away an hour ago.'

I find a lavatory in a pub up the road. After throwing up twice I feel a little better. I have neither the energy nor much interest in reclaiming my car, but nor do I trust myself on public transport. There are all kinds of ways of admitting defeat but the truth is I need help. Malo, bless him, would be useless. Instead I call Mitch.

He says he's at home in Hither Green. I have a feeling he's probably very busy but the minute he hears my voice – the hint of panic, he says

70

later, not what I'm trying to say – he tells me to stay put. He'll be there as soon as he can. I give him the name of the pub and mention the Tube station. An Uber brings him to the door within half an hour.

I'm sitting at a table where I know he'll spot me. He comes across. My glass of Perrier is untouched but I'm feeling better enough to apologize at once for calling him out.

'It's not a problem.' He's looking around. 'Do they do food here? And if they do, could you cope with me having something to eat?'

I say yes to both. It turns out he's eaten virtually nothing all day, the result of an empty fridge and an impossible deadline. He scans the food board and then goes to the bar to order a plate of pasta. By the time he comes back, Donald Trump is on all three TV screens threatening Pyongyang with fire and fury.

Mitch watches for a moment or two. It turns out he was in America this time last year to file copy on the hustings, a couple of weeks he was careful to spend with the less reported parts of the electorate.

'You had to get away from the cities. Places the media discount. West Virginia. Coal country. South Carolina. The Georgia boondocks. An hour or so off the freeway you couldn't move for Trump posters. It wasn't subtle, any of this stuff. People were pissed off, left out, and he scooped them up by the millions.'

None of this is new. I'm no politics junkie but I must have heard the same message dozens of times.

'You thought he'd win?'

'Never. But I thought he'd come close . . . much closer than the East Coast ever gave him credit for.'

'So how did you feel? When it happened?'

Mitch gives the question some thought. He'd stayed up most of the night, he says, watching the live coverage, bouncing from CNN to Fox to NBC and back again. After AP called Pennsylvania for Trump everyone knew the game was up. Clinton was slow to lift the phone and concede but she and her buddies were in shock.

'I went to sleep around dawn. By the time I was up again it was gone nine. The paper wanted a day-after piece, America waking up to President Trump, and so I left the hotel and just walked a block or two, looking for a diner. I was in New York. This is a city I know well, really well, yet it looked completely different. There's a guy called Sebastian Haffner. He was a German lawyer, wrote a wonderful book about trying to survive in the Third Reich. The day after Hitler came to power, back in 1933, he felt something similar. He happened to be in Berlin but he said exactly the same thing. It's like you're walking through some place you've never been before. Everything looks different, feels different. The people. The traffic. The cops. The bums on the sidewalk. Even the weather, even the clouds. You've shut your eyes, opened them again, and you're in the world of make-believe. A dream? No. A nightmare? Possibly. But so, so weird.'

I nod. *Some place you've never been before.*

I know exactly what he means. This has nothing to do with American politics nor New York but trying to cope with a stranger, a presence, in your own brain takes you to some very strange places. I wait for Trump to leave us in peace and then I try and explain.

'You start to doubt your own body,' I tell him. 'You think you know it and you don't because it's let you down, big time. Is that treason? Betrayal? Have you insulted it? Too many margaritas? Too much sunshine? That may be true. You have to admit it. But in that case, what *is* your body? And what is the you that is you? And where, exactly, is the line between them? I can think of no good reason why I've bred a tumour, given it house room, but there it was, making itself at home, and I'd be mad to assume it might not be back. And that changes everything, believe me.'

Mitch has lost interest in the news feed. 'You sound angry,' he says.

'I am. Take now. How come I'm throwing up? How come I can't trust myself to make it back home? How come I have to drag you halfway across London to sort me out?'

'You've had major brain surgery. That makes a difference.'

'Of course it does. I should never have left home in the first place. I understand that.'

Briefly I explain about taking my mum to Heathrow. Given the circumstances, I'm still telling myself I had no choice. A couple of drinks afterwards was probably foolish but it felt very all right at the time. When I mention the car, Mitch says he'll sort it tomorrow. All he'll need is my driving licence and registration documents.

'You don't have to do that.'

'You're right. But I want to.'

'Why?'

This turns out to be a question he's not prepared to answer. Instead, as the barman signals that his meal is ready, he gets to his feet.

'Life's always on loan,' he says. 'It's just that none of us know it.'

I watch him eat. I'm starting to wonder whether he's had some kind of encounter with cancer himself. He seems so empathetic, so prescient. Then I tell myself that these are talents that any good journalist needs. They have to listen, to understand, to be able to clamber into someone else's heart, or – God help them – head. And I know this because acting, if you want to do it right, is very similar.

No harm in asking the question, though. Cancer? Mitch looks surprised.

'No way,' he says.

'You think you're immune?'

'I think I'm lucky.' He stabs at a curl of calamari. 'You told me no radiotherapy in hospital. And no chemo.'

'That's right.'

'And that's still the case?'

'As far as I know.'

'So your hair . . .?' He's looking at my beret.

'It should grow back pretty quickly. I've been bald before. I did a film in Syria before it all kicked off out there. It was set in Palmyra, way out in the desert. The place is truly ancient. Ruins everywhere. Me included.'

Mitch wants to know more and while he finishes the pasta I tell him about the script. I played a fast-rising French business executive caught at a key moment of her convalescence. One of my buddies to make the trip from Paris to offer spiritual nourishment was an ageing leftie with whom I had unfinished business. Scenes towards the end of the movie called for us to chew the philosophical cud in the ever-lengthening shadows of an ancient Greek temple.

The film bombed and looking back I can understand why. Too wordy. Too ambitious. And too bloody long. But this was the first time I'd been to the Middle East and I had a soft spot for the desert. It was winter, freezing at night but delicious for most of the day, and I came away convinced that three weeks among the ruins of an ancient civilization were the perfect antidote to most of society's ills.

'Convalescence from what?'

'Cancer.' I touch my left breast. 'Aggressive and sadly inoperable. Hence the heavy chemo and the loss of hair. I died a beautiful death in a fifth-floor flat on the Beirut corniche. By which time most of the audience had wisely left.'

'Was the part useful? Looking back?'

'Sadly not. It sounds harsh but I never really took cancer seriously at the time. I was twenty-six. At that age you know you're immortal.'

The waitress arrives to take Mitch's plate away. We stare at each other for a long moment and then – as if by some strange biochemical accident – we both laugh.

'Well?' I say. 'Are you going to tell me?'

'About Prentice?'

'About Saucy, yes.'

'Only if you're sure I should.'

'I don't know what that means.'

'It means we both have responsibilities here. And the first is to you getting better.'

'Isn't that my business?'

'Of course. But I'd like to think I'm here to help you.'

'You are. So tell me more about Saucy.'

He holds my gaze and then shrugs. In a way I suspect this is a gesture of surrender. I get the feeling he'd spend the rest of the evening quite happily talking about something else but time, as I keep telling him, may no longer be on my side.

'Think of this as a movie,' I say. 'So far you've given me the trailer. It's a good trailer. I'm intrigued. I'm hooked. So what's all this really about?'

Another shrug. He plaits his fingers, leans forward, changes his mind, shifts in his seat, tries to relax.

'Back in the day at Antibes, you say he told you about Pompey, about Portsmouth. Am I right?'

'Yes.'

'OK. So we have the young Prentice. He's a grammar-school boy, believe it or not, but he's a tearaway as well. No patience. Bright as you like but a rebel. The last place he ever wants to go is university, which is a bit of a shame from his parents' point of view. No one in the family has ever got further than school-leaving age. Sending young Hayden to the Pompey Grammar has cost them a lot of money. According to his year tutor, university is well within his grasp, even Oxford or Cambridge, yet here he is, running with the wrong crowd, pissing it all away.'

I press for more details. The wrong crowd turns out to be a bunch of football hooligans who call themselves the 6.57 crew, a witty homage to the train they take every other Saturday morning to follow their beloved club to the four corners of the kingdom.

'He's mad about football?'

'He's mad about violence. Him and his mates go for the ruck, not the match. Before, during, afterwards, it makes no difference. The fights are pre-arranged. Pompey are playing away at Liverpool, right? That puts them on the concourse at Waterloo around quarter past nine. A bunch of thugs from Millwall are waiting for them. Before Prentice and his mates get the Tube to Euston there's debts to settle. It sounds medieval and in a way it is. This is the language of ambush, of facing impossible odds, of mateship and of never losing your bottle. Think the Hundred Years War. Think the Alamo. This is serious stuff. Chains, belts, hammers, knuckledusters. The chances of never making it to Anfield aren't low.'

'Anfield?'

'Liverpool. It's the football ground. Their destination.'

'And what then?'

'Another ruck if you're lucky, and maybe something tasty on the way home, too. Like I say, his parents were at their wits' end. This little journey was supposed to end at Oxford or Cambridge, not the magistrates' court.'

I nod, trying to associate this fierce little pageant with the man I'd so briefly shared a bed with.

'This went on for a while?'

'Yes and no. Prentice turned out to have a keen sense of where his best interests really lay. No one ever questioned his bottle. This wasn't the biggest guy you've ever met but he was mixing it with some real animals. At the same time he wasn't stupid. He knew exactly what was really going down and he was determined to be part of it.'

'Part of what?'

'Drugs, chiefly dealing. It was ecstasy to begin with but the real money was in cocaine. The six-five-seven was a gift for someone like Prentice. Put all those crews together, hooligans or otherwise, and you've got a ready-made distribution network. They fought most of the time but they still got to know each other. All it took was for some of them to get properly organized, and they did.'

'And Saucy was part of that?'

'Big time. Not the number one. Not even the number two. But Prentice took it to another level because Prentice was ahead of the game and had the foresight to ask the key question. You sort out the wholesale side. You lay your hands on industrial quantities of cocaine. This stuff was shipped out from the Dutch Antilles, Aruba in particular. You build your supply chain, your client base, and – bingo – the money starts rolling in. We're not talking thousands or even tens of thousands. Before very long, couple of years max, we're talking millions. So what happens to all that dosh? You can't drink it all. You can only drive one Bentley at a time. No, somebody has to play the magician. Someone has to wave the wand and convert all that loot into legitimate profits. On one level it's called money-laundering. The likes of Prentice would call it investment.'

'Saucy became a businessman?'

'An accountant to begin with. He did the training, passed the exams, got himself articled, sussed the way it all worked, but all the time he was looking for likely propositions, ways he could wash all the drugs money and turn yet more profit. We're talking legitimate investments here. Taxi firms. Nail salons. Cafe-bars. Nursing homes. Even a security consultancy.'

I nod. Saucy had told me all this before, or at least the bit about becoming an accountant, but only now does it make sense. The world of business, Berndt used to say, is one huge safe. Crack the combination, get inside, and you can't fail to make serious money.

'And the police?' I ask Mitch.

'The drugs operation drove them nuts. They knew exactly what was happening but Prentice and his mates were always three steps ahead. Pay attention to the small print, hire the right

79

talent, play the establishment at its own game, and they can't touch you. Not if you watch your back. Not if you're clever. And not if you keep your own house in order.'

'What does that mean?'

Mitch leans back a moment and takes a quick look round. It's Tuesday evening. The pub is half-empty.

'These guys were no strangers to violence. That's how it all kicked off. Literally. That builds a loyalty, a family bond. If you've stuck it to the Millwall against impossible odds then you're mates for life. No one grasses you up. And if they ever do, or if some other twat arrives who fancies his chances, then you wouldn't want to be around to watch the consequences.'

'Like?'

'It doesn't matter. People disappeared. And they were the lucky ones.'

I'm starting to find some of this stuff problematic. Has Saucy killed someone?

'Quite possibly. He's certainly hurt people.'

'And you can prove that?'

'Yes.'

'So why does it matter? Why does *any* of this stuff matter?'

At this point Mitch gets out his phone and summons a cab. His place, not mine. We sit in the back of a new-smelling Uber, not saying a word. The driver, who looks like a refugee from the Sixties, has recognized me. He turns out to be a big film buff. He's even watched a pirated version of my Palmyra movie on the internet.

'You speak French?' To my knowledge no subtitled versions are available.

'No way. But I'm not sure the dialogue mattered that much judging by a review I once read.'

Whether he knows it or not, this is a very shrewd judgement.

Beyond New Cross, Mitch gives the driver directions. The house, to my surprise, is detached, brick and stucco, with newly painted woodwork and a line of pot plants beneath the single bay window. All it needs for the full suburban dream is maybe a Neighbourhood Watch sticker and a poster for the church bring-and-buy sale. Mitch unlocks the front door and stands aside to let me in. He says his Syrian housemate is at work.

'What does he do?'

'Care home round the corner, cash in hand. He double shifts when he's got the energy. The guy that owns it thinks it's Christmas.'

'Why?'

'Sayid was a hospital consultant back in Aleppo, specialized in geriatric medicine. Now he's wiping arses down the road. Someone might explain the logic someday but I'm not holding my breath.'

Mitch shows me into the living room at the back of the property. The house feels warm: warm colours, warm furnishings, an essay in making a stranger feel comfortable. Nothing looks new, not the rugs on the carefully stained floorboards, not the G-plan sofa flanking the open fireplace, not the old Dansette Major record player with its stack of LPs beside it.

There's a big fish tank in a corner of the room, cleverly backlit. I stare at the bubbles, at the handful of exotic fish. They look like scraps of multi-coloured paper carried lightly on a whisper of wind.

'Lovely,' I murmur.

Mitch brews fresh coffee. Just the smell takes me back to the wholefood cafe where we first had the beginnings of a conversation. I join him in the kitchen. He wants to know how I feel.

'Better,' I tell him.

'Seriously?'

'Yes.'

I study his whiteboard beside the fridge while he attends to the coffee. A calendar hangs beside the board and September is brimful of names and times and phone numbers. One name in particular keeps cropping up.

'Who's Jennie?'

'My editor.'

'On the paper? Some magazine?'

'At the publishing house.'

I nod, realizing I'm pleased she doesn't mean more to him, trying hard not to let it show. I badly want to know whether there's another woman in his life but short of asking, I'm not quite sure how to find out. Once again, as psychic as ever, he spares me the effort.

'No girlfriend,' he says. 'In case you were wondering.'

'Any particular reason?'

'Sure. These last three years I've been more comfortable with a man.'

'Your lodger?'

'My partner. Sayid has the gift of happiness. One day you might meet him.'

'Love to.'

'Then I'll arrange it.'

The gift of happiness. I'm still looking at the calendar, fighting a tremor of disappointment at the news that Mitch is gay. My finger finds the fifteenth. It's circled in red.

'Cassini Day?' I ask.

'Exactly.'

'And we're still on for the wake?'

'Of course.'

'Then maybe Sayid should be there, too.'

We have the coffee back in the living room. I'm about to bring Saucy up again but Mitch needs no prompting.

'Prentice got very rich very quickly. They all did but the first real sign that he'd made it was the house he bought.'

'Big? Flash?'

'Not at all. That was the point. It was in Portsmouth, up on the hill on the mainland. This is an address that matters in Pompey. The views are sensational. You can see right over the Solent to the Isle of Wight but the houses themselves are pretty suburban, a bit like this place. Thirties stuff. Double bay windows. Lots of pebbledash. Nice gardens. Maybe a gnome or two. But not much else.'

'So why did he want to move there?'

'He didn't. The place was for his mum and dad. It was Prentice's way of saying there was more to life than Oxford and Cambridge. From what I can gather his mum was delighted. They've both moved to Spain now but that's another story.'

I nod. Sweet, I think. And clever. No need to brag or boast. Just hand them the keys. I'm starting to wonder whether I should ever expect something similar from Malo but I know it's unlikely. He knows I already have more money than I need. What would be the point?

I want to know more about the darker moments of Saucy's giddy rise to fame and fortune. Did these threats to his empire really disappear?

'Yes. And what's more, everyone knew it. In every case you're talking low-life chancers who never realized what they were getting into. Two of them just vanished from sight. A body part from the other guy reappeared on the beach at low tide.'

'Which body part?'

'You don't want to know. But if you're posting a message it doesn't get more graphic. Mess with us and this is what happens. End of. Take a proper look at these guys and it's hard not to be impressed. You've met Prentice. He can be a charmer when it suits him.'

Indeed. Mitch's use of the surname, Prentice, is beginning to grate.

'Why don't you call him Saucy?'

'Because that makes him what he isn't. He's not Jack the Lad. He's not one of life's treasures. He's not Robin Hood. He's a gangster with the

84

brains and imagination to have made himself very rich. He may well have killed people. He's ruthless, and bent, and refuses to take shit from anyone. All of which puts him in very interesting company. Prentice has a very short attention span. He's like the shark. He needs to keep on the move.'

'You're telling me he's bored with being rich?'

'I'm telling you he's ambitious. He's done money. Money is easy. Money was yesterday's gig. Just now he has more of the stuff than any reasonable man can possibly want. What lies beyond money is influence and maybe recognition. Prentice wants his little niche in history, his own little place on the bookshelf. Now is a good time. Now is when a bunch of guys have burst in and kicked over all the furniture. The UK's in pieces. So is the government. If you're clever, and if you know how to keep your nerve, that's a very rare opportunity and Prentice knows it. Money, if you've got enough of it, will buy you anything in this country.'

I nod. I'm beginning to sense where all this might be leading.

'We're talking politics?'

'We are.'

'Brexit?'

'Of course.'

'New faces around Saucy's dinner table?'

'Yes.'

'Anyone I might have heard of?'

Mitch won't say. Brexit, he tells me, has opened countless doors in the nether reaches of the British establishment. The people, by a laughable majority, have spoken and after the first brief moments of disbelief it's dawned on some of the major players that everything is up for grabs. There's no going back. There's no surrender to economic logic or buyer's remorse. Just a big fat chance to barge through some of these newly opened doors and help yourself to a big fat chunk of a highly uncertain future.

'That's a gift for the likes of Prentice. That's what he sussed from the start, way before the referendum. And that's why he's started putting his money where other people's mouths were. He's always had an eye for an investment. That's his genius. That's his special gift. He's nerveless and he's quick on his feet. Brexit, before the vote, was just another business opportunity. Now, it's very different.'

'Why?'

'Because people owe him. Powerful people. People who may soon be running the country. So Prentice needs to call in all those debts. He's fifty. Just. Fifty's nothing.'

'So what does he want?'

'Power. Influence. He's spent half his life shafting the establishment. In a couple of years, unchecked, he could *become* the establishment. Him and a bunch of like-minded mates.'

'You said unchecked.'

'I did.'

'So what does that mean?'

'It means we get to know the real story.'

'About Saucy?'

'About Prentice. And the company he's been keeping.'

'You mean someone grasses him up?'

'Yes.'

'Someone like you?'

'Yes.'

'By writing a book? Getting it all out there?'

'Yes.'

'To what end?'

Mitch just looks at me. I suspect we both know that this is the key question, the fast-approaching bend in the road. In some ways, like trillions of others in this country, I'm a babe in the wood when it comes to politics. But in others, when we're talking plot and motivation, I'm a whole lot sharper.

'You want to cry foul,' I suggest. 'You want another referendum. You want this Brexit thing gone.'

Eight

I sleep late next morning. It happens to be Sunday. Malo stumbles into the bedroom with a mug of tea and a letter he must have found downstairs on the mat.

'Where were you last night?' I ask him.

'Out.'

'Where?'

'With mates.'

'So when did you come back?'

'Just now.' He drops the letter on the duvet and backs cautiously out of the bedroom.

I want to know more. I want to know who these mates are. And I want to know what's happened to the little stash of ready money I use to pay my bills. Late last night I remembered to leave a tenner for the milkman in the lobby downstairs but the jam jar I keep in the kitchen was empty. Last time I counted, I was looking at more than forty pounds. All gone.

I catch up with Malo in the kitchen and pour the tea down the sink. I gave up sugar last year but he wouldn't have known that. He doesn't seem to take this gesture personally. Indeed, he seems to have forgotten he made the tea in the first place. His eyes are everywhere and nowhere. He seems to have slipped his moorings.

'Are you OK?' I'm trying my best to sound mumsy.

'I'm good.'

'So where did you go?'

He yawns and tries to shrug the question off. I'm barring the way to the door and I'm not about to move. My empty jam jar is still on the side. Challenged, Malo says he'll replace the money as soon as he can.

'Like when? How?'

'Dunno.' Another shrug.

'So what did you use it for? What did you buy?'

'Drink. Stuff.'

'What stuff?'

'Gear.'

'You mean drugs?'

'Yeah, drugs.'

'Anything in particular?'

'Cocaine.'

I'm angry, and shocked. I also feel taken for granted. Forty quid's worth of coke up your nose? No money? Just help yourself and see if she notices? All of this is pretty dire but deep in my soul I also feel a flicker of respect. Malo hasn't denied taking the money. And when I asked him a straight question he gave me the straightest of answers.

'How long has this been going on?'

'What?'

'The cocaine.'

'A bit.'

'What's a bit?'

'A bit of a while.'

'Does your father know?'

'No. He knows nothing. Nothing about me. Nothing about anything.'

'So where does the money come from?'

For the first time he falters. He doesn't want to tell me.

'Does he give you an allowance? Your dad?'

'Allowance?'

'Money. Regular money.'

'Sort of.'

'What does that mean?'

'It means I ask him for money and mostly he says yes. I've also got a couple of his credit card numbers.'

'And you can buy cocaine that way? And cannabis? And whatever else?'

'Yes.'

'How?'

He won't say. I get the impression the conversation is over. I'm looking at the empty jar.

'You know what gets to me most? The fact that you just helped yourself. I want this to be your home but it's mine, too. That means we have to trust each other. Am I making sense here? Don't go helping yourself again. Ask me first.' I force a smile. 'Deal?'

I leave the kitchen without waiting for a reply. I don't know it yet but a crap morning is about to get a whole lot worse.

Back in the privacy of my bedroom, I remember the letter. It turns out to be from my solicitor. As we'd agreed, divorcing Berndt isn't going to be as simple as he'd first suggested. My husband's Swedish solicitor is back in the game with a vengeance. His client, Berndt Andressen, is in some financial difficulty. A movie in which he'd invested heavily has gone belly-up. As things

90

stand, he's in some danger of losing everything.

I skip the small print – three dense paragraphs listing Berndt's exposure on various projects – and go straight to the meat of the letter. Your ex-husband, writes my solicitor, now wants to lay claim to half of your joint estate. That effectively means half of everything you're worth. These are still early days. We can fight fire with fire. But I'd be remiss if I didn't keep you abreast of events.

Merde. I fold the letter and slip it back into the envelope, wondering whether this is the real reason for Malo bailing out of his father's life. His prospective stepmother gone. His father's money gone. The penthouse apartment probably up for sale. What's left to keep my wayward son with a father he appears to despise?

But I know this is the least of my problems. The conversation with Malo has left me seriously worried. No seventeen-year-old should be out all night hunting for the white powder. Where did he get it? Where did he use it? Was he in company? Mates? Someone he's met more recently? Or is he the loner I've always imagined him to be? The slight figure bent over a spliff I glimpsed in the video phone only a few nights ago?

The latter thought makes me shudder. This is where the real problems start, I tell myself. This is where you fall out of love with yourself and get into seriously deep water. I know it happened to Berndt once, because he told me so. That kind of desperate cut-off-ness has also lurked on the edges of my own life from time to time. Poor bloody Malo, I think. With parents like us, the child never had a chance.

I find him watching TV. *Peppa Pig*, at half past eight in the morning, is probably worse than cocaine. I sit down beside him on the sofa and it's a moment before I realize that he's gone to sleep. His breathing is light. He jerks from time to time, tiny spasms of reflex movement. A thin dribble of saliva tracks down his chin.

I study him for a moment, knowing that something is badly wrong, then I whisper his name. Nothing. No reaction at all. I watch him a moment longer, then leave the sitting room. The spare bedroom, after my mum's careful stewardship, is a mess. Clothes everywhere, trainers that don't match, and a copy of *The Sun* open at one of the sports pages. I'm looking for Malo's phone. I find it under the duvet. Eva is listed in the directory. I copy down her number. It seems to include the prefix for Sweden.

Back in the living room, Malo is still asleep. I turn the volume up on the TV a notch or two and retire to my bedroom. I use my own phone to dial Eva. The number rings and rings before an answering machine kicks in. I'm listening to a recorded message in Swedish. It's a woman's voice, deeper and more throaty than I'd expected. It may or may not be Eva. I wonder about leaving a message of my own and then decide against it and hang up. Better to keep phoning until we can talk properly.

After I've turned off my phone, I find myself looking at the letter from my solicitor. I read it again, more carefully this time, and wonder whether to call him or not. Berndt's world appears to have imploded, a perfect storm which has robbed him of his live-in fiancée, his trophy penthouse, and now his son. His talent for raising production money seems to have deserted him and when I Google the reviews for his latest TV series I even begin to feel sorry for him. 'Vapid', 'repetitive' and 'empty' are the kinder judgements. A couple of years ago I'd have still been part of his life, telling him what a genius he is. Now, at best, I feel mildly curious. How come a stellar career like his can end so suddenly?

Because it can. Because stuff happens that way. Cassini, I think. The beckoning rings of Saturn. And next week, the final dive into oblivion. Before I left Mitch last night, at my request, he gave me contact details for Hayden Prentice. He did it with a show of reluctance which I took at the time to be phoney.

Waiting for the Uber, I asked him to be straight with me. He knew I'd once slept with Saucy. His precious book, as far as I can gather, badly needs an inside source a great deal closer to its subject. Everything he's told me about the man suggests his mates are family: tight-lipped, suspicious of outsiders, paranoid about journalists. Hence Mitch's bid to tune in on a different frequency. This happy phrase was his. Whether he admits it or not, he wants me to try and rekindle whatever brief spark existed in the first place. And after that he wants me to listen, and ask a playful question or two, and report back.

That's what last night, and all our other encounters, have really been about.

Mitch hadn't foreseen my tussle with cancer, and neither had I, but sitting on the bed I begin to wonder what difference it makes. Back in my old life, when I was well, I'd have dismissed the proposition out of hand. I was an actress, moderately successful, not a bloody spy. My life was full of opportunities and the only cloud in the blueness of my sky was Malo. His absence from my life was a running sore. On screen I could more than hold my own but as a mum I was rubbish. That hurt badly.

Now, the tide appears to have turned. Washed up on the beach is my wayward son and his bankrupt father plus a journalist I happen to respect as well as like. As long as I can remember I've always believed that things never happen by accident. Stare hard enough at the bottom of any cup and the tea leaves will send you a message. Thanks to my neurosurgeon and his team, I seem to have been granted a second chance at life. So what now?

First things first. I try Eva again on the off-chance that she may have been on another call. This time she answers. It takes several attempts on my part before she realizes who she's talking to. Her English is near perfect.

'You mean you're Malo's mother?'

'Yes.'

'Then how can I help you?'

'I understand you're coming to London. I'm just phoning to say you're more than welcome to stay.'

'London?' She sounds surprised.

I repeat the invitation. My son has moved in. She's welcome to join him. She begins to laugh, then apologizes.

'Malo told you this? About me coming to London?'

'Yes.'

'It's not true. Why would he say such a thing?'

I stare at the phone. I'm beginning to feel foolish. Maybe we should start this conversation again.

'Malo tells me that you and he are . . .'

'Friends?'

'Yes. And maybe more than friends. Have I got that right?'

'No. We have coffee together sometimes. He likes to talk. Once we went to a party together because he had no car. But no, nothing more.'

'Then I'm sorry to have bothered you.'

I'm about to hang up but she hasn't finished.

'Wait,' she says. 'How is he? Your son?'

'Why do you ask?'

'Because I know he has problems. He tells me about them. For a boy his age he's very open, very honest. Maybe too much honest.'

A boy his age.

I swallow whatever pride I have left and ask her to be more precise. What kind of problems exactly?

'I know he found it hard. The break-up.'

'And?'

'Kids can do silly things. Go looking in the wrong places for help.'

'You mean drugs?'

'Yes.'

'Cocaine?'

'No. Cocaine is expensive here. He couldn't afford it.'

'Then what?'

There's a long silence. I'm praying that we're not talking heroin. Then she's back on the phone.

'This is difficult,' she says.

I shut my eyes, trying hard not to lose my temper. This woman is playing the professional counsellor, hiding behind client confidentiality. Grotesque.

'He's your friend, not your patient,' I point out. 'And he also happens to be my son. Of course he's had a hard time. We all have. But he's arrived with a cannabis habit and he's taken to staying out all night. He says he bought cocaine. That may or may not be true. A couple of days ago I thought I knew him. Now I'm not so sure. As we speak, he's unconscious on the sofa. He's not well, Eva. Even I know that. All I want to know is why.'

Another silence. I'm trying to be patient, trying somehow to bond with this image on Malo's phone. Finally she seems to have made a decision.

'There's a form of cannabis around here we call Zombie. I think you call it Spice. It's very strong, very dangerous. It's synthetic, not from a plant. Malo uses it all the time. Say hi from me, *ja*?'

Malo uses it all the time. The drooling figure on the sofa. Zombie. The perfect description. I blink, fighting the tears. I try hard to focus on the window, on the door, on anything that will clear my vision. I have a thousand questions to ask, a thousand reasons to keep this woman on the line, but then I realize that the phone has gone dead and it's far too late.

Malo. Zombie. Spice.

I curl up in a ball, bury myself under the duvet, and try – just for a moment – to shut out the rest of the world. Hopeless. My mobile is ringing. I surface to find a text from Mitch: *Ring me soonest. Urgent.*

He answers on the second ring and senses at once that something's wrong. In this respect, as in many others, his instincts never let him down. He doesn't need to be face-to-face. Just something in my voice prompts the inevitable question.

'What's happened?'

'Nothing.'

'I don't believe you.'

'You should.' I tug at the duvet. 'So what's so urgent?'

There's a silence. He's evidently in two minds whether to continue this conversation. What little I know about investigative reporters suggests they have no conscience. In any kind of ethical toss-up, the demands of the story win every time. Wrong.

'Just tell me,' I say. 'Maybe I can help. Maybe I can't. It's about Saucy?'

'Prentice, yes.'

'So what's happened?'

'He's had an accident. He's in hospital in Dorchester. It's not life-threatening and he's not going to die but he'll be in there for at least a week. Dislocated shoulder. Suspected damage in the neck area. Broken ribs. Suspected fracture in the pelvis.'

He fills in the details. It seems that Saucy is a big supporter of Front Line, a charity that looks after injured or traumatized ex-servicemen. Yesterday he'd organized a motocross event at his Dorset estate and charged punters ten quid a head to watch. He'd called on mates and a bunch of minor celebs to turn up for the afternoon. Saucy had once ridden bikes and put himself down for the last race of the day. Cocky as ever, according to Mitch, he'd borrowed something called a Racing Warrior and come to grief on the third lap. For full coverage, I'm to go to YouTube and tap his name in.

'He's got a private room on the second floor.' Mitch is telling me about the hospital. 'The nearest ward is called Little Bredy.'

'So what do you want me to do?'

'I thought you might pay him a visit.'

'Out of the blue? Just like that?'

'You could say you've picked up the story somewhere, seen the YouTube clip. Old mates. Bunch of flowers. Whatever.'

'It's eighteen years ago,' I point out. 'He won't have a clue who I am.'

'I doubt that.'

Something in his voice prompts me to pause. He knows more than he's letting on.

'Why do you doubt that?'

'Because he's never forgotten you. And that's according to people who know him very well.

Your name comes up more than you might imagine.'

'Trophy fuck?'

'I doubt it. Apparently he's seen all your movies. That makes him more sensitive than we might imagine.'

Despite everything, I'm beginning to feel better. The thought of Saucy sitting through some of my more obscure films makes me smile.

'And supposing I go down there, supposing I get in, what do I say?'

'You empathize. You make friends again. You cosy up.'

'But what do we have in common?'

'Hospitals.'

Coming from Mitch, this is uncharacteristically blunt. Maybe, after all, he's just like every other journalist. Maybe he's as hard-boiled as the rest of them. Oddly enough, I don't protest, don't end the call. Instead I enquire what might lie further down the line.

'That's what you asked me last night,' he says. 'and to be frank I've no idea. Which is rather the point. I know a great deal about this guy. I've gone as far as the cuttings and conversations with some of his rivals will take me. What I don't know is what he's really like because only his mates and his ex-missus would know and they're not telling.'

'Which leaves me.'

'Exactly.'

'Your precious source.'

'Yes.' Another silence. 'So what do you think?'

I keep a pad and a pencil on the carpet beside the bed. I roll over, the phone still to my ear.

'Give me the name of the hospital again,' I say.

'You'll go?'

'I might.'

I spend the rest of the morning keeping an eye on Malo and having a think. Once he's woken up and I've put something legal inside him, we watch the YouTube clip together. The footage must have been posted by one of Saucy's army of punters. The opening shots show a decent crowd, hundreds certainly, massed at the start. Most of them are men and many of them are wearing an assortment of what I can only describe as combat gear: camouflage smocks, heavy lace-up boots, the whole military shtick. It's raining and the up-and-down race track is plainly a nightmare but the first couple of races come and go without a major incident. Faceless riders in huge helmets lose control and fall off but no one seems seriously hurt.

Then the guy with the camera changes position and we find ourselves looking down on a sharp right-hand bend at the end of a long descent. It's obvious from the skid marks that this bit of the course has seen a good deal of action already but nothing prepares us for the compact little figure in black leathers who comes hurtling down the slope at least ten metres ahead of the rest of the field.

In retrospect it's obvious that he's lost control already but watching the footage for the first time is like watching a movie. You know that something ugly and probably very painful is about to happen because the laws of physics tell you so, but at the same time you assume that the god of good intentions will somehow intervene. Alas, he doesn't. The figure in black goes sideways into the corner, hits the raised bank, and parts company with the bike. The riders behind him desperately try to take avoiding action but it's far, far too late. Bike after bike piles in and a second or two later we're looking at a major incident. The soundtrack alone is truly alarming, impact after impact, but in the silence that follows there comes another sound and it takes me a moment to realize what it is. Laughter.

The footage cuts to a final sequence. We're down among the wreckage. Wherever you look there are men in muddy leathers limping around, nursing their wounds. In the distance, I can hear the approaching clatter of a helicopter. Then the camera pans down to a lone figure sprawled on his back on the wet grass. His helmet lies beside him. His left hand is clutching his right wrist and there's something badly wrong with the set of his shoulder. There's blood on his face and he's obviously in pain but he's summoned a grin for the punters. Even eighteen years can't erase the memory of that grin.

Malo wants to know who he is.

'His name's Hayden. Hayden Prentice. His friends call him Saucy.'

'Why?'

'It's to do with his initials.'

'HP? The sauce?'

101

'Exactly.' I nod at the screen. 'This whole place belongs to him. He owns it.'

Malo is impressed. Both by what we've seen of the estate and by the little man's courage. I explain about the fund-raising, about Front Line. Malo has rewound the footage for another look at the crash and has now freeze-framed the face on the wet grass.

'You know this Saucy?'

'Yes.'

'Well?'

'No. I met him once a while back. Before you were born.'

'What was he like?'

'He was OK.'

'Rich? Then?'

'Yes.'

'Very rich?'

'Probably, yes. I don't know. Does that matter?'

Malo doesn't answer. He seems fascinated by Saucy. He can't take his eyes off him.

'He's mad,' he says at last. 'Coming down that hill at that speed was crazy.'

'You're right. But that's the way he's led his whole life.'

'How do you know?'

The question is sharp, proof that my poor damaged Zombie isn't quite as lost as I'd thought. I bluff about keeping up with the news but I can tell he isn't convinced. Then an idea begins to shape itself deep in my head.

'Would you like to meet him?' I ask. 'Saucy?'

'Yeah, I would.' Malo lifts his head at last and glances round at me. 'Like when?'

Nine

The next day we take a mid-morning train from Waterloo. Malo has spent the rest of Sunday searching the internet for more clues about Saucy, something I should have done myself. Among his findings are shots of his ex-wife, who happened to have been an actress. I've never heard of her but the eye-popping cleavage and split skirt are all the clues you'd need. Her name was Amanda and even without heels she must have been three inches taller than her husband, but I can't imagine physical odds ever putting Saucy off. He'd have treated his new bride exactly the way he treated Saturday's race: full throttle and fuck the consequences.

Other gems from Malo's trawl include a series of contributions from fellow tycoons he'd bested in various deals. All of them were rich and all of them were cross and when you boiled down what they had to say you ended up with the same basic complaint: that Hayden Prentice was a rogue operator who'd never encountered a rule or made a promise he didn't break. The guy was a force of nature. The guy belonged in a zoo. The guy, to be frank, was impossible.

Beyond Woking, Malo wants to know how I'm going to explain our presence at Saucy's bedside.

'I'll tell him you're my son,' I say.

'That's not what I meant.'

'I know it isn't.'

We're sitting beside the window with a table between us. I put my hands briefly over Malo's. He doesn't flinch. Last night, to my immense relief, he seemed happy to spend the evening with me in front of the TV. We even had a chat about the nonsense we were watching and when I deadlocked the front door and kept the key he didn't say a word.

Now he wants to know how I'll be handling Saucy. It's a good question, one I asked Mitch. Mitch was worse than vague but overnight I've had a thought or two.

'Your father spent some time in Angola a while back,' I say lightly. 'He may have mentioned it.'

'No.' Malo shakes his head. 'Angola?'

'It's in Africa. There was a civil war in the Nineties and the place was full of minefields. There are lots of kids in Angola and some of them got badly injured. Your dad wanted to set a film there. He spent time in the minefields to research a script.'

'It got made? This movie?'

'It did. It was called *Campos dos Sonhos.* That's *Fields of Dreams* in Portuguese. It's ironic. It's what the kids called the fields where the soldiers buried the mines.'

I made a point of finding a copy of *Campos* after Berndt and I first met. It was one of the reasons I married him. The film, shot in Angola with a Swedish crew, was a revelation. Powerful was too small a word. Kids with no arms, no legs. Primitive hospitals. Tens of thousands of crippled street orphans in Luanda with nowhere to sleep. Watch a movie like that and you despaired of the human race.

Afterwards, at Berndt's prompting, I got involved with a charity set up by a bunch of ex-squaddies who'd worked in mine demolition all over the world. They wanted profile and I was happy to add what little I could. The charity is still out there, still effective, and I still give them whatever help I can. In the earliest days of our relationship, Berndt and I had toyed with adopting a couple of these kids but then Malo had turned up, and life had bustled on, and we'd never even completed the first set of forms.

'What's the name of this charity?'

'MAG. Mines Advisory Group.'

'And Saucy?'

'Wait and see.'

We take a cab from Dorchester station. Stepping into a hospital again is something that's been bothering me for the last hour or two – the same bustle of nurses with too many patients and not enough time; the same brief glimpse of impossibly young doctors; the same drawn faces of anxious relatives waiting for news – but the experience is oddly comforting. I owe my life to a place like this. Why should I feel anything but gratitude?

It's Malo who steps out of the lift on the second floor and leads the way to the nursing station. The sister in charge is sipping a mug of tea while she scrolls through endless emails on her PC. She barely looks up when Malo enquires about Mr Prentice.

'Does he know you?'

'He knows my mum. They were big friends once.'

'Really?' This time she spares me a proper look.

I nod. Smile. Me and Mr Prentice? Best buddies. Malo gives her our names. She gets up and disappears into a side room at the other end of the open-plan ward.

A minute or so later, she's back.

'He's in a bit of a state at the moment. That's his description not mine. If you've got a sense of humour, he says you're very welcome. Otherwise he won't be offended if you bugger off.'

This raises a grin from Malo. I'm still looking at the sister.

'So how is he?'

'Lucky. Lucky to be in one piece. Lucky to be alive. You've seen the footage? Everyone else has. An incident like that we'd normally be counting the bodies. Remarkable.' She holds my gaze. 'He says you're famous. A film actress? Is that true?'

'No, not famous. Just . . .' I smile. 'Lucky.'

We head for Saucy's private room. Malo, once again, is in the lead. He knocks lightly at the door and then stands aside to let me in. The room is smaller than I've been expecting. Saucy is lying prone, his head in a neck brace, one plastered arm secured to an overhead pulley. A vase brims with flowers on his bedside table and there are more blooms in a bucket on the floor. The TV at the foot of the bed is showing some panel game though I'm not certain that he's in any position to watch. A plastic tube trails to a

106

bag beneath the bed. The bag is yellow with urine.

Malo has spotted a line of teddy bears on the windowsill. Some of them have Union Jack waistcoats. The one beside Saucy's pillow is wearing camouflage.

Saucy is aware of our presence but can't move his head. There are cuts and abrasions on his face, and swelling has nearly closed one eye. The other inspects me as I step into his view.

'Antibes,' he says at once.

'That's right.'

'Great night. One of the best. You?'

'I'm fine.'

'That wasn't my question. Enjoy it? Remember it?' He frowns. 'Who's that?'

He's caught sight of Malo. I do the introductions.

'Come here, son. Closer. The name again?'

'Malo.'

'Malo?' Saucy's eye is back on me. 'Yours, you say?'

'Mine,' I confirm.

'That makes you lucky, son. Luck is everything. And I'm the living proof.'

Malo gazes down at him. 'That's what the nurse said. We saw the clip on YouTube. Why so fast down that hill? You mind me asking?'

I've never seen Malo like this, so respectful, so coherent, so *polite.* Saucy is still staring up at him. His good eye seems to be watering. He starts to blink. Then he tries to move, wincing with the pain.

'Kleenex, son. Fuck knows where. Left eye. Quick as you like.'

Malo finds the box of tissues and extracts a couple. He has the touch of a born carer, deft, firm, unembarrassed. I can't be more proud of him. And more surprised.

'Well done, son. How old are you?'

'Seventeen.'

'Good age. *Brilliant* age.' He winces, trying to make himself more comfortable. 'Live with your mum, do you?'

'Yes.'

'Dad?'

'No.'

'Gone?'

'Yes.'

'Miss him?'

Malo doesn't answer. Saucy's good hand crabs sideways across the whiteness of the sheet, looking for Malo.

'Proud of your mum, are you? All the stuff she's done? All them movies?'

Malo nods, says nothing, but he's beaming with a naturalness I haven't seen for years. I remember exactly the way Saucy made me feel at home on the boat in Antibes and he's doing it again, in front of my eyes, as if he and Malo have been best mates all their lives. I came expecting, at the very least, awkward silences between us all. Instead I've become part of a love-in.

Malo still wants to know about the accident. How come the death dive into that final corner? Forty miles an hour. Had to be.

'Dunno, son. You want the truth? I don't remember any of it. First I knew was getting me into the chopper. Mustard, those blokes were. Thought I'd broken my neck.' This little speech comes out in brief instalments with pauses for breath in between. Berndt broke a rib once, and spoke exactly the same way, passing a message between jolts of pain.

'You don't remember a bloke with a camera?' Malo asks. 'When you were flat out on the grass?'

'No.'

'But you were grinning. You were telling him you were OK.'

'OK?' Saucy tries to suppress a cackle of laughter. 'You call this OK?'

'No, but you did. It's there. On YouTube. I saw it.'

Saucy nods and closes his eyes. Time, I sense, is strictly limited. I move Malo gently out of the way and take his place beside the bed. When Saucy opens his eye again he's looking at me.

'Enora, yeah?' His hand finds mine. It's warm.

'Enora,' I confirm.

'Pretty name. Pretty lady.' He gives my hand a squeeze. 'Nothing changes, eh? Me, the mad one. You, class act. In life, you get what you deserve. God bless you both.'

He closes his eyes again. He's obviously exhausted but when I try and free my hand and mutter something about letting him get some sleep he won't let me go.

'Why did you come?'

'We came to see how you were.'

'And what do you think?'

109

'I think you need to rest. It may take a while but I'm sure everything will be OK in the end.'

'That's what they all say. So why did you really come?'

'It's complicated. And cheeky.'

'I like cheeky.'

I explain about the mine charity, about the killing fields in Angola, about the film Berndt made, and finally about all Saucy's work for Front Line. This suggests he's into good causes.

'You want money?'

'Yes.'

'How much?'

'A hundred thousand.'

'That's a lot.'

'I know.'

He nods. He wants to see Malo again. I step aside. Malo takes his hand uninvited, asks him whether he needs more tissues. Saucy says no and then mumbles something neither of us catch. Malo squats beside the bed, gets as close as he can, his ear inches from Saucy's mouth. Another mumble. Malo is staring at him. Then he gets up. He wants a pen and something to write on. I find an envelope in my bag, and a biro. Malo scribbles something and tucks it beneath Saucy's pillow.

'Where's your mum?' Saucy whispers.

I return to his bedside. Saucy wants me to kiss him goodbye and then fuck off. His lips are dry. He hangs on to me for a moment with his good hand. He tells me to come back any time and bring the boy. Then he waves us both away.

Only in the lift returning to the ground floor do I ask what Malo had written on the envelope.

'My birthday,' he says. 'He wanted to know when I was born.'

Ten

Malo and I take the train back to London. Our fifteen minutes at Saucy's bedside have shaken me. Not because of his physical state, which was worse than I'd anticipated, nor because he remembered so much of our previous encounter, but because of his reaction to Malo. Watching them both in that airless private room, I began to wonder for the first time about my son's real paternity. The black curly hair. The broad set of shoulders. The waywardness. The refusal to listen to anyone else. And now the unspoken kinship between them. They seemed to bond in an instant in ways that only shared genes can explain. Father and son? Christ.

Malo can't possibly be having the same thoughts because he knows nothing about what happened at Antibes but nonetheless he can't stop talking about this new man in his life. How brave he is. How gutsy. How easy to talk to. How real. All of this is true and it puzzles my son because I realize how much he mistrusts wealth.

As a family, we always took money for granted. Both Berndt and I were earning loads. Yet the more comfortable our lives became the faster everything began to fall apart. I've often thought about this in the small hours – how our separate careers spun us into deepest space, leaving Malo alone in the family home. Success, I told myself, did that because success gave us money, lots of money, and money – in turn – bought us a life of infinite choices that turned out – for my poor son – to be no life at all. His mum packing her bags for yet another five weeks on some far-flung location. His father beyond reach, caged by post-production problems, by funding issues, by scripts in development. No wonder the poor soul turned to drugs.

Drugs. We've left Winchester and the train is suddenly roaring through a tunnel. In the half-darkness, I'm watching my son. If I'm right about Saucy, if he really is Malo's dad, then I'm looking at a situation rich in irony. Hayden Prentice, tearaway and apprentice drug baron, the Pompey hooligan who would learn the dark crafts of accountancy and turn bucketloads of cocaine into a legitimate fortune. Malo Andressen, conceived one drunken night in Antibes, marooned in late adolescence with no one to count on but his neighbourhood drug dealer. If Berndt were here, I think, he'd be reaching for his note pad already. Brilliant idea. Thick with possibilities.

We're out of the tunnel. Fitful sunshine. Fields of sheep. And a blur of faces as we race through one of the smaller stations. I'm trying very hard to remember exactly what happened that night in Antibes. Saucy and I definitely had sex because I could smell it the next morning. And it's true, too, that I'd abandoned birth control after some bad experiences with both the pill and a sequence of coils. Busy and distracted as ever, I'd doubtless planned to sort myself out once life gave me the chance. Then Berndt happened and I was only too glad to leave the consulting room with the test results and take the glad tidings home. Poor Malo, I think. Poor bloody child. Not Berndt's fault at all. But mine.

The next couple of days, I'm not well. It starts with a headache, a distant growl of thunder to begin with but quickly building into something that feels like a full-blown migraine. Nauseous and irritable, I give up eating and take to my bed. I throw up a number of times, a process that becomes ever more painful as my stomach empties, and I do my best to sleep. Dark thoughts lurk beyond the edges of the throbbing pain. Might this signal the return of the tumour?

Malo, bless him, does his best to comfort me. He brings tea and a slice or two of dry toast. Both help a little, as does a conversation on the subject of his smoking habits. I feel too horrible to bother dancing round the point and simply propose a deal. I'll tolerate him having the odd spliff but it has to be within our four walls, and it has to be ordinary cannabis. Thanks to the internet, I'm now one of Holland Park's experts on the evils of Spice. I know it's powerful, quickly addictive, relatively cheap, and easy to get hold of. Four reasons, I tell him, to never use it again.

'What do you want?' He's looking at my upturned palm on the duvet.

'I want you to give me whatever you've got.'

'You mean the Spice?'

'Yes, and I want you to promise me you won't use it again.'

He nods. He understands. He says it's going to be difficult.

'Of course it's going to be difficult. That's why they invented this stuff in the first place. The choice is simple. You can put yourself at their mercy or not. If it's the former, you can go back to Sweden and waste your life there. If it's the latter, we can work something out.'

'Like what?'

'Like staying here. Like getting some kind of life together. It's called looking out for each other. You could phone your dad for advice but I'm not sure he'd know what you were talking about.'

The dig at Berndt raises a smile. Malo ducks his head and picks at a loose thread in the stitching around the duvet.

'I've been thinking,' he says at last.

'Good sign. Tell me more.'

'Did you fuck him?'

'Your dad? Of course I fucked him.'

'I meant Saucy.'

'Saucy?'

'Saucy. I was watching you both in the hospital. He acted like he was used to fucking you.'

'What does that look like?'

'Like he owned you. Like you were his.'

'Then the answer's no.'

'Never?'

'I didn't say that.'

'When then?' He's abandoned the duvet. His eyes meet mine.

'A while back.'

'Like when?'

I'm reluctant to go much further but then it occurs to me that I might never get this opportunity again. My bursting head may take me back to hospital, back to the operating theatre, and to whatever may – or may not – lie beyond it. So far, Malo hasn't said a word about kicking his drug habit. One false move, one tiny miscalculation, and I might never see him again. For a brief moment I'm back beside the video phone in the hall, watching my ghost of a son batter himself senseless with another lungful of Spice.

'You know it's a prison drug, don't you?'

'You're changing the subject.'

'I don't care. That's where it comes from. It feeds off a captive market. It feeds off boredom and despair. You really think you're not better than that?'

Malo shakes his head, refuses to answer. When I finally manage to coax a reply he says that boredom and despair pretty much covers it. He's been banged up for years. With us.

My head hits the pillow. My hand claws wildly over the edge of the bed.

'You want the bucket again?'

'Please.'

Malo has it there in seconds. It smells lemony from the disinfectant he used last time he cleaned it. He helps me pull myself upright in the bed and then lean sideways as I retch a thin stream of yellow bile. It tastes foul. I'm gasping for breath. I've rarely felt worse.

116

'You want me to phone someone?' He sounds on the edge of panic. 'You need help?'

'You,' I mutter. 'I need you.'

He cradles my head, asks me whether I want to be sick again. When I say no he goes to the bathroom for a flannel and a towel. If my son does nothing else with his life he's going to make a fine carer. A second trip to the bathroom produces a toothbrush and some mouthwash.

'Use the bucket to spit in,' he says.

I do his bidding. Slowly the bitter taste of bile goes away. My face washed, my mouth rinsed, I feel a whole lot better. I pat his thin arm, a gesture of appreciation.

'I fucked him once, if you really want to know.'

'Saucy?'

'Yes.'

'When?'

'The night before I met your father.'

'And him? You fucked him too?'

'I did. Lots and lots of times. We got married soon after.'

'And Saucy?'

'I never saw him again. Until just now.'

'He never tried to get in touch?'

'Never.'

'And you?'

'I was in love.'

Malo shifts his weight on the bed. I sense he finds the phrase uncomfortable, or maybe it's the very idea. So far it hasn't served him well.

'Does Dad know about Saucy?'

'Christ, no.'

'So what does he mean to you? Saucy?'

117

It's a very good question. Only days ago, before we made the trip down to Dorchester, I'd have said nothing, zilch, *nada*. A night on the piss. An exchange of body fluids. Barely even a memory. Now, though, I'm not so sure. Seeing Saucy and my son together was a revelation. They were a perfect fit.

Malo spares me pursuing this line of thought any further. His face is very close. He thinks that Hayden Prentice could be his real dad. Might that be possible?

'Yes,' I say. 'It might. And what's more, I think Saucy knows it. That's why he asked you about your birthday. He's good with figures, Saucy. The night we had sex we were both on a boat in Antibes. He might remember the date. All he has to do then is add nine months.'

'Seventeenth of February?'

'Exactly. I was in Cannes the third week in the previous May. The dates work perfectly.'

'So it could be true? Is that what you're saying?'

'Yes.'

Malo doesn't say a word. He's looking thoughtful. Then he grins and gets off the bed.

'Where are you going?'

He doesn't reply. I hear his footsteps outside in the hall before he disappears into his bedroom. When he returns he presents me with a smallish cube wrapped in silver foil and a sealed plastic sachet containing fine shreds the colour of dry sand. This is a fairy tale, I tell myself. I want to believe it but I dread disappointment.

'Spice?' I'm looking at the sachet. Malo nods. 'And this stuff?'

'Resin. That's the lot. That's all I've got. And now it's yours.'

I gaze at him, shaking my head in wonderment. Then I open the sachet and empty the contents into the bucket. The crumbled resin comes next, the residue sticky on my fingertips. I spit in the bucket for good measure and ask Malo to do the same. He complies without protest, and then watches me give the bucket a final shake. Then I nod at the door.

'Lots of water and down the loo,' I tell him. 'No cheating.'

I listen to him doing what he's been told. The flush of the lavatory never sounded sweeter. Then he's back in the bedroom, looking down at me.

'What now?' he says.

Good question.

Mitch phones later, around six. Much better now, I thank him for leaving us alone.

'Us?'

'Me and my son. His name's Malo. I may have mentioned him.'

'You're OK?'

'I'm good.'

'And Prentice? You're going to pay him a visit?'

'We saw him a couple of days ago. Things have been a bit tricky since.'

'So how was he?'

I tell Mitch what we found down in Dorchester. I keep it brief. Saucy, in the view of people who know about such things, is lucky to be alive.

'He recognized you?'

'Yes.'

'Made you welcome?'

'Yes.'

'And?'

'And nothing. He's in a bad place. He's a mess.'

I don't tell him about my pitch for money for the mine charity. Nor do I describe his fascination with Malo. For once I'm bossing this conversation, no longer at the mercy of events, and the feeling is indescribably wonderful. Then, all too typically, I make a major mistake.

'Tell me something,' I say casually. 'If you want a sample of someone's DNA, how do you go about it?'

Mitch wants to know why I'm asking. I tell him it's a favour for a girlfriend. She wants to be sure of the link between her newborn baby and the three men in her life.

'I told her I hadn't a clue,' I say. 'But I'd make some enquiries.'

'You mean talk to me.'

'Yes.'

'Right.' There's a longish silence. I picture him thinking, trying to join the dots, trying to separate the thinness of the lie from the real reason for me asking. Silly bitch. Silly, silly bitch.

'You'll need saliva, or a nail clipping, or a hair with follicles, just a trace,' he says at last. 'And that's from the pair of them.'

'You mean the four of them. You mean *she*'ll need.'

'Of course. The technology's amazing these days. LCN. Low Copy Number. Just a used toothbrush will be enough. Extraordinary when you think about it.'

I thank him for the advice. My girlfriend, I say, might want to buy him a bottle or two of wine. What should she be looking for?

'A 2011 San Vincente Rioja.' He's laughing. 'But you knew that already.'

Malo and I are back on the train within the week. I've made a precautionary phone call to the hospital in Dorchester and have been assured that Mr Prentice is still in residence. When I asked about a possible discharge date the woman at the nursing station said the doctors couldn't be sure. At least a week, she thought. Probably longer.

This time we take a later train, arriving at the hospital in the early afternoon. Saucy's already busy with a visitor and we find a perch in the waiting room outside the ward. Malo eyes a nest of soft toys in the corner while I thumb through a battered copy of *Hello!* magazine.

So far, thank God, my son is showing no signs of the withdrawal symptoms I've been dreading – no sweats, no sleeplessness, no desperate desire to hit the streets again. On the contrary, he seems determined to make friends with me. Is this Saucy's doing? Is Malo that glad to have turned his back on Berndt? In truth I've no idea but each day seems just a little better – sunnier – than the last, and for that I'm deeply grateful.

I've just finished a breathless account of Catherine Zeta-Jones' first date with Michael Douglas when the door opens to admit a man in his early fifties. He's overweight, flushed, grey suit, purple tie, expensive-looking shoes. He spares Malo a nod and then asks me whether I'm here to give young Hayden a shake or two. When I say yes, he apologizes for keeping me waiting. Northern accent.

'He's free now,' he says. 'What he really needs is a bloody secretary.'

He laughs at his own joke and steps back outside. I've seen his face before, I know I have, but I can't think where. When I ask Malo, he shakes his head. No idea.

Saucy is pleased to see us. With the exception of the flowers, which have disappeared, not much in the room has changed. The patient is still in a neck brace, his arm is still pointing skywards, and he's still on a catheter, but the moment we step into the room I know I'm looking at a different man. He seems younger. Much of the pain that was so evident last time appears to have gone. His voice is stronger too, and he's mastered the art of speaking in whole sentences without having to stop and draw breath.

He pats the sheet for me to take a seat and pouts his lips for a kiss. I oblige on both counts. The swelling around his left eye has settled down. He's looking hard at Malo.

'Sorry about last time, son. Not at my best.'

Malo shrugs the apology away, says it's not a problem. Saucy manages a grin.

'Fucking bikes. That's over. In this life, son, you get to know your limits. Once is enough.'

Saucy asks me to pass him the cup on his bedside table. It's plastic, sealed top with a bendy straw, the kind you give to young kids. He sucks it greedily while I hold the cup. Afterwards he's dribbling what looks like orange juice but Malo is on hand again with the tissues. What a team.

Saucy seems pleased. He gives my hand a squeeze and settles back against the pillows.

'Know how many hits that piece on YouTube got?' he says brightly. 'Over a million. A *million*. In this world it pays to make enemies but a million is way over the top. Should I be flattered? Is that a compliment?'

I tell him it's a sign of the times. People love seeing others come to grief. He ignores the comment. My red beret seems to intrigue him.

'You cold or something? Why don't you take it off?'

I remove the beret. My hair has begun to grow again, a soft brown fuzz under my fingertips. Saucy is gazing at the line of stitches.

'You, too?' he says at last. 'Too quick into the corner?'

Malo laughs. I shake my head. Saucy wants to know more – demands to know more. I explain about the tumour, the operation, and coming to in a room much like this.

'You mean cancer? In the brain?' He seems to be taking the news personally.

'Yes.'

'Shit. I never knew.'

'I never told you.'

'Yeah, but . . . your *brain*? You had a headache? You couldn't think straight? Then everything went black? Is that what happens?'

'More or less.'

'And now?'

'Now's different. You take things for granted before. Plus all the wrong things matter far too much. Work. Disappointments. Crap reviews. That's all gone. Thanks to my little visitor.'

'That stuff used to get to you? Are you serious?'

'Of course. And it gets to everyone, no matter how much smoke they blow up your backside.'

He rolls his eyes. There's wonderment in his face, as well as surprise.

'But you were beautiful,' he says. 'You were so beautiful. You still are. Even fucking bald you're beautiful. Can I say that? Do you mind?'

'Not at all.' I gaze down at him. He looks like a child. He might be Malo's age when the marriage first went seriously wrong, maybe even younger. What I'm seeing, what I'm hearing, is hard to associate with the darker bits of Mitch's description. This man has killed people? Hurt people? Broken every rule in the book? Really?

'I've brought a hairbrush,' I tell him. 'It's nothing personal but maybe you need a bit of TLC.'

'Be my guest.' He sounds delighted.

Malo looks on, surprised, as I bend over the bed and begin to attack the tangle of greying curls. I work slowly, exactly the way I used to with my son, using the brush to tease out knot after knot, trying not to hurt him. His scalp is bone-white beneath the matted hair. I've nearly finished when an orderly appears at the door. He wants to know whether we'd like tea or coffee. I say tea, Malo coffee.

124

'Top work.' The orderly nods down at Saucy and then shoots me a grin. 'You want a job?'

Moments later, I'm finished. At least half a dozen of Saucy's hairs have ended up on the brush. I return it carefully to my bag and then perch on the side of the bed. I want to know what Saucy's been up to all these years our paths haven't crossed. I want to know where he lives, who he shares his life with, how he keeps himself amused. In short, I want to know everything.

'Why?'

It's a reasonable question. I'm playing this scene way too fast. I need to take my time.

'Because I'm nosy,' I say. 'And because I've never forgotten you.'

'No bullshit?'

'No bullshit.'

'And the boy?' He manages a tiny shift of his head in Malo's direction.

'He knows.'

'Everything?'

'*Everything?*' My laughter is totally unforced. 'You seduced me. You got me very drunk. And then you fucked me. That's it. There's nothing else to know. Except you made me laugh.'

Saucy is frowning. This isn't the answer he wanted. He's looking a little bruised. I lean over and kiss him again, this time on the forehead. 'No offence,' I tell him, 'but I'm still wondering about that hundred grand.'

'For the mine people?'

'Of course.'

He closes his eyes for a moment or two, says nothing.

'And there's me thinking I had you for free,' he mutters at last. 'Talk to my accountant. I'll give you the number. He'll put a cheque in the post.' The eyes open again. 'So what else does it take, apart from money?'

'To do what?'

'To stay in touch.'

I have a late supper with Mitch that night, at an Italian place in Hither Green. I called him from the train while Malo was using the toilet and described the visitor we'd so briefly met at the hospital. Thinning hair. Rimless glasses. Nice shoes. Purple tie. Purple watch strap. Now, over seafood pasta and a bottle of Soave, Mitch spreads a handful of photos beside my plate.

'Him,' I say without hesitation. I'm pointing to a suited figure on a raised stage. He has his arm around a tall, blonde woman in late middle age. She's wearing a purple rosette. They're both waving to what I assume must be an audience.

His name, according to Mitch, is Erik Dubarry, Erik with a 'k', though his real name is Derrick Johnson. He's been one of the more anonymous figures in the wings of the pantomime that is UKIP and Mitch, as ever, seems to know everything about him.

'Long-time mate of Prentice. Businessman in his own right. Yorkshire born and bred. Brewery interests in the North East and a huge property portfolio, mainly in seaside towns. This is the guy who buys all those rundown hotels that no one wants and converts them into DSS. Our masters wouldn't thank us for saying so but without the likes of Dubarry, these people would be sleeping in the streets.

'And the UKIP link?'

'He was early on the bus. I'm not sure there's a political bone in his body but he's like so many of the rest of them. Boil the offer down. Press the right buttons. *England for the English. Take back control. Don't let Brussels steal our money. Immigrants back where they belong.* You can write this stuff in your sleep and people like Dubarry didn't take much notice until UKIP started winning votes. At that point they realized that they could really get under the Establishment's skin and that's when the cheque books came out.'

'And you're telling me Saucy's part of this?'

'Prentice is part of anything that threatens to get out of hand. He can't resist a ruck, even now. That's been the appeal of UKIP. They promised to get stuck in and that's exactly what they've done. The Tories never saw them coming. Not really. They dismissed them as a bunch of fruitcakes and it never occurred to them for a millisecond that they might lose the referendum. They thought people would vote with their wallets. The one thing they never took on board was that most of those wallets were empty. That was the genius of UKIP. People had literally nothing to lose so why not stick it to the rich bastards? Prentice understood that. He got rich by screwing the poor guys. He knows the way the trick works because he understands the kind of lives that quite a lot of people lead. We're not talking drugs here. We're not even talking unemployment. You

127

can get a job these days, even two jobs, and still have trouble paying the rent. Prentice and his mates know that. They're pushing at an open door. Show them a glimpse of the Promised Land, wind them up about the fat cats, about the London political set, about the blokes in suits that make all the decisions, and they'll vote in their millions. That's music to Prentice's ears. Talk to him about the issues, about the small print, about trade treaties and preferential tariffs and all the rest of it and he'll go to sleep on you. Show him the way to give the suits a good kicking and he's your friend for life. These people have money, lots of money, and that puts them in a very special place.'

Gradually it's dawned on me that Mitch is seriously angry. He hates people like Prentice because he hates what they're doing to the country. This is mayhem for mayhem's sake, he seems to be saying. This is politics waged like the Pompey away-games where he first tasted blood. I also get the feeling that Mitch doesn't entirely trust me any more. He senses that Saucy may have turned my head again and he's exceptionally keen to make a course correction or two. He wants me to know that Prentice and his mates are out of control. They're rich. They don't care who they upset. And they have absolutely no interest in the real-life consequences of what they're up to. We're a year or two away from catastrophe, he says. And no one knows what to do.

Catastrophe is a very big word. I ask him what, exactly, it means.

'Brexit,' he says simply. 'Telling Europe to fuck off. Turning our backs on what makes life sweet. Assuming we can pig out at someone else's trough. You really think Trump won't screw us? You really believe the Indians will do a deal without a trillion work visas? This is madness. Dubarry knows it. Prentice knows it. And that makes them very happy.'

'Because . . .?'

'Because there'll be rich pickings in the wreckage and they all know it. In five years, maybe ten, there won't be a National Health Service worth the name. All gone. All privatized. All in the hands of big business. The same with education. With care of the elderly. With parks and pot holes and rubbish collection and libraries and the rest of it. The world we take for granted will be gone and all you'll hear from the likes of Prentice will be laughter. You think I'm joking?' He suddenly looks up, mid-sentence, and gets to his feet. 'This is Sayid,' he says. 'If you want to know about consequences, you're looking at an expert.'

So I finally get to meet Sayid, Mitch's house-mate and partner. He's tall. He's wearing a pair of grey trackie bottoms and a loose crew-neck top. His head is shaved and his skin is the lightest shade of olive. He moves with the grace and poise of a natural athlete and he also has what a publicist of mine once called 'a melting smile'. One could do a lot worse than fall in love with a vision like this, I think. Assuming you had any choice in the matter.

He apologizes for interrupting our meal. He's

been running on Blackheath and has somehow misplaced his keys. I'm listening hard. The clue is in the language. Not lost. Misplaced. Mitch dismisses his apologies and insists he join us. The waiter brings an orange juice and a menu. Sayid says no to food but sips the juice. After Mitch's little diatribe, the passion has gone out of the conversation but we have a quietly civilized exchange of views on the iniquities of Home Office harassment of asylum seekers.

The restaurant is barely a quarter full but Sayid is clearly ill at ease sitting here in his running gear. He keeps glancing over his shoulders at other diners, at the door, at the street outside, and as soon as he's finished the juice I push my plate to one side and tell Mitch I have to go.

'You mean home?'

'Yes.'

'You can't.'

'Why on earth not?'

'It's the fifteenth,' he says. 'Cassini left us this afternoon.'

We take an Uber back to Mitch's place. The driver seems to think the company might be in trouble in London but Mitch won't have it. Too many drivers. Too many customers. A tweak to the terms of employment and everything will be fine. Sayid says nothing during the journey. He's like an unpresence in the back of the cab, a shadow of a man with nothing to say. Even his sweat smells divine.

In Mitch's kitchen, a major surprise. Sayid turns out to be a gifted cake-maker, and he's presented his landlord and lover with a very personal take on Saturn. Strictly speaking it's only half a planet, cut through at the equator to sit neatly on the presentation plate, but the delicate shades of ochre and blue are perfectly rendered and he's even added two rings carefully sculpted from the icing he had left. Best of all is a tiny Cassini lookalike he's whittled from the remains of a discarded window frame he says he found in Mitch's shed. I stand in the kitchen, lost for words. Is there no end to this man's talents?

Mitch, I know, is touched. He's been out all day on various assignments and he'd no idea of the surprise in store. He wants to know how Sayid could possibly have kept a secret like this when their lives are so closely interlinked. Sayid smiles. He's sparing when it comes to conversation but his eyes – the deepest brown – fill in the gaps between words.

'It's a trick you have to learn,' he murmurs, 'in this country.'

'Cake making?' I ask.

'Discretion. London is a big city. I'm good at keeping secrets.'

Mitch produces a bottle of Moët. Sayid sticks to juice from the fridge. When he finds a knife for the cake he insists that I do the honours. Cutting into the perfect half-sphere, I marvel at the skill that went into its creation. This is Big Bang all over again, I tell him. A second go at confecting Saturn from the dust and debris of deep space.

'I found a mould at the care home,' he says. 'After that it was simple.'

The cake is delicious. Mitch pulls the curtains tight against passers-by before we troop into the sitting room. His anger has gone now. He's softer, gentler, something I put down to the presence of Sayid. I've acquired a lot of gay friends in my career and I've always noticed how comfortable they are around their partners. Mitch and Sayid are the same. Their obvious affection is unforced. They touch each other a lot – nothing heavy, nothing sending a message, simply a hand lingering briefly on an arm or a thigh. They sit together on the battered old sofa, companionable, enjoying the cake, sharing each other's days. Being part of this, being so wholly accepted, feels like a privilege as well as a pleasure. Nice people. The best.

I ask about Aleppo. I spent some time there before the war when we were shooting the movie in Palmyra. I remember the souk and the dust of early evening that turned the sunsets into magical shades of gold. It was a lovely city, proof that ancient civilizations can teach us how to live better lives.

'You think so?'

I can't make out what lies behind Sayid's smile. I don't want to trespass on this man's past, I don't want to ask the obvious questions about what it must be like to lose everything you count as precious, but at the same time I'm becoming horribly aware that nothing is forever. We need to ask ourselves the harder questions, I tell myself. We need to be braver, more candid. That's why I forced Malo to a decision about his young life. Be bold. Make friends with the truth. Because everything else, in a phrase that might have dropped from Saucy's lips, is bollocks.

'And Aleppo? The state of the place? Now?' I ask.

'Gone.' Sayid makes a soft, sideways motion with his hand. 'You never think it possible until it happens.'

He'd fled with his cousin and her family. I get the impression it had cost them all a great deal of money, probably his money, but he's far too classy to go into the details. At the coast they took a boat to one of the Greek islands. Waited weeks to find a place on the ferry. Walked and trained it north through the Balkans. A life of queues and freezing rain and shitting in the fields and untold misery. When we get to Calais the story stops. I assume he jumped a lorry but he isn't saying. Instead he tips his head back and stares up at the ceiling.

Mitch pours me more champagne and raises his glass.

'Cassini,' he says.

I'm home shortly after eleven. I let myself in very quietly, not wanting to disturb my sleeping son, but when I peek round his bedroom door the room is empty. Quickly, I check the rest of the flat but there's no one there. Malo has disappeared.

Eleven

I collapse on the sofa, close to tears, regretting the wine and the champagne. I can't think straight. All I can imagine, all too clearly, is the moment when the emptiness of the flat and his own inner demons crushed my poor benighted boy and sent him back to the streets. He'll have got money from somewhere. He'll have bought papers and tobacco and scored another sachet of Spice. He'll have rolled himself a big fat spliff, liberally dusted with the Zombie powder, and stumbled back into his cave. I should never have left him, I keep telling myself. Either that, or he should have come with me. My fault. My fault again. So much for motherhood.

I reach for my phone, checking in case he's left a message. My agent's been in touch about the radio play. Heal's have an autumn sale. Flights to Alicante and Murcia are mine at a knockdown price. No word from Malo. I shut my eyes, pull my knees up to my chin, rock softly to and fro. Should I get out there? Start looking for him? Start asking strangers whether they might have seen a thin seventeen-year-old with black curly hair and trouble walking straight? Or should I cut to the chase? Go to the police? Tell them I've tried and I've tried but that nothing seems to keep my precious son out of harm's way? I shake my head. None of the above, I think. Not if I'm to hang on to a shred of self-respect.

Moments later, I think I catch a noise at the front door, a strange scuffing sound. Then comes a knock, soft, then another. I get to my feet, checking the time. 23.19. Malo, I tell myself. He knows the combination to the main door downstairs but he hasn't got the key to the apartment. Another knock. I'm at the door now. I pull it open. I'm right. It's Malo.

I stare at him, not quite knowing how to handle this scene. Part of me is swamped with relief. But the rest of me is very, very angry. He's wearing jeans and the usual Einstein T-shirt. His eyes are moist and he's swaying a little. But what draws my attention is the state of his right hand. It's wrapped in a loose crepe bandage and blood is seeping through.

'You've been in some kind of fight?'

'Fight?'

I don't bother answering. The possibilities are endless. A quarrel over the deal. A fall in the street once he'd scored. A hand through a window. Any fucking thing.

I take him into the bathroom and remove the bandage. There are cuts on his palm and two of his fingers, nothing deep, nothing serious. He watches me sponge the blood away. He shows no traces of guilt. Neither, I realize, does he smell of tobacco.

'So where did you go?'

'Next door.'

'You mean Evelyn's?' I'm staring at him.

'Yes.'

'Why?'

'She came round, knocked on the door. She needed help.'

He begins to explain about her oven. It's electric and it has a special bulb that lights up when she needs to check on what's happening. The bulb goes *phut* from time to time and it's tricky to get out. I know this because Evelyn has arthritis in both hands and it's normally me who has to unscrew the thing.

'So what happened?'

'I got it out but I broke it in the process.' He's looking at his hand. 'I put another one in but there was glass everywhere so I ended up cleaning the whole oven.'

'*You* did that?'

'Me. Yeah. She wanted to give me money afterwards but I said no. She had some wine. We split a bottle.' He smiles at me. 'Maybe two.'

I gaze at him a moment and then give him a hug. My junkie son cleaning my precious neighbour's oven. When will I ever learn to trust him? When will I ever learn to trust anyone?

'Why are you crying, Mum?'

'Because I'm useless. Because I get everything wrong. But you're back. And that's all that matters.'

After I finish with his hand we celebrate with the remains of a bottle of Crianza I've got lurking in the kitchen. Malo is normally quick on the uptake but it takes him a while to realize that I'd jumped to the wrong conclusions.

'You really think I'd gone to score again?'

'Yes.'

'Why?'

'Because . . .' I shrug hopelessly. 'Just because.'

'Because you don't trust me?'

'Because I know how evil this stuff is.'

'And you think I don't know that?'

'Of course you know that. But knowing isn't enough. Not at your age. Not at any age. It doesn't matter. Come here.'

I give him another hug, clumsy this time, and spill red wine down his T-shirt. It looks bloodier than his poor hand. Poor Einstein.

'Crime scene.' I'm laughing now. 'I'll buy you another one.'

Malo wriggles free and holds me at arm's length. For the first time in years, looking at the expression on his face, I get the feeling that he might like me. Not as his mother. Not as his scold. But as a friend. He seems to be taking responsibility here, not for his own life but for mine.

'You're pissed,' he says gently. 'You need to look after yourself.'

We both surface late next day. Still in bed, I spend half an hour on my iPad trying to get to grips with DNA tests. If I want to be sure about Malo's real father then I need to submit two samples to a specialist laboratory for testing. For a very reasonable £59, an outfit called Paterfamilias will look for a match. I already have strands of Saucy's hair, all with follicles. What I need now is something from Malo. He's just got up. I can hear him in the bathroom. I wonder about stealing his toothbrush after he's used it but then I remember last night's encounter. You need to be bigger than this, I tell myself. This needs to be a team effort.

I table the proposition over a late breakfast. Malo loves the idea of Paterfamilias. He hasn't trimmed his nails for a while. Might I like to help myself?

Malo has shortish fingers, Saucy's fingers, and I use my nail scissors for the trim. I store the cuttings in an envelope and then return to the Paterfamilias website to order a DNA kit. I'm about to supply my credit card details when I notice that an extra £99 buys you a premium service: collection within two hours, a three-day turnaround, and courier delivery of the results. I hesitate for perhaps a second. £156? For acquiring a new dad for Malo? A bargain.

Back in the kitchen, Malo is looking troubled. 'What if it doesn't work?'

'You mean a negative result?'

'Yes.'

'Then you're lumbered with Berndt.'

'Ah . . .' He's frowning. 'You didn't fuck anyone else around that time?'

'I'm afraid not.'

'You're sure?'

'Absolutely.' I put a hand on his arm. 'Sorry to disappoint you.'

The courier with the DNA kit turns up within the hour. She's outside in the sunshine at the front door and Malo, after a double take, buzzes her in. Thirty seconds later she's up on the fourth floor. Malo already has the door open and stands aside to let her in. She's on the short side. She's wearing a tight jacket in dark red leather and trousers to match. Her short cropped hair is jet black, similar to Malo's, and there are hints of Aztec Indian in her face. A big helmet dangles from one hand and she has the sample kit in the other. Saucy, I know, would eat her alive.

She's given me the DNA kit. I'm in the kitchen with the door open while Malo talks to our visitor. I'm in the process of choosing a couple of his nail cuttings for one of the sample envelopes when it occurs to me he's chatting her up. He's asking her about the helmet. She says it's state of the art. Her English is perfect but heavily accented. It seems her father has connections in the world of Formula One and the helmet has come from one of the race teams. She's unzipped the jacket and she's standing in front of him, showing him how the helmet works. You input an address and it gives you audio directions via Bluetooth plus a head-up display on the visor.

Malo is impressed. He wants to put it on. She reaches out, making adjustments, telling him how to lower the visor. From where I'm standing it's hard to judge her age – early twenties, maybe younger – but there's a gleam in her eyes that tells me my son has touched a nerve. She's laughing at something he's just said. Good sign.

I'm finished with the samples. I pack them carefully into the kit, add my personal details, and seal the Jiffy bag. Next door, to Malo's visible disappointment, our courier is getting ready to leave. She takes the Jiffy bag and then checks a document. The results, she promises, will be back in three days, maybe even earlier. She does jobs for these people all the time. They're very good.

Malo wants to know whether she'll be delivering personally.

'Would you like that?'

'I would.'

'Then maybe yes.'

They lock eyes for a moment, then she's gone.

Malo and I spend the day together in town. We go to Fat Face, and one or two other stores, and I buy my son two new pairs of 501s, a rather stylish North Face jacket, a selection of T-shirts, and a pair of heavily discounted Nike trainers. In every store he seems reluctant to see me parting with money on his behalf, a trait I find oddly endearing, and when we pause for a late lunch at a Nandos he goes for the cheapest option on the menu. When I ask him why he needs to be so mean with himself he says he doesn't know. One day, he tells me, we'll go somewhere really posh, really expensive, and he'll pick up the bill. I smile. I can hear Saucy in his voice. Who needs DNA tests?

Late afternoon, I have an appointment with my agent. Malo is reluctant to come with me but I insist. She's often heard me talking about you, I tell him, and now she can meet the real thing. 'The real thing' is a phrase that seems to amuse him. We take a cab to Camden Town.

Rosa has been my agent for longer than I care to remember. She's nearing retirement now, a prospect which most people in the industry dismiss out of hand. A big woman, brisk, funny, fearless, she began life as a continuity girl out at Shepperton Studios. In time she worked on some huge movies under directors with brutal reputations but survived intact. For a while after that she ran an agency for camera crews, chiefly working for the big network TV companies, but she missed what she calls 'the talent' and started to represent us thesps. I've known her all my working life and trust her implicitly. She's done me some eye-watering deals but most of all I treasure her contempt for the vainer side of our profession. Like Saucy, she has no time for people who take themselves too seriously. And, like Saucy, she makes me laugh.

This is the first time she's seen me since I left hospital. She gives me a big hug, and then looks Malo up and down.

'He's looking after you? Your boy?'

'He is.'

'Glad to hear it. You're either lying or you're lucky. Either way it's five o'clock. Vino, or something more interesting?'

I settle for a gin and tonic. Malo asks for water. Rosa shoots him a look.

'Something the matter? You're ill?'

'Thirsty.'

'Lager, then? Peroni?'

'Water, please.'

She shrugs and sorts out the drinks. We talk briefly about the Montréal project and agree that the script looks deeply promising. When she asks me how soon I could be ready for the rigours of location work I tell her there's nothing I couldn't face with a decent wig. She's been eyeing my beret for some time.

'Do you sleep in it?'

'I sleep alone. The beret lives on the hook on the back of the door.'

'No plans in that direction?'

'None at all. I like my own company. And I have Malo.'

'Very sane. You see Berndt at all these days?'

Rosa knows Berndt well. When we were a couple we'd all run into each other at various industry get-togethers and as the years went by I had the tiniest suspicion that she quite fancied him. Something about the way she'd trap him in a corner and make sure his glass was always full. My husband, she once told me, was every thinking woman's fantasy.

'He's hit a rough patch,' I tell her. 'Shit happens. Even in Sweden.'

'Shame. I'm hearing the same stories. In his part of the wood creative talent isn't enough. You have to be clever with money, too.'

'And he isn't?' Malo is looking at Rosa.

'No, my precious, he most definitely isn't. I shouldn't be the one telling you but you've probably worked it out already. You should be proud of his work, though. He's made some fine films.'

Malo nods and then studies what's left of his fingernails. On the subject of Berndt, he has nothing more to say.

Rosa wants to talk about the BBC radio commission. The script has been adapted from a novel. It's called *Going Solo* and I get to play the wife of a pilot, widowed after he disappears mid-Channel while flying his light aircraft to France. The husband owns a couple of classic World War Two fighters, a Mustang and a Spitfire, both two-seater conversions. Between them, they've run a business offering flights of a lifetime, mainly to WW2 veterans, and now she determines to step into her husband's shoes and learn to fly.

All this, to be frank, is a bit techie for my taste, but the script brightens when she begins to suspect that her husband's death is no accident. The more questions she asks, the more troubled she feels, and as she begins to master the Spitfire she realizes that her fate rests entirely in her own hands. The play ends – improbably – with a winner-takes-all dog fight over a major air show, but by this time she's found a kind of redemption. Given the events of the past few weeks, this is something I can relate to. As one of Berndt's characters once said, we are all – in the end – totally alone.

Rosa wants to know what I think of the script. The writer, Pavel Sieger, has a growing reputation.

'I like it. I like it a lot. We're not talking Pinter or something super-edgy but just now that's a bit of a bonus. It feels quite old-fashioned but in a good way. Boys' Own with a splash of feminism. Plus I don't have to learn a word.'

This, of course, is the crux. Given my recent medical history, and all the stress of location work, it's been clever of Rosa to think of radio. She reminds me of the rehearsal dates, and the two days set aside for the recording. I assure her they're all in the diary.

'Anything else out there?'

'Not so far, sweetness. You'll be the first to know. Take it easy for a while. Watch some of those Battle of Britain documentaries. Get yourself in the mood.'

We say our goodbyes after the second gin. Malo, who's known nothing about *Going Solo*, is full of questions but I can only disappoint him. 'This is radio,' I keep insisting. 'If it was a movie you could have the time of your life on location. All those planes. All that hardware. But a radio studio is a shed with thicker walls and the closest you'll ever get to the real thing is a whole bunch of sound effects. It's all about language, dialogue, timing. Come and watch by all means. But prepare to be bored.'

We're back in Holland Park as the daylight begins to fade. I stand in the living room for a long moment, watching the big jets hanging in the dusk as they descend into Heathrow, thinking of nothing in particular. I'm still basking in the soft glow of that second gin. I'm still telling myself how lucky I am that Malo is still around, still clean, still interested. When the buzzer goes on the entry video I barely hear it. Malo leaves the room to investigate. He's back within seconds.

'It's Dad,' he says. 'What shall I do?'

Twelve

Berndt says he's come straight from the airport. It's raining now and his hair is plastered against his skull. He says he's spent his last five hundred krona on the taxi fare and a bunch of flowers from the shop on the Bayswater Road. Malo has put the flowers in the washing-up bowl in the sink. He seems in no rush to find a vase.

Berndt looks wrecked. Worse still, he looks plaintive. This isn't the man I fell in love with, the man I was crazy about, the man I married. His spirit has gone and so has the faint air of mystery that made him so irresistible. It took me years to realize just how hard he'd worked to perfect this look but even towards the end – with a half-smile or a duck of his head – he could still take me by surprise. No longer. The man sitting alone on the sofa belongs in one of Berndt's early *noir* scripts. He's become one of life's losers, deflated, defeated, awaiting the knock on the door that will finish him off. I go to the bathroom and get him a towel.

'So what do you want?' I ask for the second time.

'Help. Money. Time.' He's knotting the towel between his hands. 'Maybe a bed?'

I tell him there's no chance he can sleep here. Both bedrooms are occupied.

'The sofa?'

'No.'

'Why not?'

'Because we don't want you here.'

The 'we' hurts him. I can see it in his face. Is he acting? I can never be sure. I steal a glance at Malo. He's watching this little drama carefully, his face impassive. Dialogue, delivery, timing, I think. My boy is learning fast.

'So where shall I go?' Berndt asks.

'I've no idea. It's often best to have a plan before you make a start on the first page. That's what you always told me. So what's happened to the plan?'

'There is no plan. You want letters from the debt collectors? I can give you dozens. You want emails from my bank? My pleasure. You want a look at the message I had yesterday from Scantrax? About pulling out of the distribution deal on the Svalbard series? No problem. All of that I have in my little briefcase. But no plan.'

This is pathetic, I tell myself. He knows me too well. He knows I'm prone to lending an ear, to listening hard, to sympathizing, to nodding in agreement, to understanding, to trying to find a way through other people's problems. But what he doesn't know is that things are different. Because I have Malo now and that has changed everything.

'So why did you come?' I ask him.

'Because there's so much to discuss.'

'There's nothing to discuss. We're getting divorced. They're called solicitors, or they are in this country. They talk to each other. Sometimes they lift the phone and talk to me, and maybe you. That's what our money buys. That's what's so sweet about the deal. Arm's length. Job done. Back to square one.'

'I have no money.'

'I'm not sure I believe you.'

'Is that your solicitor speaking or you?'

'It's me,' I say. 'I'm not sure I believe you because I know nothing about the small print. My accountant tells me life is a dry river bed. Under every stone is a hidden cache of money. It's like that everywhere in the world. Business deals, tax evasion, divorces, everywhere you look. You tell me you're broke, bankrupt, whatever. How do I know you haven't hidden money away? How do I know you haven't been down to the river bed? That's why I need my accountant. Because he'll know.'

This has the makings of a speech. Malo's visibly impressed. Soon I might expect applause, but for now all I can see is Berndt shaking his head.

'More money,' he says, 'wasted on accountants. These people cost a fortune and you know something else? When the end comes, and you're through, their fees are even bigger. I hate accountants. I loathe accountants. The only good accountant is a dead accountant.'

'That bad?'

'Worse. You know something? I had a meeting yesterday in Stockholm. My accountant was there, in the flesh. I'd asked him along to vouch for me, to fend off a particular creditor, but he did exactly the opposite. He said I'd *exhausted my assets*. That was his exact phrase. He came

147

into that room as an accountant. He left it as an undertaker. Turns out he'd come to bury me. So here I am.'

This is better, I think. This is near-vintage Berndt. There's life in the old bastard yet.

'You have to go,' I say, 'because I'm not having any kind of discussion. You want to do that, then talk to my solicitor. He charges three hundred pounds an hour so you might have to keep it brief.'

I'm tempted to offer him a drink, purely out of charity, but Malo beats me to it. He offers Berndt one of the Kronenbourgs in the fridge. Watching him fetch a glass from the kitchen I feel a tiny tremor of apprehension.

Berndt opens the can and takes care to tilt the glass at exactly the right angle. This is a trick he taught me years back and I've used it ever since. Perfect head. Perfect presentation.

'*Skål.*' Berndt raises his glass to Malo. Ignores me.

Malo wants to know about Annaliese.

'There's nothing to know. The last time we talked she was on location in Copenhagen. I gather she's found herself a Danish boyfriend.'

'She's not coming back?'

'To Sweden, yes. But not to me.'

'And the apartment?'

'Gone. Repossessed.'

'So where have you been living?'

'With my sister in Norrköping. I stayed three days. By the end I couldn't work out which of us was the more depressed. It kills you, Malo.'

'What does?'

'Staking everything. Losing everything. Failing. I used to write movies about situations like these. Not for a second did I ever . . .' He turns away, burying his head in his hands. His shoulders are heaving. Small animal noises are coming from somewhere deep inside him. Impressive, I think.

Malo's face is a mask. He's totally impassive, totally unmoved. Like mother, like son.

The broken figure on the sofa seems to have regained some kind of control. He has the grace to apologize. I say that's unnecessary. Malo wants to know why he hasn't arrived with more baggage.

'Light,' he says. 'I travel light.'

'Just the one bag?'

'Yes.'

'No change of clothes? No spare jeans?'

'No.'

Malo and I exchange glances. Then Malo goes to his bedroom and reappears with one of the pairs of 501s I'd bought him on our shopping trip. Berndt looks up at him, uncomprehending. Malo asks him to stand up.

'Why?'

'I just need to check something.'

'OK.'

Berndt stands up. The carpet is wet where his feet have been. Malo holds the jeans against Berndt's still-rangy frame. They're way too short.

'Shame,' he says.

I stare at him. This is beyond subtle, beyond cruel. Whether Berndt realizes it or not, his alleged son is making a point. Different build.

Different genes. Different everything. What I'd assumed was an act of charity is anything but. Just faintly, I'm beginning to feel sorry for the man I'd once loved.

'So what will you do?' I ask him. 'Now? Tonight?'

'I've no idea.'

'You've really no money?'

'None.' He fetches out his wallet, tosses it across to me. 'Check, if you want.'

'Credit cards?'

'Insufficient funds.'

'An account with some hotel chain?'

'Those days have gone.'

I nod, think, make a calculation or two. I have a personal account with two hotel chains. I use them when I have down-time on location and I can get away for a couple of days. One of them, the Holiday Inn, has an outpost in Kensington. It's not cheap but just now it might ease my conscience.

I give Berndt the address and order an Uber. The Uber, I tell him, will be on my account. Also the hotel. Three nights, absolute max.

'And after that?'

'I suggest you go home. You have a return ticket?' With some reluctance he nods. 'Then use it.'

He looks up at me and for a moment I think we're in for tears again but then he seems to pull himself together. He's come to try and negotiate some kind of settlement and he's failed completely. Neither I nor Malo want anything to do with him. This is public failure compounded by private humiliation. This is what happens when you belittle and threaten and bad-mouth someone you're supposed to love. This is what happens when, for the briefest moment, you start to believe in your own legend. I've seen it happen dozens of times but never like this, so close, so intimate, so personal.

Malo offers to walk him down to wait for the Uber. Berndt gets to his feet and reaches for his bag. He has one question left and I spare him the indignity of having to ask it.

My bag is in my bedroom. I count £270 in notes, all I can find. I extract twenty pounds and give the rest to Berndt. He looks at it for a moment and then folds it into a pocket in his jeans.

'Don't eat it all at once,' I suggest. 'London isn't cheap.'

He looks me in the eye and then turns away.

'*Tack*,' he mutters, heading for the door.

Thirteen

That night I can't sleep. My head's full of DNA kits, of couriers in red leather, of Berndt, of Saucy. I try and visualize the passage of Saucy's hair, of Malo's tiny crescents of fingernail, through all the scientific processes, faceless boffins with latex gloves and glass pipettes, whirling machines, multi-digit read-outs, the whole mad sci-fi world which will, by Friday, announce a winner in this bizarre race to claim authorship of my son.

In my own mind, it's already a foregone conclusion. It has to be Saucy. Malo's build, Malo's temperament, Malo's fitful charm, even Malo's hair. Why did I ever suspect otherwise? Why – in seventeen long years – did it never occur to me that Saucy's sperm might have crossed the line before Berndt's? In the face of so many clues, so much evidence, why didn't I take a tiny step back and acknowledge at least the possibility that I was sharing my life with a child called Malo Prentice?

The answer, of course, was simple. I didn't want to. I was in love with a man who was taking me places I'd never even dreamed about. I was making my name as an actress. I was building a career. Only when our marriage began to falter did I start looking at Malo in a new light – as someone I had to hang on to – and even then it never occurred to me that his loathsome father might be a genetic impostor. That my precious Malo might belong to someone else.

Saucy. I can see him in hospital. I can see him on the boat in Antibes all those years ago. I think I know the kind of man he is. And this worries me greatly. Why? Because I like him.

I roll over. It's 03.34. I phone Mitch. I like him, too, and I respect him greatly, but this thing is beginning to get out of control. I want a simple answer, a couple of sentences, no more.

He answers quicker than you might imagine. He's seen my name on caller ID.

'What's the matter? You want me to come round?'

'Sweet thought, but no. Sorry to call at this time of night but just tell me one thing. What do you really want from me?'

'I don't understand the question.'

'It's about Saucy. What do you want me to find out?'

'I want to know who his mates are. I want to know who he's talking to politically. I want to know where he's putting his money. And I want to know what went down in Pompey.'

'When?'

'When he was running with the 6.57 crew. When he started making money. Friends and enemies. People who might still be around.'

'People he hurt?'

'Yes.'

'People he might have killed?'

'Yes.'

'You really believe all that stuff? Or is that where I come in?'

'Yes.'

I hear another sleepy voice in the background and then the line goes dead. I'm staring at the clock. 03.35.

I wake at nine. This time it's Berndt on my mind. It was his decision to come to London, his decision to knock on our door, but I can't rid myself of the image of my nearly ex-husband on the sofa, sobbing and humiliated, his head in his hands. Neither can I rid myself of a lingering sense of guilt for pushing him out into the night. He was never great with money. He loved ideas, scripts, narrative arcs, mould-breaking *noir* drama. He could conjure magic on the set and on location. He could, by his own account, talk any woman into bed. But when it came to making any kind of sane investment in the future his attention would wander. I learned this early. Hence my decision to look after my own financial affairs within the marriage. Alone now, he's adrift into a script he doesn't begin to understand. Maybe I should help him get his bearings.

I phone my solicitor. He's the same vintage as Rosa – sturdy, nerveless, a matchless professional happy in his own skin. His real name is Charles but I've called him Carlos since we met. He's retained the loyalty of a smallish clientele and whenever I've needed advice in a hurry he's always found the time for us to meet.

This morning is no exception. I take a bus to the Strand and plunge into the maze of streets leading down to the river. He has an office on the third floor of a building that may well have survived the Great Fire of London. From his window I can see the top of the London Eye and clouds of seagulls drifting in the wind.

Carlos is tall, slightly bent, with a big pale face framed by an explosion of grey curls. His hair always reminds me of certain pictures of Beethoven towards the end of his life, which is entirely apposite because Carlos is a gifted pianist. On boisterous social occasions, if he's in the mood, he will commandeer a piano and belt out a tune or two. When the company is more intimate, his rendition of Schubert's *Impromptu Opus 90* has made me cry.

'Well?'

I tell him about Berndt suddenly appearing at our apartment. I try my best to capture just how helpless he's become.

'You gave him money?'

'Of course I gave him money. He's in a decent hotel for a couple of nights at my expense. But that's just for now. I don't want him at my door again. I want him gone. But I want him happy, too.' I offer Carlos a bleak smile. 'So what do I do?'

Carlos briefly reviews the options. I'm filing for divorce. So far, Berndt hasn't responded. Whether or not he even has a solicitor at this point is far from certain. We can press the issue, insist on full financial disclosure, and arrive at some kind of settlement. Or we can wait.

'For what?'

'For matters to resolve themselves.'

'And if they don't? Ever?'

'Then we're all dead. Full financial disclosure will get things moving. There may be merit in that.'

'But he has no money.'

'Who says?'

I frown. This is exactly the response I expected. My accountant would say the same thing. Everyone, in the end, is unknowable. Especially someone as opaque as Berndt.

'So what do I do?'

Carlos is rolling himself a cigarette. I think he took up smoking as a protest against political correctness. With his earnings he could afford any cigar on the market. Typically, he seems to prefer shag tobacco.

'Is he still a good listener?'

'If it's in his interests, yes.'

'And he's here for how long?'

'Three days, max.'

'Then get hold of him and give him one of these.' He sorts out a card from the chaos of his desk drawer and flips it across. 'Tell him the first half hour's free. After that he's on the meter like everyone else.'

'And what will you tell him?'

'That's client confidentiality. I can't possibly say.'

'Are you serious?'

'Always.'

He gets to his feet and extends a bony hand. I thank him for his time, and for his gesture to Berndt.

'My pleasure. He made some decent films in his time.'

*   *   *

156

I take another bus, heading west this time. The Kensington Holiday Inn is on the Cromwell Road. I've tried to raise Berndt on both his mobile numbers but neither seems to work. My only option, therefore, is another face-to-face.

It's lunchtime and Kensington is buzzing. I wait for a break in the traffic to get across to the hotel. The estate agents around here don't even bother with property details in English. You need Arabic to buy anything over three million, though the photos speak for themselves. Why anyone would need a Jacuzzi trimmed in purple ermine is beyond me.

I ask for Berndt Andressen at reception. The girl behind the counter recognizes the name at once. She tells me he's at lunch just now.

'You happen to know where?'

'Of course.' She nods in the direction of the hotel restaurant. 'He phoned to book a table this morning.'

I lurk in the lobby for a moment or two, wondering if this is such a good idea, but the restaurant is busy, a sea of faces, and I tell myself there's comfort in numbers.

I step inside, trying to spot Berndt. After a moment or two I locate him at a table in the far corner beside the long plate-glass window that looks out over the street. In keeping with last night's encounter, I'm expecting him to be eating alone, picking at something soulful, perhaps deep in a book. Instead, he has company. She's facing me, unlike Berndt. She's youngish, probably early thirties, certainly younger than me. Her auburn hair is swept tightly back, exposing her face. It's an extraordinary face, perfect bone structure, wide eyes, full mouth, a face made for the camera. For a moment I wonder whether it's Annaliese but then I remember that she's always blonde.

'Madame?' It's the maître d'. He has a list of reservations on a display board. He wants to know whether one of those names is mine.

I ignore him. I can't take my eyes off the table in the corner. I've played this scene so often myself, been the willing target, the listening ear, the rapt companion, while Berndt casts his spell. I know exactly what he's at, what pitch he's making. I could even voice the dialogue, word for word. His hand reaches for hers. He's leaning into the conversation. He's pushing for some kind of commitment. Bed. Money. A role he needs playing. Anything.

'Madame?' The maître d' again, insistent this time.

At last I drag my attention elsewhere, spare him a glance, make my excuses, turn to leave.

'I have a table for one,' he says. 'Any use?'

'None at all.' I manage a smile. 'But thanks for the thought.'

Bastard. *Bastard.* I'm sitting on the bus again, inching slowly home. The sight of Berndt doing his trust-me number has brought tears to my eyes. Not because I'm jealous. Not because I'm ever going to miss him again. But because I've been so easily duped. I've no idea who this woman is. She might be someone he's known forever. She might be an actress or a model, someone he's been around lately and added to his must-have list. She might have been in the bar last night, a bird of passage, moving through. A tall stranger suddenly appears on the bar stool beside her. There comes a casual word of introduction, a name left dangling lightly between them. And then, if the prospects look promising, he'll ease into a proper conversation.

Berndt has always been brilliant at this. I must have watched him playing strangers, mainly women, a million times. The fluency of his English, spiced with a Scandi accent. The hint of his standing in the film business. The mention of a particular script or a special actor, names that will resonate and intrigue. And the whole shtick, cleverly parcelled in bite-sized morsels, complete with those sudden trademark silences that confirm what a thoughtful and reflective guy he really is. Bastard, I think again, and then, as the bus begins to pick up speed, I feel abruptly better. In real life, I tell myself, she's probably a hooker. What's left of my £250 won't buy what he's after but she's willing to join him for lunch and put up with all the arty bullshit. My poor Berndt. Reduced to a mere punter.

Thus consoled, I park my fantasies, get off the bus, walk home, and climb the stairs to the apartment. I find Malo in the living room, staring at his mobile, a huge grin on his face. Impatient as ever, he's been busy since I left. He'd made a note of the courier agency, got their number from the internet, and given them a call. The lady in red leather who delivered to Holland Park yesterday? She left her silk snood. Might

159

they give him her number so he can arrange to get the thing back to her? The agency, of course, wouldn't release her number but promised to get her to call. She's just phoned back. Her name is Clemenza. They're meeting this evening for a drink.

I nod my head in approval. This is very direct, very Saucy. No bar stool. No cosy little restaurant table. No creepy come-ons. Just a surprise exchange on the phone and a full-frontal invite out.

'You'll need money,' I tell him. 'My pleasure.'

I spend the afternoon working on the radio script for *Going Solo* and towards six o'clock I knock on Evelyn's door. Happily, she's finished work for the day and offers me a drink. I settle in and thank her for keeping an eye on my son the other night.

'I gather you thought he'd gone AWOL,' she says.

'Who told you that?'

'Malo. He thought it was funny. He's a nice lad. He's got a way with him. He knows how to listen. That's rare in my experience.'

This, from Evelyn, is praise indeed. She's merciless in most of the judgements she makes, especially where men are concerned. For the briefest moment I wonder whether to tell her about Paterfamilias, and the likelihood that Malo might belong to a different father, but she beats me to it.

'Malo told me about the DNA test. He says his real name's Prentice.'

'He's decided? Already?'

'I think it was the wine. He said he'd met his real dad twice. And then he showed me the pictures.'

'The YouTube stuff?'

'The motorbikes. The crash. He seems to think his dad was lucky to survive.'

'Malo's right. He is.'

Evelyn fetches a tube of Pringles from the kitchen. The editor in her is greedy for more detail. Work in publishing and you want the whole story.

I tell her what little I can remember. Antibes. Far too much to drink. And waking up next morning.

'You can't remember?'

'Not really.'

'How disappointing.'

Disappointing? Words are Evelyn's business, mine too, and I'm thinking particularly hard about this one.

'Disappointing's wrong,' I say at last. 'I remember feeling relaxed with him. I remember the way he made me laugh. Berndt always told me that conversation was the great aphrodisiac, getting close to someone, getting them to open up, getting them to surprise themselves. But he's wrong. What got me into bed that night was laughter. Laughter and a million margaritas.'

'Do you regret it?'

'Not at all. Not then and certainly not now.'

'What's the difference?'

'Then I knew nothing. I was a child. A naïf. An innocent. Now I sometimes think I know too

161

much. Berndt taught me that, oddly enough. Not deliberately, not on purpose. It was just something I learned by being around him, by watching and listening. The Berndts of this world are predators. Most of us wander around looking at nothing in particular. Berndt hunts. All the time. Because he can never resist the next meal.'

'That says greed to me.'

'Greed's close but it's a possession thing. Think dogs. Think lamp posts. People like Berndt always need to mark their territory, to leave their smell. Then, like any dog, they move on.'

I was suddenly back in Kensington, back in the restaurant, letting Berndt's latest little tableau sink deep into my subconscious. I know I'll live with that image for a very long time and in a way I'm grateful. Better that moment of luminous clarity than some splashy gesture on my part to try and ease his financial agonies. Trust what you see, what you know. Because the rest can only hurt you.

Evelyn enquires whether my son enjoyed helping her out with the oven.

'He did. He thought you were great. Really easy to talk to.'

'I'm flattered. So what next?'

I tell her I don't know. It happens to be the truth. At last I have a clear brief from Mitch but I have no intention of discussing that with Evelyn. As far as she's concerned, Mr Hayden Prentice is a work in progress.

'You'll see him again?'

'Definitely.'

'He knows about Malo?'

'He can't. None of us can. Not yet. Not for sure. I'm sure he's got his suspicions. Maybe he's got his fingers crossed. But that's not the same as knowing.'

'And Malo?'

'Malo approves. Malo likes him. Saucy calls everyone "son" but in Malo's case it seems to fit perfectly. After you've had Berndt as a father all your life, that matters, believe me.'

Evelyn nods, raises her glass. 'To Malo,' she says. 'Tell him the oven light works perfectly.'

Malo is back earlier than I expected, just after nine. He's toting a motorcycle helmet and a big fat smile.

'Clemenza's spare,' he tells me. 'I rode pillion. We went down to a bar she knows in Putney. She drives that bike like you wouldn't believe. People just get out of the way. How cool is that?'

Clemenza, it turns out, is the daughter of a leading Columbian businessman currently living in London. At the mention of Colombia, my heart sinks. She'll have limitless access to cocaine, probably by the kilo. Malo, when I risk a cautionary word or two on the subject, does his best to ease my anxieties. Clemenza, he tells me, is straighter than straight. Goes to Mass every Sunday. Doesn't smoke. Doesn't do drugs. Never touches alcohol. Because biking is all. And she's brilliant at it.

'You've met an angel,' I tell him. 'If I were you I'd sell tickets. Charge by the minute. You're telling me she's Catholic?'

'She is. How did you know?'

163

'Mass is the clue. Is she super-bright? As well as virtuous?'

'You're taking the piss. You should meet her.'

'I did. And I'm not surprised you tracked her down.'

'I mean properly meet her. Talk to her. She's lovely.'

'Good. I'm glad. So what next?'

'Tomorrow, same time. She's going to pick me up.'

He gives the helmet a little swing, holding it by the chin strap, and then retires to his bedroom. For the first time ever, I can hear him singing. Later I discover it's a track from an xx album. He doesn't know the lyrics and his voice is beyond flat but none of that matters. Thanks to my years with Berndt, I've learned the difference between an act and the real thing. My precious boy is very happy and that – as miracles go – is up there with the loaves and the fishes.

I remember a line from a hymn we used to sing at school a trillion years ago.

Our God, our help in ages past, I murmur, *our hope for years to come.*

Yes, I think. Yes, yes.

Fourteen

On Friday, Clemenza arrives with the DNA results. Malo has obviously shared every last detail of the story so far but she's discreet and well-bred enough to hand over the envelope and head for the door. Malo calls her back.

'Wait,' he says. 'Let's see what it says.'

The envelope is marked *Private and Confidential* and is addressed to me. He rips it open, pulls out the single sheet of paper, and gives it a quick read. Then he shows it not to me but to Clemenza. The girl, embarrassed, takes the notification and gives it to me. I'm looking at the news we've both been expecting for the last three days. Hayden Prentice, aka Saucy, is Malo's dad.

Malo is giving Clemenza a hug. Then it's my turn. Somewhere in all of this I catch the words 'thank you'. For a moment I think the poor boy's on the verge of tears. When he looks up and steps back, Clemenza has gone.

'What do you expect?' I ask. 'Making a scene like that?'

We go back to the notification. These agencies are always careful to include a health warning but we should be 98.3 per cent certain of the DNA match between Malo Andressen and Hayden Prentice. This, it seems, is a document we can use in any court of law, any passport application, any setting that requires proof of paternity. I think briefly about Berndt, about where he might be at this moment, but then decide he's not worth the effort. One day I'll have to tell him, unless Malo gets there first, but the time and opportunity will be of my choosing. For now, we have something else on our minds.

'Saucy,' Malo says. 'Dad. He has to know. We have to tell him.'

I agree. I've been on to the hospital and the news is good. There's nothing broken. His dislocated shoulder has reset nicely and the bones in his neck are stable. The hairline fractures in his ribs are on the mend, his pelvis has turned out to be undamaged, and he doesn't need a catheter any more. For weeks to come he'll be wise to take it easy but he no longer needs hospital care.

'Who told you all this?' Malo asks.

'Saucy. They're taking him home by ambulance this afternoon. He says he's over the moon. He wants us to pay him a visit.'

'When?'

'Tomorrow. We'll train it to Dorchester again. He'll have someone pick us up at the station. Take us out there.'

'You mean to his house? The big one? The estate?'

'I assume so.'

The prospect of visiting the family acres fills Malo with something I can only describe as glee. For the second time in half an hour he's close to euphoria. Less than a week ago he was sharing his life with Peppa Pig and a sachet of Spice. Now he has the world at his feet.

* * *

166

Next day, as instructed, we head down to Dorchester on the train. A woman my age is waiting at the ticket barrier to pick us up. For a second or two, looking at her, I'm furious with myself for not asking Saucy the obvious question. Is this his wife? The new Amanda in his life? Is this Mrs Saucy going to take kindly to a couple of surprise house guests, one of whom is the mother of his long-lost son?

I needn't have worried. Her name is Jessie and it turns out she's partnered with the guy who runs the estate. They live in a bungalow in the grounds of the main property and she and Andy have known 'H', as she calls him, most of their lives. This explains her accent, gruff, almost cockney, exactly the same as Saucy's.

We're in the back of a new-looking Range Rover, leaving the outskirts of Dorchester. I'm doing my best to pump her for more information but blood, as ever, is thicker than water. No, H isn't currently married. Yes, he leads a very busy life. Yes, he occasionally manages an old-times visit to Pompey. And yes, he's very much looking forward to seeing us both.

Malo is beaming. We've turned off the main road to Yeovil and he's glimpsed a handsome Georgian pile through the trees. In his jacket pocket is the good news from Paterfamilias. Life could scarcely be sweeter.

The drive sweeps up through the trees. Off to the right, at Malo's prompting, I recognize the motocross course where Saucy came to grief, a zig-zag of deep tyre ruts disappearing over a rise. Ahead is the building we've just glimpsed.

Flixcombe Manor nestles squarely in the greenness of the landscape. Golden points of sunlight reflect from a dozen windows. Smoke curls from one of the chimneys. The entrance to the place is pillared, imposing, a brilliant shade of white that draws the eye. This is a million miles from Pompey. No wonder Saucy couldn't wait to get home.

Malo has spotted Saucy emerging from the front door. He shuffles carefully forward with the aid of a pair of crutches. Game as ever, he starts to edge himself sideways down the steps. The proper place to meet guests is on the circle of gravel at the front of the house.

Face-to-face, once we're out of the car, he looks more frail than I'd been expecting. He has a kiss for me and a hug for Malo but the slightest misstep registers on his face. It happens again as he leads us back towards the house, making him wince with pain.

'Don't push it,' I tell him. 'Take it easy.'

'Easy? Bollocks,' he mutters darkly. 'Good to see you both.'

I help him on the way up to the house, Malo on his other side. For the last couple of steps we're virtually lifting him.

'Tougher than you thought, eh?' He's looking pleased.

Inside, the place is beautifully furnished, antique pieces everywhere. The smell of freshly cut flowers hangs in the air and I'm still doing a mental audit on the furniture when Saucy spares me the effort.

'Seventy-eight grand the lot,' he says, 'including

the pictures. I bought it all with the house. Bloke who owned the place knew what he was doing. Would have cost me a fortune to replace this lot.'

'What's happened to him? Where's he gone?'

'He died. Drank himself to death. I bought the estate off his eldest boy. He and his missus live out in Dubai. Can't stand the fucking rain.'

Jessie has laid tea out in one of the drawing rooms but Saucy takes us into the kitchen. He says it's the one room in the house where he feels really comfortable and looking round I know exactly what he means: wooden beams, hanging pots and pans, plenty of space, stone floor, a big range with a wood-fired Aga, and a huge old kitchen table most set designers in the movie business would kill for. Big windows look out on to a vegetable garden to the rear of the house and when I get a proper look I count half a dozen chickens peck-pecking among the onion sets.

'All you need is a dog,' I tell him. 'Who does the cooking?'

'Me.'

'*You?*'

'Yeah. I'm not too handy just now so Jessie helps with the heavy stuff. I just did a load of flapjacks, though. In your honour.'

The flapjacks are delicious, moist as well as crunchy, a difficult trick to pull off. Malo sits beside us at the kitchen table. When his hand goes to his jacket pocket I tell him to wait until the three of us are alone.

At last Jessie leaves us. This is Malo's cue.

Saucy has near-animal instincts. He knows something's going on. He can smell it.

Malo is flattening the Paterfamilias results against the grain of the table. Saucy squints at it, then tells Malo to fetch his glasses. Hall table. Next to the door.

'OK, Dad.' The word doesn't seem to register. Malo waits a moment longer for a reaction and then heads for the hall.

'What's all this about?' Saucy is looking at me.

'I'd prefer if Malo tells you.'

'Tells me what?' There's an edge in Saucy's voice I haven't heard before. He doesn't like surprises.

Malo is back with his glasses. They're nice enough – rimless, inoffensive – but when he puts them on Saucy looks ten years older. He reaches for the Paterfamilias document, scans it quickly, then reads it again.

'Fuck me,' he says softly. 'Who'd have thought?'

It's at this point that it occurs to me that Saucy probably doesn't have any kids of his own. Another unasked question.

'All right, Dad?' It's Malo again. He loves the word.

Saucy is still studying the document, reading the small print, exactly the way a businessman might. He wants to make sure he's got this thing right. Finally his head comes up and he takes his glasses off. He's looking at me, not Malo.

'Give us a kiss,' he says.

I get up and circle the table, settling beside his

chair and putting my arms round him. He feels softer and perhaps more frail than I'd been anticipating. I kiss him on the lips. His eyes are closed. He's smiling.

'How long have you known?' he asks.

'Since yesterday.' I nod at the document.

'But really? In here?' His head sinks to my chest.

'A couple of weeks. It started when I saw the pair of you together in hospital. Peas in a pod. You couldn't miss it.'

'Not before?' He sounds disappointed.

'No. Things have been difficult recently. In fact things have been bloody awful for quite a while.'

'Anything I should know about? Anything you want to tell me?'

'No. Maybe later. Maybe one day. But not now.'

I get to my feet again and take a tiny step backwards. This should be Malo's day, not mine. Saucy reaches out to him, then circles my waist with his other hand.

'Family,' he says softly. 'Right?'

We both nod. Malo wants to know what he should call him.

'Dad,' he says. 'What else?'

Malo looks slightly crestfallen. I'm not sure what kind of reaction he's been expecting but it certainly wasn't this. There's almost an air of entitlement about Saucy, as if he'd been expecting the news.

'Tell me you're surprised,' I say. 'Tell me it's made your day.'

171

Saucy says nothing. He glances at Malo, then chuckles.

'Who's the lucky one, son? You or me?'

This, thank God, breaks the ice. Saucy calls for champagne. Jessie appears. When Saucy shares the glad tidings she looks amazed.

'You old dog,' she says. 'You never said.'

'I never fucking knew.'

'But it's true?' She's putting the question to me. I nod at the Paterfamilias confirmation, say nothing.

Jessie picks it up.

'D'you mind?'

'Not at all,' I say. 'Help yourself.'

The news puts a big smile on her face. She wants to tell Andy. She wants to start hitting the phones. She wants the world to know.

'Steady, gal.' Saucy's looking alarmed.

'Steady? You have to be joking. Party time. We'll get some people up. Sort out some invitations. Your fiftieth and now this. Brilliant.' She departs to lay hands on a couple of bottles of Moët. My gaze returns to Saucy. Content isn't a word I'd ever associate with my son's new dad but just now it comes very close.

'Get a few people up from where?' I ask him.

'Pompey.' he says. 'Where else?'

'And what should I call you?'

'H.' He blows me a kiss. 'Like everyone else who ever fucking mattered.'

And so H he becomes. In a way I'm sorry because I liked 'Saucy'. It chimed exactly with the personable chancer I met down in Antibes, and the more Mitch told me about the mad days of his youth, the more the name seemed to fit. Now, though, his circumstances call for a different persona. Not because he's rich. Not because his eye for a deal has won him this glorious house and countless acres of prime real estate. But because new friends and a bigger address book call for something a little more dignified. The Hayden Prentice that Mitch suspects of keeping interesting political company will never turn his back on the mayhem that was his past. But I'm beginning to understand that H – clipped, intimate, gently assertive – is a whole lot closer to the essence of the man than 'Saucy'.

H, I think. Close to perfect.

We agree to stay for a couple of days. H spends a great deal of time on the phone in the small upstairs room he uses as an office. He invites me up there on a couple of occasions for a chat about Malo, and how things have been for both of us, and I'm surprised by how bare the room is. The only items worth a second glance are the view, which is sensational, and the desk. The desk is far from antique but I fall in love with it at first sight. It's huge and purposeful, deep drawers on either side, and a spread of dark green leather on the top. I run my fingers over the leather, tracing a path around the big PC screen.

H is delighted by my interest. He tells me he lifted it from Pompey dockyard back in the day when no one was looking. It belonged in the big quayside building where the Naval Writers worked. He fancied it because his dad had been in the Navy and was looking for something half decent for the new house on Portsdown Hill. With a mate he'd man-handled it down three flights of stairs and smuggled it out of the dock-yard in the back of a plasterer's van. His dad had used it to keep track of his paperwork and once he'd passed on, H had reclaimed it.

'So when did he die? Your dad?'

'Years back. Asbestosis. These days they give the family a whack of money in a case like that, but back then you'd bury the poor bugger and try and make the best of it. It was my mum I felt sorry for. She was lost without him.'

'And she's still alive?'

'No. She turned her face to the wall. Once he'd gone that was it. Finito. End of. Sad as you like. Here . . .'

He stabs at the keyboard, opening an icon on his screensaver, and moments later I'm looking at a black and white photo of a couple in what I take to be their early sixties. These are faces from a different era – work-seamed, shy, peering uncertainly at the camera. H's dad looks taller than his son but his mum is tiny, a little pudding of a woman.

'Their names?'

'Arthur and Gwen. Nicest people you'd ever meet. Never deserved a son like me. I gave them nothing but grief. At least in the early days.'

I smile, returning to the photo. Arthur has his bony arm around his wife, at once proud and protective. It isn't hard to imagine their

174

bewilderment when their young scrapper of a boy began to come home with serious money.

'What about you?' he asks. 'Your folks?'

I tell him about my mum. When he realizes she was French, and that I spent part of my youth in Brittany, he seems pleased.

'I never knew that,' he says. 'When we were on the boat I had you down as a toff, private education, posh school, university, whatever. That's where I figured you learned French, that fancy accent of yours.'

'And now you know different?'

'Too right. You lived there. That's allowed. You fucking *are* half-French. That turns you into a human being.'

'So you fucked me because you thought I was posh? You're telling me this was class war?'

'I fucked you because you were pretty. Not pretty, beautiful. Then I started watching some of those movies of yours and I twigged you were fucking bright as well, really talented. Thick old me, eh?'

I half expect a hand on my arm, or maybe somewhere else, but to my relief he's only interested in conversation. He wants to know about Malo, about the lives we've made for ourselves over the last decade and a half, about what kind of boy he really is.

'Troubled,' I say at once. 'But these days that comes with the turf. Every mother says the same thing. Which means it's probably our fault.'

'Troubled how?'

I tell him about the lives that Berndt and I used to lead – busy, pre-occupied, neglectful.

'We both made a point of trying to involve him in the showbizzy bits, take him on location, show him around the set, introduce him to people he could boast about later. We thought that was enough. In fact we thought he was lucky, spoiled even, because that was way more than any other kid ever got. What he really wanted was a new skateboard and mum and dad somewhere close, somewhere he could rely on, somewhere he could call home. We never sussed that.'

'Because?'

'Because we were stupid. Because we were selfish. And because we never paid him the right kind of attention. Had we listened hard enough all the clues were there but somehow we never had the time.'

'*Made* the time.'

'Exactly. Does that make you feel guilty? Of course it does. But then it didn't seem to matter.'

'And this Berndt?'

'He was the same. He does a wonderful guilt trip but that's because he's a much better actor than I am.'

'He's gone now? Fucked off?'

'Yes.'

I tell him briefly about the depths we hit once the marriage had collapsed. I don't mention Berndt's recent visit.

'You hate him?'

'I used to feel sorry for him. Now I'm indifferent. Indifference hurts someone like Berndt more than anything else so maybe he's getting what he deserves. This is a man who needs to be noticed.'

'And the boy?'

'Berndt stole him from under my nose. Made promises he never kept. Malo's brighter than me. It didn't take him long to see through all that bullshit. Kids can be unforgiving. After Malo bailed out, Berndt was history. That hurts him too. He only thinks in the present tense.'

'Nice.'

'Nice what?

'Nice phrase. You really do hate him, don't you?'

We hold each other's gaze for a long moment. Then I nod.

'I do,' I say. 'You're right. Which is why this paternity thing really matters. I don't know whether you know it but Malo has been like a kid at Christmas. Life hasn't done him too many favours recently but suddenly he's looking at the present of his dreams.'

'You mean me?'

'I do.'

'Shit.' He spares Mum and Dad a glance on the screen. 'No pressure, then.'

'You're disappointed?'

'Not at all. How could I be?'

'You're worried? Intimidated?'

'*Intimidated?* Fuck, no. Never.'

'You think he might be a bit of a burden? A bit surplus to requirements?'

'No. If you want the truth it's not him I worry about, it's me.'

'I don't believe you.'

'Try. I have no kids of my own. I'm clueless. I don't know where to start.'

177

'You could start by talking to him, by getting to know him. Don't tell me you're shy.'

'Of course I'm not shy. I can talk to anyone. Just ask Jessie, Andy. Ask any of the geezers we're gonna get up from Pompey. Ask the guy who's coming to dinner next week. He's like you. You'll see his name in the paper. No, it's not shyness. It's something else.'

'Like what?'

'Like what happens if I get it wrong? You say he's troubled. You say he's damaged already. What if I can't put that right?'

I wonder whether this is the moment to tell Malo's new dad about his son's dalliance with Spice, but decide to adopt a slightly harder tone.

'You make him sound shop-soiled,' I say. 'He's not. Underneath, he's just a kid. He's confused. He wants a middle to his life.'

'You mean us.'

'I mean you. I'm his mother. I'm also recovering from a brain tumour. That, believe it or not, is a bit of a wake-up call. He has my full attention. It might be a bit late but he knows I'm there for him.'

'But you'll help me, yeah?' He sounds almost plaintive. 'You'll be around when I fuck up? You'll be around when I'm getting it all wrong and he thinks I'm just another cunt? You'll do that? For me?'

'For us.'

'Promise?'

'Of course. As long as you make an effort.'

He nods, thoughtful. Then he looks at the screen again. He looks, if anything, a bit lost.

I put my arms round him, kiss his temple, hold him close. What I want is a commitment. Not to me but to Malo.

'It's just parenthood,' I murmur. 'Piece of piss.'

'You really think so?'

'I do.'

'OK.' He offers me a rueful grin. 'I'll give it a go.'

Fifteen

He's as good as his word. So far, we've spent three days at Flixcombe Manor. On the morning of the fourth, as I'm packing my bag to return to London, I get a call from my agent. Rosa tells me the BBC have had to rejig the rehearsal and recording schedule for *Going Solo* because the male lead has gone down with whooping cough. I won't be required for at least a week, probably a lot longer. This is very good news indeed because H and his new son are beginning to bond and it gives me a great deal of pleasure to be on hand to watch it happen.

It begins, fittingly enough, with one of H's trail bikes. H doesn't want Malo to end up in hospital like his dad and so he tasks Andy, Jessie's partner, to teach Malo how to ride the thing properly. Andy, it turns out, is a genius when it comes to dealing with kids Malo's age. He has the looks – tall, stylish, fabulously unshaven – and his patience is seemingly limitless. He has the kind of dry wit, often cruel, that kids adore and he knows how to offer praise when it will make a difference. He's also a natural on two wheels, gunning the mud-caked machine around the estate course while the three of us – Malo and his mum and dad – look on.

Towards the end of the first lap, where H came to grief, Andy brakes late, slides the machine into a perfect turn, and then accelerates hard for the climb out. The bike snakes left and right before the rear tyre bites and then he's gone. Malo is open mouthed. Me too. While H, remembering the price of getting it wrong, just shakes his head.

After this display, it's Malo's turn in the saddle. Andy has taken him to the flattest part of the estate where he can fall off to his heart's content. Watching him clamber on to the machine and listen to Andy carefully running through each of the controls, I wonder how much of him is thinking about Clemenza back in town. She, he's told me, is an artist on two wheels and now he's about to find out how tough it can be.

The briefing over, Malo puts on his borrowed helmet and lets Andy make the final adjustments. Then, more carefully than I ever expected, he revs up and heads for the figure-of-eight course that H has already coned out. For the rest of the morning, with a pit-stop to refuel, he slowly masters both the bike and the trickier corners. At noon, H calls a halt. Jessie has done lunch. Over egg and chips around the kitchen table, H and Andy take it in turns to analyse where Malo might be having problems. Both of them are careful to let him have his say when he doesn't understand something or even disagrees and by the time we're back outside Malo seems to have found a real confidence. They're treating him like a grown-up, like an adult, and he loves it. For the first time I wonder why Berndt never tried something similar.

That night we all watch *The Dam Busters* in

the little cinema H has had installed. This turns out to be H's all-time favourite movie. To my shame I've never seen it before but I've had dealings with one or two of the actors, now in their dotage, and a story of mine about the tail gunner in one of the bombers that doesn't make it reduces H to fits of laughter. As the second dam begins to crack and the music on the soundtrack swells he takes my hand in the half-darkness. Malo is aware of this and when I let it happen I catch a tiny nod of approval. Malo wants us all to be friends and just now I know he's right. Aside from anything else, my poor boy deserves a little affection in his life.

The following evening, we have company at dinner. H has already mentioned a special guest and I've been tempted to ask for more details. Visitors like this, of course, are exactly what Mitch needs for his precious book – a taste of the milieu H is trying to make his own – but already I'm starting to understand something that Mitch, in one of his *Guardian* articles, called Stockholm Syndrome. This has nothing to do with either Berndt or Malo but refers to that strange about-turn that often happens to kidnap victims. You get taken at gun point. You get banged up by your captors. You have no doubts that they're thoroughly wicked. But somehow you start to see it their way.

This, I know on my nerve ends, is beginning to happen to me. I'm not a prisoner in this house. I'm not here against my will. But H has been on the receiving end of a thoroughly bad press and somehow, in my heart, I'm not altogether sure he deserves it. He's also the father of my only son and that matters more than anything.

Our guest for dinner turns out to be a UKIP politician. His name is Spencer Willoughby. As H has anticipated, I dimly recognize his face from some newspaper or other, or maybe the telly. He's tall, quite articulate in a shouty, superficial kind of way, nearly good-looking, and drinks far too much of H's burgundy for his own good.

Jessie serves fillet steak with veggies from the garden. We know by now, thanks to Willoughby, that H has been more than generous with his contributions over the past few years. A cheque for a hefty sum ahead of the 2015 election. Another to help fund the push to win the Brexit vote. This draws nothing more than a curt nod from H. The relationship between the two of them has been obvious from the start, with H emphatically in control, and when Willoughby starts naming specific sums of money H does nothing to shut him up.

This collusion on H's part is, I suspect, for our benefit. He wants to show me, and perhaps Malo as well, that he bankrolls some of their efforts, that he puts his money where his mouth is, and that he's therefore become something of a player in a high-stakes political game. Willoughby's mission this evening is clearly to leave with another cheque. UKIP are about to name a new leader and they want to claw back territory and profile they lost in the last election. Nothing, it seems, comes cheap in the world of politics.

By the time we get to H's contribution to the meal, a workmanlike baked Alaska, Willoughby is drunk. This doesn't please H at all. He didn't invite this loudmouth to dinner to make a fool of himself and when Willoughby leans across the table to suggest that half a million from his host might make all the difference under the new leadership, H starts to lose it.

'So what the fuck will you do with all this dosh? Supposing it ever happens?'

Willoughby is having trouble keeping anything in focus. I think he knows H has a short fuse but he adores the sound of his own voice.

'Home truths,' he roars.

'What the fuck does that mean?'

'Blacks. Browns.' He leans forward over the table. 'Even the fucking French.'

'What about them?'

'We have to be honest. We have to listen to the people. We have to chuck these leeches out. There's serious votes in immigration. That's how this whole thing started.'

This is a big, big mistake. H isn't racist and – given my presence at the table – he definitely likes the French.

'You need to get a grip, my friend,' H growls. 'Since when did the frogs do us any harm?'

'That's not the point. They've got their own country. They're different to us. That's what got us over the line last year. That's what won us the referendum. We need to build on that. British jobs. For British workers. British laws. British courts. Taking back control means what it says. We need to look after our own.

When did you last sit on a bus and hear a conversation in proper English?'

I doubt whether Spencer Willoughby has been on a bus in years but that's not the point. He's thinks he's addressing some meeting or other and he's not going to stop. He's also after H's half million quid.

'You want to know what we're really about? How we're going to pull it out again? This is just you and me, Hayden. Inside track stuff. Strictly embargoed. *Comprende?*'

H gestures for him to go on. He obviously thinks that money on this scale should buy him the odd party secret which seems, to me, entirely reasonable.

Willoughby reaches for what's left of the burgundy and refills his glass. The Tories, he tells us, are in deep shit. Theresa May, surrounded by headbangers, is a hostage in Downing Street. A lost vote in parliament, more treachery from the likes of Boris Johnson, no movement in the Brussels negotiations, and we could suddenly be facing another election. When that happens, Labour will be after loads of constituencies in the north. That's where the election will be won or lost. These are people who voted for Brexit. People who've had enough. The last thing they should be doing is putting a fucking cross against the Labour candidate.

'So you take them on again? Is that what you're telling me?'

'Not at all. We're having quiet conversations with all sorts of people, top Tories all over the country. We have lots in common. When it comes to Brexit we're there to keep them honest, to hold their fucking feet to the fire, to make sure they deliver. There are places up there where we'd still poll well, have lots of support. The Tories could use those votes because the punters have got nowhere else to go. Labour want to stay in the EU. They won't admit it but that's the truth. So when the election happens, if the deal is right, there are places we'll simply stand aside.'

'You mean a deal?'

'I mean no UKIP candidate in key selected constituencies.'

'You're telling me you'll throw in the towel?'

'Exactly. As long as the Tories do what they're told.'

H is toying with the remains of his baked Alaska. He's trying to make sense of all this. Finally he looks across at Willoughby again.

'So I'm bunging money to the Tories, is that what you're saying?'

'You're bunging money to us. To make sure that Brexit happens the way we want it.'

'But the Tories spend it? To help win all these constituencies?'

'In effect, yes. It's nothing we'd ever own up to, and they won't either, but that's the way these things sometimes work. Means and ends, Hayden. We keep the Tories in Downing Street and we make sure we get out of Europe on our terms. That's what it's about. Just like always.'

H nods, says nothing. Even I understand the dark logic of the plan. I'm thinking of Mitch.

He should be here at the table. He should be listening to all this.

I steal a glance at Malo. He's trying to stifle a yawn. Just for a moment, Willoughby appears to have stopped banging on. I take advantage of this brief silence to make my apologies for beating a retreat. Malo's had a heavy day. I'm exhausted. Much better that you two have the rest of the conversation in peace.

H looks up at me. His wine is virtually untouched.

'Fucking good idea,' he says. 'Leave this clown to me.'

Sixteen

I come down early next morning after a sleepless night. I find Jessie in the kitchen. She's filled the dishwasher with last night's dirty plates and now she's drawing up a tally of names on a big foolscap pad. I suspect this is the guest list for the celebration bash that H is determined to throw to mark his fiftieth birthday, and – much more importantly – the surprise acquisition of a son. It turns out I'm right.

'How many?' I enquire.

'Dozens. Hundreds. Thousands. H isn't short of mates in Pompey.'

'Seriously . . .'

She shoots me a look. I sense we've become friends but I'm learning fast that being part of H's teeming ménage is something you'd never take for granted. There are unspoken rules, lines you should never cross, and one of them is the need to keep your curiosity under control. There might be lots of questions you want to ask but you'll never get the answer until H is good and ready.

This I'm beginning to understand. What comes as a surprise is Jessie's own enquiry.

'Did you really only meet him that one time?'

'Yes. How did you know?'

'H told me. France, wasn't it?'

'Antibes. Celeb land, even then. Not us. We

were cheap hires on a movie, ten a penny if you want the truth.'

'So what did you make of him?'

'I thought he was funny. And bold.'

'That's H. Still is. Though he doesn't laugh as much as he used to. Nice man underneath it all. Heart of gold.'

I nod, tell her I'm glad to hear it. She reaches for her pen again, remembering yet another name. Then she looks up.

'You will be here, won't you? For the party? H likes to pretend it's all about being fifty and about finding Malo but I'm not sure that's true.'

'I'm flattered.'

'You should be. H isn't an easy man to get close to.'

That morning, Malo takes a break from learning to ride a motorbike. Instead, Andy takes him shooting in the woodland that fringes the estate to the west. All morning, sitting by an open window in the big library downstairs, I hear distant gunshots and by the time the two of them return for lunch, Malo has bagged his first pigeon. With some pride he shows it to his dad.

'Top job, son. Spot of red wine gravy? Game chips? Lovely.'

I later find the poor dead thing on the compost heap beyond the vegetable garden but that doesn't matter. What's infinitely more important is the ease with which my son appears to be settling into his new life. Neither of us know how long we'll be staying. The subject is never broached and in any case, apart from the BBC radio play, neither of us have other commitments. And so the days roll by, the weather holds, and Jessie and H between them conjure delicious meals. In the evenings, when we're not watching yet more movies, we play Monopoly, or backgammon, or maybe a card game. As I say to H at the end of the first week, it feels like an endless Christmas.

'Is that a compliment?'

'Definitely. I've always loved Christmas. Malo does, too. You're spoiling us rotten. We like that.'

H nods. That slight defensiveness I'd noticed earlier has gone completely.

'It's convalescence,' he says, 'For all of us.'

On the following Monday I take a call from Mitch. I happen to be out on my morning walk, something I've adopted to try and keep my weight down in the face of so many meals. From where I'm standing, the house is a grey dot in the distance.

'Are you OK?' I ask him.

'I'm fine. Busy but fine. Where are you?'

'H's place.'

'Who's "H"?'

I laugh. This is the measure of just how far Malo and I have come. I explain about Saucy's new name. I can tell from Mitch's voice that this isn't altogether good news. I sense I'm supposed to keep him at arm's length. Not succumb yet again to the gruff Prentice charm.

'You're OK with him?'

'I'm a house guest, Mitch. And so is my son. If you want the truth it's a bit of a break for

190

both of us. Think Jane Austen. I'm in temporary residence. I spend most of the day with my nose in a book. I might even take up crochet-work. Aside from that I do what a good spy's supposed to. I watch and I listen. That's when I'm not bloody eating.'

'And?'

'I'm getting fat.'

'That's not what I meant.'

'Of course it isn't.'

'So? You've got anything for me?'

I don't answer, not immediately. First I want to know why he's phoned me.

'We have to meet,' he says. 'I've been getting some grief from my publisher. He needs to know when I can deliver.'

'Which is what you're asking me.'

'Indeed.'

I tell him it might be difficult. 'We're down here for a while.'

'But I thought you had something to do for the Beeb?'

'I have. It's been postponed.'

'I see.' There's a longish silence. Then he's back with a proposition. He has to go to Salisbury tomorrow for a meeting with a source. We could have lunch afterwards.

I tell him that might be possible. I've no idea how far Salisbury is and I've even less idea how I might get there but H is in the business of making things happen so I say yes.

'I'll phone to confirm,' I tell him. 'And you can tell me where to meet.'

Back at the house, an hour or so later, I broach

the idea to H. I have a friend I need to see. We want to meet in Salisbury. Any ideas? As it happens, Jessie is going to an interior design agency in Romsey tomorrow to discuss some plans for one of the rooms upstairs. Romsey is near Southampton. She could drop me in Salisbury and pick me up on the way back home.

'Sorted?'

'Sorted.'

That night we're back in the cinema. At Malo's request, we're watching a movie called *Gravity*. Sandra Bullock and George Clooney, in fetching space suits, cavort in orbit while the gods of weightlessness do their best to wreck the party. The plot line is non-existent and the dialogue is beyond parody and even the special effects aren't enough to keep me awake. The movie over, H gently shakes me back into something approaching consciousness.

'Who won?' I mutter.

'The Germans. On penalties. Same old fucking story.' H peers down at me. 'You want me to come? Tomorrow?'

'Not really. It'll be fine.'

'You're sure?'

'Yes. But thanks for the thought.'

He studies me a moment longer, half-expecting me to change my mind, then gives my elbow a little squeeze.

'Take care out there, yeah?'

Late next morning, around twelve, Jessie drops me outside the hotel in Salisbury where I'm due to meet Mitch. We've chatted for most of the journey from Flixcombe Manor. H, she says, gives her all the freedom she wants when it comes to decoration. She loves muddy colours, dark greens and browns, and H indulges her passion for wood panelling, of which the house has a great deal. Budget-wise, unless she gets really silly, he simply signs the cheques.

Towards the end of the journey, with the city's cathedral spire in sight, I'm starting to wonder whether she thinks I'm going to be some kind of threat to her monopoly on interior decoration and before she drops me outside the hotel I try to offer a little reassurance.

'I'm Malo's mum,' I tell her. 'Nothing else.'

The hotel is called the White Hart. There's a bit too much red velvet and polished brass for my taste but I'm not here for the decor. I find Mitch at a table in the lounge. He makes his excuses about not being able to stretch to the restaurant down the hall but I tell him that the bar menu will be fine. Something light with salad? Perfect.

He fetches me a gin and tonic. I notice he's drinking Perrier.

'Liver packed up? Or are you driving?'

He says he took the train down, working non-stop on his laptop.

'The woman opposite me was raving about the countryside. Said Wiltshire in autumn was close to perfect. I had to take her word for it.'

'Poor you. Sayid?'

'Sends his best. He's had a bit of a cold these last few days. In fact we both have.'

I nod, sympathize. I've been wondering why he looks so peaky. He wants to know what Malo is doing with me down at Chateau Prentice.

'He came for autumn,' I say lightly. 'Like your lady on the train.'

'You're kidding.'

'You're right, I am. He's keeping his mum company. It happens sometimes. It's a parent thing.'

'But he's a city kid, no?'

'Of course.'

'So isn't he bored?'

'Far from it.'

I've been wondering whether to tell Mitch the whole story about Malo and this would be the perfect opportunity, but it's still something I want to keep to myself. On the other hand he already knows about Antibes and he might have drawn one or two conclusions of his own. Either way I'm keen to move the conversation on.

'You mentioned your publisher on the phone. Is there some kind of problem?'

'Yes.'

'Like?'

Mitch checks left and right before answering. I find this unsettling. Life in the country has been so simple.

'Why do you want to know?' he asks.

'Because there are ways I might be able to help.'

'With the publisher?'

'With the book. You've told me it's about Prentice and some friends of his. You called them "like-minded folk". It was an interesting

194

phrase. I remembered it. What, exactly, does it mean?'

'It means people who think the way he does.'

'Politically?'

'Yes.'

'Coming from the same kind of background?'

'The same pedigree, yes. Not the same city, even the same area. But the same mindset.'

'We're talking rich people?' I ask.

'By definition, yes. Without money, serious money, none of this would matter.'

'None of what?'

'Influence. Leverage. Putting your money to work.'

'In the interests of what?'

'Of yourself, in the end. But en route you kid yourself it's for the good of the nation.'

'You mean Brexit?'

'Of course. But we've talked about that.'

I nod. He's right. We have. I remember the pub in Ealing the day when my poor Peugeot had been towed away. On that occasion Mitch was nice enough to get it back for me, something I shouldn't forget.

'H had a politician to dinner the other night,' I tell him. 'His name was Spencer.'

'Spencer Willoughby? UKIP?'

'Yes. Is he big? Important? Should I have known about him before?'

'He's middling. Probably less important than he thinks. But he's certainly ambitious.' Mitch stoops to the bag beside his chair and produces a pad. 'So what happened?'

I tell him about H's contributions to the UKIP

fighting fund over the last couple of years. Mitch appears to know about this already but when I mention Willoughby's fresh bid for yet another cheque, Mitch scribbles himself a note.

'Did he say how much?'

'He wanted half a million.'

'And Prentice?'

'He didn't say anything. Not while I was there.'

'So it might have been a yes?'

'Might have been. There was something else though, nothing to do with money.'

I tell Mitch about Willoughby's plans for fighting the next election. How UKIP planned to leave the Tories a clear run in constituencies they might not otherwise win. And how H's money might help make that happen.

'You mean the money would go straight to the Tories?' His pen is poised over the pad.

'That wasn't clear. You'd have to ask him. This is Willoughby talking. That's all I can tell you.'

'Did he mention any constituencies in particular?'

'No. Except that most of them were in the north.'

Mitch nods. He seems to think that Willoughby might be out of his depth. The word he uses is 'flaky'. UKIP, he says, were virtually wiped out at the last election and it isn't clear why the Tories would ever be listening to them.

I'm desperately trying to remember some of the other things Willoughby said that night at H's table.

'He thinks they still have a direct line to the grass roots. He told H they're still plugged in.

The way he saw it, only UKIP could guarantee a proper Brexit. Does that make sense?'

'It does. UKIP always claim they were there at the birth, and they're right. They also did most of the heavy lifting when it came to the referendum. That's where donors like Prentice were so important. Now, the Tories don't need UKIP marking their homework. They've got enough headbangers of their own.'

'So Willoughby . . .?' I shrug. 'Am I wasting your time here?'

'Not at all. Especially if you're right about Prentice's money ending up with the Tories. You think it did? You think that's true?'

'I've no idea.'

'Can you find out?'

The question couldn't be more direct and it puts me on the spot. Do I steal a look at his cheque book? Access his online bank account? Wait until his office is free and root through the drawers in that wonderful desk?

'I don't know,' I said. 'I suppose I could try.'

'That would be helpful. Especially if you took a photo or two.'

'Of the cheque stub? If there is one?'

'Yes. And maybe some shots of the house, too. We call it "colour" in the trade. It sets the mood. Shows the reader just how far our Pompey boy's come.'

Mitch gives me a shopping list: photos showing the house in the landscape, the sheer size of the estate, the motocross circuit where H came to grief. He also wants as much as I can get from inside: the baronial hall, the main reception room, the library, the newly installed cinema, the kitchen, even a taste of the bedrooms upstairs. This, of course, would be much easier for yours truly but I'm not at all sure I want to do it.

Mitch offers me a sheet of paper from his pad and a pen. He thinks I should be making a list.

'I've got a perfectly good memory,' I tell him. 'I think I know what you want.'

'Am I pissing you off?'

'Yes, you are.'

'So what's changed? I was pushing at an open door when you were in London. Or at least I thought I was.'

'It's just . . .' I'm trying to marshal my thoughts. 'None of this is easy . . .'

'You're bloody right it isn't. Try being on the sharp end. Try getting anywhere even half close to these people.'

'These people?'

'People like Prentice. Self-made. Powerful. Minds of their own. They know exactly what they're after and they don't care who they hurt on their way. They might corrupt the political process in getting there and you might not think that matters but there are still some people who do. Forgive me, but I assumed you were one of them. Which just goes to show how wrong us fucking scribes can be.'

Mitch very rarely swears. He's as angry as I am. I get to my feet. I've had enough of this. It wasn't me who made the phone call in the first place, who stood outside my flat and suggested breakfast. It wasn't me who's been on my case ever since, pushing me gently towards H and his mates.

198

'You've been very kind to me,' I tell him. 'You've been there when it mattered and I really appreciate that. You've probably got me down as a spoiled celeb with more money than sense. For the record I do care about democracy and the health service and pot holes and libraries and all the rest of it, but where we're heading at the moment is, to be frank, just a wee bit personal. So you'll forgive me for skipping lunch.'

'And this?' Mitch nods at his pad. 'Willoughby? The cheque? All that?'

'We'll have to see.'

'That might not be an option. My publisher's anticipating an election within the next six months. We have to get our ducks in order. Otherwise I've just wasted a year's work, probably more.'

This is emotional blackmail and both of us know it. I'm still lingering by the table, wishing I'd hadn't heard that last little speech.

The stand-off is becoming awkward. The barman is eyeing us with some interest. I think he may have recognized me but I can't be sure. Finally, it's Mitch who breaks the silence.

'This is about Malo, right?' He gestures at the chair I've just abandoned. 'Do you want to talk about it?'

I stare down at him. Then I shake my head.

'No,' I say. 'I don't.'

Seventeen

I'm back at Flixcombe Manor by mid-afternoon. H has spent most of the day in his office conferring with his accountant on a business plan for new insurance products for the over-sixty-fives. Two recent developments, he tells me, have told him there's squillions of quid to be made. One of them is the fact that older souls – both men and women – are a great deal fitter than they used to be. They still want to push themselves. They're still hungry for physical risk. Yet older bodies break more easily, hence the call for extreme sports insurance cover to put them back together again without, he says, costing an arm and a leg. Ho ho.

'Did you dream that up in hospital?'

'Yeah, as a matter of fact I did. If you hurt yourself in this country it's not too bad. If it happens anywhere else, you're stuffed. I might call it Easy-Mend. What d'you think?'

I laugh dutifully and enquire about his other wheeze. This also has a great deal to do with abroad. The day after we leave the European Union, millions of ex-pats are going to find themselves suddenly stripped of medical care. For the elderly, he says, this is going to be a real problem. Accessing the local clinic in Provence or Malaga won't be cheap but H and his accountant are busy cooking up ways these orphans can avoid selling up and coming home.

'I've been in this business years,' he says. 'I've got the contacts. I know what I'm about. Brexit is a big fat pay day if I get it right.'

A big fat pay day if I get it right.

I'm suddenly thinking of Mitch. For weeks now he's been telling me what a disaster awaits millions of Brits both here and abroad. How b its of the country will implode post-Brexit. And how the likes of Hayden Prentice are lurking in the shadows, waiting for the dust to settle, making their plans. Now I'm hearing it from the horse's mouth. *Easy-Mend.* Very funny.

H is watching me carefully. He's abandoned the paperwork on his desk.

'Go well, did it? That little lunch of yours?'

'It was lovely. Girlfriend I haven't seen for years. Bit of a catch-up really.'

'Great.' His hand lingers briefly on mine. 'Jessie's finished that list of hers for the weekend. You want me to talk you through it?'

Jessie has typed the list out and sent it to H. A couple of keystrokes and it hangs on his PC. Nearly sixty names, not one of which I recognize. H is scrolling slowly through them, a smile on his face, and it occurs to me that in some respects this little gathering – assuming they all come – will be like one of those regimental reunions.

My stepfather's dad was in the army and saw service in Korea. His regiment had a hard time in a particular battle at some river or other. I remember him telling me they were holding a hill against the Chinese. A third of them were killed or wounded and the rest of them spent the next two years behind the wire. At the war's end they made it back to the UK, all damaged to various degrees, and every year that followed – on St George's Day – they got together to pay their respects to the dead and get roaring drunk.

Is H doing something similar? Am I in for a night of war stories and a monster hangover?

H has settled on a particular name. Mick Pain.

'Top bloke,' he says fondly. 'Hard as you like. I dug him out of the shit the morning we got ambushed by the Millwall. Waterloo fucking station. Just down that little alley behind the arches. Cunts were waiting for us. Hundreds of them. Mick was out front. Chinned one of their generals. Huge bloke. Went down like a sack of cement. Bad move on Mick's part because the Millwall never liked us taking the piss. There were some nasty bastards there but we still gave them a hiding.' He shakes his head. 'Brilliant.'

Another name. Tony Morse.

'Classy guy. Still is. You'll love him. Clever as fuck and likes you to know it. Once we started making serious moolah we couldn't do without him. Wised us up. Taught me stuff I'd never have known otherwise.'

'Another hooligan?'

'Fuck, no. Bloke was a solicitor. Retired now, thanks to us. Lovely guy but silly around women. Three wives? That's fucking careless.'

The list goes on. A woman called Leanne who rose to the challenge of running a string of themed wine bars, all funded by cocaine loot.

A planner, Alan Ransome, who knew every short cut in the book when it came to making development applications. And a streetwise bodybuilder, Wesley Kane, who H still calls The Prefect.

'Wes kept things nice and tidy,' H tells me. 'Any problems, Wes would sort them out. We bought him a house in Fratton for the day job. The sound insulation cost us a fortune but an hour with Wes in that back room and you wouldn't fuck about any more.'

I edge my chair back an inch or two. I'm beginning to get the picture here: a bunch of football thugs with a limitless appetite for violence discover the joys of drug dealing and hit the mother lode. The money rolls in and sensibly they use some of it to buy proper advice: Solicitors. Accountants. Planners. All helping themselves.

'And the police?' I wonder aloud.

H shoots me a look and reaches for the mouse again. Scrolling backwards he settles on another name. Dave Munroe.

'Fat Dave,' he says. 'DC on the drugs squad. Kept us abreast of events. Most of the time the Filth had their heads up their arse, totally useless, but times when they became a nuisance Dave would mark our card.'

'And you paid him?'

'We did. Money mostly, because Dave had a bit of a gambling habit, but women too. Dave loved big black women. We could help him out there. Jamaican called Gloria who ran a couple of knocking shops.' He laughed. 'We'd bought

203

one of those big seafront hotels by then. Dave had screwing rights in a room on the top floor. She used to eat him alive.'

'And the police never realized?'

'About Dave? Never. In the end he retired on full pay. These days he's on the Isle of fucking Wight drinking himself to death but once he knows our booze is free he's bound to turn up. Here's someone else you might meet . . .'

Marie Mackenzie. H is staring at the name. His mood has darkened.

'Lovely woman,' he says softly. 'Real class.'

'So how come she liked football?'

'She didn't. She married into it. Worst decision she ever made except she loved him.'

'Who?'

'Bazza. Bazza was our top guy. Bazza was King. Bazza was someone you'd never fuck with. Mad cunt but clever. The Filth spent years trying to nail him but never got close. The way these things work, you need a leader, someone with a brain in his head, someone who knew the difference between taking a risk and pissing it all away because you've made the wrong fucking call. Bazza was on top of that, all day, every day. He was the one who took us all legit. He was brilliant in business, brilliant in everything. Fucking sad.'

'What happened?'

'He made one mistake. Just one. Bloke called Winter. Paul Winter. He was Filth to begin with, drugs squad again, and a real pain in the arse because he was the only cunt who knew what he was doing. They stuck him undercover and then got him blown because they were so fucking useless, so he had a meet with Bazza and told his bosses to fuck off. Bazza thought that was funny. So funny, he offered him a job.'

'With you lot?'

'Yeah. Some of us thought Bazza had lost it. Big mistake. And in the end we were proved right.'

'He was still undercover?'

'Not at all. He did the biz for us for years. He was good. And he was funny, too. Then Bazza got ideas above his station, stood for parliament. Daft move. Absolutely insane. He was king of the city already. Why become a fucking politician?'

'He went through with this? Campaigned?'

'Yeah. And didn't do bad, neither. But that wasn't the point. Him and Winter fell out, big time, and the next thing Bazza knows Winter's grassed him to the Filth. That was the end of it. Even Bazza couldn't survive that. Served him right in a way. He should have listened to us.'

'He's still around? Bazza?'

'No.'

I want to know more. I want to know exactly what brought this stellar career to an end, but H won't tell me. All I need to know, he says, is what I see around me. The house. The estate. The cars. The bikes. All the other toys that make life so sweet. Not just for him, not just for Hayden Prentice, but for so many of the names on Jessie's invitation list. All this, he seems to be saying, is down to Bazza and there isn't anyone on the planet that can touch any of it. That's how fucking good he was.

He's staring at the PC screen. Marie Mackenzie. 'You think she'll come?'

'I doubt it. She hates us now.' He falls silent, shakes his head, rubs his face. 'We'll have a minute's silence on Saturday night,' he says. 'Before we all get too pissed.'

While H tidies the last of his paperwork, I go for a walk. Through no fault of my own, unless you count Antibes, I appear to have ended up in a weird cult of ex-gangsters who've made their money but still can't quite believe it. I know very little about drug dealing and even less about putting all that loot through what H quaintly calls 'the laundromat' but I can only take H at his word.

We live in a free market. You source something that people need badly. You charge the earth, watch your back, and make a fortune. Everything you do, everything you touch, is illegal but if you hire the right advice and pay the right money you're home free. This is the kind of conjuring trick that makes good guys like Mitch Culligan froth at the mouth – and I don't blame him because even to me the implications are troublesome.

It can't be just Portsmouth. This must be happening all over the country. Name any city and you'll find a Bazza, and an H, and a bent solicitor or two, and rogue cops, and corrupt accountants, and a bunch of crazies with far too much money. That's how the trick works. That's why capitalism is such a lovely word.

Should I phone Mitch? Should I apologize for

walking out on him at lunchtime? Should I tell him he's right? That Brexit is a disaster in the making? That the entire country has suddenly found itself at the mercy of Hayden Prentice and his brethren? Or should I wait until Saturday, and put on my best dress, and settle in for the Command Performance? Make a few notes, keep my phone on Record, play the spy for real?

In truth, I'm out of my depth. This is a role I've never been offered before, and don't much want, but I am where I am and there's something shaping in the wreckage of my poor brain that feels suspiciously like duty. I owe it to a number of people to try and figure out what's really going on here. One of them is obviously Mitch. Another, far more important, is Malo. I pause to phone him. I need to get my bearings. Or, more precisely, his.

When he finally answers, he tells me he's busy. A local farmer has lost his stockman to an attack of flu and after a call to Andy, Malo has been drafted in to help get his cows to the dairy.

'You're OK with that?' I ask.

'It's fine. Cool. Cows? You've no idea how big they are. Amazing.'

I can hear cattle lowing in the background and the slow clop-clop of hooves on a tarmac road. An act of simple neighbourliness, I tell myself, has opened yet another door in Malo's young life and who am I to get in his way?

Standing in the middle of this huge estate, listening to my son trying to get some action out of a cow, it's hard not to remember that moment on the video phone that still haunts me, his thin

207

body bent over a Spice-filled spliff. Down here he has a million distractions, a trillion million better things to do, and that very definitely matters. On the other hand, although he doesn't know it, we owe this sudden whiff of redemption to the narco biz, to drugs money.

Impossible, I tell myself. Just what does a girl do?

I allow myself the beginnings of a smile. This little irony would be music in my ex-husband's ears. Berndt would be on it in seconds. He'd block out the story, add a cast of low-life characters, write a trial scene or two, hone the dialogue, and doubtless find a backer. And within less than a year, if all went well, I'd find the resolution to my little dilemma on screen.

I shield my eyes against the low sun. I'm probably kidding myself but several fields away I think I can hear cattle.

'Mum?' It's Malo. 'What's going on?'

'Nothing,' I tell him. 'As long as you're OK.'

That evening, H gets Jessie to drive us to a gastropub he likes in a village down the road. This is excellent news, partly because there are questions I need to ask, but mainly because I'm starving hungry.

The pub is full but H has made a reservation. The woman in charge of the restaurant gives him a careful hug and asks how he's getting on. H's accident has evidently been the talk of the village and she tells me to take great care of him.

'Boys will be boys,' she says. 'But there are limits.'

Quite. Our table is beside the fire, which is mercifully unlit. The nearest couple to us are locked in a fierce debate about the Tory party conference which takes place next week. The husband – tweeds, brogues, fine-spun hairs on the backs of his hands – thinks Theresa May's useless. His wife predictably disagrees. Our PM, she says, has the measure of the cabinet rebels. She'll see them off without any great fuss, exactly the way she glided into Downing Street in the first place.

'Stole,' the husband says. 'She stole into Downing Street like a thief in the night. I give the bloody woman until Christmas. And that's if she's lucky.'

H is rolling his eyes. When he reaches for the menu I ask him just how much of this stuff really matters to him.

'You mean politics?'

'Yes.'

'Most of it's bollocks. Most politicians are on the make except for the Labour lot and they're fucking lunatics. The steak here is brilliant. Fill your boots.'

I order fish with hand-cut chips and a dish of veggies. H sorts out a bottle of Chablis largely, I suspect, for my benefit. While we wait for the wine, I go back to the matter in hand. The couple next door, mercifully, have paid up and gone.

'You told me this Bazza stood for parliament. You give loads of money to UKIP. If most of it's bollocks, how does that work?'

He's dismissive. 'It's a game. Sometimes you

like seeing these people dancing for your money. Toss them a quid or two and they'll do anything.'

'What about Bazza? Standing for parliament takes some doing.'

'He was taking the piss. Seeing how far he could get.'

'I don't believe you.'

'You don't?' I've caught his interest at last. 'So what's your take, then? You don't think I've got better things to do than ponce around in suits all day?'

'I think you want power.'

'I've got power. It's called money.'

'But political power. Calling the shots. Making the odd law.'

'Law?' He's laughing now. 'Laws are there to be broken. I've built a whole career on that. You might have noticed.'

'So why UKIP?'

'Because they were the underdogs. Because they were a load of old dossers in ties and blazers with lots to get off their chests. If my dad had ever been into politics he'd have been a Kipper. I know these people. I know the way they think. I know what gets under their skins. They're not toffs like the Tories and we're not talking Nazis like the English fucking Defence League. They just wandered into politics like you or me might go shopping and they decided to make a noise. They don't much like abroad, and they definitely don't like Pakis nicking their seat on the bus, and given half a chance they'd shut their doors and spend the rest of their lives listening to the fucking Archers. Do I have a problem with any of that? No. Do I think the country's going to the dogs? Yeah. And the sooner the better. Because then we can have a proper sort-out.'

I nod. I've heard Mitch say something similar, especially the last bit. He called it anarchy.

'So did you give them the half million in the end? UKIP?'

'No way. I wrote them a cheque for five hundred. That's bye-bye money for old times' sake. Spencer Willoughby is a twat. Even the Kippers can do better than that.'

The waiter arrives with the wine. After he's gone, H raises his glass.

'Let's talk about something interesting,' he says. 'Here's to the boy.'

'To Malo.' We touch glasses.

H leans back in his chair, trying to ease his shoulder. He's been with his son a lot these last few days and he likes what he's seen.

'He loves it down here,' he says. 'He really does. It's opened his bloody eyes. He's even put a bit of weight on.'

'I know. I've noticed.'

'You're telling me that's a bad thing?'

'Not at all. Far from it. He hasn't been in a good place recently.'

'Really? You want to tell me more?'

I explain about the fall-out with Berndt, about the phantom affair with Eva, about turning up in London with a stash of cannabis and a Spice habit.

'*Spice?*' H looks horrified. 'That's low-life. That's B fucking wing. You're serious?'

'I am. He could have been one of your customers back in the day. How does that make you feel?'

This sounds more aggressive than I intended but it was hard to resist the temptation. Live by the sword, die by the sword.

'Nice one. It wasn't around at the time but we'd never have touched Spice. Nor smack. Nor a whole load of other rubbish. We were there to spread a little happiness. We wanted people to love each other up. That was always Bazza's line.'

H is grinning at me. Uppers, not downers, he says. Loads of ecstasy and as much of the laughing powder as Pompey could handle. I smile back. He rides the punches well. But he still wants the full story.

'About what?' I enquire.

'Malo.'

I tell him as much as I know: my son slipping his moorings, my son disappearing at odd hours, my Zombie boy back at the door, totally wasted.

'Wasted is fucking right. That stuff's evil. Which is why he's best off down here.'

'Where you can keep an eye on him?'

'Exactly.'

To be fair, this is a proposition I've been half-expecting but now he's spelled it out it makes me anxious. Stockholm Syndrome, I think. My son held hostage for a second time, first by Berndt, and now by his real father. Is this really what I want?

'What about Malo?' I say. 'What does he think?'

'He's up for it. Room of his own? Learn how to drive a car as well as a bike? Money in his pocket? The boy can't wait.'

'You're buying him off. That's too easy. There has to be more.'

'Of course there fucking does. He needs a project. Something he can run with. A bit of responsibility. If I make it sound a doss, it won't be. No one gets a free pass. Not here. Not anywhere.'

'So what will he do?'

'I dunno yet. I've got a couple of ideas. We'll see.'

'Do I get any clues?'

'No.' The glass extended again. 'Happy days, eh?'

Happy days. I'm starting to get a feel for life in H's boiling wake. He hasn't recovered yet, far from it, but the pace he sets is still blistering. He's up by half past seven, a cup of coffee and two slices of white toast. He summons a series of business associates and sundry others for brainstorming sessions in the downstairs reception room he's reserved for get-togethers like these. On more than one occasion I watch the faces of these people as they leave. They look dazed. They look as if they've been under sustained bombardment. And they probably have.

By now I've realized that H isn't one of life's democrats. He mistrusts discussion and he has no time for the word 'no'. So far, I've only seen the softer side of him, and it's Andy, of all people, who marks my card.

213

'He wants to get you down here,' he says. 'As well as Malo.'

'And he thinks that's possible?'

'He thinks anything's possible.'

'So what would you suggest?'

The question takes him by surprise. I know he likes me, maybe more than that. I've seen it in his eyes, and in the odd aside from Jessie. I suppose I'm a bit exotic. I come from a different world, the world of feature films and the theatre and the odd TV series. That might be interesting in its own right but more importantly it keeps me at arm's length from H. I owe him nothing, at least not yet, a situation I might – in Andy's phrase – be wise to hang on to.

'H likes to own people,' he says. 'Half the time he doesn't even know he's doing it. It's just part of his nature. He wants you on the journey. He wants Malo, too. He wants all of us. With H, it's black and white, all or nothing. This is a guy with no gearbox. It's stop or flat out. And stop bores him stupid.'

That's nicely put. I make a mental note. What other tips does he have?

'Don't let him shag you. He wants to. Badly. Do I blame him? Of course I don't. But he knows he's done it once and he sees no reason why it shouldn't happen again.'

'What about me? Do I get any say in this?'

'Of course you do. But you asked me a question. H is a creature of habit. He's also impatient, and headstrong, and sees no point in fannying around. What you see is what you get.'

I nod, and thank him for his time. This is

sensible advice. We're talking in the meadow beyond the kitchen garden where Andy has been tipping poison down badger holes. This spot, as far as I can judge, is invisible from the house.

Andy hasn't moved.

'Does he ever let you out at night?' he asks.

'Never. I'm gagged and bound. That's the way he likes me best.'

'Fancy a drink at all? Whenever it suits? There are some neat pubs I know. Yeovil isn't far.'

I study him for a long moment. Good face. Good eyes. And the kind of smile any girl would enjoy waking up to. I beckon him closer. This is confessional stuff.

'You know what that makes you?' I ask. 'Apart from brave and reckless and quite attractive?'

'Tell me.'

'It makes you crazy. I've spent all morning trying to imagine the wrath of Hayden Prentice and it does nothing for my peace of mind. I suspect you've known him forever. Otherwise you wouldn't be here. So why are you coming on to the mother of his long-lost son?'

'Because I can.' He grins. 'And because we'd get away with it.'

'That's supposition. You're delusional. And you know what?' I lean forward and kiss him lightly on the lips. 'That makes you just like H.'

The following day I have to stage a brief return to London for a conference with my agent. Jessie drives me to Dorchester but my attempts to spark a conversation come to nothing. At the station I wave goodbye but she doesn't spare me a

215

backward glance. She's been watching Andy, I conclude. Very wise.

Rosa, when we go to lunch, shares the latest news from Montréal. The movie to which I've attached my name is definitely going ahead, but before I sign any contract Rosa has to be sure about my medical status.

'I need more tests,' I say at once. 'Do you want me to ask for a schedule?'

'It might be more complicated than that. We have to do the usual with the insurance forms. I've no objection to lying but if you collapse on set it might get awkward. The Montréal people are thrilled to have you but the word seems to have spread. They need to be certain you'll last the course.'

Last the course. After my break in the country I'm suddenly back in the world of movie budgets, and deadlines, and very probably another session with my neurosurgeon.

'When do they want to start?'

'After Christmas. Montréal? Wrap up warm.'

Christmas is nothing. Less than three months away. How will I feel? Where will we all be?

I call my neurosurgeon for advice. His secretary says he's busy at another hospital. I tell her I'll call back later and she says early next week would be best because he's up to his ears. Rosa has been half-listening to the conversation.

'You'll be around tomorrow?' she asks. 'It'd be nice to get this thing wrapped up.'

Tomorrow is Saturday. I shake my head and tell her I have a pressing social engagement in deepest Dorset.

'Party time?'

'In spades.' I nod. 'Wish me luck, eh?'

It's Jessie who picks me up at Dorchester station but this time she has Malo in the car. It's raining hard and his Wellington boots have left mud all over the Range Rover's rubber matting. He talks non-stop on the drive back to Flixcombe Manor, mainly about tomorrow's party. He and Andy have taken the trailer to the big Tesco Extra in Yeovil. He's a bit woolly about the details but between them they've plundered shelf after shelf of canapés, sausages, crisps, cold chicken, plus five packs of plastic glasses and a mountain of booze.

'Mainly Stella,' Jessie says drily. 'And bourbon for afters.'

I press Malo for more news. 'How many might be coming?'

'Forty-eight so far,' Jessie confirms. 'And counting.'

Forty-eight guests is a small crowd. Or maybe a big riot. Forty-eight people will need an awful lot of looking after.

'Where will they all sleep?' I enquire.

'Where they drop.' Still Jessie. 'I don't think sleeping's on the agenda. If push comes to shove I've had Andy put straw down in the barn.' She shoots me a look. 'He may have mentioned it.'

'Sadly not,' I say. 'But it sounds very practical.'

By now we've taken the turn from the main road and Jessie floors the accelerator as the back of the Range Rover shivers on the wet mud. The big grey house appears through the trees. Malo has glimpsed it already.

'Home,' he says absently. 'That was quick.'

We spend the evening brightening the house under H's direction. Between them, Jessie and H have dug out countless photos and mementos from the glory days in Pompey. A pile of football programmes will greet guests on their arrival. In one of them is a travel voucher for a month in Mauritius, H's idea for warming up the party from the off. I flick through a couple of the programmes, trying to grasp the magic appeal of Fratton Park, the legendary stadium where H's journey began. Andy helps me out.

'Fortress Fratton,' he says. 'Think Alcatraz on a wet day. Back to the Eighties. Back to the Seventies. Rule one: the old days were even better than you thought. Real football. Blood, sweat and shit meat pies. Ring any bells?'

'None,' I say. 'Roland Garros was about my limit.'

'Roland what?'

'Garros. It's in Paris. It's French for Wimbledon.'

Andy loves banter like this. Twice this evening he's confessed to being a closet thesp, deeply frustrated, and I'm beginning to believe him. Of Jessie, for the moment, there's no sign.

Andy has found a cutting from a French news-paper. He can't resist asking for a translation.

I take a look. The cutting comes from *Le Havre Libre*. The date is badly smudged. Nineteen eighty-something. At the top of the story is a black and white photo of a cafe. My first impression is that the Vikings have paid a visit. The place has been sacked: tables on the terrace overturned, windows smashed, glass everywhere. Andy is standing beside me. I can feel his presence, the heat of his body. His finger rests briefly on the top of the photo.

'The clue's in the name,' he says.

Café de Southampton? I'm none the wiser.

'Southampton's up the coast from Pompey. The two cities hate each other. Anyone from Southampton is a Scummer. Anyone from Le Havre is even worse. The local frogs are twinned with Scummerdom. Something like that, you don't need an excuse.'

'For what?'

Andy describes the cross-Channel expedition. Bazza and H and the rest of them jumped the ferry in Pompey and made the crossing to Le Havre. They attended a pre-season friendly, Pompey against the French lads, and then descended on the cafe. The rest, he says, is history.

'You were there?' I'm still looking at the photo.

'No. I was late to the party. Nineties boy.' He picks up the cutting. 'This became a battle honour. Bazza couldn't stop talking about it, H too. Run with these guys and you realized anything was possible.'

'Even a place like this?' I gesture round the wood-panelled walls.

He laughs, looks at me. We're alone in the big reception room, surrounded by memorabilia. The door is shut. Very politely, he asks for a kiss. I tell him no.

219

More photos. More faces. More tattoos. Episode by episode the story H wants to celebrate unfolds. Some of these young faces, mostly pissed, will reappear tomorrow night. They'll be older, maybe wiser. Some of them might even be semi-respectable, investing all that narco-loot in a wife and a family and a decent address.

Slowly piecing together this pageant, I begin to wonder about all our lives. Berndt and I never did drugs, not seriously, but showbiz and the whole creative shtick is just as narcotic. Applause, like a good review, can become addictive. You start to yearn for the approbation of your friends, for that arty three-page profile in *Cahiers* that says you've arrived, for the whisper at boozy gallery openings that you've been down to Cannes not once, not twice, but umpteen times. H and his army of marauding cavaliers were chasing their dream as hard as we were chasing ours. What right do I have to raise an eyebrow or wag a finger? To suggest that we were perfect parents? Proper human beings?

It's at this stage that Malo steps into the room. Andy, mercifully, is on his knees on the polished wood floor, arranging a grid of photos. I'm aware that this is priceless stuff from Mitch's point of view but I can't bring myself to get my phone out and take a shot or two.

Malo says that H wants to call a halt. He thinks we've done well. He wants us to get in the mood for tomorrow night. The parallel is obvious. I can't resist it.

'You mean some kind of rehearsal?'

Yes. And yes again.

220

We drink vintage Krug in the kitchen. Jessie has done two big bowls brimming with chips. We have a choice of sauces, red or brown. By ten o'clock, as H has doubtless anticipated, we're blind drunk.

After a final round of Jim Beam, Jessie steers Andy towards the door. Malo has already beaten a retreat, coshed by the champagne. That leaves me and H. Dimly I'm aware that this is a repeat of Antibes without the bougainvillea and the heat.

I'm sitting on H's lap. It's his idea and I'm trying very hard not to hurt him. He's telling me that he thinks he might be in love with me, which is definitely something I don't remember from the last time, but there's a cautionary, slightly provisional note in his voice.

'You are or you're not?' I let him suck my finger for a moment.

'Yes,' he says.

'Yes what?'

'Yes, please.' He starts to laugh. The laugh has an innocence I find wildly attractive because I've never heard it before. He's laughing like a child. He's laughing like Malo used to.

'You're pissed,' I tell him gently. 'It's nice.'

'You want to fuck me?'

'I don't know. Tell me why I should.'

The question seems to floor him. For the first time ever he doesn't know what to say.

'You weren't this way before.'

'You never told me you loved me before.'

'Might. I said might.'

'Yeah. And that's what I said back.'

221

'So what does it take?'

He's trying to juice me through my knickers. I remove his hand and give it a little squeeze.

'Is this some kind of negotiation?' I ask him. 'Some kind of business thing?'

'Not at all. I wish it fucking was.'

'Why?'

'Because you've got me. You've nailed me. That's not supposed to happen. Not to me. Not to H.'

Our faces are very close. He has a tiny smudge of brown around his mouth. I moisten a fingertip and remove it. Saucy, I think. HP.

'It's the Krug,' I tell him. 'You'll get over it.'

'I don't want to get over it. I want it to go on and fucking on. You don't have to do it. You don't have to fuck me. You don't even have to sleep with me. I just want you to be honest. I just want to know where we are.'

'We're here,' I tell him. 'You're Malo's dad and we're the ones who made it happen. Isn't that enough?'

'Yeah.' He pauses for a think. 'Yeah, it is.' He looks up at me. There's a lostness in his eyes. The last time I saw anything similar was with Malo, very recently, back in London. 'You're good with me, right?'

'I am.'

'You don't think I'm a twat?'

'Never.'

'You mean that?'

'I do.'

'And you'll stay here? Move in?'

'No.'

'Never?'

'I never say never.'

'One day then?'

'It's possible.' I kiss him properly this time. 'You're a good man. All you have to do is believe it.'

Eighteen

No one gets up next morning until way past ten. I prowl around the kitchen trying to remember where Jessie keeps the Sumatra strength five coffee. Footsteps on the stairs falter, resume, then come to a halt. I find Malo in his boxers holding his head. He thinks he might be dying. He asks me to check. I know exactly how he's feeling. It's probably a genetic thing.

By mid-afternoon, with the exception of Malo, we're combat-ready again. The food is laid out under cling film, including the stuff that has to go into the oven, and H has liberated yet more bottles of Krug. Souvenirs from the old days have penetrated every corner of the house until it's started to resemble a museum. This seems to please H no end. All his life, I suspect, he's hankered after an event like this, an opportunity not just to showcase his precious house but to prove that he can father a son. He even appears to have forgiven me for not sleeping with him. Either that, or it's slipped his mind.

Our first guest arrives early. To H's surprise, it's Marie Mackenzie. She must be in her fifties but she's kept her looks. She's blonde and slightly gaunt, testimony to a gym addiction. She wears a Balenciaga three-quarter-length dress, in the subtlest shade of a burnt autumnal red, a woman with taste as well as poise, and I catch a whiff of Coco Mademoiselle as she offers H a token hug. By now I know that Bazza is dead, because H – very drunk – has told me so. At the first opportunity, once I've been introduced, I offer her a tour of the house.

It turns out that this woman has recognized me. She's a big fan of the kind of movies I've been involved in all my professional life, which – given what I know about Bazza's social life – comes as a slight surprise.

'You speak French?' I ask her.

'*Oui.*'

'And you liked the films?'

'Very much.' We happen to be in H's bedroom. She looks me in the eye. 'So what are you doing here?'

'I have a son by Hayden.' I see no point in lying.

'He's the boy downstairs?'

'Yes. A one-night stand. Eighteen years ago.'

She nods. Some of the iciness has gone. I sense she's beginning to warm to me.

'It's hard to miss the resemblance,' she says. 'Poor boy.'

'You think Hayden needs a makeover?'

'Not at all. It's the inside I always worry about.'

I blink. This woman was married to the legendary Bazza, who was by all accounts H on steroids. What right does she have to badmouth Malo's dad?

She's looking at a display of trophies neatly arranged on H's bedside table. They include a brown chunk of turf ripped from the Wembley pitch when Pompey won the FA Cup, and a beer glass liberated from the Café de Southampton.

'They were all crazy,' she murmurs. 'You know that, don't you?'

I nod, say nothing. She's looking at the bed now. Before she draws any conclusions I assure her that I sleep in a room on the next floor.

'Very wise. These men like to take scalps. There comes a day when you realize they're all dogs. They still follow their dicks, believe it or not, and you're talking to someone who knows.'

'You're still fighting them off?'

'I am. The professionals are the worst. Give a man a law degree and he thinks you can't resist him. There'll be some of them here tonight so don't say you weren't warned.'

'You still live in Portsmouth?'

'Of course.'

'So why don't you move, if it's so awful?'

'Why should I? It's my home. My kids are there. And their kids. Maybe it's become a habit. Maybe I've become too idle. But I happen to like it.'

'And now? Here? Why make an appearance?'

'Good question.' She walks across to the big window where H probably stands every morning, surveying his estate. She looks out at the view, silent, reflective. Then she turns back to me.

'My husband would have wanted me to be here,' she says. 'This is for his sake, not mine.'

I nod, say nothing, trying to weigh whether or not to put the obvious question. In the end I realize I have no choice. I may never get the chance again.

'So what happened?' I ask. 'To your husband?'

She looks me in the eye. Not a flicker of emotion.

'The Filth killed him,' she says.

'Filth?' I've heard H use this word, but somehow I don't expect it from Marie.

'The police. Down in Portsmouth. Bazza should have paid a little more attention. He could be a lovely man sometimes but he never listened. He was hopelessly outnumbered. He could have surrendered, handed himself in, but that was never his style. I understand that one bullet was all it took. Not that anyone ever tells you the truth.'

She shoots me an icy smile and moments later she's gone. I hear her footsteps on the staircase. Then comes a murmur of voices in the hall before the front door closes behind her. H struggles up the stairs and appears at the open door.

'What was that about?' he asks me. 'Why won't she stay?'

I wonder whether to be honest, to tell him that her take on the last thirty years might be at odds with his, but then I decide against it. Tonight is, after all, his party.

'Previous engagement,' I say lightly. 'Early drinks with friends.'

By mid-evening, the party is beginning to rev up. Malo, chastened by last night's Krug, is taking it easy on Pepsi with a splash of bourbon. I'm doing something very similar, except I won't let anything alcoholic near my lime juice. I drift from room to room with H in attendance, trying

227

to put faces to the names on Jessie's list. One of the earliest guests to arrive has been Dave Munroe, the bent cop. He's easy to spot because he's in a wheelchair, testament – I imagine – to his failing liver. He's a balloon of a man, tiny head perched on a huge body, affable, garrulous, with a winning smile and a habit of patting everyone's extended hand. Once captured, it's difficult to get free but I squat beside his chair for a minute or two while he quizzes me about exactly what I've seen in H.

'He's the man of my dreams,' I tell him. 'Everything a girl could ever want.'

I get a special pat for that and a big wink. This is someone, I suspect, who loves complicity and can spot a lie a mile off. I fetch him a couple of sausage rolls and we agree to have a proper chat later.

By now, the big rooms downstairs are filling up as more guests pile in. Malo is manning the bar in the entrance hall. So far the gender balance is heavily skewed, men everywhere, middle-aged, heavy-set, baggy jeans and a variety of eighties T-shirts, and most of them go for the Stella. None of them seem to have wives or partners but according to H this is deliberate. They've left their women at home. Tonight, like the old days, is strictly for the blokes.

H introduces me to Mick Pain, his comrade in arms when they battled rival hooligans the length and breadth of the kingdom. Mick has a can of Stella in either hand and looks truly scary. He has a deep scar along the line of one cheekbone and far fewer teeth than the usual complement but in conversation he turns out to be a real softie. On weekends he works as a volunteer, helping to maintain an old fishing boat moored in a Pompey dock. He also has a passion for bird watching and he's telling me about a nature reserve on the Isle of Wight which is dreamland if you happen to like little egrets.

It's at this point that someone cranks up the music. Mick taps his ears and shakes his head, a clue that further conversation is impossible. Other guests are having the same problem so I set out to look for Andy, who spent most of the afternoon setting up the audio.

I find him DJ-ing in a corner of the hall towards the back of the house. He lifts one earphone and asks me what I think of his playlist. To be honest I'm no expert when it comes to Eighties indie music, headbanging or otherwise. I've never heard of The Beat nor The Pixies. Neither can I hear what Andy's trying to tell me unless I get very close indeed. I'm pressed up against him, trying to suggest that a little less volume might help the party along, when I catch sight of a face through a mill of guests. It's Jessie with a plate of sausage rolls. She's moving from group to group, trying to exchange banter, share gossip, catch up, but every now and then she shoots us the kind of look that leaves little room for ambiguity. She plainly doesn't trust Andy. And neither, after a promising start to our relationship, does she much like me.

A minute or so later, the sausage rolls gone, she's at our side.

'Hate to break this up,' she yells, then whispers

something to Andy and disappears. This turns out to be a cue for H. Andy at last winds down the volume until the music dies under the buzz of conversation. Then comes a double blast on an air horn and H mounts an antique dining chair in the middle of the hall. He's calling the party to order. First he wants to introduce someone very special. I'm trying to attract Malo's attention, to warn him to take a bow, but it turns out that H means me. This is something I haven't expected. Whistles and cheers greet my name. I imagine that most of the people in this room haven't got a clue who I am but it doesn't seem to matter. Listen to H, and you might think I'm the toast of Hollywood.

'She's come to raise the tone,' he says. 'And about fucking time.'

At this point the main door opens and Gloria appears. This is the woman who's been making Dave Munroe so happy all these years. She's very black, with a huge chest and a Caribbean dress the colour of sunset that's probably visible from the moon. In tow, behind her, come a bevy of girls, mainly Asian, laid on as a present for H. The fact that they're all dressed in Pompey strip – red, white and blue – raises another storm of applause. Gloria blows H a kiss and says she's sorry for being late. Borrowed minibus. Puncture on the motorway.

The girls begin to circulate while H gets on with his speech. This time it's Malo's turn. H doesn't bother to gild the lily.

'Nearly twenty years ago,' he says, 'I had the pleasure of sharing an evening with this lad's mum. Fuck knows how but he turns out to be the junior version of me. Malo, son, you're very welcome in our house. And you know why? Because it's your house as well. And these people here tonight will be your mates forever. Because they'll make it their business to look out for us both.'

This might not play well in cold print but tonight, in this company, H's little announcement truly touches a collective nerve. His mates aren't used to seeing H so natural, so sincere. There's a kind of humility, as well as pride, in the way he doffs his cap to our son and I know from the expression on his face that it means the world to Malo. At the news that H has become a dad, there's a stir among the watching faces, first astonishment, then delight. Dave Munroe calls for three cheers for Malo. The roar that follows fills the house.

But H hasn't finished. He has one last thing to say.

'Not everyone has turned up.' He's looking round. 'And that's their fucking loss. But there's one guy that should be here and will never make it. So a minute's silence, boys and girls, for the one man among us that we'll never forget.'

'Bazza.' This from Dave Munroe.

Heads bow. Feet shuffle. The Asian girls stop giggling. Then there's total silence. I'm still thinking about Marie, and her errant husband's private Alamo, when H's head comes up. This is a signal to Andy. He hits a button on his master board, pushes the volume paddle to its limits, and suddenly we're listening to Tina Turner.

I nod. I never met Bazza but it's hard not to choke up. *Simply the best.* What could be more perfect?

People are singing now. They're world class on the lyrics. They belt it out, line after line, linking arms, swaying with the music, punching the air as the song explodes towards the big finish, and then they throw their arms around each other as the music dies.

'Fucking wonderful,' H says, as he dismounts from the chair. And he's right.

Much later, past midnight, I find myself alone in the barn with Tony Morse. Tony is the gang's solicitor, the sleek legal eagle charged with transforming decades of Bazza's narco-loot into money he can safely spend without courting arrest. In his prime, I suspect, Tony was a real looker. He's still attractive – tall, nearly slim, with a mane of greying hair and greeny-blue eyes he uses to some effect. He's also wearing a beautifully cut tuxedo with a red velvet bow tie, which certainly marks him out from the sea of denim we've left behind in the house. I especially like his cuff links, solid gold, weighty, yet somehow discreet.

'Why the dolphin motif?'

'They were a present from Bazza and Marie. Marie was the one with the taste. Bazza wanted her to find something that would appeal to me and this is what she came up with.'

'Was she right?'

'She was. I like company, just like dolphins. I'm also partial to crowds. If you're practising

232

as a criminal lawyer you have to be a bit of a performer. You're in court. Whether it's the magistrates or a jury you have to make an impact, you have to get people onside. It's persuasion. It's hearts and minds. It's what dolphins do. Am I ringing any bells here?'

'Of course you are. It's exactly the same in my business. Except no one's life hangs in the balance.'

Like me, this man is stone-cold sober. It was his idea to get out of the house, mine to wander into the barn. Buy enough booze, play the right music, invite like-minded people, and there always comes a moment in any party when things start to get out of hand. Judging by the noise we can still hear through the open windows, we've made exactly the right decision.

'You're driving back tonight?' I ask.

'Sort of.'

'What does that mean?'

'I've got a room booked in a hotel in Shaftesbury. You're more than welcome if it appeals.'

It's a civilized invitation and I appreciate the absence of pressure. Stepping away from the house I'd briefly watched two of the Asian girls servicing a lone partygoer in the back of Gloria's minibus. I suspect that H would have preferred them to use one of his many bedrooms but old Pompey habits obviously die hard.

Now I ask my new friend about the wilder extremes of Bazza-land. People, I say carefully, talk about serious violence. Are they making it up? Or did the likes of Wesley Kane really play the Enforcer?

The question seems to amuse him. He lights a cigar, looks for somewhere to lose the match among the loose hay without setting the barn on fire.

'Wesley was an animal,' he says. 'Still is. Did they tell you about the house they bought him in Fratton?'

'They did.'

'He's still got it. He's off the reservation now, freelancing for anyone with debts to settle. Last time I heard he was into kettling.'

Kettling Pompey-style, it turns out, has nothing to do with riot control. It needs nothing more than an electric kettle, a chair, and a length of rope. First you do a spot of tying up. Then you boil the water. Then you ask a question or two. If the answers aren't to your liking, the water goes over the guy's lap.

'It's very effective. Especially when you drive him to hospital and dump him outside A&E. By this time, if you've got it right, the skin is off his todger. People who know Wes tell me he loves punch lines. He thinks that's one of the best.'

'I think it's horrible.'

'That puts you in a minority of just two.'

'Me and you?'

'Indeed.'

I gaze at him for a moment and then ask about what exactly happened to Bazza Mackenzie.

'He died. Took a bullet for his sins. There were cops in Pompey still celebrating a week later.'

'But how? Where?'

'There was a bent cop called Paul Winter

234

who'd gone over to the dark side and decided to work for Mackenzie. In the end they fell out. Big time.'

'Why?'

'Mackenzie thought Winter was screwing his wife.'

'You mean Marie?'

'Yes.'

'And was he?'

'No. But Winter was clever. It was his job to light Mackenzie's fuse and that's exactly what he did. They ended up in the middle of the night in a shop that sold reptiles, mainly snakes. Deeply appropriate.'

'And?'

'It was all a sting. The cops had wired Winter. By the time they got there, Mackenzie had Winter all trussed up. He'd lost it completely. As I understand it, he was about to fill Winter's mouth with expanding foam, the stuff you use to seal double glazing. One verbal warning to Mackenzie, and then they shot him dead. Bang. End of.'

'How do you know all this?'

'The officer who pulled the trigger told me later. Over a drink.'

'You always talk to both sides? Play both ends against the middle?'

'Of course.' He's smiling. 'I'm a lawyer. That's what lawyers do.'

I'm still staring at him, totally hooked. First kettling. Now death by expanding foam. Tony takes my arm and walks me towards the big open doors and the fresh air. Further away from the house, we pause in the shadow of a huge elm tree. The wind's got up and tiny lanterns are dancing against the blackness of the sky. Tony's head is back. He draws on the cigar and expels a plume of blue smoke. I've always loved the smell of cigars.

'One more question,' I say softly. 'Then I'll let you go.'

'That would be a shame.'

'It's about H.'

'Surprise me.'

'Did he ever kill anyone?'

There's a long silence. My arm is still linked through his. From outside the house comes the clunk of the minibus door sliding open. I'm still waiting for an answer.

'No,' he says at last. 'Never. Not to my knowledge.'

'Did he ever come close?'

'That's a different question. Why do you want to know?'

'Because H intrigues me. And because he's the father of my son.'

'You've got your doubts about young Malo? You think he might fall into bad company? Take to killing people?'

'Not at all. Doubts? No. Hopes? Plenty.' I put the gentlest pressure on his arm. 'H is a good man. When people tell me otherwise I need to know why.'

'Maybe they have their own debts to settle. Theirs was a rough old world. They broke every rule in the book and they certainly hurt people. That came with the territory. What I'm not going to discuss are individuals. To work for Bazza was to pay your dues and button your lip. If you think it's a Mafia thing you wouldn't be far wrong. *Omerta, capisci?'*

Omerta. The code of silence. I nod. I understand.

I hesitate a moment. Part of me says I owe Mitch nothing. But one more question wouldn't hurt.

'So you're not going to tell me? About H?'

'Of course not.' He smiles down at me. 'And that's for your sake, not mine.'

Nineteen

The morning after is predictably glum. I come downstairs to find bodies everywhere. In a movie this would be a crime scene, lots of scary music and lingering close-ups. Bodies curled in corners. Bodies hogging sofas and armchairs. Even a body glimpsed through the kitchen window, gently swinging in H's favourite hammock. Of Gloria and the Asian lovelies there's no sign, and when I check outside the minibus has gone.

Back in the house no one has stirred. Then Malo joins me. Between us we lay hands on a couple of big shopping bags and start the clean-up. Thank God Andy invested in all those plastic glasses. With no need to trouble the dishwasher, we move from room to room, picking up cans, smeary paper plates, olive stones, plastic knives and forks. There's been a major crisp spillage in a corner of the library. I despatch Malo to look for a dustpan and brush while I take a wet cloth to a mysterious stain on one of H's fluffy white rugs. When I sniff my fingertips it turns out to be lime pickle.

H himself appears at exactly the moment when we're starting to win. He must have had some kind of accident last night, or maybe took a fall, because he's walking with a limp. He's wearing a pair of black pyjamas. He gives the nearest body a poke with a bare foot. The body grunts, rolls over, goes to sleep again.

'Scrambled eggs,' H grunts. 'I'll sort these tossers out.'

Malo and I retreat to the kitchen. Someone, probably Jessie, has had the foresight to invest in three big trays of eggs. Malo finds half a dozen loaves of sliced white in the pantry while I raid the fridge for butter and marge. In minutes, we're ready to feed the small army of casualties next door. Waiting for our first customers to appear I tell my son we could make a living out of this.

'Disaster relief,' I say. 'All we need is a big tent and a couple of film crews.'

Malo shoots me a look. He isn't convinced.

The first faces appear, pale, largely silent. I do the eggs while Malo butters the bread. Soon the half dozen chairs around the kitchen table are all occupied and more and more people are piling in. Most of them want nothing but coffee. H takes it upon himself to spoon instant coffee into the plastic glasses we never managed to use last night and then gets the kettle on. Watching him pour the boiling water it's hard not to think about Wesley Kane.

With the kitchen full, H takes the opportunity to make another little speech. Last night was great, he says, but nothing comes for free. Later today he'll be circulating details of another little wheeze he's dreamed up to raise some moolah for Front Line. This time he has no plans to end up in hospital. The joke raises a chuckle from Dave Munroe but no one else has a clue what

H is talking about. Pressed for details, he says he just wants people to pile in and help.

'I'm after six volunteers,' he says. 'At five grand a pop. If you can't manage that kind of money then find someone who can.'

Five grand for what? He won't say. Just wait for the email, he says. Just be fucking patient for a change.

Later in the day I get a chance to corner him. Everyone but Dave Munroe has pushed off. Dave's waiting for his carer to arrive and has holed himself up in the library with one of H's true-crime books. I fetch him a coffee and we have a chat. H has told me he lives on the Isle of Wight. How come?

'No choice, really. My lovely colleagues always suspected I was on the take but no one could prove it so once I retired I didn't want to hang about in Pompey. I had a thing going with this woman down in Ventnor. She ran a B&B and the invite was there to move in. So I did. Best move ever. She looks after me a treat. Heart of gold. Lucky me, eh?'

When he asks for sugar, I return to the kitchen and find H sitting at the table. He says he wants a word or two about Malo. I take the sugar to Dave and rejoin H.

'It's about this project,' he says. 'You remember in the pub the other night we agreed he needs something to get stuck into? Something to put his smell on? I think I've got just the thing.'

Put his smell on. Very H.

'And?'

'I was talking to Mick Pain. Turns out he works

on an old boat in the Camber Dock. Makes sense in a way. He's a decent chippie.'

The boat, H says, is a Brixham trawler, old as you like, lovely thing according to Mick. It's owned by some charitable trust or other and they're always looking for ways of trying to raise money to cover the upkeep.

'I thought you said Front Line?'

'I did. Here's the deal. They can take six paying guests. They charge a grand each for a long weekend. We find six punters, five grand each, and off we go. We pay the trust people their whack and the rest goes to Front Line. That's more than twenty grand if I've got the sums right. Not bad for a weekend's work.'

'Go where?'

'France. Normandy. This is November. We push off on the tenth. The eleventh is Remembrance Day. We take lots of flowers. We look smart. We find a war memorial on one of those invasion beaches, and pay our respects. Then we have a beer or two and come home.'

I nod. I see the logic. Clever.

'It's mustard,' he says. 'And the boy will be doing the work, keeping it together, keeping the show on the road. I've already mentioned it. He loves the idea. Big fucking smile on his face.'

'Five thousand pounds is a lot. What makes you think people will pay that kind of money?'

'You.'

'Me?'

'You're coming, too. Star of the show. Three days with a movie queen? Cheap at the price. Can't fail.'

I'm speechless. I've never much liked boats, and I detest being the centre of that kind of attention. Neither reservation makes any difference. H will be booking the boat tomorrow. Everything else falls to Malo.

'Do it for him,' H urges me. 'You can't let the boy down.'

I shake my head. Try to think of other excuses. But H is right. If Malo is to spend his days doing something useful then this sounds near-perfect.

'This boat's got a name?'

'Yeah. *Persephone*.'

'*Persephone*?' I start to laugh. I did a Greek tragedy once on a bare clifftop stage near Land's End.

H wants to know what's so funny.

'You know about Persephone? You know who she was?'

'Tell me.'

'Queen of the Underworld.'

H is staring at me. Then he shakes his head as if he can't quite believe it.

'Brilliant,' he says. 'You couldn't make that up.'

For the rest of Sunday we're in a bit of a trance. H mutters about Post Traumatic Stress Disorder and Dave Munroe departs when his specially adapted van arrives to collect him. That evening, deep into a showing of a Clint Eastwood movie, I get an apologetic email from Rosa, my agent. The actor playing against me in *Going Solo* has recovered. The producer wants to start rehearsals on Tuesday. Can I manage that? I text her a yes and mention it to H once the film's over. Either he doesn't hear me properly or he doesn't care.

'Whatever,' he says.

On Monday, Jessie once again runs me to the station in Dorchester. I try and dream up ways of convincing her that Andy hasn't got into my knickers but I sense she's in no mood to listen. Only when I mention that I might be away for a while does she brighten up.

'Take your time,' she says. 'We'll look after Malo.'

Back in London I phone my neuro-consultant and explain the issue over the insurance for the Montréal movie. He's sympathetic but can do nothing until I've had the three-month scan. Only then can he be sure of my prognosis. I relay this news to Rosa, who isn't best pleased. I suggest that maybe we can skate round it somehow. She says she'll try.

I spend the evening going through the BBC script. Rehearsals start the following morning in a basement studio in Broadcasting House. I've never done radio before and I like it a great deal. It feels very intimate and I love playing from a script I can see in front of me. The producer is young, fresh out of Cambridge, and he reminds me a little of Berndt in his earlier days. He has a delicate way of suggesting changes of nuance and tone in delivering particular lines and I quickly learn to trust him. By lunchtime we've made a great deal of progress and the afternoon goes so well that he thinks we might make a start on the recording a little earlier than planned.

That night I take Evelyn to a play I know she

wants to see at the Harold Pinter theatre. In a way it's a thank-you for all the support she's given me over the past few weeks and I know she's touched that I've managed to lay hands on a couple of tickets. The play – *Oslo* – is excellent, richly deserving the rave reviews in every corner of the press, and she insists on treating me to a late supper in an Italian place she knows in Covent Garden. The place is buzzing and we linger over coffee and a couple of brandies after the meal. I tell her about Malo, and a little about the party at the weekend. A family reunion doesn't really do it justice but that's the story I'm sticking to. Evelyn might be incredibly well-read but deep down I suspect she's a woman of tender sensibilities. I don't want to shock her.

'So what's this Hayden person like?'

It's hard to do justice to H. In a way he belongs among the pages of a novel.

'He's larger than life,' I tell her. 'He's bold and he's loud and what you see is pretty much what you get. But Malo seems to think the world of him and that's good enough for me.'

'Malo's happy down there?'

'Very.'

'That's good. I'm glad.'

She asks about my journalist friend. She's met Mitch on a number of occasions and I think she approves. I tell her we met recently for lunch but again I spare her the details.

'You don't think you two might . . .?'

'No.'

'Shame. I just wondered . . .'

'I'm afraid not. Just now I'm trying very hard

just to stay in one piece. You've no idea how wearying that can be.'

'And the radio thing?'

I tell her about today's rehearsal. The sound effects, in particular, I find astonishing. Half close your eyes during various flashback sequences and you could have been living in the Blitz. This makes Evelyn laugh. She settles the bill and I splash out on a cab back to Holland Park. We say our goodbyes outside her door and I give her a hug.

'Thank you,' I say, 'for everything.'

When I let myself in my answerphone is flashing red in the darkness. I turn on the lights and press the play button to access the message. It's Mitch. He's been trying my phone all evening but I've obviously got the thing switched off. We need to talk. It sounds urgent.

I reach for the phone, then have second thoughts. A check on my mobile reveals two more messages, both from Mitch, but he's right, I've been unobtainable. I fetch a glass of water from the kitchen and make myself comfortable on the sofa. I know I should phone him. I know it's what he wants. But there's something inside me that is weary of playing the agent in enemy territory.

I'm sure that H has been up to all kinds of mischief in his life, but as far as Malo and I are concerned he's been nothing but generous. Is it really my job to hazard all that? No matter what Mitch tells me about UKIP, and the perils of Brexit, and all the rest of the doomster nonsense? Shouldn't I simply be grateful that fate has given my son a father who really cares about him?

I think of the trawler down in Portsmouth and my adolescent boy suddenly handed responsibilities he could never have dreamed of. A couple of weeks ago he was slumped on this same sofa, totally Zombied. Now he's tasked with extracting a great deal of money from people he barely knows. That's a steep learning curve, something Berndt would never have dreamed up, and when I've drained the glass I decide to call it a night. Mitch will have to wait. Maybe I'll phone him first thing tomorrow. Maybe.

I don't. For whatever reason I fail to hear the alarm clock and by the time I'm properly awake I have barely an hour to make it to Central London. I swallow a bowl of cereal and skip my make-up. By the time I make it to the basement studio, the rest of the cast and production crew are already eyeballing the day's first scene. I mutter my apologies and slip into my chair in the recording booth.

My script is still on the music stand where I left it. I find my place and we kick off. Mercifully the male lead has a protracted coughing fit which gets us all wondering whether he's really better. The producer fetches water from the nearby washroom. It doesn't do the trick and so the producer calls a break while the male lead pops out to the nearest chemist for throat lozenges. With nothing better to do I ask the recording engineer if I can take a peek at his paper. It happens to be the *Guardian*.

I briefly scan the first couple of pages and I'm about to turn to the arts section at the back when

I take a second look at the photo beneath the main story on page four. It shows a UKIP politician snapped on his own front doorstep. The last time I saw Spencer Willoughby he was roaring drunk at H's dinner table. Now he's opened the door to a press photographer and he looks less than pleased.

The accompanying story has been lifted from Mitch's Finisterra website. It reveals that UKIP may be standing aside to give Tory candidates a clear run in the next general election. Not only that but sizeable donations to the Kippers are alleged to be ending up in Conservative Central Office. The most recent donation is alleged to be half a million pounds. More details on the website.

My heart is sinking. I use my smart phone to access the full story from Finisterra. An old photo of H shows him inspecting a vast gin palace at the Southampton Boat Show. I'm not aware of any plans on H's part to acquire this trophy motor cruiser but that's far from the point. This single image has done untold damage to the Tory party, to UKIP, to Spencer Willoughby and to H himself. Anyone who suspects that democracy has been handed to the fat cats need look no further. My eye drifts to the Finisterra byline. The name of the journalist responsible for this damning exclusive? Mitch Culligan.

Rehearsals begin again with the return of the male lead. Mid-morning, the producer calls a break. I step out of the studio and call Mitch. I've read the story again and I'm beyond angry.

I ask him what the fuck's going on.

'I've been trying to contact you,' he says.

'I know.'

'Since yesterday.'

'Yes. So what did you want? Were you trying to warn me?'

'I needed to let you know.'

'And if I'd objected? Asked you to think again? Asked you not to publish?'

'That might have been difficult.'

'*Difficult?*' I'm ready to explode. 'I gave you that information on trust. You told me it was for your book. That's what I believed. That's what you said. A book we can sit down and talk about. In a book you can put all this stuff at arm's length. Now I find it all over the fucking internet. And it's wrong, by the way.'

'What's wrong?'

'The figure you quoted. The half million pounds.'

'That's what you told me.'

'I said "may". I said "might". I said I couldn't be sure. If you want the real figure it's five hundred quid. That might keep UKIP in beers for an evening or two but it's not half a million. You should have checked.'

The phone goes dead. He's cut me off. Bastard. Then I start to wonder about H. Did he really mean five hundred? Or has he been stringing me along as well? These questions are impossible to answer, especially now. The studio manager is beckoning me inside. My day job awaits. Shit, I think. Shit. Shit. Shit.

We break for lunch at one. So far cast and crew have shared adjoining tables at the Broadcasting

House canteen. On this occasion I skip the Beeb salad and head out to the street where I can try and get my teeming thoughts in order. When I check my phone this time there are a couple of texts, both of them from people I've never heard of. I scroll slowly through them. They're both demanding a call back, I've no idea why, then I pause on a name I recognize. Spencer Willoughby. The message is blunt. I've grassed him up. He thought he was in discreet company at H's table and it turns out he wasn't. Very shortly I may be hearing from his solicitor. Over and out.

Worse and worse, I think. Little me in the middle of a media shit storm with nowhere to hide. I phone Mitch again. He apologizes at once for hanging up on me.

'Someone more important to talk to?'

'Something like that.'

I ask him again why he chose to publish now and not later. This time he's blaming his publisher.

'They wanted advance publicity,' he says, 'for the book. It's Theresa May's big speech tomorrow, up in Manchester. We needed to get in her face.'

Part of me marvels at the little party tricks these people get up to. Shafting the Tories. Winding up the Maybot. The rest of me is still very angry. Angry and betrayed.

'Betrayed? How does that work?'

'I trusted you.'

'Trusted me how?'

'To protect our interests. Mine and my son's. I won't bother you with the details but I dread to think where this thing is going to end.'

'I don't understand.'

'Yes, you do. You asked me to keep my eyes open. To look around. To report back. And that's exactly what I did because I assumed you'd act like any decent human being when it came to using any of this stuff. Instead, I find myself all over a national paper.'

'Nonsense. You're not mentioned anywhere.'

'And you really think that matters? You really think there aren't people out there who might draw the odd conclusion?'

I tell him about the text from Willoughby.

'So what's he going to do about it?'

'I've no idea. Until his solicitor tells me.'

'He's brought in the lawyers? Already?'

'So he says.'

'He's bluffing. They all do that. Forget it.'

Forget it? I explode on the phone. Tell Mitch what a snake he is. All the time I thought he had my best interests at heart. Now this.

There's a long silence. I'm watching a couple snatching a kiss across the road and for a moment I wonder whether Mitch has hung up on me again. Then he's back on the line.

'This is about Prentice, isn't it? And about Malo?'

'I don't know what you mean.'

'Is he your son's father? All I need is a yes or a no.'

'Why? What would you do with either?'

'That's immaterial. I just want to get the story straight. Do I hear a yes?'

'You hear nothing.' It's my turn to hang up.

I feel like crying. I feel like setting off west

250

and taking the long way home. I feel like spending the entire afternoon blanking myself off from my phone, from my army of new friends, and from anything else that can hurt me. Instead, as I must, I go back to the studio.

By early evening, we've made a decent start on the recording. Another day and a half should see it finished. The male lead suggests a drink in a pub he knows nearby. Exhausted, I accept.

He buys me a large gin and tonic. He settles into the chair across the table. He's drinking Guinness.

'You look terrible,' he says.

'Thanks.'

'What's the matter?'

I shake my head. Everything is blurring. Everything is slipping out of focus. Unusually for a man, he's carrying a handkerchief.

'Here.' He's trying to be gentle. 'Blow your nose.'

I try and dry my tears. It's hopeless. He slips into the chair beside me and I feel myself collapsing against him. Pathetic, I tell myself. Pathetic and unnecessary. He puts one arm round me, offering comfort. Mercifully, he doesn't ask me what's wrong.

The great thing about London is that nobody else seems to care. I'm not talking about the male lead. I'm talking about everyone else in the pub. I'm sobbing my heart out and no one even looks up from their smart phones.

When I've finally stopped crying and got some kind of grip I bring this to the attention of my new companion.

'Don't you think that's remarkable?' I ask him.

He smiles and asks me whether I'd prefer otherwise. Anonymity is bred deep in this city's bones. Speaking personally, he thinks that's rather wonderful.

'But you're an actor,' I say. 'And we're all show-offs. It's in the job description. The last place we need to be is off the fucking radar.'

The fucking radar is a phrase he says he'll cherish. Praise is a currency actors tend not to waste on each other and for the first time I start taking a proper look at this man. In the studio, as scripted, he's pulled off an American accent with an underlying hint of German and done it with some style. He's maybe five years older than me but he laughs a lot and has a fund of good stories about his days in Australian soaps. Now he's wondering about another drink.

'Yes, please.' I fumble for my bag. 'And make mine a double.'

We stay in the pub most of the evening. Supper is three bags of crisps, one of them shared. When he asks me where I live he says his flat is a lot closer. I've told him nothing about Malo, about H, about Flixcombe Manor, about Mitch, about Spencer fucking Willoughby, about Brexit, and I feel a great deal better. Drunk but better. His flat turns out to be a ten-minute walk away. It's small, cosy and very male. As we strip, I establish the rules of engagement. We'll fuck until we go to sleep and at some point after that I'll get up and go home. No commitments. No regrets. Not a whisper of this to anyone else.

'Perfect.' He's on his knees, easing my thighs

apart. He has a busy tongue and he knows exactly what he's doing. Hours later, dressed again and waiting for the Uber, I wake him up.

'How come you can afford an address like this?'

He peers up at me, still groggy with the Guinness.

'Australian soaps,' he says. 'You won't believe the residuals.'

Next day, in the parlance, we put *Going Solo* to bed. Neither I nor my male lead betray the slightest evidence of our night together and after a second take on the final scene we all share a couple of bottles of Prosecco brought in by the producer. We toast the health of the production, offer effusive thanks to the producer for his hospitality, have a hug or two, and make for the street. It's only on the bus home that I realize that in all likelihood I'll never see my one-night stand again. I know his name, Desmond Reilly, I dimly remember where his flat is, but I have no contact details. Nice man. Gifted lover. Amusing stories. End of. Of this, believe it or not, I'm strangely proud and it's only when I'm walking home from the bus stop that I realize the real irony. Eighteen years ago something similar happened in Antibes. And look where that took me.

Back in the apartment, I call Malo. I want all his news, especially how he's getting on with Project *Persephone*, but as well I'm keen to know about H.

'He's fine. Just like always.'

'Not upset in any way?'

253

'Not at all. Why should he be?'

I know I can't take this line of enquiry very much further, not without betraying my hand. Malo, it turns out, is in Portsmouth with Andy and H. They've spent most of the day aboard the old fishing boat, talking to the people from the charity. H has secured a handy discount on the hire fee, releasing more money for Front Line, and Malo has lots of photographs he can use for his presentation to would-be passengers. I'm about to ask him what happens next when he puts me on to H.

'You OK?'

I tell him I'm fine. Malo's right. He sounds as blunt and bouncy as ever. Maybe he never reads the *Guardian* or Mitch's fucking website. Maybe he hasn't had an earful from Spencer Willoughby. Maybe the media shit storm has passed him by.

He wants to know how the BBC thing went. I tell him it's in the can.

'They're pleased?'

'I think so.'

'Anything else you have to do up there?'

'Not much.'

'So when are you coming home?'

'Home' is the key proposition here. He's used the word before, glancing references *en passant*, but this is the first time he's put it in lights. Home. Unadorned. Unqualified. Unambiguous. The place where you hang your hat. The place where your heart is. Home.

'I'm at home now,' I say lightly. 'You must come up some time, pay me a visit. It's not Flixcombe Manor but I'm very fond of it.'

'We miss you,' H says. 'Especially the boy. Exciting times, this *Persephone* thing. We need to get our shit together.'

I agree. We certainly do. There's a hiatus, a moment or two of silence, slightly uncomfortable. Then he's back.

'That's a deal, then. Friday? End of the week? Just the three of us? No Tina fucking Turner? Give me a bell. All I need is a train time.'

He's gone. I'm back with my son. It seems he's very busy. He has to find out about the weather in mid-November and the shipping lanes off the French coast. The people he's talking to are very nice and – just for the record – he's loving what he's seen of Pompey.

Pompey? He uses the term as if he's lived there all his life. He uses it the way you might refer to a much-loved relative. Is this genetic, too? Something he's inherited from his dad?

'Take care,' I say. 'See you soon.' But already he's gone.

As it turns out I'm on the train again, as ordered, on Friday. Even in the early afternoon London is emptying ahead of the weekend and every carriage is packed. At Dorchester station, to my relief, there's no sign of Jessie. H is alone at the wheel.

'Your doctor's signed you off?' I ask him. 'No issues with driving?'

'Issues? You want to take the bus?'

We leave Dorchester. He drives fast but the deeper we get into the countryside, the narrower the roads, the more carefully he gauges every

255

corner. This is a man, I remind myself, who's successfully eliminated every possible risk in his life. Not from an excess of caution but by being consistently smarter than the enemy. His luck may have run out on the trail bike but when it comes to dealing with threats on two legs he appears to be beyond reach.

We chat about Malo, about *Persephone*, about the job our son's doing on the task H has handed him. H has located a graphics consultancy in Yeovil, people with a real flair for marrying images and text. Malo spent most of yesterday with them and came back with some impressive ideas.

'They've sourced a load of pics of your lovely self,' H says without a hint of irony. 'We thought we'd leave the final choice to you.'

I nod, say nothing. I want, very badly, to find out whether he saw Tuesday's *Guardian* but I can't think how to ask. Minutes before we hit the turn-off for Flixcombe Manor I enquire whether he saw anything of May's big speech at the Tory conference. A joker in the front row presented her with a P45 when she was in mid-flow, a clip that made countless news feeds within seconds.

H saw it. Thought it was funny. Along with the cough sweet and bits of the backdrop falling apart. He especially liked the man with the P45.

'Same bloke presented Trump with a bunch of golf balls when he was over here on business. Each one had a swastika on it. That's my kind of politics. Get under their skins. Give the bastards a poke. Everything goes tits-up when you take these clowns seriously.'

'And does the same go for Willoughby?'

'Willoughby is a prat. The field's pretty thin just now but he can't even make it as a politician. That man's out of his depth in a fucking puddle.'

And that's it. No more mention of politics, of *Guardian* exposés, of fictitious six-figure donation to UKIP funds. Case closed.

We spend a very civilized weekend helping Malo shape the pitch he wants to make to lure paying passengers aboard *Persephone.* As H promised, the graphics people in Yeovil have found umpteen photos of yours truly and I spend one of the nicest evenings of my life in the downstairs library with my son as he goes through them. What were you doing in Rome with Liam Neeson? How old were you when they shot the adaptation of *The Reichenbach Falls*? What does it feel like to walk that red carpet into the Leicester Square Odeon? I answer each of these questions as best I can, aware of H cocking an ear in the background. Many of these locations I've virtually forgotten, lost beneath the drift of the years, but when we get to a shot towards the bottom of the pile, the memories put a smile on my face.

We were shooting, in all places, on the Isle of Wight. It was a biopic about a famous Victorian photographer, Julia Margaret Cameron, and I was playing one of the younger models she used to perfect various lighting techniques. It was a lovely time of year, late spring, and we were staying in a hotel – the Farringford – which had once belonged to Tennyson.

My role was undemanding and I treated the location a bit like a holiday. I'd get up every morning shortly after dawn and take the path down through the fields and up on to the long fold of chalky turf that stretched west towards The Needles. It was called, appropriately enough, Tennyson Down and I'd spend a glorious hour or two in the company of rabbits, marauding seagulls, and the odd hare without once laying eyes on another human being. Those were the weeks, I tell Malo, when I truly fell in love. Not with someone else but with that sense of kinship, of belonging, of being mysteriously entwined with something infinitely bigger than I'd ever be.

I'm not sure Malo really understands what I'm trying to say. Neither am I making an especially good job of describing what, in the end, became moments of transcendence. But after Malo discards the shot of me dressed up as a nine-teenth-century photographer's model, and moves briskly through the photos that remain, I catch sight of H sprawled in his armchair. He offers me a nod of what I suspect might be approval. Praise indeed, I think.

On the Sunday, H takes us all out for lunch. It's a different pub this time, more down-to-earth, and Jessie and Andy come too. Jessie, for some reason, seems to have become more comfortable in my company. I can't say she's forgiven me because there's nothing to forgive, but we manage a half-decent conversation when we're waiting for the mains. The men are talking football. Pompey, it seems, are struggling a bit but Manchester City, according to Andy, are a joy to watch.

Jessie rolls her eyes. She's never had much time for football, which must be a problem if you're living with Andy, but she tells me about another expedition she made only days ago. The Romsey interior design place she visited when I was last down turned out to be a real disappointment but she's found an interior design outlet in Salisbury that has exactly what she's been after. I listen to her rhapsodizing about granite worktops, and soft-close drawers, and clever solutions to crockery storage, and all the other bits of kitchen porn, and agree that our parents' generation were lucky to survive without a walk-in freezer. Then, as the men's attention turns to the approaching waitress, I feel the lightest touch on my thigh.

'Watch out for yourself,' Jessie says softly.

Watch out for myself? I fork my way through a plateful of slightly overcooked scampi and wonder what on earth she means. Andy and H have done football by now and we're all discussing last weekend. A torrent of emails, most of them obscene, have been flooding in after the party and as far as H can judge it seems to have been a roaring success.

'Only you would know,' I suggest.

'Yeah?' He turns to eyeball me. 'And what's that supposed to mean?'

I shrug. I've meant no offence. All I'm saying is the obvious. That these are people H has known most of his life. They're friends, buddies, mates, brothers-in-arms. They must have been

259

through a lot together and a closeness like that can only breed loyalty. No wonder the weekend went so well.

H frowns. He seems to be exploring the notion in his head, putting it to the test. Finally he picks up the remains of a lamb chop and gives it a chew. Then he licks his fingers and gives his mouth a wipe on a paper napkin.

'You're right,' he grunts. 'Loyalty? Nothing fucking like it.'

I'm back in London for the start of the new week. Jessie's warning still bothers me but I'm doing my best to ignore it. I spend a lovely afternoon drifting around the Singer Sargent exhibition at the Dulwich Gallery and return with a bag of crumpets from the Londis round the corner. I make tea, toast the crumpets, watch the evening news, try calling Malo. He's on divert so I leave a message asking him to phone, nothing urgent, then settle in to let the evening drift by. By ten I've decided I deserve an early night. By half past I'm asleep.

It's five in the morning when the phone rings. Thinking it might be Malo, I fumble for the mobile. It's Mitch. He sounds terrible.

'What's happened?'

'We have to talk.'

'Where?'

'My place. Soon as you can. Please.'

Twenty

I'm in Hither Green within the hour. The Uber drops me outside Mitch's house. Dawn is breaking over the rooftops across the road. Mitch has the front door open before I've even made it through the gate. He's fully dressed and he has the look of someone who's been up all night. Exhausted. And fearful.

'What's happened?'

He gets me into the house and checks the street left and right before shutting the door. I hear the slide of two bolts. Then we're in the kitchen at the back and I'm looking at what appears to be a business card on the work top. I recognize the Met Police logo. Not a good sign.

'Sayid,' he says.

I put my arms round him. I think he needs to cut loose, let everything out. I tell him to take his time. Deep breaths.

He nods, tips his head back, gulps. I suggest we both sit down. Does he need a drink?

He shakes his head. No drink.

'I got home around ten,' he says. 'I couldn't understand why the lights weren't on. Sayid should have been home. He never runs on a Monday. Never.'

He let himself in and looked for a note. Nothing. He waited ten minutes or so, thinking Sayid might have gone out for milk or whatever,

261

and then he phoned the care home. The manager on duty said he'd left as usual around seven. As far as he was aware he was heading straight back home.

It was now half past ten. Sayid, he tells me, always left his shoulder bag down beside the sofa. When Mitch checked, it wasn't there. This was seriously worrying. Sayid has very few friends. He likes his own company. Apart from running, he rarely goes out.

'I was tempted to call the police,' he says. 'But they get funny around people like Sayid.'

'So you waited?'

'Yes.'

'And?'

'The phone went. It must have been around eleven. Caller ID said Sayid. I can't tell you how relieved I felt. Then I realized it wasn't him. It was another voice. Nothing like Sayid. He said to go to the end of the road. It's a cul-de-sac. There's waste land at the foot of the railway embankment. The kids are always up there. Drinkers, too. Loads of empty cans.'

'What sort of voice?'

'Male. Rough.'

'Accent?'

'Might have been London. Might not. Hard to tell.'

Mitch left the house. He's not built for running but he says he was at the end of the road in seconds and I believe him.

'The street lighting's shit up there. I should have brought a torch but I didn't. I had a look round, couldn't see anything, and then a train came by. He was less than a metre away. I don't know how I missed him.'

'Who?'

'Sayid.' His head goes down. He covers his face with his hands. There are few sights harder to cope with than a big man sobbing.

I do my best. I tell him once again to take his time. Finally he reaches for a tea towel and mops his face. The tea towel is a souvenir from Weston-super-Mare. Odd how these details settle in your brain.

'At first I thought he was dead. They'd beaten him up, smashed his face. There was nothing left, nothing I could recognize. Then I realized he was still breathing. Jesus . . .'

He phoned 999. An ambulance, happily, had been on standby in Lewisham and arrived in minutes.

'The guys were amazing. Two of them. They worked on him for a minute or two and then got him into the ambulance. It was obvious he was in a bad way. They'd found a pulse but he wasn't responding. King's is close that time of night. We were there in less than ten minutes.'

I nodded. I know King's College Hospital. It's next door to the Maudsley. I used to pass it when I was visiting a friend with breast cancer.

'So what happened?'

'They fast-tracked him. A&E. He's still alive but only just.' His eyes settle on his mobile. 'They said they'd phone me if there were any developments.'

'You didn't stay?'

'The police arrived. Took a statement. They

wanted to know everything about Sayid. Thank God he's legal.'

'So what are they going to do?'

'They'll obviously search the embankment. Beyond that they might do house-to-house down the road, CCTV, put out some kind of appeal, whatever. The bloke who did most of the talking told me not to hold my breath. He didn't actually say it but that's what he meant.' At last he looks me in the face. His eyes are red. His cheeks are shiny with tears. 'Foreign-looking bloke? Alone on the street at night? The story writes itself. You know that.'

'But it doesn't. You took a call. That's not some accident.'

'I know. That's exactly what I told them. Then they said they couldn't find a phone, not on Sayid. That's when they really started in. People he might have upset. Enemies. Some grudge or other. Maybe drug debts. *Drug debts? Sayid? Are you kidding?*'

It's a mess. But then, according to Mitch, it gets a whole lot worse.

'They wanted to know about our relationship. Whether we were close. Whether we'd had some monster row. Whether I had any previous for violence.'

'You're telling me you're a suspect?'

'I'm telling you exactly what happened. This morning we're going to go through it all again. Brixton police station. Half nine.' He nods at the card on the work surface. 'DC Brett Daltrey. My new buddy.'

'You want me to come?'

'No.' He shakes his head. 'Thanks, but no. You being here now is enough. I can't tell you. A time like this, you think you're going mad. It's like a nightmare. It's like a truly crap movie. Except you end up playing the key role and having bugger all to say. You know something? I used to think I'd been around a bit, seen a few things. I used to think nothing could ever take me by surprise, touch me, hurt me, whatever. And you know something else? I was wrong. Such a handsome guy. So gentle. So fucking *luminous*.'

I hold his gaze for a long moment. He looks wrecked. There's a big fat question mark hanging over this conversation and both of us know it. This isn't about Sayid at all. He's not the kind of person to upset anyone. It's about Mitch.

'So who made the call?' I ask him. 'And why?'

He won't answer the question and in a way I don't blame him. All he wants is to be held, to be comforted, to have someone reassure him that there might – one day – come an end to this madness. That Sayid will recover. That the damage will be repaired. That their relationship will take them somewhere safe and perhaps a little brighter.

I do the motherly things. I make tea. I offer toast. I lend a listening ear. Mitch has started to ramble a little. He wants to tell me about the good times he and Sayid have had, about the day they met at a seminar at the LSE, how they took a trip down the Thames on a tourist boat that same afternoon, surrounded by foreigners, how the relationship slowly deepened until Sayid was sharing Mitch's kitchen, and finally his bed. This is all depressingly past tense, as if Mitch's lover has died already, and I keep reminding him of the miraculous reach of modern medicine, how gifted strangers can reach deep into your brain and make you better.

'You'd know, of course. I'm sorry. That's crass.'

'No problem. I don't blame you. All I'm saying is that he's still alive. Otherwise they'd have phoned you.' I reach for his hand, give it a squeeze. 'No news? Good news? Isn't that the way it goes?'

I leave him around half past seven. He wants a shower and a change of clothes. He'll call me if anything happens. He hopes I don't mind. I tell him again that I'm there whenever he needs me. As I close the front gate behind me I can see him in the front room, a ghost of a man. He lifts a hand, waving goodbye, and then he's gone.

Instead of looking for a bus stop or summoning an Uber, I take a walk to the end of the cul-de-sac. Access to the railway embankment is barred by an unmarked white van and a length of Police Do Not Cross tape that dances in the wind. Three men in forensic jump suits are combing through the grass where the embankment meets the scabby tarmac. I watch one recover a can of what looks like cider and sniff it before putting it carefully to one side. An assortment of other cans and bottles await sorting and bagging. This little tableau is beyond bleak. No one deserves to have been fighting for his life in a setting like this.

Thoroughly depressed, I finally phone for an Uber. By nine o'clock, after the slow crawl north, I'm back in Holland Park. At this point I truly don't know what to do. Unless Mitch has upset someone else, there has to be a connection between the *Guardian* article and what happened last night.

Beating Sayid nearly to death is a very neat way of getting to Mitch. H and his mates may be much subtler than I've ever suspected but that puts us all in a place I never want to go. Maybe Spencer Willoughby was behind last night's attack. Maybe he's opened his cheque book and hired a bunch of thugs and made himself feel a great deal better in the process. Or maybe the Tories took umbrage at Tuesday's article and did something similar. Whatever happened, I realize I will go to very great lengths not to believe any of this has anything to do with Malo's new dad.

I've been at home for a couple of hours when the phone rings. Thinking it might be Mitch I don't bother to check caller ID. Silly mistake. Easily done. It's H.

'I'm just walking up your road,' he says. 'Posh-looking block? Four floors? Have I got that right?'

He's at the front door within the minute. I buzz him in and wait for the lift to arrive. He's whistling a tune I don't recognize. This is something new. I've never known H whistle before.

'Nice.'

I've invited him in. He's left his briefcase on the table and he's having a look round, exactly the way you might if you were planning to put in an offer. He seems very cheerful. The limp has gone and when I tell him to take a seat there's none of the caution that's attended every movement since he left hospital.

'Well?' He's beaming up at me. 'Everything shipshape?'

This is a stupid question and I suspect we both know it. Since the moment I heard his voice on the phone I've realized what a bizarre conversation this is going to be. Deep inside, no matter how hard I fight the conclusion, I know that H must have had something to do with Sayid. It carries his fingerprints. In TV drama cop-speak, it's very much his MO: clever, effective, ruthless. Yet the last thing I want to do is start any kind of conversation about Mitch Culligan because I've no idea where that might lead. Malo is still Malo. Malo is my son. And just now he seems to belong to H.

'Shipshape?' I query.

'Here.' H has opened his briefcase. Out comes a sheaf of artwork. He spreads it on the table. What happens next stretches my acting skills to their absolute limit. The artwork is themed around a single word: Remembrance. Sepia shots of *Persephone* under full sail bleed artfully into black and white photos from the D-Day landings. Five thousand pounds will buy you the once-in-a-lifetime chance to pay your respects to the hundreds of thousands of Allied soldiers who were killed in the Battle of Normandy, and to the countless millions who died in both World Wars. The voyage has the blessing of a number of regimental associations and all proceeds will go to Front Line. There's a promise of a four-course gourmet lunch afterwards in a top Normandy restaurant plus on-board silver service on both legs of the crossing. Better still, every guest will have the chance to get to know *Persephone*'s guest of honour. Me.

I tell H it looks great. I tell him Malo's done a fabulous job. I've absolutely no doubt that the voyage will be over-subscribed within weeks and that Front Line will be mega-grateful. I'm trying very hard to make this burst of enthusiasm sound both spontaneous and genuine, and I think I've done OK, but all I can really think of is that poor bloody man fighting for his life. Is now the time to step out of role and have a proper conversation? Or do we carry on the masquerade?

H is looking pleased. He wants to know what I think of the photo Malo has chosen. H has his finger on it.

'You mean of me?'

'Yeah.'

'It's fine. I was ten years younger then. Can these people handle disappointment?'

H thinks that's funny. He also thinks I'm wrong.

'Beautiful women always age well,' he says. 'And you're the living fucking proof. It's not the boat that will get them on board. It's you.'

I'm not at all sure I want to be the come-on for a bunch of ageing war-junkies with time on their hands and far too much money, but that's a different conversation. For now, all I want is to get H out of my apartment. I suspect he senses this. His feral instincts never let him down.

'Busy, are we?'

I glance at my watch. Nearly half past eleven. I can invent a lunch date. I can say that Evelyn needs some groceries. I can bring this little exchange to an end in any way I like. Except I know it's not going to happen.

H has produced a bottle from his briefcase. It's very early for Krug.

'Little celebration,' he announces. 'A toast for the boy's efforts.'

I fetch glasses from the kitchen. This is a bit like surfing, I tell myself. You try and spot the right wave and then see what happens.

'Malo . . .' H has his glass raised.

I murmur my son's name and do the same.

'I'm surprised he's not with you,' I say.

'He is. I dropped him at a courier place. Woman called Clemenza? Ring any bells?'

'Of course. I've met her. He's crazy about her and I'm not surprised. She's lovely.'

'So why didn't you mention her before?'

'She's Malo's business, not mine. Or yours for that matter.'

This sounds harsher than I intended. I try and soften the impact with a smile but H seems oblivious.

'Anything else you haven't told me?'

'I don't know what you mean. In what respect? You want to know about my girlfriends? My marriage? My all-time favourite movie? Only this could take a while.'

'Don't play games, gal. Not with me.'

'Gal' is new. 'Gal' comes loaded with menace. This is a new H, a different H, and he is, to be frank, scary. I'm trying very hard not to think about that embankment. Or Wesley Kane. Or expanding foam.

I ask H how long he's been up in town.

'We came up last night,' he says. 'M and me. Took him to a casino. Stayed at a nice hotel. Made a fuss of the boy. He loved it.'

I nod, reach for my glass. No longer Malo but 'M'. My son has been rebadged. M.

'You should have phoned,' I tell him. 'You could have stayed here.'

'Didn't want to disturb you. Didn't know what you might be up to.'

He lets the sentence hang in the air.

'I could ask the same,' I say.

'But I just told you. Casino, something to eat, something to drink, another couple of twirls on the roulette table, then bye-byes.' He counts each of these little adventures on his thick fingers and then looks up. 'You want to check? See the receipts?'

'Why would I want to do that?'

'Fuck knows. Just wondering.' He gets up and starts to prowl around the living room, pausing to stare at the odd photo, inspecting my collection of paperbacks, my DVDs, my music. I know he's playing with me, building up a certain tension. It's a trick Berndt used to use all the time in his darker scripts. The victim was always a woman. The camera would linger on her face until the moment came when she broke. This would usually be the cue for some kind of confession. This isn't going to happen to me, I tell myself. Never.

H has ended up at the window. He has his back to me. Something in the street below seems to have caught his attention.

'I sent Jessie to Salisbury the other day,' he says. 'To look for some stuff she wants for that room upstairs.'

Salisbury. I briefly close my eyes. *Watch out for yourself.* Shit.

'And?' I say brightly. 'Any luck?'

'Yeah. She got it sorted quicker than she thought. Had a bit of time on her hands.' He turns round at last. 'So where do you think she went?'

'I've no idea. Should I?'

'Place called the White Hart. Place she dropped you the other week. And you know what? She popped in, had a word with the bloke behind the bar. Good girl, Jessie. Been on the team for a while.'

'What team?'

'My team. The top team. The A team. Is there any other?'

I ignore the dig. I know exactly what's coming next. Jessie warned me in the pub at the weekend. I should have sussed it. I should have thought it through. In a way she was trying to help me, trying to head off this scene. *Watch out for yourself.* I should have been bolder, cannier. We should have talked.

'Did she go for lunch?'

'Of course she fucking didn't.'

'Just a drink, then? One for the road? Something soft?'

H isn't amused. He leaves the window and steps towards me. He's very close now. I can smell mints on his breath.

'Your problem, gal, is that people remember you. Bloke behind the bar turns out to be a fan. That's nice unless you're dicking someone else around, especially if that someone happens to be me. Are we on the same page here or do I have to spell it out?'

I say nothing, telling myself there's too much at stake. H is back beside the window, checking the street again. Then he spots his son.

'M is back early,' he says. 'That makes you one lucky girl.'

'Is that a threat?'

'Not at all. It's over. Done. Sorted. We'll never mention it again. Deal?'

I don't know what to say. No script of mine ever ended this way. H is beyond clever. He holds all the aces, including my son. No wonder they went to the casino.

'You mean Malo is back early,' I say.

H is laughing. It's not a pleasant sound. At last he turns back from the window.

'No,' he says. 'I mean M.'

Twenty-One

Malo joins us in the apartment. He missed Clemenza by minutes at the courier agency, which didn't please him, but he's made contact by phone and he's fixed to see her this afternoon before he and his dad go back home.

This news floors me completely. Home. Flixcombe fucking Manor. Malo has spotted the artwork on the table and wants to talk me through it. I notice that H doesn't offer him any champagne but is keen to top up my own glass. Our troubles, he seems to be saying again, are over. We've had a bit of a ruck, he's said his piece, we know where we stand, and that's the end of it. This begs one or two of the larger questions but for the time being I have no choice but to listen to my son.

He's explaining why this element works and this one doesn't. He's pointing out why some images are a lot stronger than others. And he's agreeing with his father that the lads in Yeovil have got to do a whole lot better. This is a new Malo, a Malo I've never seen in action before. He must have picked up a lot of this stuff in barely days and yet his grasp of the language is genuinely impressive. But what's also obvious is that he shares H's steeliness in negotiations, in business. There's no question of compromise, of accepting second best. The

274

presentation has to be tone-perfect. It has to be exactly *right.*

I wander through to the kitchen to put the kettle on. The Krug has gone to my head and it's a moment or two before I realize that H has followed me.

'No hard feelings?'

I shoot him a look. At least he's not calling me 'gal'.

'This isn't the time or the place,' I tell him. 'And you know it.'

'For what?'

'For . . .' I shrug. I feel utterly hopeless. There's nothing I can say, nowhere I can go. H has ordered a punishment beating to mark Mitch's card, exactly the way that gangsters do, and Sayid may yet die. Most of this appears to be my fault and that makes me feel a whole lot worse. In the meantime, artfully, he seems to be holding my son hostage. Not only that but Malo is very visibly thrilled by the prospect. What the fuck have I done, I wonder. First Berndt, and now someone altogether more terrifying.

I pour Malo's tea and step past H to get back to the living room. When I suggest to my son that he might like to spend a night or two in his own bed he shakes his head. Wrong time. Too busy. Too fraught. He has to get the *Persephone* project up and running.

Barely weeks ago this would have been music to my ears. My son engaged. My son motivated. My son eyeballing a learning curve steep enough to delight any parent. Instead, though, I can think of nothing but getting him back. That and what's left of Sayid's face once H's thugs had filled their boots.

H and Malo leave within the hour. We have a civilized chat about where next for the *Persephone* project and I'm absolutely certain that Malo has no idea of what's happening between his mum and dad. Much of this, to be fair, is to H's credit. I've been around actors all my working life but I've never met anyone with H's gift for crashing the emotional gearbox without stripping a cog or two. Sunshine and rain, I think. The blackest of moods one moment, Mr Affable the next. Probably bipolar.

H and Malo gone, I collapse on the sofa. When I call Mitch, he's at the hospital. I ask about Sayid. 'How is he?'

'Still out.'

'Unconscious?'

'Yes.'

'So what are they telling you?'

'It's early days. He has hairline fractures to his skull and his brain has swollen but it's not bad enough to operate. I think that means they won't take the risk. Not at his best doesn't really cover it.'

This tiny spark of humour I take to be a good sign. When things get truly horrible, as I know only too well, there's nothing left but the darker jokes.

'What about his face?'

'They say they can rebuild most of it. Teeth. Nose. Cheekbones. Jaw. That's if he survives.'

'And the police?'

'Hang on . . .' I picture Mitch leaving Sayid's

276

bedside. The rest of our conversation needs to be away from listening ears. 'You're still there?'

'Yes.'

The police, Mitch says, have started behaving like human beings. The case has escalated up the food chain and is now in the hands of a Detective Inspector. Mercifully, she's a woman. She appears to be ready to accept that Mitch may not have kicked his partner half to death, which comes as a relief, and she's also pursuing a number of lines of enquiry with some vigour.

House-to-house calls, alas, have yielded no sighting of an unfamiliar vehicle going up the cul-de-sac and a proper CCTV trawl is pointless without clues on a likely target. Officers are in the process of contacting train drivers in case they might have noticed a parked car or van at the foot of the embankment and the enquiry team may commission posters for display on stations along the line asking the travelling public to come forward with any information. The forensic team are still trying to tease some kind of time-line out of the scene while analysis on Sayid's phone hasn't thrown up any usage since the call to my number.

'They think the phone got binned after that. They can track these things if they're switched on but there's been no signal.' He pauses. I can hear a lift door clanging shut in the background. 'You know something really sick?'

'Tell me.'

'I'm starting to wonder if Sayid would get even better service if he'd died. The DI's virtually admitted it. We're talking GBH, maybe even attempted murder, but these attacks are ten a penny in London. Homicide would have moved things along. That's her phrase, not mine.'

I tell him I'm confused. The work the DI's already commissioned seems pretty impressive to me.

'That's because she knows I'm a journo. The Met aren't shy when it comes to getting a good press.'

Mitch wants to know whether I could bear to pay Sayid a visit.

'What would be the point?'

'He liked you. He liked you a lot. Apparently a voice at the bedside can make all the difference.'

'You mean he might come round? Wake up?'

'It's possible. It's unlikely but he might. Would you mind?'

'Of course not.'

We fix a time. He says early evening would be good. Sayid is in Critical Care. The very phrase makes me shudder. We agree to meet downstairs in the main reception area at half past six. He'll walk me up. I ask whether he'll be with me at Sayid's bedside.

'No,' he says. 'One visitor at a time. House rules.'

I get down to Brixton with half an hour to spare. Hospitals seem to have become part of my life recently. First me. Then H. Now Sayid. I step in through the main entrance. The waiting area is crowded, visitors everywhere, but I find myself a chair by the water cooler. I'm deep in a book by Stefan Zweig just now and in less than a paragraph or two I'm back in the dying days of the Austro-Hungarian Empire.

'*Beware of Pity*?'

It's Mitch. I look up, startled. He knows the book well, loves it, along with most of everything else Zweig wrote.

'You know his story? What happened at the end?'

To my shame I don't. Mitch squats clumsily beside me. He seems calmer, even rested. Zweig and his wife fled the Nazis, he says, and made a new life in Brazil.

'They were Jews?'

'Of course.'

'Home safe, then.'

'Hardly. They had a suicide pact. Died of barbiturate poisoning. Took their own lives. 1942.'

He delivers this news without any explanation, any hint of why they'd chosen such a death after surviving the attentions of the Nazis, and I'm still trying to work it out minutes later when we emerge from the lift and make our way to the Critical Care unit.

Mitch pauses at the entrance and points inside.

'Second to last bed on the left,' he says. 'They get a bit edgy if you stay too long.'

I nod. Even from here the atmosphere in the unit is sepulchral, a heavy silence punctuated by the whirring of what seems like a million machines. I've no plans to stay a moment longer than I have to. A couple of minutes of one-way conversation, of trying to penetrate the darkness

279

of Sayid's swollen brain, and then an honourable retreat.

A nurse steps across from the nest of desks in the middle of the unit and asks my name. Mitch has already warned her to expect me and she leads me down the line of beds until we're looking at Sayid.

'How is he?' It's an instinctive question, almost a reflex.

'Not too bright, I'm afraid. He's ticking along. I don't think we're going to lose him. It's really a question of what's left if and when he comes round.'

What's left? I swallow hard. We're standing at the bedside. There's nothing of the handsome, playful Sayid I recognize. His face, the colour of ripe watermelon, has ballooned. Blood has crusted around his mouth and nose. God knows what they did to the rest of him but everything else is hidden beneath some kind of cage that has tented the single sheet. He's breathing with the aid of a tube inserted into his throat. Another feeds him nutrients. A catheter drips urine into a bottle beside the bed.

What's left? Yuck. This lovely man escaped the nightmare that was his home city and fled to what he judged to be the safety of what we still call civilization. Now this.

'Mitch wants me to have a word or two,' I tell the nurse. 'He thinks it might be useful.'

'By all means. Help yourself.'

I wait for her to go back to the nursing station before I draw up a chair and position myself beside the wreckage of Sayid's face. I've done countless acting exercises in my time, little games we play to explore this dramatic possibility or that, but I've never tried anything like this. Just what do I say? Just how might I trigger a memory or two?

'Aleppo,' I say very softly, then break the word down. *'Al–epp–oh.'*

Nothing. I try again. Same city. Same birthright. Same nest of memories. Intently, I watch what I can see of his face. Not a flicker. His eyelids are closed. His thin chest rises and falls beneath the fold of sheet.

'Syria.'

Nothing.

'Daeesh.'

Nothing.

'Islamic State.'

Nada.

Then I remember the Greek island where he and members of his extended family paused in their journey towards mainland Europe.

'Lesvos,' I say. Still nothing.

I'm concentrating very hard now, alert for the faintest sign of recognition and I haven't heard the nurse returning to Sayid's bedside.

'Try using your name,' she says. 'Pretend you're introducing yourself.'

Good advice.

'It's Enora,' I whisper. 'Enora Andressen. We met in the Italian restaurant. You had an orange juice. We went back to Mitch's place.' I pause. I'm wondering quite how far to take this. Then I have a brainwave.

'Enora. Enora Andressen,' I repeat. 'Cassini.'

The nurse is laughing softly. Like everyone else in the world she's seen the pictures on the TV. Saturn. Those amazing rings. The tiny twinkling dot that is planet Earth. And little Cassini.

'He made us a cake,' I tell her. 'It was beautiful. A work of art. Tasted even better.'

'Again.'

'What?'

'Again.' She's looking hard at Sayid.

'OK.' I lean forward, my mouth to Sayid's bloodied ear. 'Cassini,' I say. 'Cassini.'

'There.' It's the nurse.' She's definitely seen something. 'Say it again.'

'Cassini.'

'And again.'

'Cassini.'

Now I see it too. The merest flicker of an eyelid, something so brief, so fleeting, that you'd have to work in a place like this to recognize it.

'You think he heard that?'

'I do. Try again.'

I lift my head a moment and look down the ward. Mitch is still at the entrance, still watching our every move.

'Cassini.' I'm back with Sayid. For a second, maybe less, one eye flicks open. There's no sign of recognition, or understanding, and try as I might I can't trigger any sustained reaction. 'Cassini,' I whisper. Cassini, Cassini. But nothing happens.

It doesn't matter. The nurse is already on the phone to one of the doctors. Mr Abdulrahman is showing signs of consciousness.

I linger a moment at Sayid's bedside and then bend quickly and plant a kiss on what used to be his face. His flesh feels warmer than I'd expected. I only know one word of Arabic but it feels all too fitting.

'*Inshallah*,' I murmur. And leave.

Twenty-Two

Mitch and I find ourselves in a cafe-bar in the middle of Brixton, a five-minute walk from the hospital. It's small, and quietly intimate, and on a Tuesday evening we are, by far, the oldest people in the room. I'd shared the good news about Sayid the moment we left the ward but so far Mitch hasn't said much. He seems neither pleased nor relieved, a reaction I find, to say the least, troubling. Only when we've split the first carafe of red wine is he ready to talk.

'All this is my doing,' he says. 'My fault.'

'What is?'

'Sayid. What happened.'

I nod. This is hard to deny and I've no intention of letting him off the hook, not least because I'm equally to blame. No H, no snooping around Flixcombe Manor, no covert meetings in a Salisbury pub, and Sayid would still be pulling on his Nikes, still heading out into the half-darkness of Blackheath. Life is rarely fair. I've known that for a while. But why the wrath of H should descend on someone as blameless and lovely as Sayid is beyond me. Except that he matters a great deal to Mitch and that, in turn, has put this lover of his in the firing line.

I'm toying with my wine glass. Overpriced Rioja is doing absolutely nothing for me.

284

'H came round to my place this morning,' I tell Mitch. 'He's been in town since yesterday.'

'Surprise, surprise.'

'You think he did it?'

'Not personally, no. That's never been his style. He gets on the phone, calls in a favour or two. He'll have known my name from the Finisterra website. After that the script writes itself. All he needs is my address and someone keeping an eye on the house to join up all the dots.'

'Have you seen anyone?'

'No, but then I've been away a lot lately. And in any case I haven't been looking.'

'You never anticipated something like this?'

'No, not this extreme, not this clever. No.'

'*Clever?*'

'Getting to me through Sayid. People like Prentice know which buttons to press. That hurts. Believe me.'

This is a deeply strange thing to say, all the more bizarre because Mitch seems oblivious to its implications. Sayid, his lover, his best friend, has nearly died. Yet the real damage, Mitch is suggesting, lies closer to home.

'So was it worth it?'

'Of course not.'

'So will you stop now? Call a halt?'

'Stop what?'

'The book. Maybe another article. Bothering the world with all this Brexit shit. You told me recently the people in the shadows have the real power . . . and guess what?'

'I'm right.'

285

'Exactly. So might now be the time to admit it? To close the file? To move on?'

'Why on earth would I ever do that?' He looks genuinely shocked.

'Because it nearly got Sayid killed and even now he may end up a vegetable. Life support for the rest of his days? A bed in some godforsaken nursing home? Faces he'll never recognize at his bedside? Every meal spoon-fed? Is that really worth saving democracy or whatever else you've got planned?'

Mitch is staring at me. This is the last conversation he needs.

'It's what he would have wanted,' he says.

'How do you know?'

'Because we used to discuss everything together. I never came out of an interview or a session on the internet without sharing it with him. We were in lockstep. Total agreement.'

Mitch's use of the past tense is beginning to upset me. He clearly regards Sayid as dead already.

'What if he starts to get better? What if he needs lots of support, lots of looking after, lots of making things right again?'

'Then I'll be there for him.'

'But you don't think it's likely?'

'I don't know. I'm not a brain surgeon.'

'But do you really *want* him to get better?'

My question is beyond hurtful but I'm getting really angry now. So far there hasn't been the slightest hint that Sayid's recovery might be more important than the fucking cause. Mitch is giving obsession a bad name.

286

I press him again but he won't respond, won't answer my question. His glass is empty. He signals the woman behind the bar for another carafe. Then he's back with me.

'Finding Sayid on the embankment was the worst moment of my life,' he says slowly. 'You'd only understand that if you were me, if you had a relationship that close. The moment I saw him – saw him properly – I knew what I'd done. Putting him in harm's way. Making him a target like that. Do I regret it? Of course I do. Does it make me feel like shit inside? Yeah, just a bit. But is there any part of me that's tempted to chuck it all in? No. And you know why? Because those evil bastards will have won.' He pauses. Looks away. Shakes his head. Then he's back in my face. 'Edmund Burke? Ever heard of him?'

I shake my head. Never.

'*The only thing necessary for the triumph of evil is for good men to do nothing.* That's me, my creed. That's what I believe in. That's what made me phone you in the first place. You have to do something. Backing down isn't an option. And you know something else? If Sayid was here he'd be the first to agree.'

The woman behind the bar has arrived with a new carafe. Mitch spares her a glance and then pushes his chair back and gets to his feet.

'Second thoughts.' He shakes his head. 'I've had enough.'

The moment I get home I hit Google. The wealth of information on Edmund Burke doesn't help me at all. Rebellion in the American colonies.

The impeachment of Warren Hastings. The iniquities of the French Revolution. The sanctity of property rights. But there, towards the end, is Mitch's quote again. *The only thing necessary for the triumph of evil is for good men to do nothing.*

This is heavy stuff. I've had a glimpse or two of what might be H's default setting, and it chilled me to the bone, but evil is a very big word and has some uncomfortable implications. If H belongs in this box, does that make Malo – H's precious M – the spawn of evil? And if it does, what should I be doing about it?

The short answer is that I've no idea. I toy with phoning H, with asking for a little honesty. *Did you really order the attack on Sayid? Were you there when it happened? Are you aware of the state of the man as we speak? And if so do you really think that Mitch's wretched article could ever justify that kind of savagery?*

A conversation like this is probably overdue, but however hard I try I can't for a moment imagine H bothering me with the truth. He's already made it clear that this is strictly business. It might, regrettably, have been over the top but it should never intrude into what he's now delighted to call family life. That's me. And Malo. And his gangster dad.

Around eight, I'm starting to drive myself crazy. I seem to be bound hand and foot in a situation way beyond my control. I feel totally helpless. Compared to this, another brain tumour might come as a merciful relief. I chase the questions around and around – about Mitch, about Sayid, about H, about M – until there's nowhere left to go. I need a wiser soul to tell me what to do.

Evelyn is watching television when I tap at her door. I apologize for the intrusion. Some other time, I say. Maybe tomorrow.

She takes one look at my face, reaches for the remote, and invites me in. The television goes off. I take a seat and say yes to a glass of Sauvignon blanc. Evelyn offers a cautious toast to good times, whatever that might mean, and asks me what's wrong. I tell her everything. If she's shocked it doesn't show. Just getting the right facts in the right order makes me feel slightly better. I'm probably kidding myself but I sense the return of some kind of control.

Evelyn wants to know how she can help. It's a reasonable question.

'Advice, maybe?' I suggest.

She nods. I have options, she says. I can do my best to support Mitch. I can share visits to the hospital, try and relieve the pressure he must be under. At the same time, I can have it out with H, demand an explanation for the attack on Sayid.

I tell her I know this won't work. But even if it did, and he admitted it, then what?

'You go to the police.'

'And Malo?'

'Malo will do whatever Malo does. If his dad gets arrested I'm assuming the lad will come back here.'

'I doubt that. The two of them are really close. Malo's the age when you're not thinking straight.

It won't matter what his dad's done, Malo will stick by him.'

'Sweet.'

'But that's not the end of it. Malo will know why his dad's been arrested because his dad will tell him. I can hear it now. *That mum of yours grassed me up.* That will matter to Malo. I'll be lucky to see him again.'

Evelyn nods, sips her wine. I may have a point, she seems to think. In this sorry mess, motherhood trumps everything.

She asks again about Sayid. Exactly how bad is he?

I've already described the injuries. True, there's been just a flicker of consciousness, a brief flaring of the candle that was once Sayid. But the prognosis would still seem to be grim.

'You think he might die?'

'Yes.'

She nods again, glances at my glass, reaches for the bottle.

'So you think H must have had something to do with it and, on the evidence, you might be right. I'm assuming he has ways and means of ordering the beating. He doesn't have to do it himself. Let's imagine these people had killed Sayid in the first place. That's murder. What would you have done then?'

I'm staring at her. Oddly enough, in the chaos of the last couple of days, this is one scene I haven't played in my head. Sayid lying dead on the railway embankment. What then?

'The police,' I say slowly. 'In the end they'd

probably come for me anyway so I wouldn't have an option.'

Evelyn is pouring more wine. I sense this part of the conversation has run its course. Then comes another toast.

'Here's to better times,' she says. 'For now I suggest you wait and see.'

Good advice. Sayid, mercifully, doesn't die. On the contrary, he begins to recover. I go to the hospital daily, always contacting Mitch to make sure our visits don't coincide. Mitch is pleasant enough on the phone, and readily accedes to the arrangement, but there's an unspoken acceptance on both our parts that what's happened to Sayid has come between us.

Try as I might, I can't forgive Mitch for not putting all his baggage aside. Crusaders, I want to tell him, belong on a horse. They wear fancy armour and head for Jerusalem and look no further than the tips of their bloody lances. Human beings, on the other hand, put friends and lovers first. This is a conversation we don't have, not yet, and every time I arrive at the hospital, I'm truly glad that Mitch won't be there.

Sayid leaves Critical Care after the third day. His injuries have turned out to be less serious than doctors at first feared. He's fully conscious now, and his various tubes have been withdrawn. His jaw is wired up, and he'll need the attentions of a dental surgeon before too long, but the hideous swelling that deformed his lovely face is fast subsiding. We're able to communicate by a series of grunts and gargles, nods and shakes of his head, and tiny squeezes of my hand. To my delight there seems to be no evidence of permanent brain damage and as the days pass, the light returns to his eyes. When his consultant judges that the time is right, two detectives spend an hour at his bedside but they leave the hospital no wiser about the thugs who put him there. Of the beating that left him on the embankment, he has no recollection.

Malo, meanwhile, appears to be going from strength to strength. He phones me on a near-daily basis, largely to keep me abreast of the latest developments in the *Persephone* project. His father is giving him a great deal of latitude, which gladdens me no end, and I start to antici-pate his calls with something I can only describe as glee. He reminds me of a faithful spaniel, in from the weather, determined to share the spoils of the hunt. As our conversations get longer and longer, I can picture him down in Dorset, his eyes bright, his tail wagging, his coat ever more lustrous as the days spool by.

To begin with I suspected H's hand in all this. After what happened to Sayid he wants to make amends, to put the darkness back in its box, to glue our little family together again. No bad thing, I tell myself. Especially if it's turning my wayward son into someone I barely recognize. Those long-ago days of slagging off his teachers, of not bothering with his homework, of drifting round bits of West London instead of attending school, have gone. This is emphatically a new Malo.

On the day when Sayid takes his first hesitant

steps down the ward to the lavatories at the end, I return home to find a message on the answerphone. Malo sounds breathless, excited.

'Cracked the Pompey end, Mum,' he reports. 'Give me a ring.'

Cracked the Pompey end? I barely have time to get my coat off before the phone rings. It's Malo. He's given up waiting for me to call.

'Where have you been all day?' he says.

'Out.'

'But you're always out.'

'I know. It's an actress thing. Never turn a job down.'

'Anything interesting?'

I invent a small lie about another BBC job. Malo will never listen to radio drama so I don't think I'll be caught out.

'Is there a date on this? I need to be sure you're still on for the cruise.'

'Of course I'm on for the cruise. It's in the diary. Rosa knows the dates are sacrosanct. Not only that but I'm looking forward to it.'

This is another lie. I'm not one of the world's natural sailors and the more I find out about the kind of weather we can expect in mid-November in the English Channel, the more queasy I feel. Googling 'Brixham trawlers' was another mistake. *Persephone* might have survived intact for over a century but these fishing boats were obviously built for men with a high tolerance for primitive living conditions, constant soakings, and the lurking possibility of the rogue wave that might end it all. Sooner rather than later we're going to have a serious conversation about safety drills and on-board comforts, but in the meantime Malo wants to tell me about Southwick House.

'Southwick what?'

'It's where they planned for D-Day. It's not in Portsmouth, not in the city. You drive north. It's about twenty minutes. General Eisenhower was there. It's private now. It's some kind of college. But like I told you, I've cracked it.'

It turns out Malo has been worried about value for money. Five thousand pounds a berth, he says, is a lot, even though most of it is going to charity. He wants people to think they've had a proper time of it and so he's been thinking of ways to make more of the experience. He's started using phrases like 'the offer', and 'value-added'. This amuses me at first but I quickly realize he means it. Not only that, but he's very definitely got a point. H, in his blunt way, probably thinks it's enough to bang six strangers up in a quaint little bit of seafaring history and let them get on with it. Malo, on the other hand, is determined to do a whole lot better than that.

H has always referred to punters. Malo now calls them guests. They'll all meet, he says, in a place called the Camber Dock in Old Portsmouth. This will be the day before departure for Normandy. There's a D-Day museum on Southsea seafront and he's fixed a late-morning visit once everyone has got to know each other. After lunch at a seafront hotel a minibus will take the guests up to Southwick House on the mainland.

'For what?'

'I'm working on a presentation. There's a guy

I've found at the university. He's a historian. He's really good. He knows all about D-Day, especially what happened at Southwick House. They've got a special room there. It was all about the weather. D-Day was supposed to be the fifth of June. They had to hang on for a day because it would have been so rough. Did you know that?'

I didn't. But what's far more interesting for little me is where all these ideas came from. Who dreamed up the visit to the museum? Who got the permission to use the special room at Southwick House? And who knocked on the university's door and recruited this star academic? The answer, in every case, is Malo. When I tell him how impressed I am he just laughs.

'It's easy,' he says. 'Dad says you just turn up and be nice to people. Having Front Line on board is good. People love all that. And me being so young is a massive help as well. It's like as soon as they see you, they want to make it happen.'

'And your guests? Is anyone confirmed yet?'

'Three, so far. There's a couple from London, Alex and Cassie. He's just retired. Dad said he was some kind of top civil servant. His wife is really nice. I've talked to her on the phone and guess what? She's a really big fan.'

'Of what?'

'You. That's why they're coming. It's her birthday. Like a present thing.'

'So what is she expecting? Apart from yours truly?'

'That's something else Dad says we need to

talk about. There's a brand-new place in the Camber Dock, a huge building, really cool. I had a tour with Dad the other day. They built it for the America's Cup, the sailing thing, and I've managed to blag a little presentation suite they've got. So the night before we leave we have drinks and eats and stuff in a pub down there and then watch one of your movies. Just to get in the mood. We thought you might have an idea which one. Dad's favourite is *The Hour of Our Passing.*'

This doesn't surprise me. *The Hour of Our Passing* is a period piece set in Nantes during the wartime occupation. A couple of Resistance fighters gun down the top Nazi in the city. Berlin demands retribution and a hundred hostages are taken on pain of death unless the killers are delivered to justice. I play a Resistance heroine trying to keep the peace between the headbangers – all communists – and the gentler souls. There's an important love interest and the script called for a scene towards the end when I and the male lead are together for the last time. It was my first taste of sustained on-screen nudity and according to Malo it made a big impact on his dad. Would I mind if he got hold of a copy to show the guests on the eve of departure?

A moment's thought prompts a yes on my part. I made the movie nearly fifteen years ago and I remember parking Malo with my mum in Brittany while I was doing the location shoots down in Nantes. I had a decent body in those days, firm in all the right places, and I'm genuinely curious to see how I made out in the scene. My recent tussle with the Grim Reaper has stirred many memories and I'm more than happy to make room for one more.

'And the other guest?'

'Sadie Devine. She's a journalist on the *Daily Telegraph*. She wants to write a piece about what people will do for Front Line and Dad thinks that's cool. She kicked up about the money but Dad wouldn't budge. He's happy to have her along but only if she pays up. Dad says the *Telegraph* is rolling in it. No freebies.'

I'm smiling. Sometimes my son can be so transparent, so guileless. Just now I can hear H in every phrase.

'Three down,' I say. 'Three to go.'

'No problem. Easy. We're spoiled for choice.' He says the first mailing produced over a hundred expressions of interest, of which he reckoned at least half were ready with a deposit.

'So what do you do? Audition? Score them out of ten?'

'Sort of. Dad and I met this Sadie woman when we were up in London. Dad has met the MoD man, too. He thinks it's all going to be down to the chemistry on board. All it takes is one bad apple, he says. Do you think he's right?'

I do, but this emphasis on careful vetting comes as another surprise. H's interest in inter-personal chemistry normally boils down to people doing what they're told. I saw him in action over the party weekend down at Flixcombe. This is not a man well-versed in the nuances of human behaviour. What H says, goes. End of.

'So your dad's happy with the way things are coming together?'

'Yeah, I think so.'

'And you're getting on OK?'

'Massively. We've put in for my driving test. If I pass, and this whole thing goes OK, he'll get me a car.'

'That's good to know,' I say lightly. 'You can be my chauffeur, drive me around.'

Malo laughs but says nothing. Then he mentions another trip he's planning to London.

'When's this?'

'Next week. There's a guy Dad wants me to go and see. He's an Indian businessmen. You know the *Hot* chain? That's him.'

I nod. *Hot* is a mega-successful bid to scoop up the younger generation and give them a life-long passion for Kashmiri cooking. *Hot* as in bird's-eye chillies. *Hot* as in eye-watering interior decor schemes, designer Mumbai lagers, and a soaring share price. The week before my tumour was diagnosed, Rosa took me to the branch in Covent Garden. *Pas mal.*

I wonder aloud whether Malo might find time in his busy schedule for a coffee and a proper chat.

'Yeah, Mum, and that's the point. Dad's bunged me a wad of money. He wants me to take you somewhere nice. This Indian guy has an office off the Tottenham Court Road.' He gives me an address and hangs on while I find something to write with. Then I'm back on the phone.

'Half twelve OK? Next Friday?' he says. And then he's gone.

Twenty-Three

Over the days to come I spend most of the morning at the hospital. Sayid has an aversion to television. He doesn't much like what's on screen and despite my offer to pay the exorbitant fees to give him access to any channel he fancies, he much prefers to read a book. The physical act of reading, he says, gives him headaches just now. This appears to be a consequence of what he's been through but his consultant says the headaches will resolve themselves as the brain settles down.

This is good news but has still left Sayid without a book. I offer to sort out some audio recordings but he shakes his head. What he really wants is for me to read to him. Might I do that? This is clever on his part because a longish book will bring me back to his bedside again and again, but by now I know I'm as dependent on our time together as he is and so I say yes. Watching his face recover day after day does wonderful things to my self-esteem. It was me, after all, who helped get him into this mess and the knowledge that I might be playing some small part in getting him better is a real tonic.

I've left the choice of book to Sayid. He settles on Stefan Zweig's *Beware of Pity*, partly because I've been raving about it, and partly because he likes the title. He's been through a great deal in his life, especially over the past few years, and he's had to learn the difference between practical charity – money, visas, clean water – and the hand-wringing ministrations of what Berndt once called the grief-porn lobby. The latter, according to Sayid, want to share your misery, to feel your pain, but not too much, and certainly not too often.

And so I've started the book all over again, an interesting exercise in its own right because knowing it well already has given me an insight into the more important characters, something I can carry into the way I read it aloud. The story itself is very simple. A young soldier in the Austro-Hungarian army, just months before the outbreak of the First World War, finds himself posted to a small provincial town. There he finds himself invited to the local castle for dinner. Afterwards there is to be dancing. The owner has two daughters. The voluptuous Ilona and her crippled sister, Edith. A little tipsy, and ignoring all the clues, our hero asks Edith whether she would care for a dance, an invitation which sparks a reaction of some violence. In one sense, the entire book is pre-figured in this single incident. The soldier blames himself for the crassness of his mistake and resolves to do whatever he can to make amends. This commitment, over the hundreds of pages to come, proves catastrophic on a number of levels. Hence the title.

This narrative device, of course, has parallels to my own presence at Sayid's bedside, though mercifully only I'm aware of it, and as the days go by, and the comforting beat of Zweig's prose takes us deeper into the soldier's quandary, a smallish knot of other patients enquire whether they, too, might draw up a chair and listen.

By now, Sayid is occupying a bed in a general ward and for his sake I'm delighted that Stefan Zweig has brought him new friends. One of them, slowly recovering from complications after an operation on her lower gut, takes a shine to Sayid. Formerly, in another of life's little ironies, she's been dead set against anyone foreign but the more glimpses she gets of Sayid's inner grace, the more she begins to change her views on immigration.

'If we had that referendum again,' she confides to me one afternoon, 'I'd be a bleeding Remainer.'

I carry this thought home and wonder about sharing it with Mitch. I know he's been going to the hospital most evenings because one of the nurses has told me so, but when I try and imagine the reality of even a phone conversation I know it wouldn't be fun for either of us. It's not that I dislike the man. On the contrary, I have some very fond memories of how generous and how kind he was. It's just that his single-mindedness, once glimpsed, has left a very deep impression. Beware of Causes, I tell myself. No matter how worthy.

Friday arrives. I limit myself to ten pages at Sayid's bedside and take a bus to Trafalgar Square. The Indian entrepreneur, whose name is Amit Iyengar, has a walk-up suite of offices in a narrow street off the Tottenham Court Road. There's no plaque on the door downstairs, no sign of the distinctive *Hot* logo, just an entry phone that connects to a woman with a heavy cold.

I give my name and wait for her to open the door. In keeping with his restaurants I was rather expecting something a little edgier from Mr Iyengar, certainly a lot grander, and while I wait for my son in the dingy cubbyhole that serves as a reception area I wonder why he hides himself away like this.

Malo, as ever, has the answer. This is a guy, he tells me over lunch, whose working day rarely starts without a death threat. For whatever reason, people out there hate success, especially when it comes in the shape of a great deal of money, and most especially if the lucky recipient happens to be foreign. 'Out there' is an interesting phrase, one I've not heard Malo use before, and I wonder if he's acquiring the same sense of embattlement I sometimes associate with his father. Either way, it certainly explains Mr Iyengar's interest in keeping his head down.

'So have you signed him up?'

'Big time. He thinks it's a great idea.' Malo pats the front of his leather jacket. 'He wrote us a cheque on the spot. When I looked at it properly I told him he'd got it wrong. It's five thousand, not ten, but he said it didn't matter, we could keep the change. He also offered me a job if I ever fancied it.'

'Deliveries? Like Clemenza?'

'Business development. He wants to open big in France.'

'But the French hate spicy food.'

'That's what I told him. When he realized I

could speak the language he said I was wasting my time doing all this charity crap. If I was smart I'd work for him.'

'And?'

'I took the cheque and said thank you.'

I'm looking hard at the leather jacket. It's obviously brand new because I can tell from the smell but it also has that deceptive slightly rumpled pre-aged quality that comes with top-end leather. Hundreds of pounds, I think. Another little present from his doting father. Along with the off-white Nikes and the rather nice CR7 skinny jeans. Is this gangster chic? Or a look that Malo has conjured for himself?

I ask him about the rest of the guests. He tells me, with a hint of pride, that every berth is now taken and paid for. Alex and Cassie, the recently retired couple from London, and Sadie, the journalist, I already know about. Next to make the cut is Ruth, a young lawyer with the Crown Prosecution Service. She works down in Bristol and she wants to make the trip in homage to her grandfather who died on one of the invasion beaches back in 1944.

'She wants to visit his grave, too, so that's something else we have to fit in.'

'You know where it is?'

'She does. She's been there before. She gave me the details.'

'Is she nice?'

'She's awesome. Quite pretty. But you wouldn't fuck with her. She even managed to keep Dad quiet. Impressive or what?'

'You both went to see her?'

'Yeah. That was Dad's idea. Two pairs of eyes. Two minds.'

'So why isn't he here today? Scoping out your new Indian friend?'

'I think they've talked on the phone a lot. Dad sussed he might be up for paying over the odds. I'm just here to collect the cheque.'

We're in The Ivy, one of my favourite restaurants, and I'm picking at my champagne and wild mushroom risotto. Malo, in keeping with his new jacket, is wolfing his Ivy hamburger. I've been keeping score as far as the passenger list is concerned and we're still short of a body.

'Rhys,' Malo says. 'He's Welsh and he's been around a bit. This time last year he was working on a shrimp boat in the Gulf of Mexico. He knows all the really cool places to go in New Orleans. Top bloke. Dad loves him.'

'I can imagine.'

'Seriously. We met him in this pub in Plymouth. He told us to come down by train and I never realized why until they started drinking. I had trouble getting Dad into the taxi afterwards. He'd have stayed there all night.'

I nod, watching Malo tidy the remains of his *pommes allumettes* and dill relish into a neat pile at the side of his plate. Not just a tour organizer. Not just a well-turned-out youth who knows how to sweet-talk the big money. Not just an instant expert on D-Day and the ins and outs of Brixham trawlers. But a mate and carer when his Dad hits the rocks.

'Impressive,' I say quietly.

By now we've finished our main course. Malo insists we call for the dessert menu.

'Dad says to fill your boots,' he says. 'And he's paying.'

I order a salted caramel fondant but only manage half of it while Malo tucks into Bramley apple crumble pie. There's an actress at a nearby table I haven't seen since we were both in a Tennessee Williams in Newcastle and on the way out I pause by her table and have a brief chat. She's much taken by Malo, whom I introduce as my toy boy. She looks him up and down with frank approval and hopes he knows how to make an older woman very happy. All three of us know it's a joke, and even Malo laughs.

We say goodbye on the street outside. This is the first time for a while that I've had my son to myself and I've loved every moment. Seeing him like this from time to time, dipping into his busy, busy life, I'm aware of him maturing in front of my eyes.

He gives me a hug and turns to leave but then stops. His hand goes to his jacket pocket.

'I nearly forgot. You have to fill this in, especially the medical bits. It's for the insurance.'

He gives me a form and I skim-read it quickly. All the usual questions – name, gender, DoB, contact details, then some more pointed stuff. *Do I know how to swim? Am I currently under medical supervision? Is there any other health reason why I shouldn't embark on the voyage?*

'You had this drawn up specially?'

'Yeah. Dad said not to take the medical bits

too seriously. We don't want you to be turned down for the insurance.'

'You're asking me to lie?'

'Not me. Dad.'

He gives me a peck on the cheek and leaves me with the form. I watch him loping away down Litchfield Street, a moment – on my part – of real pride. When H took me to the pub that first time, and talked of the need to enrol our son in some project or other, I never dreamed it would be something as complex and challenging as this. At Malo's age I would have had neither the raw nerve nor confidence to put myself in front of all these people, to confect knowledge I probably didn't have, to make sophisticated judgements about their personalities, about their prepared-ness to take a risk or two, about how well they'd adapt to each other in what might turn out to be testing conditions.

Then, as he disappears round the corner at the end of the street, I tell myself I'm wrong. At seventeen I'd begun to think seriously about being an actress, a performer, downstage in front of hundreds of people, or – even more daunting – in front of a camera and a director and a tech-nical crew. That took nerve, too. Plus the guile to play a part, to inhabit someone else's skin, someone else's persona, and all in the cause of making people laugh or cry or maybe just think a little bit harder.

That, in a sense, is what my boy is doing. The bravura, the *chutzpah*, the sheer cheek, he gets from H. But some of the rest surely comes from me. This is a thought I can live with for a while, a conclusion that makes me very, very happy, and as I head for the bus stop, still clutching the insurance form, it takes me a moment or two to realize that I haven't once thought about Sayid, or Mitch, or fucking Brexit for at least two hours.

Happy days, as H would say. From the top floor of the 94 bus, I send him a text. I thank him for The Ivy, trail five kisses across the screen, and then add a postscript. *We should both be very proud of Malo*, I text. *Just look what we've done.*

Twenty-Four

Sayid is discharged from hospital two days before we're due to set sail. *Beware of Pity* is a long book – 454 pages – and once we know when Sayid is to go home I speed up the readings a little and spend longer at his bedside. We get to the final page on the eve of his departure and a relative of one of the group of fellow listeners turns up with a home-baked cake, suitably iced and decorated, to mark the occasion. A single toy soldier guards the lone candle. Sweet gesture.

By now, Sayid is on his feet, fully mobile. He won't be running for a while but he's learned to put a sentence together through his broken teeth and still-wired jaw. Mitch, he says, will be coming in the morning to take him back to Hither Green. I hold him for a long moment. We've shared a lot these past few weeks and I know he's grateful for me coming to the hospital so often, but as ever he's thinking not of himself but of me.

'Have fun on that boat of yours,' he says.

I've told him all about the voyage, and our complement of paying guests, and I've shared my misgivings about crossing the Channel. I've had a peek at the Met Office advance forecast for the next few days and although I'm no expert it doesn't look great. The surface pressure charts show a whorl of isobars in mid-Atlantic, a sign of strong winds, maybe even gale force. This depression – an interesting word – is coming our way and there appears to be another one brewing up behind it. On the phone, Malo has been dismissive when I played the feeble mum. Boats like *Persephone*, he told me, can live with any kind of weather. This may be true, and I didn't say anything on the phone, but it isn't *Persephone* I'm worried about.

Sayid accompanies me to the door at the end of the ward. He wishes me God speed and tells me to take care. Then he touches his own head.

'You're OK in there?'

'I'm fine.'

'And in here?' His hand slips down to his chest, covering his heart.

'In there is fine, too.'

I mean it. After the *Guardian* shitstorm and everything that followed, my daily visits to Sayid's bedside have achieved what a true penance should. I feel rested, calmer. I feel comfortable with myself. On an especially good day I can even see myself crossing the Channel without spending most of the voyage throwing up.

I leave the hospital and take the bus home. After consulting with *Persephone*'s skipper, Malo has circulated an information pack for all our guests plus myself and H. Among the items I need to take on board are a heavy-duty wind-and-waterproof jacket, trousers made of the same Gore-Tex, plenty of insulating layers for underneath, slip-proof foot-wear, and heavy woollen socks. A lifejacket will be waiting for me in my cabin.

We'll all be meeting on the morning of 9 November at the Camber Dock. Onboard safety and house-keeping brief. Pre-lunch drinks in the saloon with a lightish meal to follow. Visits to the D-Day museum and Southwick House in the afternoon followed by dinner in a local pub and a very special screening of *The Hour of Our Passing. Moi* to introduce the movie.

Persephone, Malo has written, loves to put herself in the hands of first-time matelots. She can be a challenge to sail – lots of sweat and effort – and once we've left Portsmouth on the following day there'll be plenty of opportunities to teach us novices exactly what to do. The skipper plans to slip from the Camber Dock in the late morning to make the most of a hefty spring ebb tide. Nautical twilight is expected around 17.01. Dawn, at 08.02 French time, should find us within thirty miles of landfall. With a fair wind and a measure of luck we should be berthing in Ouistreham in time for lunch. *Bon appetit!*

The information pack goes on to detail the schedule once we've arrived in France. Courtesy meetings with various civic dignitaries. *Un vin d'honneur* with members of the Caen/Portsmouth Twinning Association. A promising succession of meals. Our second day, 11 November, is to feature a wreath-laying on a beachside memorial at Arromanches, followed by a visit to a war graves cemetery for the benefit of Ruth. In the evening we shall be dining in a top local restaurant, a must for seafood buffs. At first light on the twelfth, weather permitting, we'll be slipping our moorings in Ouistreham and putting to sea for the return leg to Portsmouth. Home safe in the Camber Dock in time for breakfast the next day.

This was a lot to digest in one sitting and I remember being impressed yet again by Malo's attention to detail. The sheer precision of the schedule. His apparent mastery of time differences and tide tables. Phrases like *spring ebb* and *nautical twilight.* Just where did all this stuff come from? And how come my clever, clever son is such a quick study?

Back in Holland Park I complete my packing and re-check the train times for tomorrow. An early departure from Waterloo should put me beside Portsmouth Harbour by nine o'clock. Plenty of time to make my way to *Persephone*, meet my new shipmates, and join the trip to the D-Day museum and Southwick House. I book an Uber for 5.45 next morning and retire early. Malo texts me just after nine. He's laid hands on some new seasickness pills the skipper swears by. *Dors bien. A demain.*

Sleep well. See you tomorrow. His message makes me smile. My precious boy thinks of everything.

Next morning another text awaits me. It's Sayid this time, wishing me *bon voyage.* I take this as the best of omens and struggle downstairs in the darkness to throw my bags in the back of the waiting Uber. By half past nine, in a thin drizzle, I'm paying off another taxi driver down in Portsmouth on the very edge of the Camber

Dock. *Persephone* rides easily below me, nudging the harbour wall. I appear to be the first to arrive.

I'm struck at once by *Persephone*'s good looks. Sturdy? Yes. Workmanlike? Definitely. But graceful, too, a lyrical poem in carefully varnished timber. Gifted shipwrights, I tell myself, must have evolved the shape of boats like these. Chosen the wood, laid down the keel, made her ready for the ocean and the decades of heavy-duty fishing that will follow. Malo has already blitzed me with dozens of sepia shots of trawlers like *Persephone* in their prime, wallowing down-Channel, hauling huge nets, the trapped fish attracting clouds of quarrelsome seagulls. In those days, he told me, the three-man crew had nothing but sails to see them through. No engine. No navigation aids. Just raw muscle and the kind of inbred knowledge that passes from generation to generation. These days, looking at the array of aerials on top of the mast, I suspect it must be a whole lot easier and for that I'm duly grateful.

I'm still debating how to get out of the rain when a slight, diminutive figure appears below. It turns out to be the skipper. Her name is Suranne. She's barefoot on the wetness of the deck. She's wearing patched jeans and puffer gilet over a black T-shirt. She has an elfin haircut, a strong jaw line, and is sucking on a thin roll-up. I throw her my bags and then, under her direction, clamber down the iron ladder.

'Welcome.' She's laughing. 'Haven't I seen your face before?'

She takes me through the doghouse where she

says all the important stuff happens and then down another set of steps to the saloon. The key word here is cosy. There's a tiny galley and a biggish dining table lapped by leather-covered banquettes. There are two cabins at the back of the boat, another midships, and four berths in the bow. The crew, all four of them, live somewhere else.

The next hour or so, as crew and guests gather, is a blizzard of names I dimly recognize from conversations with Malo. Malo himself is in the very middle of it all, working the crowd, pressing the flesh, carefully deferring to the skipper. At first glance, Suranne might be in her late twenties. However, given the responsibility she carries, she must be a good deal older. She's direct, and likes to share a joke or two, but she's learned the knack of establishing the pecking order without a hint of pulling rank. Clever. And impressive.

Persephone's first mate is taller, and fuller, also a woman. Fresh-faced and super confident, Georgie divides us into smaller groups and walks us through a list of dos and don'ts. The key location are the two loos. She calls them heads. There's a pump arrangement for disposing of the effluent and she squats on the toilet seat in this sentry box of a lavatory and demonstrates exactly what we're expected to do. Numbers are evidently the key to a happy boat. Twenty pumps to fill the bowl. The flick of a switch. Twenty more to empty it. Alex, the ex-civil servant, happens to be in my group. Like all of us, this is his first brush with onboard authority.

'Not a motion more, not a motion less,' he murmurs.

I think it's funny. I'm not sure Georgie even heard the comment but one thing is already uncomfortably clear. In any kind of weather, or 'blow' as Georgie calls it, spaces like these will quickly become somewhere you'd probably best avoid.

By midday, after a full safety brief up on deck, we return to the saloon. The cook, a cheerful teenager called Esther, is making what she calls a winter soup. The fourth member of the crew is Jack. He's a strapping gap-year youth with hands the size of plates and a winning grin, and his pre-lunch job is to make sure we all have drinks. The soup is delicious and the rolls that come with it are hot from the oven.

By now, we're starting to get to know each other. Sadie the *Telegraph* scribe has yet to turn up while Alex and Cassie tend to hang back a little. Ruth, petite, pretty, has an icy smile and clearly dislikes direct questions. Whether this comes with being a CPS lawyer, I've no idea, but I make a mental note to avoid anything too playful or light-hearted. Amit Iyengar, the man the media have dubbed Mr Hot, does his best to hog every conversation and will clearly become a pain. Meanwhile Rhys, the Welsh roustabout, earns my undying affection for having exactly the same pre-voyage reservations as me.

We find ourselves side by side at the table, dunking rolls in the soup. He's taking a long look round, sizing up this cluttered space we're about to call home. Then he beckons me closer.

'Not a lot of room to throw up,' he says in his Welsh lilt. 'Best to kip on deck.'

We spend the afternoon being grown-ups at the seafront museum and later at Southwick House. We learn about the five invasion beaches and everything else that followed on behind. Floating harbours. Oil pipelines. And a huge July storm that did almost as much damage as the marauding Germans. The latter, at Southwick House, offers our university friend a chance to analyse the 1944 weather in detail. His PowerPoint presentation features surface pressure charts that shaped the forecast on 5 June. To me it could be a duplicate for what we might expect tomorrow. Except that tomorrow is November. And then was sunny June.

By now, Rhys and I are bosom buddies. He, too, has seen the latest pressure charts. Back in the day, Eisenhower called a twenty-four-hour delay. Why can't we do something similar?

'Fuck knows.' He looks resigned. 'That was a war. This is for charity. You tell me the difference.'

That evening we all eat fish and chips together at a harbourside pub. Sadie, the *Telegraph* scribe, has at last arrived and it's obvious at once that Amit is besotted. He games the seating arrangements so they're sitting side by side. Judging by their conversation, they're old mates. When it comes to any excuse – the ketchup, the salt, the vinegar – he can't keep his hands off her.

Later, when I say a word or two ahead of the screening of H's favourite movie, I'm aware of

Amit trying to canoodle in the half-darkness and I'm wondering when Sadie's going to do something violent. Then the lights go down and the movie begins and I watch H bend quickly and have a word in his ear. It takes less time than the brief exchange of dialogue in the opening scene, and after that Amit doesn't lift a finger.

That night I share a cabin with Sadie. She must be ten years older than me but she's managed to preserve her looks. I'm wondering how much of that is down to money and careful exposure to cosmetic surgery when she confesses that this assignment might be her last chance to live the dream.

'Dream?'

'Telly. Channel Five are looking for a presenter. It's a travel show. Your son's offered to shoot a trial piece to camera. Lovely boy that he is.'

A trial piece to camera? My son? I shake my head in wonderment. To my knowledge Malo has never done anything like this in his life but I'm sure that wouldn't stop him for a moment.

Later, once we've put the lights out, I mention Amit. She's obviously met him before. Nice guy.

'Wrong.' I hear her rolling over in the bunk below. 'Amit is an arsehole.'

We set sail next day earlier than planned. Our skipper has spotted what she calls a window in the onrushing weather and wants to be in Ouistreham at first light tomorrow. Accordingly we sail at high water, missing the ebb tide that Malo has promised. We slip out through the harbour narrows with the thump-thump of the engine beneath our feet. A gauzy sun is visible through the blanket of high cloud and the sea is the colour of pewter. There's a whisper of wind coming up the Solent from the west but Suranne decides to wait until we're off the Isle of Wight before hoisting the sails.

I sense we're all aware that this will be our first real test. Suranne eases the engine into neutral and we all gather beside the main mast for instructions. This is a totally new world, the realm of jackstays and Samson posts, of lizards and cleats, of scuppers and deadeyes and something – improbably – called 'baggywrinkles'. I've come across some challenging scripts in my life but this is the most bizarre.

We split into two-man teams. Georgie shows us how to hoist the sail up the mast by hauling on the main halyard, a thickish rope, one big tug at a time. This isn't as simple as it looks. Most of us are game enough but it's heavy work. Even H tries to lend a hand but his shoulder is still far from perfect and it's Malo who gently tells him to stand aside. I, thank God, am teamed with Rhys. He's done all this before, understands exactly where to put his weight, and our sail races up the mast.

By mid-afternoon, with the light beginning to die, we've cleared the Isle of Wight. There's a biggish swell from the south-west and *Persephone* wallows along at a stately five knots. It's cold in the freshening wind but most of us have preferred to stay on deck rather than go below. We huddle in little groups, white-faced, slowly getting to know each other.

I spend a couple of hours with Alex and Cassie, gladly sharing some of my experiences on various movies. Cassie is very astute when it comes to particular films of mine. Her judgements are more than sound and she's keen to understand what led to this interpretation or that. Like H she rates *The Hour of Our Passing* very highly, though probably for different reasons, and she's especially keen to know whether I had any input into the original script. When I say no she seems disappointed but all three of us agree to meet for drinks before we eat.

Dinner is at seven o'clock. It's been dark for a couple of hours. Down below, the roll and dip of the boat is harder to cope with and some of my shipmates are beginning to look queasy. The smell of roasting lamb from the galley doesn't help and I notice that Rhys is one of the few takers when Jack clatters down from the doghouse to enquire about drinks. Rhys is a Guinness fan. Most of us are wedged in various corners of the saloon, mostly around the big table, but he drinks on his feet, his long body effortlessly in tune with the motion of the boat. I envy him this and tell him so.

'Practice,' he says. 'I've been at this game a while.'

I remember Malo telling me about Rhys shrimping on the Gulf of Mexico. He says it's true. He did it for three years and his last trip clipped the hurricane season. The first big storm was called Anthea.

'We knew she was coming and we made a run for New Orleans. Worst night of my life. Just

318

made it. Another couple of hours and we'd have been breakfast for the 'gators.'

The rest of us exchange glances. The wind is definitely picking up. We can hear it every time someone steps into the doghouse from the deck above us. It's a low keening noise in the rigging, punctuated by a wild flapping of sail every time the boat wallows. I catch Cassie's eye. Like me she's probably wondering whether there are alligators off the Normandy coast.

Supper comes and goes. Nobody, except Rhys and Malo, eats very much. Even H seems to have lost his appetite. Already both loos are occupied and when Sadie emerges, pale, haunted, I suspect all is far from well. She did her test piece to camera in the last of the daylight and it was crap so maybe she wasn't feeling too bright even then.

Malo's anti-seasickness tablets seem to be doing the trick. I risk a couple of mouthfuls of lamb and a baked potato washed down with red wine and feel fine. Malo, bless him, is doing his best to keep our spirits up and I'm happy to perform when he asks me for a couple of location stories. My new friends around the table are nice enough to listen and respond with a question or two and it's nearly midnight when my turn comes to stand watch.

This time I'm teamed with Amit and Ruth, the CPS lawyer. Ruth, I've noticed, has tucked into a decent plate of food but Amit hasn't touched a thing. For once, thank God, he has nothing to say.

We put on our life jackets and make our way

up to the doghouse. Suranne is bent over a chart of the central portion of the English Channel, logging our progress south. Inconceivably we aren't even halfway across but she's anticipating a break in the weather and thinks we should still make landfall by breakfast time.

Mention of breakfast does nothing for Amit. I think I hear a groan when we make our way out into the heaving darkness. We're all wearing safety harnesses and we clip into lines laid specially on the deck. I can see Georgie standing at the big ship's wheel, fighting the wind and the waves, her face shadowed by the red glow of the binnacle. She gestures me closer, asks whether I might relieve her for a while. All I have to do is keep my eye on the compass.

'Steer one hundred and sixty-seven degrees,' she says, 'more or less. She responds very slowly so don't overdo any input. I'll be in the doghouse. Shout if you need me.'

Shout if you need me?

This is beyond belief. I tally up the numbers. Suddenly, without any warning, I have sole responsibility for twelve souls, in the middle of the night, with wave after wave roaring out of the darkness. The biggest of these break over the boat in an explosion of white spume, soaking us all.

Georgie is still beside me. She makes sure I'm comfortable at the big wheel, feet apart, body weight nicely balanced, and tells me not to grip the wheel too hard.

'Treat it like a friend,' she says. 'Be firm but gentle. Tough love, *quoi*?'

320

This is the first time I realize she speaks French. Nice. I like this woman. I love her competence. And I'm in awe at the degree of trust she seems to have.

She lingers for a second or two longer, eyeing the oncoming waves. Then she picks her moment and disappears into the doghouse, leaving me at the wheel.

I look round for my watch-buddies. Amit has tucked himself into a corner of the crescent of bench at the stern. His head is in his hands and I suspect he's just thrown up. Ruth, on the other hand, can't wait to have her go at the wheel. She's watching my every movement. She's probably been doing this half her life, I think, just like Rhys. She's probably marking me out of ten.

I concentrate very hard on the soft red glow of the binnacle, trying to keep the central line locked on 167 degrees. This is a lot harder than it might seem but as the minutes tick by I begin to get a feel for the boat. Georgie's right. It's a living thing. It needs constant attention, endless small course corrections. Then from nowhere arrives a truly big wave, smashing the bow sideways until the sails begin to flap, and I have to haul on the wheel to get her back to where she belongs.

By now, I'm soaking. Cold water has got in around the hood of my anorak and through the folds of scarf around my neck and I can feel it trickling down my back. I'm concentrating so hard that none of this really matters and I'm aware with something close to euphoria that

I'm managing to hack all this when Georgie returns. When she checks the course on the binnacle compass I catch an approving nod of the head. Then it's Ruth's turn.

Our watch ends at four in the morning. We make our way back down to the saloon. Amit gives the hot chocolate a miss. There are bodies everywhere, most of them in a bad way, fighting the boat's motion. By now I've sensed that the key to survival in a situation like this is to roll with the punches, to break down every little task into its component bits. If you really need to go to the loo, do everything slowly, deliberately, consciously. Unpeel your waterproofs. Drop your knickers. Don't rush things. Relax.

To my delight, it seems to work. Forty pumps later I'm back in the saloon contemplating an hour or two's sleep in my cabin. When Rhys suggests that going back on deck with himself and Malo would be a wiser option I ignore him. A zig-zag course across the saloon, thrown left and right by the motion of the boat, takes me to bed. Sadie is showing no signs of life. I struggle out of my clothes, towel myself dry, pull on a new T-shirt and trackie bottoms, and wriggle into my sleeping bag. Moments later, no kidding, I'm asleep.

Dawn finds us in the Bay of the Seine. France is a low grey line on the horizon and the English Channel appears to be a friend again. The wind has dropped and the remains of the swell sweeps us towards Ouistreham.

We dock shortly after eight o'clock. The sound

of Malo confirming our mooring with the marina boss in fluent French puts a huge smile on my face. H, especially, is deeply impressed. We're standing on the deck together while Georgie and Jack make fast our lines.

'Top job, my son,' he says, as Malo hops back on board.

'Our son,' I tell him.

The smell of frying bacon has revived flagging spirits. We all gather down below to attack Esther's breakfast. Crossing the Channel, us ladies agree, is a bit like childbirth. Bloody painful and immediately forgotten. Rhys begs to differ.

'You were a pro,' he tells me. 'I'd take you to the Gulf of Mexico any day.'

After breakfast, in a burst of team spirit, we help with the washing-up while Sadie sweet-talks Malo into a second take on the piece to camera. I watch from the deck as she preens on the dockside, lifting her face to the thin winter sun while Malo sorts out his new iPhone. He's using the phone to shoot the video and H smiles when I ask him where Malo got it.

'Another present?' I suggest.

'Present, bollocks. Essential tool is the way I look at it. Great screen. Brilliant camera. Shoots videos. Water-resistant. The lot. The boy's a credit to himself. Just look at him.'

H is right. Sadie has to be more than twice his age. According to H she's a seasoned feature journalist, a tough old bird who knows how to mix it with the best of them. Yet here she is, putty in my son's hands as he tells her to relax, to be more normal, to treat the camera like a friend.

This line seems to startle H.

'Where the fuck did he learn that?' he asks.

'He got it from Berndt,' I tell him. 'And from me.'

We spend the day in a minibus, driving from invasion beach to invasion beach and meeting an assortment of local worthies. Malo sits at the front, chatting with the French driver, telling him what we're up to. At Pegasus Bridge, where the first British paratroops dropped out of nowhere, we pause for coffee and inspect a display of military bits and pieces before Malo describes our D-Day heroes taking the Germans by surprise and establishing a position to protect the flank of the Allied bridgehead. Once again, with little visible effort, he seems to have mastered his brief. Fields of fire. Mortar crews. Artillery support. And all this delivered with his now-trademark confidence.

Gradually, our little gang is sorting itself out. Alex and Cassie are locked in conversation with Ruth, the young lawyer, while Sadie and Amit appear to be friends again. Jack, the ship's mate, has been given leave of absence from *Persephone* for the day and is eager to see the invasion beaches. He and Rhys are the naughty boys at the back of the bus, where I, too, have a seat. We laugh a great deal and get peaceably drunk over a four-course lunch at a seaside resort called St Auban.

By nightfall, we're all exhausted. Rhys proposes

a game of Spoof around the saloon table after yet another meal while Cassie and I chat more about the movie business. To my relief she wants to move on from my own films and I'm more than happy to share gossip about actors and actresses that have always interested her. One of them is Liam Neeson, whom she suspects of wasting a huge talent, and I do my best to defend him. Liam, I tell her, parlayed his gifts into some fine movies and a small fortune, something much rarer in La La Land than she might suspect.

The weather, to our surprise, perks up for Remembrance Day. Bright sunshine greets us when we de-bus at Arromanches. Malo and H have paid a visit to a *fleuriste* in Ouistreham and the resulting wreath is a clever interlacing of deep red hypericum berries with green leaves and twists of white lilies. Now, it's Ruth who carries our offering up the steps of the D-Day memorial at Arromanches. This is where the Allies established their floating harbour and Malo has managed to attract a decent scatter of local print reporters plus a film crew from a Caen-based TV station.

One of my proudest all-time memories will be Malo and Ruth being interviewed together while the rest of us gathered in the background. Towards the end of the interview, asked why someone of his age would be remotely interested in an event that had happened seventy-three years ago, Malo paused for a moment and then suggested that bad things always happened when the world was looking the other way. This was a phrase that came straight from Berndt but I didn't care. It sounded respectful, and wise, and would play wonderfully on French regional TV.

That afternoon, we accompany Ruth to her grandfather's grave and then return to the boat. Our final run ashore takes us to the fish restaurant in Ouistreham that Malo has been promoting since our arrival. In a much-appreciated gesture of thanks, H insists that *Persephone*'s crew join us. The meal is sensational, especially the *loup de mer en croûte,* but the mood around the big table is oddly flat. I can't make up my mind whether we're all exhausted or simply dreading the journey back. The weather forecast, once again, is far from promising but back on *Persephone* Suranne assures us that a good south-westerly blow will have us home in no time. It's this thought I take with me to bed and it's a moment or two before I realize that Sadie and her two bags have gone.

I find Malo sitting in the doghouse with Suranne. Our skipper has spent the day attending to maintenance jobs around the boat and she's now plotting tomorrow morning's course.

I ask Malo about Sadie. He says she's had to take the train to Paris for a meeting. From there she'll return to London by plane.

'She bottled it, more like.' Suranne doesn't look up from the chart. 'Bloody journalists are all the same. Show them a bit of serious weather and they can't take it.'

Malo and I agree our skipper is probably right. From my point of view I couldn't care less whether Sadie made the return leg or not. Having our cabin to myself will be a deep pleasure.

I give Malo and Suranne a hug and retire to bed. Once again, I'm asleep in seconds. Eight hours later, I'm awoken by a movement beside the twin bunks. I rub my eyes and reach for my torch. The battery is low and it's several seconds before I get a proper look at the face beside me.

Mitch Culligan.

Twenty-Five

'What are you doing here?'

He doesn't answer me. He hasn't shaved for a while and the beard has altered the shape of his face. He's inspecting the lower bunk. He wants to know if this belonged to Sadie.

'You know her?'

'Yes.'

'She's left something? You've come to pick it up?'

'I'm sailing back with you.'

'You're *what*?'

This is the last thing I expected. Not just Mitch Culligan appearing from nowhere. But Mitch Culligan choosing to share this boat with someone determined to hurt him.

I'm up on one elbow now, staring down at him as he opens his rucksack and tugs out a bundle of wet-weather gear.

'But why are you here?' I say. 'What's the point?'

'Every story deserves a proper end. Especially this one.'

'I don't understand. Are you pissed or something? You're making no sense.'

He doesn't answer. From somewhere he's found a pair of yellow wellies and a red woollen hat with a bobble on the top. Absurd.

'How did you get on board?'

328

'Your son met me on the quayside. Sadie phoned him late last night, explained I'd be taking her place on the voyage home. Nice lad. Looks just like his dad.'

'And Malo was OK with that?'

'He was fine. I'm paying. That's all that seems to matter.'

'And H? Does he know you're here?'

'I've no idea. I gave your boy a different name. Prentice won't have a clue who I am. Neither will Malo.'

'H will have seen photos.'

'I doubt it. I never use a picture on bylines and I'm not on social media. I'm Mr Nobody. Cadging a lift home.'

Worse and worse. Whose responsibility is it to tell H about the cuckoo in our nest? Mine? Then comes another thought, even more pressing.

'But what about Sayid? Who's looking after him?'

'He's back in his care home. As a client, this time.'

'And you're happy with that?'

Mitch shoots me a look before heading for the door.

'He is,' he says. 'And that's all that matters.'

We gather for breakfast as dawn breaks. Mitch is calling himself Larry Elliott. He offers a hand across the table by way of introduction and apologizes for not being Sadie. This sparks a ripple of laughter. Rhys, who's just seen the latest weather forecast, hopes our new friend has a sense of humour, while Cassie offers to share

329

her dwindling supply of seasickness tablets. The mood, unlike last night, is buoyant. The trip is nearly over. It's been testing in parts, occasionally worse than that, but we've learned a lot and now we're going home.

H is the last to arrive for breakfast. There are still curls of bacon left, and a couple of croissants, and Esther offers to scramble more eggs but H shakes his head. I can tell he's had a bad night. His shoulder seems to be hurting him and there are a couple of tiny cuts on his chin where his razor slipped.

Rhys pours him a cup of coffee and makes room on the sagging banquette. H stays on his feet. He's looking at our new shipmate and something in his face tells me that he's far from convinced.

'This is Larry, Dad. He's a mate of Sadie's.'

'Is that right?' His eyes haven't left Mitch's face. 'He's here for breakfast?'

'We're taking him home.'

'Why?'

Mitch stirs. He's sitting beside me. The sight of H in the flesh hasn't disturbed him in the least.

'Sadie got sidetracked,' Mitch explains. 'I happened to be in Paris. I'm not due back in the UK until next week. EasyJet or a Brixham trawler under full sail? Tough call.'

I'm aware of people exchanging covert glances around the table. After the rigours of our recent crossing I suspect most of them would kill for a seat on easyJet.

'You've sailed before?' H asks.

'Never.'

H nods, eyeballs him a moment longer. No handshake.

'Good luck my friend.' He grunts. 'You're gonna need it.'

By mid-morning, we've cleared the French coast. The distant smudge of Le Havre lies off to our right, or starboard as I'm learning to call it, while the Normandy beaches are disappearing astern. We've broken sweat hauling up the sails and Suranne has dispensed with the engine. The wind is blowing from the south-west, exactly as predicted, and *Persephone* is making the most of a gathering swell.

I'm standing with Mitch up in the bow, away from listening ears. He's brought a pair of binoculars and he's looking for dolphins.

'Malo tells me you're the come-on for the punters,' he murmurs.

'That's right. My pleasure.'

'And all this money really goes to good causes?'

'That's what I'm told.'

'And you believe it?'

'Every word.'

'Really?' He spares me a sideways glance.

I nod. For most of our brief relationship Mitch has let me pretty close. He's been supportive when it mattered, frank about his private life, passionate about his political beliefs. But this is a different Mitch. He's become solitary, withdrawn. He's retired behind his new beard. And when I press him about his real reason for being on board, for becoming Larry Elliott, he won't answer me. Most of the time he avoids my gaze but just occasionally, like now, I sense real anger in his eyes. *The only thing necessary for the triumph of evil,* I remember, *is for good men to do nothing.*

I ask Mitch whether he's planning some kind of confrontation. He's abandoned the hunt for the dolphins.

'Confrontation?' He seems quite taken by the idea.

'You and H.'

'Because of Sayid?'

'Of course.'

'And you think that might help?'

'I've no idea. I'm asking you.'

He shrugs, turns back to the view, leaning on the rail, absorbing the slow roll of the boat. Then I'm aware of another figure making his way towards us. It's H. He's carrying two mugs of coffee. He pauses beside us.

'Here, gal.'

I take the coffee. Mitch turns back from the rail, expecting the other mug. H lifts it, takes a sip. His eyes haven't left my face.

'Cheers.' He wipes his mouth with the back of his hand. 'Happy days, eh?'

For the next few hours we pick our way carefully through the busy shipping lanes off the French coast. I spend some of this time alongside Suranne in the doghouse, watching her monitoring the screen that charts the movement of passing vessels. When their course and speed indicate the possibility of a collision, she gets on the radio to alert them to our presence in case

332

they haven't seen us. Earlier generations of fishermen, I think, would have killed for technology like this.

By nightfall, as the wind begins to rise, we're forty-three nautical miles north of the French coast. In a couple of hours, God willing, we'll be halfway across. Esther announces an early supper for those who want it while Mitch, hunched in a corner of the saloon, makes occasional entries in the *Guardian* crossword. I'm sitting beside Ruth. She's deep in a John Grisham thriller when something prompts her to check the time.

'Shit,' she says.

She produces her mobile and scrolls through her directory before trying to make a call. It doesn't happen. Mitch pauses beside us.

'We're out of signal range,' he says. 'Patience is all.'

This could be a line from an Agatha Christie movie, a handful of near-strangers banged up on an ancient trawler at the mercy of the elements, and of each other. I've spent most of the day keeping a watchful eye on both H and Mitch but so far they've behaved themselves. This I interpret as a blessing but the real test, I suspect, will come later. Darkness, especially on a heaving deck, can invite all kinds of retribution and I have a quiet word with Suranne, suggesting that she try and keep H down below for the crossing. When she asks why I blame his shoulder.

'He'll never admit it,' I tell her. 'But he's in agony.'

Supper is soup with freshly baked rolls and

fish pie to follow. Out here in mid-Channel we're fully exposed to a wind that appears to be rising. Rhys has volunteered to take the wheel, to give the crew a chance to eat. The swell has given way to a succession of big rollers, each breaking wave thumping into the wooden hull. The old trawler is corkscrewing now, plunging into one trough, shaking herself dry, then disappearing into another. The motion is acutely uncomfortable and there are few takers for either the soup or the fish pie. People are nervous again. You can sense it, even smell it. They know exactly what to expect because we've been here before and they dread the hours to come.

It's at this point that I hear a commotion on deck above our heads. Raised voices. Heavy footsteps. Someone screaming. Malo is on his feet, following Suranne up the steps to the doghouse. I stay put, waiting on events. No point getting in the way, I tell myself. No point playing the hero.

Around the table, apprehension about the weather has given way to alarm. Something has obviously gone badly wrong and we're in that scary zone where things abruptly become unreal. Cassie has found her husband's hand. Amit's eyes are huge in his face. Ruth is frowning. What's happened? What the fuck's going on? Only H and Mitch appear unmoved.

Another scream. Then comes the thump of something heavy from the doghouse and a blast of freezing air from the open door to the deck. Mitch is sitting beside me, rolling with the motion of the boat. He has perfect line of sight to the steps leading down from the doghouse.

The first pair of legs to appear belong to Rhys. He's obviously surrendered the ship's wheel. He's still in his lifejacket and wet-weather gear and he's dripping water everywhere. He gives us a nod and then turns back to the ladder as another body descends. Battered Nikes. Torn jeans, soaking wet. A filthy once-white T-shirt. And finally a head. His mouth is open, gasping for air. His teeth are very white in the blackness of his young face.

The boy stares at us. He's shaking with cold. He seems to be in shock. For a moment there's nothing but the howl of the wind in the rigging and a groan from the hull as another wave bears down. Then I get to my feet. My cabin is closest. Sadie has left a black quilted anorak hanging on the hook behind the door. I grab it and then judge the moment to get back to the saloon.

Rhys has already yelled at Esther to get something hot to drink. He has his arms around our surprise guest. It's a clumsy embrace because of the life jacket but it's exactly the right thing to do. I take over from Rhys. Mitch has found a towel from somewhere and I wrap Sadie's anorak around the newcomer before mopping his face with the towel. I need a name. When I ask in English he doesn't seem to understand.

'*Votre nom? Comment vous appelez-vous?*'

'Mbaye.'

'*Vous venez d'où?*'

'*Un petit village. Près de Dakar.*'

Mbaye. From Senegal. A stowaway.

I pass the message for everyone else's benefit. We make space at the table, sit him down, make him drink the hot tea. First he warms his hands on the mug before taking a sip or two. Then he looks at me. Huge eyes. A deep scar down the left side of his face. Tight curls of black hair laid flat against his skull. Young. Maybe Malo's age.

'*Sucre?*' he asks.

There's sugar on the table. I give him the bowl. He tips most of it into the mug. He's still shaking but he manages a nod of thanks.

'*Merci,*' he says.

H has been watching the boy carefully. 'How did he get onboard?' he asks.

I point out that we were all at the restaurant last night and that the boat was locked up but unattended. H isn't interested in my opinions. He wants me to put the question to the boy.

I ask him exactly what happened. He mutters an explanation in rapid, heavily accented French. I'm not used to the Senegalese *patois* but I manage to pick up most of it.

'I was right,' I tell H. 'He'd been watching the boat for a while. When we all went off to the restaurant he took his chance and got on board. He says there's a pile of tarpaulins up towards the bow. He hid under there until he got so wet and so cold he couldn't bear it any longer.'

'I saw him on deck just now,' Rhys says. 'Just a movement in the darkness. I called Jack. He took care of it. There was a bit of a struggle but Jack calmed him down. Bloke could have been overboard in a flash, just like that.'

H nods, his eyes returning to the boy. H seems to have appointed himself Chairman of the Board, which in a way I suppose he is.

'Ask him if he's hungry.' I put H's question in French. The boy nods. 'Then give him something to fucking eat.'

There's still fish pie in the oven. Esther dishes it out. The boy eyes it for a moment. Then a pair of thin arms emerge from the folds of Sadie's anorak and he wolfs the entire plate. He's uncomfortable in our company but the shaking has stopped.

Ruth wants to know what happens next. Do we turn round? Take him back? Rhys laughs. With a wind like this turning round wouldn't be for the faint-hearted and after that we'd be facing hours of grief from the onrushing waves.

'Home, then? We hand him over when we dock?'

I'm aware of everyone looking at H. In law I imagine this must be Suranne's call. It is, after all, her boat, her kingdom, but by the sheer force of his presence at the table this decision appears to fall to H. Mitch is watching him with some interest.

At length, after a huge wave takes the boy's empty plate skidding off the table, H yawns and asks Esther for a coffee.

'Early days,' he says. 'Let's see what happens.'

Early days? I'm not the only one who finds this declaration puzzling. The situation couldn't be plainer. We have a stowaway on board, a refugee, an illegal. He's seen the flag on our stern, listened to our chatter from the quayside, knows we're English. From my mum, I've gathered that France is unpopular among refugees, even French speakers like Mbaye. Work is hard to come by and there's a lot of racism. Across the Channel, on the other hand, Mbaye could find some kind of job, maybe plead his case, maybe avoid deportation, start a whole new life. The attraction is obvious.

H is looking at Alex. He knows he was recently at the Home Office, bossed an entire department, understands the rules.

'What's the score then, Alex? With the boy here?'

Alex takes his time. I know he loathes heavy weather because Cassie's told me so, but he seems to welcome this new development. Something to think about. Something to chew over. I also know the depths of his despair at a job he once cherished. Another confidence from Cassie.

'The regulations are tricky,' he says. 'How old is the lad?'

I put the question to Mbaye. *Dix-huit ans.* Eighteen.

'Then forgive me but it's black and white. If he's eighteen, he goes home unless there's some pressing reason he might come to grief there.'

I ask Mbaye why he left Senegal. He says his life was boring. He was a fisherman with his father and two of his brothers but the fish have gone. In town there was no work, nothing to do. With a bit of money you could buy somewhere to squat in the back of a truck and head north across the desert to Libya. Everyone was doing it.

Alex shrugs. He doesn't need a translation.

'Economic migrant,' he says. 'We'd put him on the plane.'

H wants to know if he's carrying a passport. Mbaye says no. H shoots a glance at Alex. I know what's coming next.

'Then what if he lies about his age?' H growls. 'Pretends to be sixteen? Fifteen? Whatever?'

'Then he can stay until he's eighteen,' Alex says.

'And how does he get by?'

'We look after him.'

'And then?'

'He makes an application to stay, which he'll lose, and then he goes home.'

Ruth intervenes. I can tell there are elements in this conversation she finds difficult. She is, after all, a lawyer.

'But the boy's eighteen.' She's looking at H. 'He's just told us so. Alex is right. It's black and white. Eighteen years old. Economic migrant. *Adieu.*'

Amit is nodding with some vigour. He, too, would march Mbaye to the airport and put him on a plane home. Odd, I think, how a fellow immigrant might be hardest of all to win over in this strange debate. Last in. First out.

Rhys has at last shed his life jacket. He steadies himself against one of the pillars in the saloon and then looks at H.

'You're right, boyo,' he says softly. 'We take care of the lad. Make sure he comes to no more harm.'

No one calls H 'boyo', but Malo's dad, our

onboard gangster, looks strangely untroubled. Suranne has arrived from the doghouse. She slips on to the banquette alongside Mitch. Mitch updates her with the boy's name and the rest of Mbaye's story. When Ruth enquires again about returning our stowaway to French jurisdiction, Suranne confirms what Rhys has already told us. The barometer is falling fast. The weather is guaranteed to get worse, the wind strengthening and veering westerly to bring the waves beam-on. There's no question of danger, or even of heaving to and riding out the next few hours, but neither does it make any sense to turn round and go back. We're in for a rough night.

Ruth nods. Suranne has redrawn the watch list as I requested and Ruth will be up on deck between two and four, along with Mitch, Malo and myself. Suranne offers us all the chance to say no but none of us will hear of it. I've just taken the last of the tablets and my helping of fish pie is staying where it should, but I've learned enough now to know that Rhys is right: weather like this is best endured where you can see the next big wave coming.

Ruth hasn't finished. She wants Suranne to confirm that she'll be handing Mbaye over to the authorities when we berth in Portsmouth. I'm sure that Suranne hears the question but she has one ear cocked for noises that might indicate trouble. Every storm, I suspect, has a soundtrack of its own and the best skippers, the ones who survive, are the ones alert to every hint of danger.

Ruth puts the question again. She's beginning to get under H's skin. I can sense it.

'We have to,' Ruth repeats. 'We have to stick by the rules.'

Suranne nods absently. Her body language speaks volumes. At the moment, she has more than enough on her plate. First things first.

She tells Esther to make sure the boy rehydrates properly. If he's still hungry give him something else to eat. Unthinkingly, I pat Mbaye on the arm. He's our charge now, our responsibility. The boy returns my smile and huddles closer. Every time the boat lurches sideways, falling off a wave, I feel the thinness of his body pressing against mine but unlike most of us, now he's warmer and fed, he has no problem with the plunge and roll of the ancient trawler.

I ask him about life at home in Senegal. He's already told me he's worked on the family fishing boat. He has no fear of the sea, he says. It's always been a friend, a source of food, a living. You have no money? You fish. And that way, if the gods are kind, you survive.

H is nearby, doing his best to monitor our conversation. I translate as best I can but H is greedy to know more. How many brothers? How many sisters? Does he miss them all? What else does he know how to do apart from fishing? And how's life been since he jumped on the back of the lorry and headed north?

I put all these questions to the boy and he's happy to fill in the details. He has four sisters and five brothers, one of whom died recently in a traffic accident in Dakar. Yes, he missed his family, and his friends too, especially when the trip north got rough. The desert, he says, goes on forever. The smugglers rip you off. And beware of soldiers with guns.

I ask him about Libya. How was it?

'*Affreux.*' His head goes down and he covers his eyes. '*Vraiment.*'

Even H doesn't press him any harder at this point but what's really interesting is Alex, the ex-civil servant. I'm not at all clear what role he played at the Home Office but he certainly knows a great deal about asylum seekers, appeal tribunals, and the mechanics of deportation. At the same time I'm getting the impression that this may be the first time he's seen a refugee on the run, the first opportunity he's had to translate all those Home Office statistics into flesh and blood.

H, too, is aware of this. He's never less than direct.

'So what do you think, Alex?'

'About?'

'Our friend here. And all those mates of his. Are we right to put them on the plane? Send them back? Or have the Germans got it right?'

Alex has been watching Mitch out of the corner of his eye. He seems to be as interested in the reply as H.

'You want the truth? We're civil servants. We're there at the bidding of our masters. Our masters are the politicians. And to be frank, as far as immigration is concerned, they haven't got a clue. That's point number one. Point number two is related in a way. Because those same politicians always want something for nothing. They chop us down all the time. They call it austerity. But when it comes to the police, or the Border Force, or the prison service, God help it, there's no flesh left on the bone. We have fewer bodies behind fewer desks and so we're making bad decisions all the time. About a hundred people a month get letters ordering them to leave the country when they're perfectly entitled to live here. That's shameful enough but I'm afraid it's not just the Home Office. Whitehall is a shambles and it's about to get a whole lot worse. So it doesn't matter what the politicians think they want. It won't happen.'

'That's not what they tell us.'

'Of course it isn't. Most of them have only got one thing in mind. They need to stay in power. You want the immigration numbers down? They'll promise you the earth. Do they ever tell you how complex this stuff is? Never. Will they ever get their way? No.'

This is beyond blunt. Mitch is nodding. I bet he's memorized every word. H is only interested in Mbaye.

'So say our friend here makes it.'

'Makes it?'

'Gets ashore. What then?'

'That depends. If he's on a watch list the police might go through the motions. It's unlikely but they might.'

'And the numpties in the Border Force?'

'If he's already made it they'll be looking the wrong way.'

'Home safe, then?'

'Almost certainly.'

H nods. Says nothing. Ruth is staring at Alex.

Then the boat rears up and falls sideways off a huge wave and we can hear nothing but the gunshot flapping of the sails. Some of us have tumbled off the banquette. Mbaye, Mitch, H, and myself are in a heap on the floor. I can hear water dripping through cracks in the decking overhead and sluicing down the companionway from the doghouse. Then the boat rights itself and comes slowly on to the wind again.

H and Mbaye are nose to nose. H is holding his shoulder.

'Fucking madness, mate,' he says. 'Love it.'

Mbaye doesn't understand. He looks to me for a translation. I shrug. I think H is talking about the Home Office but in truth I can't be sure. I glance at Mitch. He's eyeballing H.

'I could swear you're starting to bond,' he says softly.

'With fucking who?'

'Our friend here. Mbaye.'

'And so what if I am?'

'Nothing,' Mitch shrugs. 'I'm just surprised, that's all. Stowaway black kids aren't to every-one's taste. Neither are other refugees. Like Syrians, for instance.'

'You're talking about people like me?'

'Yes.'

'So what are you trying to say?'

Mitch won't answer the question. I know he has a name on his lips and I'm praying it gets no further. Sayid. Sayid Abdulrahman. Is this why Mitch has stolen aboard? To exact a little revenge for what happened at the foot of the railway embankment in Hither Green?

H has had exactly the same thought. I can see it on his face. The way his eyes have narrowed. The set of his jaw beneath the three-day stubble.

'You want to sort it out now, son? Up there? On deck?' He nods towards the doghouse as the boat takes yet another lurch. The fiction that is Larry Elliott hasn't fooled him for a moment.

Mitch holds his stare, then permits himself the faintest smile.

'No, thanks,' he murmurs. 'Not yet.'

We're on watch from two o'clock in the morning. The waves are beam-on now, exactly as Suranne predicted, and walls of water loom out of the darkness. We huddle on a bench on the lee side of the boat, sheltered by the doghouse from the worst of the weather, not really knowing what we're supposed to do. Georgie and Jack share turns at the wheel, trying to keep the heavy old boat on course, hanging on for dear life as *Persephone* lurches sideways. Conversation has died. Ruth sits beside Mitch, her hands dug between her thighs, her eyes shut tight.

Between me and Mitch is H. Despite my carefully laid plans he's refused to stay below but so far, to my immense relief, both men seem to have forgotten their earlier conversation. Maybe the sheer force of the storm has blunted their appetite for a helping of extra violence. Maybe there's some prospect of getting them both home in working order. Either way I'm not sure I care that much any more. Wet through, freezing cold, all I'm counting are the minutes between now and the moment when I can struggle below and get warm again.

Relief comes earlier than we expect. Suranne, bless her, steps around the corner of the doghouse with a flask of hot coffee. She says she's worried about our welfare. She doesn't want any of us to end up with hypothermia. We nod, too numb to say anything. Ruth is the first to get carefully to her feet. She doesn't want the coffee. She's clipped on to the safety line and when yet another wave nearly tosses her towards the boiling ocean it's Mitch who grabs her flailing arm and hauls her back. A glimpse of her face tells me everything. She's terrified.

I watch Mitch hauling her towards the doghouse, reaching out for the sliding door, making sure she gets safely inside. Then he turns again and heads back towards us, fighting the pitch and heave of the boat, and for the first time I realize that he isn't clipped on to the safety line. Another huge wave rolls the old trawler sideways. The deck on our side is awash, practically underwater, and there's nothing Mitch can do about it. He's on his knees now, half submerged, and the wire guard rail saves him from going overboard but I know that one more wave will pitch him into the darkness.

H is watching him carefully, still motionless, but the moment I lunge towards Mitch, both arms outstretched to try and help him, H is on his feet.

'Sit down, gal,' he shouts. 'Fucking leave this to me.'

Leave what? Leave my son's gangster dad to finish the job? To wait a second or two for the

346

next wave? To toss this upstart journalist into oblivion?

I turn on H. No way will I let this happen. I'm trying to push him. I'm trying to fight him. I'm trying to get him back to the safety of the bench we've all been sharing. H's face is inches from mine. I swear he's grinning at me. Not because I amuse him. But because he is, in some unfathomable way, impressed.

'Leave it out, gal,' he growls. 'I'm going to save his fucking life. Not that he deserves it.'

And that's exactly what happens.

Moments later, after I've helped H wrestle Mitch back across the deck, I leave them both on the bench. Mitch, his head in his hands, is throwing up. H even has his arm around him. I watch this little tableau, still trying to make sense of what's just happened, but then decide to leave them to it. One day I might understand men but not tonight, and certainly not here.

With great difficulty, one step at a time, I make my way back to the doghouse, fighting the chaos around me. Suranne, as ever, is concentrating on the GPS read-out on one of the screens. We're twenty-one miles south of the Isle of Wight. Thanks to the sheer force of the wind, progress has been faster than she'd anticipated. Soon we should pick up the lighthouse on St Catherine's Point.

St Catherine's Point, I think. England.

I know I should stay on deck. For whatever reason peace appears to have broken out, but I know I should try and make sure that neither H nor Mitch or even both of them end up in the sea, unmissed for minutes, maybe longer, and almost certainly lost. But I'm simply too cold to think straight.

Down below looks like a scene from a war movie. There are bodies everywhere, pale-faced, slack-mouthed, grimly hanging on to anything solid. Mbaye is the only exception. He's wedged in a corner of the banquette and he appears to be asleep. Still cocooned in Sadie's anorak, he has a smile on his face. Remarkable.

I stay as long as I can. I make it to the cabin and towel my face dry. I'm tempted to get out of my wet-weather gear but if anything happens I know it would take me forever to put it on again. And so I slip on to the bottom bunk and close my eyes but it's impossible to sleep. Every next wave throws me against the side of the hull. Water is pouring through cracks in the deck, soaking the top bunk and then dripping on to my face. The pillow is wet. The bedding is wet. My whole world has surrendered to an eternity of wetness.

By now, I've run out of tablets. After a while, I've no idea how long, I know with a terrible certainty that the fish pie was a huge mistake. Either I get back out on deck or this slum of a cabin will be awash with vomit. I make it to the door. It takes forever to lay a course towards the steps up to the doghouse. I climb them one by one, taking advantage of those tiny moments between the boat's recovery and the next roll. Suranne is where I last saw her: squinting up at the GPS screen, making notes on a pad on the desk.

'Two miles off Ventnor,' she murmurs. 'Past Shanklin it might ease off.'

Ventnor? Shanklin? Ease off? I've no idea what she's talking about and now is no time to find out. I throw myself towards the door and wrestle it open in time to vomit into the darkness beyond. Slowly, a figure at the wheel swims into focus. It looks like Jack but I can't be sure. Then I feel a comforting pressure on my arm. It's Georgie, the first mate. She's looking concerned.

'You have to clip on,' she says.

I bend and try but I'm useless. My fingers, already stiff with cold, won't work. She drops to her knees and does it for me. Then she takes me by the arm again and begins to lead me into the shelter of the lee side. Sweet, sweet girl.

My stomach half-empty, I'm feeling a whole lot better. I'm trying to thank her when I hear a shout from the wheel. Definitely Jack.

'Starboard forrard,' he yells. 'Big container.'

A second or two later the boat shudders from a huge impact. Over the shriek of the wind I hear a splintering of wood. Instinctively I reach for the grab rail around the doghouse and peer into the teeth of the wind. Our precious *Persephone* seems immobile a moment and then slowly rises to the next wave as the enormous metal box disappears into the darkness.

Georgie tells me to hang on. Moments later she's back in the doghouse. The windows are streaming with water but I can see her and Suranne heading down the steps into the saloon. Jack is still on the wheel but he seems to be having trouble holding course. I want, very badly, to do

349

something to help. The other end of the safety line runs to the wheel. Judging my moment, I lunge towards him, just make it.

'Take the wheel,' he yells. 'Steer three hundred and twenty-two.'

I do my best, peering at the compass. Three hundred and twenty-two degrees. We need four pairs of hands, I tell myself. But then Jack has gone, swerving nimbly towards the doghouse. The door open, I can see that Suranne's back from the saloon. She has the VHF radio in her hand. I've no idea what's happening but the very pit of my stomach tells me that this is a real disaster. Not just a stowaway. Something infinitely worse.

I fight the wheel and the weather for what seems an eternity. The course I've been given, 322, quickly becomes a joke. With every wave the compass swings wildly left and right, and with every slow recovery, the boat feels heavier. Every few seconds, off to port, I can see the long white finger of what I presume is a lighthouse. It stabs into the darkness, slowly revolving, bathing us in a brief moment of clarity before moving on. Then, lurching out of the doghouse, comes another figure.

It turns out to be Rhys. He's come to relieve me at the wheel. When I ask him what's happening he says there's water pouring into the forepeak. Georgie and Jack will be back on deck in a moment to try and rig a spare sail over the damage in the hull, a kind of Band-Aid solution that just might work. For now, though, they're sorting out a pump.

'Pump?'

'The bilges are filling.' Rhys nods down at his feet. 'Technically we call that sinking.'

Shit. I'm staring at the compass: 354, then 350. Then, very, very slowly, 346. Rhys is right. We must be carrying tons of water already.

I snatch a look at the doghouse. Suranne has stirred the engine into life. I can feel it throbbing beneath our feet. Now, she's talking on the radio. A life boat, I think. A real fishing boat. A passing ferry. Santa fucking Claus. Anything to get us out of this mess.

Rhys puts me out of my misery. Suranne, he says, has a plan. She's called a Mayday but these things take a while. There are no harbours on this bit of the Isle of Wight, nowhere to find shelter, and so she wants us to head for the nearest beach which happens to be Ventnor. There, *inshallah*, she'll drive the boat up on to the pebbles.

A plan? I nod. Then I have another thought.

'Malo?' I yell.

Rhys has the wheel now. The new course is 299. He thinks Malo might be with his dad on the lee side. I nod, grateful. I have to be with him. I have to be with my son.

Still clipped on to the safety line, I make my way around the doghouse. All the water down below has helped stabilize the boat. Movement is easier. Crouched together on the bench I find Malo with his dad, which is a huge relief. To my shame I don't even ask about Mitch.

H wants to know what's happening. I tell him about the container, the bilges filling, and

Suranne's bid for us to end up on the beach at Ventnor.

'Where?'

'Ventnor.'

In the darkness I faintly detect what might be a smile on H's face. Then, above the shriek of the wind in the rigging, I hear my name. It's Rhys. He wants me back on the wheel. I get to my feet, steady myself, check my safety harness, and wait for that fleeting moment of steadiness when I can move again. Rhys has managed to maintain the new course. The pump is working, and so now he has to go below to help organize a chain of buckets while Georgie and Jack do their best with getting the spare sail over the hole in the hull.

'Two hundred and ninety-nine.' Rhys nods at the compass, gives me the wheel.

By now, I've lost all track of time. Dimly I'm half-expecting dawn in the east but whenever I check in that direction I can see nothing but darkness. The boat is wallowing, the water almost close enough to touch, but the wind is filling the sails and with the help of the engine we're still making progress. The lights of what I assume must be Ventnor lie directly ahead. I can just make out strings of coloured bulbs dancing on the promenade and in the throw of the streetlights I can see curls of surf pounding the beach.

A huge wave throws the boat sideways. Ventnor now lies off to port. The wind bellies the sails again and no matter how hard I try and wrestle *Persephone* back on course, it doesn't happen.

The wheel seems locked. There's nothing I can do to shift it. Fighting the tons and tons of water below is beyond my strength.

Then, from nowhere, comes a movement. It's Mbaye. He's emerged from the doghouse, still wearing Sadie's anorak, and he seems to dance towards me. He's nimble, light as a feather. He has the experience to anticipate the boat's every movement. He can read this mad score, recognize the music, conduct the orchestra. Unlike the rest of us, he's totally in tune.

Beside me now, he takes the wheel, tests it, looks up at the set of the sails, then peers out at the blackness of the night.

'*Vers les lumières,*' I yell, pointing at the lights of Ventnor off the port bow.

'*Les lumières?*'

'*Oui.*'

He nods. Judging his moment, waiting for a particular wave, he eases the boat to port, holds tight, then manages to spin the wheel again as another wave lifts us high. His touch, his knowledge, is instinctive. He doesn't spare the compass a second glance. His gaze is fixed on the lights in the darkness ahead. He's even smiling. White teeth in the darkness, I think. Our salvation.

I shout at him. I want to know how I can help. He shakes his head. *Tout va bien.* Everything's going to be OK. Trust me.

Ventnor is bang on the nose again. In the darkness up near the bow, Georgie and Jack are bent over the rail, wrestling with the spare sail. In the meantime, another figure has appeared in the open door of the doghouse. It's Alex, our honcho from the Home Office, our expert in winnowing the genuine refugees from the chaff. He's carrying a brimming bucket which he empties towards the lee side. Then he catches sight of Mbaye at the wheel. He pauses a moment, puts the bucket down, and then begins to applaud. It's a gesture I'll take with me to my grave.

The next few minutes bring more buckets, all emptied by Alex. There must be a succession of willing hands, I think, stretching down into the saloon, my shipmates doing their best to save us from sinking. Seconds later, another figure appears.

It's Suranne. She's animated, full of life. She makes it across from the doghouse and gives Mbaye a hug. Then she has the wheel. She's looking up. She's cursing the set of the sails, how untidy everything is.

Untidy? Shit.

She's yelling at Alex and Georgie. No more buckets. Forget the spare sail. We're minutes from beaching. She wants everyone up in the bow, ready to jump.

The boat is corkscrewing again but very slowly. If this was an animal, I think, we'd be talking death throes. I find Malo and his dad where I left them.

'You OK?' I shout.

H is studying his phone. Malo nods.

'And Mitch?'

Malo shrugs, gestures back at the doghouse. Maybe he's below. Maybe. Then I feel a tug on my arm. It's Rhys again. He wants us all in the bow.

We make our way forward and join the tight little knot of crew and passengers crouched against the wind and the curtains of spray. The beach is very close now, yellow pebbles, steeply shelving. It must be high tide, I think vaguely, which might or might not be good news. There's no sign of police or an ambulance but in the distance, shredded by the wind, I can make out the howl of a siren.

I look at the faces around me. Amit appears to be talking to himself. Ruth is tight-lipped, a coil ready to spring. Alex and Cassie are holding hands. Then Mitch, to my huge relief, joins us. We swap glances. I'm glad he's still alive.

A hundred metres to go, maybe fewer. Jack is standing in the bow, ready to jump. Georgie is beside him. She'll be handing us up on to the lip of the bow. Her instructions, as ever, are very clear. We'll jump on her command, not before, not after.

'Land and roll on the pebbles,' she says. 'Make like a paratrooper.'

Amit, I can tell, isn't convinced. Suranne is driving the boat as hard as she can, riding a huge roller. I can feel the deck lifting beneath my feet. Then, very suddenly, the beach is upon us and there comes a grinding noise from deep in the hull as the old trawler spears into the pebbles, pushed to safety by the breaking wave.

On board, there's a moment of silence. All we can hear is the thunder of the surf astern. Jack must have jumped because he's gone. Georgie is looking over the bow. She steadies Amit and then – when he refuses to jump – gives him a push. Next is Ruth. Then Cassie and Alex. Malo, Mitch, H and I are looking at each other. Rhys has just disappeared over the bow. A big wave lifts the stern and then the boat settles at an angle. Georgie isn't pleased. Time is precious.

'For fuck's sake.' She's looking at me. 'Just do it.'

I clamber up on to the bow. See the ring of white faces beneath me. Shut my eyes. Brace myself. Then, without waiting for her command, I jump.

I hit the pebbles hard. Coldness. Wetness. And the enveloping roar of the surf. Unseen hands pull me up the beach. Then come more bodies jumping out of the darkness until we're all on our feet, still swaying slightly, orphans from the storm.

Suranne is doing a head count. Georgie goes from face to face, asking, checking, making sure we're OK. Then Suranne tallies up the numbers a second time before calling us all to order. We stare at her, still numb, still in shock.

'Mbaye?' she asks.

Twenty-Six

Dawn has broken. It's nearly eight o'clock. Suranne has notified the police about our missing stowaway and while coastguards begin to search the rocky foreshore beyond the beach at Ventnor, a lifeboat is en route from neighbouring Shanklin. The assumption, I suspect, is that Mbaye jumped from the boat and probably drowned but everyone is hoping against hope that he made some kind of landfall. In no time at all, this young asylum seeker has acquired an almost mythical status. A handful of us saw him at the wheel – assured, fearless, immensely competent – and when Alex wonders whether he might have helped save our lives, I find myself nodding.

As the tide recedes down the beach, Suranne organizes the offload of our gear from the boat. Now, dry at last and nearly warm, we take it in turns to inspect the damage to the hull.

The wound is ugly. According to Rhys, a corner of the container must have ripped into the hull just below the waterline. The planking is stove in, the wood splintered around the edges of the gash. The impact of the beaching shifted the mattress that the crew had used to try and plug the hole and if you stand on tiptoes at a certain angle you can see into the saloon. Had the hole been even ten per cent bigger, says Rhys, we would have been history because neither a pump nor all those buckets would have coped. As it was, we dug ourselves out of an early grave and this knowledge has produced a real bond. We did it. We survived.

A journalist has arrived. Mitch tells me she's a freelance stringer. These people apparently spend their working lives monitoring the emergency channels and now she's here to ask that eternal media question: what was it *like*?

We shuffle around on the shingle and exchange awkward glances while she readies her little camera, but the truth is we can't wait to get it all off our chests. Amit admits he was scared to death. He prayed for his wife and his two kids. Ruth describes moments when the storm was at its height, water everywhere, the boat thrashing around, while Alex makes a point of telling the journo what a brilliant job the crew did. There was absolutely no panic, he says. Simply a succession of practical measures carried out in the teeth of impossible conditions. Just watching the crew in action made you believe in your own survival. Outstanding.

Rhys agrees. He puts his arm round young Jack and gives him a kiss. On camera. On the lips.

'Saved our lives, boyo. Put *that* on your CV.'

Suranne happens to join us at this point. She's been up on the promenade working her phone. The charity that owns *Persephone*, she tells H, will be despatching a couple of carpenters from Pompey and they should be with us by midmorning. Mercifully, the spring tides will be receding from now on and, barring another

358

storm, the old trawler should be safe for the next couple of days while the hull is made watertight. At that point, she'll be refloated and returned to the mainland for a proper inspection.

Interviewed on camera, Suranne fends off any suggestion that attempting the return leg was reckless or even unwise. The winds, she points out, were forecast Force 4, gusting 5, conditions that most trawlermen would consider a breeze. In the event, the depression turned out to be a little deeper but even so *Persephone* would still have made it safely across. Had the container not intervened, by now we'd all be having breakfast in the Camber Dock.

The journalist is happy with her interviews. When she asks for onboard smartphone footage, a number of hands go up. Mitch's isn't among them. Interestingly, no one has mentioned Mbaye. As far as our young stowaway is concerned, we're all complicit.

Suranne organizes breakfast at a big seafront hotel called The Imperial. At H's insistence, the food is served in a function room away from the main restaurant. I'm not the only one to find this puzzling but the moment the waitress leaves us alone he's on his feet. He thinks this may be the last time we're all together. Arrangements are in hand to return us to the mainland and so now is the moment to thank Suranne and her crew for, in H's phrase, digging us out of the shit. Speaking personally, he's been in some dodgy situations in his life but nothing to compare to the last couple of hours. When he first set eyes on our skipper he thought she must

359

be a truant bunking off school. Now, thank Christ, he knows different.

He gestures Suranne to her feet, then the rest of the crew, while we stand and applaud. It's a graceful gesture on H's part, nicely done, and I detect a glint of tears in Cassie's eyes when we exchange glances.

'I'm going to miss all this,' she whispers. 'Can you believe that?'

After breakfast, I meet H at reception. He's booking a couple of rooms.

'Why?' I ask him.

'The boy,' he says briefly. 'We need to find him.'

'You mean Mbaye?'

'Yeah.'

'But he's probably dead.'

'You really believe that?'

'I do, yes. You were there. Those waves? The state of the sea? Did I imagine all that?'

H shakes his head. He draws me aside. Not for the first time, he seems to know more than I'd assumed.

'He jumped at the last minute,' he says. 'I was with him. He went off the stern before we hit the beach.'

'And?'

'The lad's a survivor. He's been swimming all his fucking life.'

I nod. True, I think. But then I remember how thin he was, how vulnerable, skin and bone wrapped in Sadie's sodden anorak. It's November. It's freezing cold. He's wet through. Where would he go? How could he possibly survive?

I put these questions to H. We've found a sofa in a corner of the reception area beneath a potted palm. Outside, it's started to rain again.

'M gave him his mobile, told him to ring Fat Dave. We gave him money, too. Quite a lot of money.'

Fat Dave Munroe? The bent cop? I should have guessed. He lives here in Ventnor with his wheelchair and the new woman in his life. She runs a B&B. I try and imagine her coping with a surprise visitor in from the street. An open door, a hot bath and plenty of home comforts to follow.

'You've phoned him? You've been in touch?'

'Of course I fucking have. I belled him from the boat before we hit the beach, as soon as you told me about Ventnor. Fat bastard never answered so I had to send a text.'

'And now? You've phoned Dave again?'

'Three times.'

'And?'

'Dave's heard nothing. The boy's gone to ground. He's biding his time. Or maybe he's moved on already. Four hundred quid goes a long way.'

I gaze at him for a moment, then shake my head. Fantasy, I think. H isn't stupid. He can read my mind.

'You think it's wrong? Me doing all this? You think we should have just handed him over?'

'Not at all. I think what you've done is great. Let's hope he's alive. Let's hope he's on some ferry as we speak. Did you give him any other contacts?'

361

'Yes. Ours.'

'You mean Flixcombe?'

'Of course. He can stay forever. M told him that. Last night.'

Stay forever. I'm thinking of Sayid at the foot of the railway embankment. Sayid in hospital. Sayid trying to coax an entire sentence through his broken teeth. How, in H's teeming brain, does any of this add up? Then I notice Mitch coming in from the rain. He spots us in the corner and comes across. He's looking for Suranne.

I get to my feet. I happen to know where she is. H watches us as we cross the reception area and head for the manager's office. The two men haven't even looked at each other but I know H isn't pleased.

Suranne is sitting behind the manager's desk. She's on the phone when we step in. She gestures for us to take a seat before finishing the conversation.

'That was the Lifeboat secretary,' she says moments later. 'They're after search parameters.'

She's told them what little she knows. The last she saw of Mbaye was when she relieved him on the wheel. After that it was guesswork. He may have gone overboard a couple of hundred metres out. It may have been closer. He's certainly not still hiding aboard because she and Georgie have had a good look.

'He jumped when we were about to hit the beach,' I say quietly.

There's a moment of silence. Then Suranne asks me how I know.

'Someone told me.'

362

'Who?'

I shake my head. Another silence. Then I sense Mitch stirring beside me.

'Prentice,' he says. 'Has to be.'

'Is that true?' Suranne is still looking at me.

'Yes.'

'Why? Why did he let that happen? And why hasn't he told anyone?'

'Because he wants the boy to be safe.'

'*Safe?* In a sea like that?'

'He thought he'd make it. He liked him. He thought he had guts.'

'And he thinks he's still alive?'

'Yes.'

Suranne nods. She liked our stowaway, too. But she's a realist.

'I'm sure he had the best of intentions,' she says, 'but Hayden probably killed the lad.'

Mitch agrees. He's here to tell Suranne that he's been in contact with a diver he knows.

'His name's Joe Cassidy. He runs an outfit in Southampton. They have contracts in the oil business, mainly in the North Sea. He happens to be a friend of mine and he owes me a favour.'

Joe, he says, still dives himself. On the phone Mitch has explained about Mbaye and about the likelihood that the boy went overboard. Joe's getting some gear together and should be in Ventnor by mid-afternoon. If the coastguards and the lifeboat draw a blank he's happy to have a go himself.

'Go at what?'

'Finding him. Joe used to be in the Navy.

363

Clearance diver. He knows all the tricks, believe me.'

'We're talking a body, right?'

'Yes.'

'And you want me to pass this on to the lifeboat people?'

'Yes, please.'

While Suranne reaches for the phone I ask Mitch whether this is the guy he wrote the book about. The one he gave me when we were at his agent's place. He nods.

'The man's a legend. If anyone can find the lad it'll be Joe.'

This seems to imply he'll be dead. I'm still trying to hang on to H's belief that Mbaye may somehow have survived but Mitch tells me I'm delusional. The conditions were evil. The least we owe Mbaye is a serious attempt to recover his body. Then we can pay our respects and say a decent farewell.

Suranne's off the phone. The lifeboat people, she says, are keen to stress that Mr Cassidy is welcome to conduct whatever search he might deem appropriate but will be working at entirely his own risk. Meanwhile, if there are any developments, Suranne will be the first to know.

Mitch and I leave the office but linger in the corridor outside.

'I gather you're staying the night,' he says.

'Who told you?'

'Malo. I'll be around, too. I've booked into a B and B. Maybe dinner together?' His smile is icy. 'All of us?'

Minutes later, back in reception, I find Malo

364

and his dad on the sofa. Malo has shipped all our gear up from the beach and now needs to take it upstairs to the rooms H has booked. There are two of them, both doubles.

We take the lift and H unlocks the first of the bedroom doors. This is a sizeable suite, tastefully appointed. A Battle of Britain theme runs through the paintings on the wall and a notice beside the TV draws guests' attention to a collection of accompanying World War Two DVDs. While H inspects this little treasure trove, Malo and I drift across to the view.

The weather outside is still horrible but, even so, the long stretch of beach fills the big picture window. *Persephone*, our precious home for the past few days, sits forlornly on top of the pebbles. She has a list to port and local workmen have already shored her up with heavy baulks of timber. Both of us stare at the old trawler for a long moment. Then H tells Malo to leave our stuff by the bed.

'*Our* stuff?' I'm still looking at the view. No one says a word. Not to begin with. I glance back at H. He's still on his knees beside the library of DVDs. His face is a mask. Then Malo tells his dad they'll be sharing. There are two beds pushed together. He'll occupy one single, H the other. H shoots me a look.

'Is that what you want?' he asks me.

I nod. After *Persephone*, a bit of privacy is exactly what I want.

'No offence.' I bend to pick up my bags. Then, as an afterthought, I tell H about the diver we can expect. This is Mitch's idea. I'm still calling him Larry Elliott.

'When's he coming? This bloke?'

'This afternoon.'

'They're staying over? Him and your friend?'

'My friend?'

'Mitch fucking Culligan.'

Malo appears to have lost the plot. His gaze goes from each of our faces. He's never seen his Dad in a mood like this. So dark. So full of menace.

'Who's Culligan?' he says.

'Leave it out, son.' H is still staring up at me. 'I asked you a question, gal. Are these numpties here tonight?'

'Yes. As far as I know.'

'And they're staying in the hotel?'

'I doubt it.'

'OK.' H at last struggles to his feet. 'Then get them round here tonight. Half seven. I'm in the fucking chair.'

Twenty-Seven

A sense of dread stays with me for the rest of the day. I rest up in my hotel room, lying full length on the bed while the last of the light drains from the sky outside. I have no idea what to expect from the hours to come but I'm certain none of it will be good. Mitch and H have been on a collision course since the *Guardian* article appeared. God knows what happens next.

We've planned to meet in one of the two hotel bars for drinks. The rest of Malo's guests are already off the island thanks to a hired minibus, while Suranne and her crew have found somewhere much cheaper to stay, waiting for the boat to be repaired. I've told Malo that Mitch Culligan is a journalist and a good man and he appears to be happy with that. Now he and I are reliving various moments of the storm when Mitch and his diver friend appear. H, according to Malo, is still upstairs watching *Reach for the Sky.*

I recognize Joe Cassidy from the photos in Mitch's book. He's a broad-set man, not an ounce of spare flesh. He has a bony face, receding hair, and gnarly old hands I last saw on a gardener H occasionally employs at Flixcombe. The jeans, boots and lumberjack shirt give him the air of someone who's wandered into this swank hotel by mistake, a role I suspect he enjoys. He walks with a certain stiffness, as if he'd overdone some exercise or other, but there's no indication that half his left leg is missing. He must be in his sixties at least but it doesn't show. This man, I tell myself, is full of mischief.

Malo fetches drinks from the bar, putting them on his dad's account. Mitch is drinking Perrier, not a good sign, while Joe sips at a brimming pint of Guinness. We're still discussing what might have happened to Mbaye when H appears. Both Malo and I can tell at once that he's not in a good mood. When Malo gets him a chair he shakes his head. He says he's asked for the function room again. No point hanging around.

Mitch refuses to be hurried. He's no longer pretending to be Larry Elliott and he's deep in conversation with Joe. His diver friend seems to know a great deal about the way the tides work around this bit of the island and he's still drawing lines on the tabletop with his huge forefinger when a waitress appears with a menu. Chef, she says, will be busy tonight with a coachload of Americans signed up for his tasting menu and would appreciate an early order. Heads bow around the table. H is first to make a choice. Fillet steak, rare.

'What are *pommes allumettes*?' he asks.

When Mitch shrugs, Malo steps in.

'String chips, Dad. You'll love them.'

The meal ordered, we follow H through to the function room. Use of this facility has been a recognition on the hotel's part of the ordeal we've all been through but I sense their patience is wearing thin. This, of course, is lost on H.

He sits us down. Shuts the door. In truth, I'm

expecting the worst. This is the moment I've been dreading, the moment when the brittle civilities of the last few hours descend into something more visceral. H hates being taken for an idiot. The thin fiction of Larry Elliott was a serious mistake on Mitch's part.

'You're Culligan, aren't you? Just fucking admit it.'

'Yes.'

'The cunt that wrote the drivel in the *Guardian*.'

'Yes.'

'Then why fanny around? Why all this Larry crap?'

'Because I wanted to be on that boat when it left.'

'And you thought I'd throw you off?'

'That was a possibility, yes.'

'You're right, I might have done. But you know something else? I'd have been wrong. I had you down as a devious little bastard, the kind of twat who gets other people to front up and ask all those tricky questions you know I'd never answer direct. Spencer fucking Willoughby. UKIP. Stuff about the old days in Pompey. How I got all that money in the first place. What I do with it now. That was you talking to Enora, wasn't it? That was you helping yourself, taking fucking liberties, taking fucking *advantage*. The poor bloody woman's just been through brain fucking surgery and I bet you were there at her bedside. Flowers. Chocolates. Whatever. Am I getting warm here, my friend? Isn't this the way it happened?'

I risk a glance round the table. Malo is spellbound, his glass untouched. Joe Cassidy is studying those huge hands of his. H, I suspect, should really be in Berndt's line of business. He has an instinctive nose for a compelling story well told. All the better if it happens to be true.

Mitch clears his throat. He wants to say something. Or maybe he feels the need to defend himself. But either way it doesn't much matter because H hasn't finished.

'So you made friends with her, right? You got her onside. And then you pointed her in my direction. What I need to know is why. That's what's been on my mind. That's why I invited you over tonight. That's what you're doing here. I need you to spell it out to thick old me. I need you to explain what made all that effort worthwhile. Because one of the things you don't seem to understand is that blokes like me go back awhile. We have history. We have mates. We've done stuff together. We're like shit on the shovel. We stick by each other. And so when one of these mates comes to me and says there's some numpty asking whether I've ever killed someone, not frightened them, not even hurt them, but fucking done a nut job on them, then I start to get seriously interested. Does that sound reasonable? Or am I the one taking liberties here?'

He lets the question hang in the air. I'm looking hard at the ceiling, trying to affect indifference. Tony Morse. The night of the party. The conversation in the barn. And the question I popped afterwards. Not on my account but Mitch's.

Fuck.

'So have you?' This from Mitch.

'Have I what?'

370

'Killed anyone?'

'No I haven't. And even if I had, you'd be the last person I'd ever fucking tell. You're doing some book, right? You want to make your name? You want to be famous? You want to be rich? I have no problem with any of that. But it's not fame, is it? And it's not even money. I know about you, Culligan. I know the kind of life you lead, the kind of company you keep. I know how to hurt you, too, but that's a different story. What this is about is why. Why go to all this trouble? Why lean on Malo's mum? Why put yourself in the fucking firing line? When all you're guaranteed is grief?'

Dimly, through the fog of obscenities, I begin to understand H's drift. Deep down, he's asking exactly the same question I put to Mitch after we left Sayid's bedside that first time at the hospital. What, when you peel everything else away, really matters?

'We're talking motivation, right?' Mitch is toying with his Perrier.

'Right.'

'Then it's simple. I do what I do because I believe in certain things. They include all the stuff about liberty and the rule of law we're lazy enough to take for granted. Just now the wreckers are at work. You're one of them, big-time. You're not at the sharpest end. That's for the politicians. But you help make it happen. Whether you realize the consequences of what you're doing, I dunno. In one way it probably doesn't matter because when the shit really hits the fan you and your rich mates will clean up. What's round the corner for the rest of us, millions and millions of us, is immaterial. We'll get poorer, just like the country. We'll lose interest in what really matters because we'll all wake up one morning and realize that we've been suckered, that we're helpless, that there's sod-all we can do, that we're in the hands of a bunch of gangsters who call themselves politicians but who couldn't care a toss. In posh-speak we're collateral damage. But in real life we're fucked.'

I resist the temptation to applaud. H, I suspect, is losing the plot.

'This is about UKIP?'

'Partly, yes.'

'Me and UKIP? Bunging them all that moolah?'

'Of course. Along with others.'

'But UKIP were always a joke.'

'Then why support them?'

'Because that way we could give all you posh twats a poke in the fucking eye.'

'Just for the fun of it.'

'Of course. What else is there?'

What else is there? Brilliant. I'm back at Flixcombe, back at the party, back watching a roomful of grown men weeping to Tina Turner. H, by accident or design, has got to the very heart of it. In a world growing more complex by the nanosecond, we're all helpless. All we can do, all we can manage, is to try and raise our voices, try and make a fuss, crack a joke, get briefly in the face of the people who make things happen. *What else is there?* Clever man. Clever, clever man.

So far, Joe Cassidy hasn't said a word. His

glass is empty. He pushes it towards Malo who nods and leaves the room. Then he turns to Mitch.

'You know about me,' he says. 'And the proof's there in that book of yours. It was excellent. It was a terrific job. It even made me sound half-interesting. My wife, if she was still around, would have loved it. You listened to what I had to say about my Navy days, about all those Falklands dits, about clearance diving, about setting up in business afterwards, and all this is all the more remarkable to me because I wasn't altogether honest with you. There was stuff I never talked about. Stuff I withheld. Stuff that might make better sense on an evening like this.'

'Like what?' Mitch is watching him carefully.

'Like the Falklands War. You're a journalist. You guys love stories. We all know that. You also happen to have a bit of an agenda and that was obvious, too. So when you asked about certain incidents, I was happy to tell you what you wanted to know.'

'We're talking Sheffield?'

'Yes.'

There's a moment of silence. I haven't a clue what these two are talking about. Did the Argies bomb South Yorkshire?

H comes to my rescue. He's word-perfect on the details. He tells me that HMS *Sheffield* was the first Royal Navy ship to go down in the war. She was hit by an Exocet missile which set her on fire and killed twenty blokes. Everyone knew there were fuck-ups, because that's what happens in every war, but at the time the papers were full of our brave lads doing their best in the face of the enemy.

I ask Joe whether he was on the *Sheffield*. He says yes. He also says that fuck-ups were the order of the day. The ship wasn't prepared for a missile attack because no one could properly understand the huge intelligence assessment that had recently arrived onboard. The key warfare officer didn't believe the Argie aircraft had the range to launch any missiles. When a warning came from a neighbouring warship, this officer was having coffee in the wardroom while another was taking a leak. That left just two juniors on the bridge, neither of whom had a clue what to do.

According to Joe they just stared at the incoming missiles. No evasive action. No turning towards the threat to minimize the bulk of the ship. Just a huge bang in the galley and bodies and smoke everywhere.

'Shit.' This from H.

'Exactly. Mitch asked all the right questions. He knew we'd fucked up. But I never told him how bad things really were. Shiny *Sheff* was just one example. I could give you hundreds more.'

Mitch nods. He's beginning to look uncomfortable. H wants to know what any of this has to do with what we've been talking about.

'Everything.' Joe again. 'My point is simple. I've been around a bit. I watch. I listen. I remember. I pick things up. I join the dots. And what I learn tells me that government, big government, isn't too clever. They get far too many things wrong, far too often. After I left the Navy I went into business. Business teaches you everything. It teaches you to stand on your own two feet. It teaches you to get things *right*. And unless you do that you'll end up like *Sheff*, burned out, sunk, abandoned, royally fucked. So Mr Prentice here is more right than we might think. If this is about Brexit then you're looking at someone who voted yes. Why? Because it puts us back where we belong. On our own two feet.'

Another speech. H is looking at Joe with something close to wonderment.

'Shit,' he says quietly. 'Why aren't there any politicians like you?'

The door opens. In comes Malo with a pint of Guinness. Joe contemplates it for a moment and then asks what everyone else is drinking. I know from Mitch's face that he's itching to get stuck in again, to argue his case, to paint H as the bad guy, to make all the important points about the imperfections of democracy and the threat of the Deep State and the power of money and all the rest of it, but H has another idea. He leans across and puts his thick fingers on Mitch's forearm.

'There's one thing I never mentioned,' he growls. 'It took guts to get on that boat in France, no matter what fucking name you used. Believe it or not, I admired that and I still do. All the rest of what you're about is total bollocks and one day we'll meet in the street or some fucking place and you'll admit it, but for now let's get some serious drinking in.' He glances across at Malo. 'Son?'

375

Malo is well trained but I think he needs some help. I follow him out of the function room and back to the bar. It takes no time at all to organize four bottles of Moët. By the time we're making our way back towards the function room I can hear laughter through the half-open door.

Malo pops the first bottle and I'm on hand with the glasses. Joe is sticking to Guinness.

'A toast?' I suggest.

H nods. 'Here's to our little black fucker.' He raises his glass. 'Wherever he might be.'

Twenty-Eight

The following morning, I have an early breakfast with Mitch at a cafe in Ventnor. The invitation has come from him and I've been very happy to accept. Joe, he says, has gone to talk to a local fisherman about the recent storm and about a reef along the coast. Later he'll take a look at the foreshore, hire a dive boat, and decide where to start.

'You think he'll find the boy?'

'Yes.'

'You *know* that?'

'Yes. Nothing that man has ever told me has ever been wrong.'

'Except by omission.'

'Of course. But even then, I can see his point. He knew what I was after at the time and he gave me enough to make the book work but there were other issues in play.'

'Like?'

'Loyalty.'

'To?'

'The Navy, I guess. It wasn't perfect but these were blokes he loved.'

This, from Mitch, is a major concession. Flesh and blood trumping Mitch's headlong gallop towards the truth.

'And last night? Brexit? All that?'

'He has his point of view. He's wrong, of

course, but I'd never question his right to believe it.'

'And H?'

'H is different.'

I'm staring at him. This is the first time Mitch has called Hayden Prentice by his nickname. H. Progress indeed.

'Different how?'

'Different because I'm sure he did kill someone. His name was Darren Atkins. I can't prove it and there's no way H will ever discuss it, but the circumstantial evidence is pretty convincing. The guy disappeared, just went off the radar. He'd stitched up a guy called Mackenzie on a big consignment of cocaine. He'd brought it in from Aruba and about two hundred grands' worth had gone missing. He blamed it on the Colombians, who'd sold it in the first place, but Mackenzie knew that was bollocks. It turned out Mackenzie was right. He had H and a couple of other guys turn Atkins' place over. They found the stash in a lock-up in the north of the city after they'd had a little talk. No one ever saw him again. Apart from the remains of a left foot washed up on Southsea beach. Atkins used to be a decent footballer in his day. Always scored with his left foot.'

Mackenzie. Aruba. A little talk. And the signature warning on the wet pebbles for any apprentice drug runner with similar ambitions.

'Bazza,' I say softly. 'And a guy called Wesley Kane.'

'You know about this?' Mitch has stopped eating.

378

'Of course I do. I'm part of it now, whether I like it or not.'

'And do you?'

'What?'

'Like it?'

I give the question some thought. As ever I prefer the subjunctive mood to anything truly decisive.

'I might,' I say. 'It depends.'

It's mid-morning before Joe has the information he needs about the reef. Malo has acquired a boat from a local crab fisherman and Joe drives his van down to the promenade to offload all his gear. I help him and Malo carry the heavy equipment down to the waiting crabber while H looks on. According to Malo, his dad awoke with a thumping headache but a pint or two of water and a Percocet from yours truly seem to have done the trick.

Aside from the boat's owner, there's only room for three aboard. H and I find a seat on the prom while Joe strips to his swimming trunks. He wears a false leg below his left knee and we watch him perched on the side of the boat while Malo helps him with the dive suit. Next comes the heavy cylinder of compressed air, a weight belt, and a single fin. Joe's helmet has a built in LCD light with an attached camera. According to the crabber's skipper, the set of the offshore current at the time we speared into the beach would have taken Mbaye away to the east, towards the reef. After his walk along the fore-shore, Joe has already decided on his first dive site. Now he pivots on the thwart and makes himself comfortable while Malo gives the boat a shove seawards and hops in. Moments later, Malo gives us a wave and then they're off.

H and I watch them in silence until the boat disappears. The carpenters from Pompey are at work on the trawler and from time to time the sound of their hammering echoes around the shallow curl of the bay. It's grey and miserable and there's a dampness in the air. H is wrapped in the big sea-going jacket he wore for the crossing. I think he's cold. I think he wants to go back to the hotel.

'Tell me about Sayid Abdulrahman,' I say. 'Did you do that yourself? Or did you leave it to someone else?'

H doesn't answer. He's staring out to sea. I put the question again. And I tell him he owes me an answer.

'Why?'

'Because I know that man. And what you did should never have happened. It was horrible. It was worse than horrible. It was evil.'

H nods. He appears to agree but I can sense there's no way he's going to take this conversation any further. For a few minutes we sit in total silence, watching the men at work on the trawler. Finally I try another name.

'Darren Atkins,' I say softly. 'Tell me about him.'

For a moment H doesn't react. He's still hunched on the bench, hands dug deep in the pockets of the jacket.

'You've been talking to Culligan,' he says at last. Statement, not question.

'You're right.'

'How much did he tell you?'

'Enough.'

'Enough for what?'

'Enough to make me wonder.'

'About me?'

'Of course.'

'And? Supposing whatever he said is true?'

I shut my eyes. This is typical. I'm on the back foot. Again.

'He thinks you killed him,' I say carefully. 'All I want is a yes or a no.'

'And if it's a yes? Will you go running off and tell Culligan?'

'Absolutely not.'

'So what difference will it make? To you and me?'

'I don't know.'

This isn't the answer he wants. He seems pained by it as if I've somehow let him down. He's about to ask me something else, to maybe take the conversation in a new direction, but then he has second thoughts.

He stirs on the bench and then struggles to his feet. I'm looking up at him.

'So is that a yes?' I ask. 'You're telling me you killed a man?'

He gazes down at me for a long moment and I realize how much the last few days have taken out of him. He looks haunted, gaunt, somehow diminished. The last thing he needs is me on his case.

'I'm going back to the hotel,' he grunts. 'Bell me if they find the kid.'

* * *

Joe and Malo return a couple of hours later. I've walked the length of the promenade twice and had a brief conversation with an elderly woman in a motorized buggy who very much liked a movie I did a couple of years ago. I've also made contact with Rosa in case she's picked up news of our adventures on *Persephone*. It turns out she hasn't but insists on a full report. I tell her most of it but skip the bit about Mbaye. My description of taking the wheel at the height of the storm has her in fits of laughter. I gave her a lift once when I was driving a little 2CV and she got out after less than a mile. We agree to talk again as soon as word comes from Montréal on the Canadian movie and before she hangs up she gives me a transmission date for the radio play.

'The male lead's been in touch,' she adds as an afterthought. 'He wants your contact details.'

'Tell him nothing,' I say.

Now, I hurry down the beach to meet the boat. Malo hops off and hands me a rope. Joe needs something from his van, parked up on the promenade. The first dive was fruitless and he had to abort the second because his regulator was malfunctioning. Waiting for Malo, Joe and I have a brief conversation. He says that visibility is better on the reef than he anticipated after the heavy weather. He has three more dive sites in mind, with a day in hand, after which the search might get problematic. I'm still wondering quite what this might mean when Malo returns with a replacement regulator. Seconds later, after a hefty push from yours truly, they're off again.

By now it's early afternoon. I make contact with Mitch, who is en route back to an important meeting in London, and confirm that so far we haven't found any trace of Mbaye. Then I find a seafront cafe with a view of the beach and settle down in front of a bowl of lentil soup.

My last conversation with H has disturbed me. I know I should never forgive him for what happened to Sayid, but even so I seem to have succumbed to something I find difficult to describe. Charm is too feeble a word. H himself would hate it. A kind of animal magnetism comes closer. This is a man with total self-belief, a man for whom life holds no fears. That makes him brave, as well as reckless, and it also makes him very rare. Like it or not, thanks to Malo, Hayden Prentice has become part of me. Never, I realize with a sudden jolt of surprise, have I regretted that evening in Antibes.

Leaving the cafe, I walk to the hotel to check that he's OK. I can't find him anywhere and when I enquire at reception the girl tells me he's retired for a nap. Strictly no calls, she says. I nod and return to the beach. This is worrying. H never naps.

By the time the boat returns for the second time, I've nearly given up waiting. A low duvet of cloud has hung over us all day and by half past four it's getting dark. I hear the boat before I see it, a putter-putter growing louder by the second. I walk down to the waterline, aware of the presence of *Persephone* on the shingle. The carpenters are doing a fine job on the gash but are now packing up. Queen of the Underworld, I think. As sorry-looking and beached as H.

The moment I see the expression on Malo's face, I know the news isn't good. He's crouched in the bow, ready with the line, but there's a tightness in his mouth that tells me everything I need to know.

'You've found him?'

He nods, throws me the rope. Joe has the underwater footage. There's a laptop in his van. We all need to watch.

I accompany Joe and Malo back up the beach, helping with the equipment. Joe has strapped on his false leg and manages the pebbles better than me. At the van I wait on the pavement while Joe stows the gear. I'm wondering whether to try and put a call through to H but before I can make any decision Joe emerges with his laptop. He's transferred the footage.

All three of us settle on a nearby bench. Joe opens the laptop and finds the footage. The camera is built into his dive helmet and acts like a second pair of eyes. The image on the screen is pin-sharp and I watch, fascinated, as he takes a final look at the crabber and then submerges. Light drains from the screen as he swims deeper until he triggers his LCD and suddenly we're above the reef in a world of yellows and dark greens. Sediment hangs in the water. Tiny creatures drift past. Then comes a glimpse of a pocket of sand as he touches the bottom. Ahead is a wall of darkness. Slowly, stroke by stroke, I can make out the shape of individual rocks, heavily barnacled. I see a starfish. Something brown with big eyes. A torn fragment of fishing net, a bright synthetic orange. Joe is moving slowly along the outer wall of the reef. His passage stirs tiny plumes of sand from the bottom. Then, very dimly, I sense a different shape, softer, slowly coming into focus. This has to be him, I think. And I'm right.

I sit back a moment, overwhelmed. Then I force myself to watch again. Mbaye has been trapped by one foot in a gap between the rocks. The rest of his thin body hangs in the yellow light, gently moving in the current. His head is down, his chin on his chest, while his arms float free. Joe is circling the body. The boy's eyes are closed and his mouth is slack. Those teeth, I keep thinking. The startling white of those teeth.

Joe has frozen the image. He wants to be sure. Malo confirms it's Mbaye. I nod, saying nothing. Joe closes the laptop. He's buoyed the site and tomorrow he'll inform the police.

'So what happens?' I ask. 'To Mbaye?'

'They'll recover him at low tide. The weather should be OK. There'll be a post-mortem, then an inquest. The body will belong to the Coroner. Once the legals are over, I imagine he'll release it.'

Release it. Not him. It.

I get up and walk to the edge of the promenade where it drops away towards the beach. I want very badly to be alone. It's dark now but in the throw of the seafront lights I can make out the shape of the old trawler on the shingle. I shut my eyes a moment. It takes nothing, no effort on my part, to be back on that heaving deck, with the waves roaring out of the darkness and nothing but fear in the pit of my stomach. I can feel the icy bite of the wind, hear the distant thunder of the surf, flinch at the crack of the sails, and then comes another image, altogether more comforting. That thin little figure at the wheel. How he took over. How clever he was. And how brave.

Twenty-Nine

The same fisherman, with the aid of Joe and the police, recovers Mbaye the following day. Malo, H, and I are on hand when the grim little party carries the grey body bag up the beach towards the waiting undertaker's van. H has spent an anguished evening at the hotel trying to decide what to do next. When I tell him that an inquest could be months away he doesn't seem to be listening. He needs to put the lad to rest.

It's Malo who suggests a local funeral and then maybe cremation. We could scatter the ashes at sea. We could buy an urn, something nice, and find somewhere suitable to keep it. I like this idea but when I suggest Flixcombe, H shakes his head.

'We have to take him home,' he says. 'We have to take him back to his own people.'

This is easier said than done. All we have is a Christian name. No passport. No home address. No next of kin. Just Mbaye's word that he came from a big family in a fishing village near Dakar. All too sadly, Mbaye is just one in a squillion young refugees jumping on smugglers' trucks and disappearing north. If H really wants to find his family, just where do we start?

To this question H has no answer. We're in the hotel bar, having a night cap. H is staring glumly at his glass of malt when he suddenly brightens.

'Son?'

Malo is on his smart phone, scrolling through his emails. He doesn't look up.

'Dad?'

'It's gonna be down to you. Your project. Your call. I'll fund it. I'll pick up the costs. You find the boy's folks. Deal?'

Malo nods. He's replying to one of the emails.

'Deal,' he says absently.

I return to London the next day while H and Malo drive west to Flixcombe. All three of us have left our contact details with the police who will forward them to the Coroner. In due course, explains the desk sergeant, the Coroner's Officer will be in touch to get statements from each of us. We may also be summoned to attend the inquest. When H pushes for some kind of date, the sergeant shrugs. Could be a while, he says. Sad business, all these young lads.

In London, I pick up the threads of my former life. The events of the past week or so have made a far bigger impact than I ever anticipated and the more time slips by, the harder it is to rid my mind of some of the more vivid images. We could all have gone down with that boat, every single one of us, H, Malo and me, a little gene pool wiped out forever, and the more I think about this the gladder I am that we all managed to pull through. None of us are perfect, least of all H, but I like belonging to these people. They've brought colour and a whiff of something dangerous into my life, and that matters a great deal. H, very much on the mend now, also makes me laugh. Which I suspect is just as important.

Towards the end of November, Mitch gets back in touch. At his suggestion we meet at an Indian restaurant in Clerkenwell. He arrives late but I'm still pleased to see him. He tells me that Sayid has been back home for a while now and is almost completely recovered. Last week, for the first time, he put on his Nikes and managed a gentle mile and a half around the block. Next week, God willing, he'll try and make it to Blackheath. Only towards the end of the meal do I raise the issue of the book. Mitch has already told me that he's been working all hours to meet a deadline on a major piece on Universal Credit. After that he fancies something ecological. Scientists have reported a seventy-five per cent wipe-out of insects in nature reserves across Germany. This appears to be down to the widespread use of pesticides. If something similar is happening here the longer-term consequences to life on earth could be catastrophic.

This is the old Mitch, the crusading doomster who stepped into my life with the offer of breakfast and changed pretty much everything.

'And the book?' I ask.

'Book?'

'Brexit? UKIP? All of us fucked?'

Mitch shakes his head. This is a question he's probably anticipated but doesn't much like. He mumbles something about the cowardice of publishers in general and his in particular. Not his fault. Theirs.

'So what's happened?'

'They pulled out.'

'Why?'

'They said it was legally imprudent to carry on.'

'*Imprudent?* How does that work?'

'Prentice threatened to sue. They also had calls.'

'From who?'

'They never knew but that wasn't the point. These people were promising to set them on fire and they believed them.'

'You mean arson? Torching the premises?'

'Murder. Torching them.'

'Shit. Didn't you try any other publishers?'

'Of course I did. Same story. Publishing's a small world.'

'You mean they're frightened?'

'Terrified. Game, set and match to your H. Will all that stuff ever see the light of day? I doubt it. Not between hard covers. Does that matter? Of course it does. But there comes a time when you realize that no one cares, not out there where they should. Same old story. Shit wages. Shit telly. Shit lives. What else is there? Fuck all. Because nothing matters.'

Because nothing matters. This is resignation on stilts which must be tough for Mitch.

'So is that it? All that research? All that work? Having sources like me passing out on you over breakfast?'

Mitch offers me a tight smile. He's not a good loser and it shows.

'There's a satirical rag based in Paris I've been talking to,' he says. '*Le Canard enchaîné.* You may even have heard of it. They're braver than our lot and they might stretch to some kind of serialization. I think they want to stick it to *les rosbifs* and who can blame them. A French publication telling the truth about the Brexit lot?' He shakes his head. 'That's beyond irony.'

I nod. *Le Canard enchaîné* is venerated by certain sections of the French intelligentsia but its readership is tiny. If Mitch has been dreaming of mass-market sales figures, he's about to be disappointed. I want to sympathize but when I reach for his hand he flinches. He has no idea what's coming next and he finds that alarming.

'Don't be frightened.' I'm smiling at him. 'I just want to say thank you.'

'For what?'

'For H.' I give his hand a squeeze. 'And for Malo.'

In early December, bad news arrives from Montréal. Everything is on schedule for location filming to begin shortly after Christmas, but the principal backer, for reasons that no one can fathom, has suddenly pulled out. The shoot has therefore been postponed indefinitely until other funding is in place.

'Are we dead in the water?' I ask Rosa on the phone. 'Be honest.'

'We are, my precious,' she says. 'But something very interesting has just popped up in Belgrade.'

She doesn't volunteer any further information and I don't ask because I've long trusted this woman with looking after my best interests.

Either a script will arrive in due course or it won't. Whatever happens, I have more important things on my mind.

My three-month check is due this same week. I attend first for an MRI scan. I've been through this procedure before and there's a real feeling of coming full circle as I make myself comfortable on the scanner table and allow the assistants to slide me into the machine. The next forty-five minutes are painless but incredibly noisy. It's important to keep your head still and I try very hard to remember what a yoga teacher once told me about trying to imagine every inch of my body in fierce detail. I've got as far as my left knee when the machine is switched off and I'm free to go.

I return to the hospital three days later. My neurosurgeon has had a cancellation on an earlier patient and he's waiting for me at his office door when I arrive. He invites me in and we sit down. My MRI scan is already hanging on his white board. He asks me how I've been recently and seems surprised when I say fine. He scribbles himself a note and then directs my attention to a darkish area around the site of the first operation. The news, he says, is not good. These are still early days but there appears to be an indication that the tumour has returned.

'Really?' I'm still looking at the scan. I don't feel the least bit shocked, or even disappointed. Just curious.

I ask him why this might have happened. He says he can't be sure. Maybe he didn't excise enough of the diseased brain tissue. Maybe we're dealing with a brand-new bunch of rogue cells. Either way there are decisions to be made.

'You want to operate again?'

'Not really. Not unless I absolutely have to. We'll try radiotherapy first. And a couple of cycles of chemo.'

I have a fear of chemo. Too many friends of mine have emerged from treatment with horror stories about hair loss, throwing up, and industrial strength exhaustion. My neurosurgeon is nice enough to assure me that the drugs are getting better every week. So far, to my relief, he hasn't mentioned the Grim Reaper.

'So when do you want all this to start?'

He consults his calendar. Christmas is fast approaching. Best, he says, to leave it until the New Year.

'Is that OK with you?' He's on his feet already, his hand outstretched.

'That's fine,' I say. 'Something to look forward to.'

I walk the three miles home, partly to test my newfound resilience in the face of bad medical news, and partly because I don't want any kind of company. I've learned a great deal about myself over the past few months and one of the conclusions I've drawn is the need to be ruthless about time. Time, in the end, is all we've got. And when someone in the know suggests it might be limited, it's better to spend it wisely.

I get home mid-afternoon. I know that Malo and H have been out in Senegal these last couple of weeks, trying to locate Mbaye's family. Malo has taken a couple of screen grabs from his smart phone, shots of Mbaye he took on the boat, and armed with these he and his dad have been driving along the coast from village to village, trying to find someone who might recognize the boy.

Malo, bless him, has been phoning me every other day with what began as progress reports but as the calls got shorter it became obvious that neither of them were falling in love with West Africa. On the one occasion I found myself talking to H, he left little to the imagination. The people were OK, he said, but there were far too many of them. Dakar was a shit heap and some of the outer townships were worse. Malo had had a run-in with a rogue prawn and spewed his guts out for forty-eight hours. The weather was too hot, even in December, and they were both sweating like a bastard by midday.

'It's costing me a fortune,' he said before handing me back to Malo. 'And that's just for a new fucking shirt every morning.'

Now, I phone Malo. They've been back at Flixcombe since last night, plenty of time to recover. The phone rings and rings until my son finally picks up.

'Mum?' he says. 'Is that you?'

It's lovely to hear his voice. We haven't talked for nearly a week. I ask him how he is.

'Great. Knackered but OK.'

'Stomach all right?'

'Yeah.'

He badly wants to tell me about the back end

394

of the trip, what they got up to those last few days in Senegal, but I ask him to save it.

'For what? For when?'

'For tomorrow,' I say, 'if you can make it. Maybe the day after if you can't.'

'Make what? What is this?'

I tell him I have a little expedition in mind. I want him, need him, to carve out a couple of days in his busy, busy life.

'What for? Where?'

'The Isle of Wight.'

'Is this the inquest? Have they brought it forward?'

'Not at all. It's got nothing to do with the inquest. They're talking the New Year now. It could still be months away.'

'Then what's up? Why the island?'

I'm not prepared to say. All I want him to do is promise to meet me at Portsmouth either tomorrow or the next day. The weather forecast is glorious. We'll take the ferry to the island. We'll travel by bus or cab. We'll be away for one night. Then he'll be back home again.

Something in my voice must have told him to say yes because the barrage of questions abruptly comes to a halt. He agrees to meet me at Portsmouth Harbour station around noon tomorrow.

'Are you sure that's OK?' I ask him.

'That's fine, Mum. Twelve o'clock. Skinny guy. Quite suntanned.'

Next morning he's waiting for me on the platform at the harbour station. Expecting us to take the catamaran across the Solent to Ryde, he steers me towards the main exit. Outside I pause to admire the view. Last time I was here it was pouring with rain and I was about to embark on *Persephone*. Now, under a cloudless sky, sunshine dances on the big, blue expanse of the harbour. A tug fusses around a huge warship. A pair of yachts motor slowly towards the harbour mouth. Flags flutter and snap in the wind.

Malo is tugging me away. Time, it seems, is short.

'Where are we going?'

'The car ferry.'

We've come to a halt. I'm looking down at a smart Audi convertible, dark blue. It looks brand new.

'This is yours?'

'Yeah. Present from Dad. I think he wanted to make up for all the hassle on the boat.'

We get in. Firm leather seats. Fancy audio set-up. Even a camera at the back for getting out of tight spots, doubtless invaluable if you happen to be a son of H.

'Like it?' Malo is beaming.

'Love it. What time does the ferry go?'

We drive to the car ferry terminus. As the ferry slips her moorings and rumbles towards the harbour mouth, we're both on the upper deck, enjoying the sunshine. From here, we have a perfect view of the Camber Dock.

Malo spots her first. 'There, Mum.'

I follow his pointing finger. *Persephone* is tied up at her usual spot beside the harbour wall. Nothing I can see from the ferry would give me the slightest clue to the trauma she's been through. A line of washing from the doghouse aft indicates that someone must still be aboard. I look a little harder. Skimpy black knickers. A child-size T-shirt. Definitely Suranne. The ferry is making a turn now and as the old trawler begins to disappear I linger as long as I can on the big wooden steering wheel aft. Mbaye, I think. My last ever glimpse of him alive.

An hour later, we're bumping off the ferry boat ramp in Fishbourne. Malo gets rid of the roof and I settle down for the ride. The seats have electric heating. I feel glad, and cosseted, and very much alive. I'm also within touching distance of the most important man in my life, a bonus I've only ever dreamed about.

I've asked Malo to take us to Ventnor. We drive down through the town and park on the promenade. It's low tide. The beach is empty apart from a couple walking a dog and I fancy I can see an indentation in the pebbles where *Persephone* came to rest. Malo laughs and tells me I'm making it up. He's shading his eyes against the slant of winter sunshine. I suspect he thinks we're going to The Imperial. He's wrong.

'Freshwater Bay,' I say.

'Freshwater what?'

'Bay.'

'Anywhere in particular?'

'The Farringford.'

He punches the word into his sat nav, grunting with satisfaction when the directions appear. Then he pauses.

'I've heard that word before,' he says. 'Recently.'

'You have.'

'You made a film there? Am I right? When you were playing the photographer's model?'

'Yes.'

I'm delighted. Half my work is done. I want to draw my precious son to the very heart of me, the very middle of me, and this is the perfect start.

The sun is beginning to set as we head west. The road follows the line of chalk cliffs that stretch way out towards The Needles. At any time of year this is a spectacular journey but in mid-winter, in weather like this, it feels ultra special. We have the road to ourselves. At every next bend, with no sign of traffic, I'm starting to wonder whether we have the entire island to ourselves. Away to the right, on rising ground, the green smudge of a forest. On our left, still blue, still lightly flecked with waves, that same English Channel that nearly killed us. Ahead, softened by the haze on the far horizon, the dying orb of the sun.

Accommodation at the Farringford comes in the shape of self-catering cottages in the grounds. I've booked one of the two-bedroom versions. Access to the house itself is restricted at this time of year, which is a shame, but that's not why we're here.

Malo has parked the car in front of our cottage. There's still a blush of orange in the west but dusk is falling fast. Malo is looking back at the house. This once belonged to Alfred Lord

Tennyson. To me it has perfect proportions, just two floors in soft grey stone. One end of the property is covered in ivy and a magnificent cedar tree frames the view towards Tennyson Down.

'This is where you stayed, right?'

'Yes. I had the bedroom at the top there, third window from the left. I got up early every morning to catch the sunrise. I'll never forget it.'

We eat that night at a pub in the village. At H's insistence, I'm spending Christmas down at Flixcombe Manor, but I want this evening to be our own special celebration, just Malo and myself. My son sorts out the drinks and takes our food order to the bar. There's a comfortable buzz of conversation from the surrounding tables and locals attend to the wood-burning stove when it needs a new log or two. Perfect.

Over loin of pork and roast potatoes, Malo fills me in about his two weeks in West Africa. Only towards the end of the trip, he says, did his dad really get any kind of handle on the place. Until then, he'd been certain that they could find Mbaye's family, pay their respects, bung them a quid or two, and offer to organize repatriation of the body. The latter gesture, I suspect, wouldn't be cheap and when I ask Malo how much he says nearly £3,000. The body must be embalmed. It must also be free from infection and transported in a zinc-lined coffin to provide a hermetic seal. Lots of documentation includes a copy of the death certificate and the findings of the Coroner.

'And you'll be organizing all this?'

'Yes. But that's not the point. We looked high and low for the right village. There are loads of them, boats drawn up on the beach, everyone sitting on their arse, kids everywhere. In the end we gave up on finding the right one and just chose the prettiest.'

'The *prettiest*?'

'Dad's idea. We tracked backwards. There was one beside an estuary, a bit nicer than the rest. Dad got me to go and find the priest. He turned out to be a really good guy, quite young. I explained about Mbaye, and not finding anyone who seemed to recognize him, and then I asked him whether it would be OK for him to do the honours.'

Honours? Once again I tell him I don't understand. Malo grins.

'Take care of him. Find a plot. Have a grave dug. Put a headstone in, something decent, something nice with just the name. Mbaye. Plus the date he left us.'

The date he left us. Monday 13 November. Written on my heart.

'And?'

'He was a bit doubtful at first but then Dad arrived and took him aside. You know the way he does that?'

I nodded. Oh, yes.

'Dad said he'd pay for it all, the grave and everything, plus he'd give some money to the village for whatever they needed, maybe like a medical centre or something, I dunno.'

'A medical centre? How much money are we talking here?'

'That's what I asked Dad. He said half a million.'

'Half a *million*?'

Malo nods. Half a million pounds. Instead of UKIP, I think, a medical facility in a remote West African village. Instead of mischief-making in the UK, something truly worthwhile. And all in the memory of a boy we'd known for less than a day.

I resist the temptation to phone Mitch. He'd hate news like this.

'So what happened?'

'The priest said yes. Only too happy. That night he introduced us to the elders in the village. Weird. I thought we might be in for some kind of ceremony, some tribal thing, but all they did was sit round and talk about how poor they were. Dad was really disappointed.'

I'm smiling. I can imagine this scene, H feeling short-changed by a bunch of West African whingers. Then another thought occurs to me.

'So we have no family for Mbaye?'

'That's right. None.'

'Then how are you going to lay hands on the body? The Coroner won't just give you the keys to the mortuary. It doesn't work that way.'

'I know. That's what I told Dad. I took advice. Mbaye's family have to come up with proof that he was their son.'

'Is H aware of this?'

'Of course. I told him. I got advice. I spelled it out before we went.'

'And?'

'He said it wouldn't be a problem. We'd find the family and sort it.'

'And now?'

'I dunno. He never listens, Dad. Maybe he'll just end up giving the priest the half million. Call it quits.'

'Conscience money? For getting the boy killed?'

'Maybe.'

We finish our main course and study the desserts board. Malo settles for treacle tart while I order a sorbet. When Malo returns from the bar he finds something waiting for him.

'What's this?'

'Open it.'

'But what is it, Mum?'

'Call it an early Christmas present. Call it what you like. Just open it.'

He nods, reaches for a knife, folds back the wrapping paper. Inside is a box. He lifts it out and studies it. It's American. I found it in a gift shop I especially like off the Cromwell Road.

Malo opens the box. Inside is a container the size of a dinner plate. It has two halves that fit together, both concave, both silvered on the inside. The top half has a circular hole cut in the top.

Malo is staring at it from every angle. He hasn't a clue what he's looking at. I delve in my bag for another present, much smaller this time.

'This goes with it,' I say. 'I'll show you how.'

Malo does some more unwrapping. This time it's a soapstone figure, jet black, beautifully carved, a bird-like shape with a long curved neck.

'It's a loon,' I tell him. 'Made by Inuits.'

'Is it precious?'

'Very.'

'So what do I do?' He gestures at the first present. I position it in the middle of the table and lift the top lid. The carving sits snugly inside. I give the top lid to Malo and tell him to replace it.

He does what he's told. The lighting, thank God, is perfect.

'Now sit back. Any angle. It doesn't matter.'

I hear the scrape of the chair. He's looking hard at the container, at the hole on the top, at the loon magically hovering above. He reaches forward for it, tries to trap it in his fingers, but it's made of nothing.

'It's an illusion,' I tell him. 'In French we'd call it a *trompe-l'oeil*. What you see isn't what you get.'

He's still staring at the loon, daring it to move, to disappear, but it's still there, a beautiful black nothing. I love the expression on his face. He could be seven again.

'Happy Christmas,' I say.

Next morning I get up before sunrise, find something warm to wear, and tiptoe out of the cottage. My feet are bare and the dew is icy on the grass. I've been canny enough to pack a heavy sweater as well as my jeans and I wait beneath the cedar for the clouds to part. The forecast doesn't let me down. The sky to the east is already on fire and I tilt my face to the sun as shadows slowly appear all round me. When I was on location here, so many years ago, it was high summer but the feeling of aloneness, of privilege, of somehow being the only human being on the face of the planet, is no less powerful. I linger for a while, enjoying the first hints of warmth, before returning to the cottage. My son, bless him, is still asleep and to my deep satisfaction he has the loon tucked beneath his pillow.

We set off for Tennyson Down an hour or so later. I lead Malo around the edge of two fields, exactly the path I took every morning all those years ago, and then I find the gap in the hedge that leads up on to the Down. Someone's installed a new-looking stile but apart from that I've stepped into a time warp.

The springy turf seems to go on forever. The sun is behind us now and our long shadows sometimes seem to coalesce into one. Gulls are soaring and wheeling overhead, turning to ride the wind that blasts up the cliff face. There are rabbits everywhere, scuttling away for cover, and twice Malo swears he's seen a stoat. These are magical moments, moments of pure bliss. Ahead of us lies the Tennyson Monument which marks the highest point of the Down.

We pause beside it. The briskness of the walk has brought colour to Malo's cheeks. He looks alive. He looks so well.

'So what do you think?' I nod at the view west. The Needles are invisible from here but the bony whiteness of the sheer cliffs are promise enough.

'Brilliant,' he says. 'No wonder you loved it so much.'

I nod. He's understood. That's all I wanted.

And now he's shared that feeling, that wild exaltation, and that's even better.

'Come with me.'

I take his hand. It feels very natural. We're walking towards the cliff edge. He trusts me completely. I know he does. The wind is blowing in from the sea, hitting the cliff face, funnelling upwards. From maybe ten metres away, you can feel its force. Look up, and those same gulls are stationary above us, weightless, riding this invisible column of air.

I stop at the cliff edge and peer over. My son does the same. We can see the creamy swirl of breaking waves among the rocks at the bottom of the cliff. They look so small, so distant, so tempting. One step. Just one. Then oblivion. Cassini, I think. My batteries running out. Our final plunge. Then nothing but silence in the vastness of deep space.

Malo is shivering. I can feel it. He wants to know what happens next.

'Good question.'

We step back and then head on west towards The Needles. I want to keep this matter-of-fact. No drama. No tears. No concessions to anyone else's script. Just one promise from my lovely boy.

I motion for him to stop. The sun is on his face. I have some news, I tell him. I've been to see the consultant. I've had another scan and the results aren't great. I feel fine in myself, no real symptoms, not like the last time, but there appears to be a chance the Grim Reaper might come calling.